Acclaim for Mi

"A poignant, cautionary tale that peels back layers of the soul. This beautifully written, heart-wrenching journey takes us into both the familiar and unfamiliar, reminding us that no one is perfect or immune to life's harsh realities and challenges. Raw and real, yet infused with hope, the beauty within this book will touch your heart and stay with you long after the last page is turned."

—CATHERINE WEST, AUTHOR OF *THE THINGS WE KNEW*

"This moving story of one family's struggle with the human cost of following God's call will resonate profoundly. As is so powerfully illustrated in *Of Stillness and Storm*, sometimes the sacrifices we make for God can cause others to suffer in ways He never intended. Like Michèle Phoenix, I am an MK and am passionate about protecting children. I urge you to read this gripping cautionary tale, listen for God's voice, and take to heart what is so close to our Father's heart—caring for *every* precious child He has placed in our path."

—DR. WESS STAFFORD, PRESIDENT EMERITUS, COMPASSION INTERNATIONAL AND AUTHOR OF *TOO SMALL TO IGNORE: WHY THE LEAST OF THESE MATTERS MOST* AND *JUST A MINUTE: IN THE HEART OF A CHILD, ONE MOMENT CAN LAST FOREVER*

"You will be captivated by this story of heartbreak and triumph. *Of Stillness and Storm* is an important book for anyone who has heard that still, small voice saying this is not right—and mustered the strength to make a change. A must read."

—ANITA LUSTREA, PODCASTER, SPEAKER, MEDIA COACH, AND AUTHOR OF *WHAT WOMEN TELL ME*

"*The Poisonwood Bible* for a new generation, stark yet with a subtle hope. Michèle Phoenix's hauntingly beautiful prose depicts a family in deep turmoil as they try to follow God's will. *Of Stillness and Storm* is a disturbingly poignant look at how godly people can become dangerously dysfunctional. This novel touched deep places in my soul, as a thirty-year-veteran missionary in Europe who works in Member Care. Michèle got it right and unabashedly shares the horrors one family descends into as they seek God's will. A must-read for those contemplating missions and for all those who pray for missionaries and their children (MKs) who are scattered around the world."

—ELIZABETH MUSSER, AUTHOR OF *THE LONG HIGHWAY HOME*

"In *Of Stillness and Storm*, Michèle Phoenix bravely tackles what appears to be a great paradox in Scripture—that Jesus says we are to follow him despite the cost to self or other relationships, yet later we read that those who do not care for their families are worse than infidels. How can both principles be operative at the same time? Through a beautifully written and compelling account of one family's struggles to understand the implications of these statements within the context of 'real life,' Michèle causes us to take a fresh look at our own stories as well. You will be both challenged and encouraged as you read this gripping tale."

—RUTH E. VAN REKEN, INTERNATIONAL SPEAKER AND CO-AUTHOR
OF *THIRD CULTURE KIDS: GROWING UP AMONG WORLDS*

# of stillness and storm

MICHÈLE PHOENIX

THOMAS NELSON
Since 1798

Published in Nashville, Tennessee, by Thomas Nelson. Thomas Nelson is a registered trademark of HarperCollins Christian Publishing, Inc.

The author is represented by MacGregor Literary, Inc.

Thomas Nelson titles may be purchased in bulk for educational, business, fund-raising, or sales promotional use. For information, please e-mail SpecialMarkets@ThomasNelson.com.

Publisher's Note: This novel is a work of fiction. Names, characters, places, and incidents are either products of the author's imagination or used fictitiously. All characters are fictional, and any similarity to people living or dead is purely coincidental.

Library of Congress Cataloging-in-Publication Data

Names: Phoenix, Michèle, author.
Title: Of stillness and storm / Michèle Phoenix.
Description: Nashvillie : Thomas Nelson, [2016]
Identifiers: LCCN 2016028401 | ISBN 9780718086428 (softcover)
Subjects: LCSH: Self-realization in women--Fiction. | Married women--Fiction.
| Marital conflict--Fiction. | Domestic fiction.
Classification: LCC PS3616.H65 O35 2016 | DDC 813/.6--dc23 LC record available at https://lccn.loc.gov/2016028401

Printed in the United States of America

16 17 18 19 20 21 RRD 6 5 4 3 2 1

To my parents for the immeasurable
gift of growing up MK

Acknowledgments

CHIP MACGREGOR, MY AGENT, THANK YOU FOR PAVING THE way to my new home at Thomas Nelson. Your tireless effort and belief in this novel made miracles happen.

Becky Monds, my editor, your inspired expertise enhanced and refined Lauren's story. I can't imagine a more supportive or collaborative experience. Thank you.

Chris, Leslie, and children, your love for Nepal shines bright and true. Thank you for introducing me to its bewildering beauty—and to its traffic, its monkeys, and its power outages.

Prakash, my Nepali friend, your life is a testament to dreaming big and bold. Compared to what you've done to bring education to remote regions, your contribution to this book may seem insignificant to you, but it's invaluable to me.

Renée, Mrs. Dailey, Lauren, Greg, Myrna, Gail, and Mom, *Of Stillness and Storm* wouldn't exist without you. Thank you for reading that messy first draft and encouraging me to persevere.

I couldn't possibly list all the Missionaries' Kids who have breathed purpose, challenge, and beauty into my life—but you know who you are. You have galvanized and fulfilled me, and I thank God for each of you.

Prologue

I HESITATED AT THE GATE, AFRAID THAT MY MERE PRESENCE would seem sacrilege to death's inmates. This was a place of interrupted conversations, where lichen grew and strangled sculpted stone. Abbreviated eulogies etched like scars on granite graves denied death's perpetuity. All words were mute here. Only the trills of hidden birds punctuated the dull hum of silence.

A polished stone reflected racing clouds and filtered sun. I knelt and traced the contour of his name.

Part One

ABSENCE

one

THE SOUND OF THE FAN COMING ON BROUGHT ME OUT OF A heavy sleep. Its initial slow clicks accelerated into a whoosh that covered the growls of dogs facing off by the *pasal* outside our gates. I squinted at the battery-powered alarm clock on Sam's side of the bed, its numbers barely illuminated by the moonlight shining through the window. Just after two in the morning.

When the moon wasn't out, nights were black in our part of Kathmandu. No street lamps. No lighted signs outside shops, along empty streets, or on deserted corners. When the electricity went off—and sometimes stayed off for ten hours a day—the windows of Nepali homes hung like empty eye sockets from the brick walls that held them.

Living with unpredictable power was a skill I was still trying to master. Even after two years, I'd leave a light switch or two in their on position after the bulbs had flickered out. So when the fan hummed on and the old fridge shuddered back to life downstairs, I'd set off on my nearly nightly game of turn-off-the-lights. From the darkness of the house, I could tell that I'd done better than usual tonight, but I assumed the bare lightbulb hanging from the ceiling in Ryan's bedroom would be on when I got there.

3

As I reached for my robe, I wondered where Sam was, what he would see when the sun crept over the mountain peaks four hours from now. Though the weather was unusually warm for February in Kathmandu, I knew it was much chillier at the altitude where he lived during his weeks away from us. But the cold never seemed to bother him. Wherever this trek had taken him, he'd be lying in his tent or under the stars on his side, arms crossed, a thin blanket pulled shoulder-high, impervious to the temperatures, filth, and hunger that would have daunted lesser men.

Though I'd gotten used to waking up without him, I missed the sameness of living alongside Sam. His routines were as familiar to me as my own. Every morning he was home, his eyes would open at dawn—those pale blue eyes that stood in stark contrast to the ruggedness of his features. He'd glance up and gauge the time from the brightness of the sky, ignoring the clock that sat on the nightstand next to him. Then he'd throw back the blanket and swing his legs out of bed in one smooth movement, pulling on the baggy Nepali pants he'd left stacked on the floor like a fireman's uniform the night before.

The lights and fans turning on in the middle of the night wouldn't have woken Sam. They never did, when he was home. Nor was he bothered by the ringing of copper bells at six o'clock each morning, attempts by the pious to earn the favor of their gods. He slept like a sated baby, with two folded T-shirts for a pillow so he wouldn't get "soft" during his days with us.

I glanced at Sam's picture on the dresser under the window. How little he'd changed in nearly twenty years. With age, his features had become sharper. His cheekbones more prominent, his mouth set off by deeper creases at its corners. The youthful glow of our first encounter had tightened into something less naïve—something more lived-in.

Sam would be home in a few days. Back under this roof. Back in our lives. Back in my bed. I tried to muster up the swells of anticipation that had preceded his returns in the early stages of our life in Nepal. But I couldn't manufacture the longings. Not anymore. They'd faded gradually, in almost imperceptible ways. On nights like these, I feared that I had too.

I ran my fingers through my hair as I left the bedroom, expecting to feel sleep-tangles, but was surprised—again. The cropped hairstyle had been more resignation than aesthetic decision. It had underlined a shift in my worldview. A relinquishing. A submitting.

"Cut it all off."

It was three months into our Kathmandu transition. I'd just stepped out of the shower and had called to Sam to bring me a pair of scissors.

"Cut it all?" He looked puzzled. "Lauren, are you sure?"

Appearance was utterly unimportant to Sam, but he knew my hair, thin and straight as it was, was one of the few features I actually liked about myself.

"It's too hot. And too much hassle. And it never really feels clean." I gathered it, wet and dripping, into a tight ponytail and took stock. I looked different without its fullness framing my face. My skin looked paler, my neck thinner. I felt exposed, but I knew this moment had been weeks in the making. Months, perhaps.

"Cut right above where I'm holding it," I instructed Sam, "and I'll fix it when you're done." My hand shook where it gripped the ponytail.

Sam positioned the scissors, but his expression was still uncertain. "Lauren, are you absolutely sure?"

I nodded. "New life, right?" I said, attempting optimism, trying to make of this action a decision—not a capitulation.

"New life, new look." The knot in my stomach contradicted my self-deception.

Sam smirked. "And fewer hair products to pay for."

How typical of Sam to measure this moment on a financial scale. I stared at my reflection and felt a chapter slamming shut. There was a flutter in my chest that might have been excitement or dread. "It's just a haircut," I said—a feeble assertion. Then I nodded at Sam to begin cutting.

I didn't feel any freer as I took the scissors from his hands minutes later and saw the approval on his face. I combed my hair straight and snipped the ends into an even bob as change seeped its uncertainty into my resolve. Then I snipped some more. Out of victory. Or maybe spite. Resignation. When I was done, the bob had become a short, spiked cut that symbolized more than I was willing to admit.

With a flashlight lighting the way, I crossed the threshold to Ryan's room and tried the door. He lay spread-eagled under his pile of blankets, his mouth slightly open, one hand dangling off the edge of the mattress. With sleep softening his features, he looked his age again. Thirteen and vulnerable. He stirred as I turned off his overhead light and reached for his alarm.

"Electricity came on," I whispered.

"What time is it?" His voice was sleep-rough and bothered.

"A little past two. Try to go back to sleep."

He groaned and let his head fall back onto his pillow. "Can you make baked oatmeal?" Semiconscious and still thinking about food.

"For breakfast?"

"Yeah." He burrowed deeper.

"Sure."

He turned toward the wall and pulled the blankets close around his face, the way he had since he was a child. I smiled and resisted the impulse to find the edge of his bed in the darkness and sit there, listening to him breathe. I wanted to run my hand over his hair until he fell into a deeper sleep. But I couldn't do that anymore, not even in the middle of the night, when slumber weakened his resistance.

Though there were still moments of connection between us, they'd grown scarcer with each of Sam's returns, and every time he left again, I lost more of our son. Ryan pretended not to miss his dad and went out of his way to let me know how little he cared. About anything. It wasn't so much in words as in the absence of words—overfull silences.

But he'd spoken to me without scowling just now. I felt my heart constrict as I pulled his bedroom door shut.

There was no need to tiptoe as I headed downstairs in my rubber-soled slippers, though I did anyway. The floors and stairs were made of cement. No creaking boards or sagging steps— only cold concrete and colder feet. I circled through the living room on my way to the kitchen, pulling a blanket off the back of the couch and wrapping it around my shoulders to ward off the February chill.

After two winters, the penetrating dampness still surprised me. We had no central heating, just a small electric radiator we used on rare occasions, when the cold got bad enough to warrant the power usage. Even then, it was only effective in the tiniest of rooms. I'd taken to wearing layers inside the house— sweats, long-sleeved T-shirts, zip-up sweaters, and fleece jackets. Sometimes, I'd add fingerless gloves to the vagrant look. All three of us slept with hot water bottles in our beds. Anything to ward off the creep of shivering discomfort.

For our twice-a-week showers, we'd drag our radiator into the downstairs bathroom and use it just long enough to hop in and out of the cement tub. We kept mouths and eyes closed to the bacteria in the thin trickle of water drawn by gravity from a cistern two stories above.

I flipped the switch that pumped water to the roof, knowing we would run out if I didn't take advantage of our hours of electric power. Then I placed an empty pitcher under the filtration system that hung above the kitchen sink and turned on a slow stream to fill it, lining up several other pitchers for later use. I set a pot of filtered water on the gas stove to heat for tea and installed myself at the dining room table, lifting the laptop's lid.

One of my middle-of-the-night activities was using my laptop when the faster Wi-Fi signal from the NGO next door had fewer users sharing it. I knew Sam disapproved of my "borrowing" it, but I told myself the occasional midnight usage was harmless.

I didn't spend much time communicating with the past. It seemed healthier not to keep too connected to what had previously fed and defined me. But on nights like these, in the silence of a sleeping house and with much-needed water refilling our rooftop cistern, I had time to spare and nowhere to go.

I opened my Gmail account. A couple of promotional e-mails about discounted photo books and vitamins. The weight loss ads I'd started receiving after clicking on a site hocking raspberry ketones. And a note from Sullivan.

Sullivan.

We'd met in Austria—her Southern belle exuberance an odd match to my Midwestern wallflower reserve. And for reasons still mysterious to me, we'd become friends. She was as self-promoting as I was self-effacing. As flamboyant as I was restrained. As outspoken as I was measured. She quoted *Steel*

Magnolias like I quoted C.S. Lewis. And somehow, in a tiny Bible school perched on a mountain in a town named Sternensee, where our presence was as illogical as it was providential, we'd recognized in each other an odd-shaped missing piece.

If someone had told me when I started college that I'd get to spend a semester in Europe studying theology in a chalet with twenty students from around the world, I'd have doubted the prediction. Granted, my growing-up years had been steeped in youth groups and church services and prayer meetings and outreach projects. But as I grew into my teens, my faith had become more circumstantial than intentional. There were moments along the way when something indefinable hinted at a soul connection. A flutter of spiritual yearning. A dependence on the divine. But those occurrences had remained mild and fleeting until college, when a new circle of believing friends had awakened my desire to learn and experience more.

So I'd searched for a school where I could bolster my beliefs with knowledge and where living in another culture would broaden my worldview. I'd found both in Sternensee's quirky Christschule, an English-language Bible school where international students came to study and ski—sometimes in reverse order. I'd spent a semester there, basking in a foreign world and accumulating credits that would somehow count toward my bachelor of arts from an American college.

I'd met my husband there too—something Sullivan had predicted nearly from the moment she met Sam.

When was it that she and I had started communicating again? Two years ago? Nearly three? Life had gotten in the way after college, and multiple moves had put an end to the Christmas cards that came slipping into the mailbox between Thanksgiving and New Year, leaving sparkles on my hands and a strange wistfulness in my mind.

I opened Sullivan's e-mail, bracing for the effusions of enthusiasm I'd come to expect. Three days ago, she had twisted my arm into opening a Facebook account. *Chickadee. Chick-a-dee!* she'd written. *You have got to come over to the dark side. I've found every single member of the Sternensee gang, and I've got to tell you, while I've been maintaining my girlish figure and youthful countenance, these people have gotten appallingly old. Listen, I know you're not into this sort of thing, but you're the only one missing from our little reunion page.* I could picture her waving a hand in the air as if dismissing something trivial. *Just give it a try, will you? You won't need to sign your name in blood or anything. The gang'll be thrilled to hear from you!*

Sam was suspicious of Facebook and its power to monopolize one's time, and though I didn't have any moral convictions about it, I'd resisted the social networking phenomenon mostly because I disliked fads. But I knew Sullivan. Her powers of persuasion were well honed and irresistible. The timing of my crossover to the "dark side," as she called it, might have been in question, but the inevitability of it was not.

So on a quiet evening three nights ago, I'd clicked the Facebook icon and, taking a deep breath, begun to fill in my information. Twice I'd closed the page, telling myself it was the wise thing to do, and headed to another room to grade some papers. Twice I'd returned to the computer, berating myself for my misgivings, and set about entering the information again. *The gang'll be thrilled to hear from you!* Sullivan's words prodded me on.

As soon as the deed was done, I'd clicked out of the app and gone about my business as usual. I hadn't opened it again in three days—partly to prove to myself that I was capable of restraint and partly out of nervousness about reconnecting with "the gang."

Whatever qualms I'd had, Sullivan's latest e-mail put them to rest. *You did it! What a kick in the pants! Welcome to the realm of the connected and addicted, Chickadee. I promise you will* not *regret it.*

She might as well have sent a voicemail. Her accent, intensified perhaps by the passage of time, drawled out of the screen as I read.

Here's something you may not realize: sites like these are most effective if you actually visit them, which I know requires a bit of a leap into the unknown. So I've sent you a message on Facebook—a personalized guided tour. I could charge you for the Sullivan Geary Facebook Tutorial, but since you're a pal o' mine, it's yours for free. So head on over there and open my message. Now. (Are you still reading this? I said—now!)

I stepped back into the kitchen, just a few feet away from the dining room table, to change out the pitchers. Then I took the pan of boiling water off the stove. With steaming tea in hand, I returned to the dining room.

I opened Facebook, typed "Sullivan Geary" in the search bar, and scrolled down to her thumbnail to click on it.

Sullivan's profile picture, a black-and-white shot of the socialite holding her beloved three-legged Dudley, was perfect. Her hair was stylishly tousled, her makeup impeccably applied, and her smile as orthodontist-straight as any movie star's, but the dog she held—a mix of unknown origin, one ear higher than the other, with the stub of one foreleg unapologetically displayed—said more about my friend than any professional portrait could have.

This was the Sullivan I loved: a polished, charismatic woman in full command of her world, who wielded her status like authority and served on the boards of countless charities, demanding donations by the sheer magnetism of her spirit. And a softhearted empath who had stopped her white convertible on a torrid Savannah day to rescue a stray who'd been hit by a car. The veterinary bills had been astronomical and the outcome uncertain, but she'd fought for that little life like a mother for her child. And Dudley had survived.

I moved my finger on the trackpad until the cursor hovered over the blue message icon and clicked, then I followed Sullivan's instructions to a T, choosing my privacy settings, deactivating e-mail notifications, and trying to figure out the difference between walls, newsfeeds, profiles, messages, and instant messages. Despite Sullivan's strong recommendation, I balked at uploading a photo and declined Facebook's offer to help me find friends.

After an hour or so of stumbling around the site with little evidence that I'd accomplished anything, I took one last sip of my cold tea and prepared to sign out. That's when I noticed that another red number had appeared on the message icon at the top of my screen. I checked the laptop's clock. It was almost eleven at night in Savannah. Surely Sullivan, whose beauty rest was a nearly religious concern, was long asleep.

I clicked the icon and frowned. Aidan D? Then I put down my cup and stared at the screen, my breath catching.

Aidan?

I clicked to open the message. The thumbnail next to Aidan's name was a blur of primary colors, but I didn't attempt to get a closer look. The words next to it were enough to make me shove the laptop away, incredulous, then draw it closer again.

hey, ren. is this really you?

I stared at the words. Willing them to tell me more. Willing them to shift into the shape of his face and confirm that it was he. Ren. No one called me Ren, an odd abbreviation of Lauren I hadn't heard since—Aidan.

I shut the laptop's lid, pushed away from the table, and retreated to the kitchen. Then I laughed at the impulse. I didn't know much about technology, but I was pretty sure that a computer couldn't follow me to another room.

"This is absurd," I mumbled out loud, a hand pressed to my chest, my eyes still on the laptop sitting on the dining room table. I shook my head. "Ridiculous, Lauren." Marching back into the dining room, I lifted the lid and squinted at the single line of writing.

hey, ren. is this really you?

My fingers shook a little as I moved the cursor over Aidan's name and clicked. I sat back and took in the information on his page. The banner at the top was blank, but the smaller picture, the one I'd seen as a thumbnail next to his message, was a rugged tree painted in stark, textured red. The brash, unapologetic nature of the art convinced me that this Aidan was the same I'd known from childhood until . . . I frowned again and felt my heart rate speeding up.

Aidan.

two

January 1997

Sullivan squealed as she stopped in a spray of snow and ice, her skis mere inches from mine and perfectly parallel. "Gracious, when that sun drops behind the mountain, visibility turns to mud!"

It would have taken me half the time to get the same sentence out, but Sullivan's Savannah drawl turned warm-honey words to cold-morning molasses.

"I told you another run would be pushing it."

"And that's exactly what sent me back up there, Chickadee!" Sullivan said with a flourish of her ski pole. She flashed her Miss Berkeley County second runner-up smile. "If it ain't risky, it ain't fun."

I laughed and pulled my red knit hat farther down over my ears, wishing I could radiate a fraction of her zest for life. "I'm going to remind you of that when you're destitute, married for the fifth time, and all banged up from a skydiving accident."

"Bring a bottle of bourbon to my bedside and you can remind me of anything you like." She pointed a pole toward the barely visible hostel on a hill across the mountain village, a building nearly one hundred years old that had been converted by an American organization into a short-term Bible school. Its windows gleamed softly in the darkening evening. "As many great explorers before us have said," Sullivan declared in a well-modulated, theatrical voice, "Mush, darlin', mush!"

15

From her lips, the words sounded more like an invitation to decadence than the starter pistol for our long trek home.

"Whatever you say, Sullivan." I tucked my scarf more tightly into the neck of my jacket and used my ski poles to push off in the direction of the footpath that led from the slopes to the village. Sullivan followed close behind. Lights were flickering on in the chalets of the Austrian village, and plumes of white smoke rose from their chimneys. Three days into my stay in Sternensee, the sights and sounds of the village still enchanted me. Their beauty lulled me and their otherness surprised me.

People stopped to stare as Sullivan and I headed home. We'd taken off our skis where the snowy path met the road and carried them on our shoulders, the *cuh-cuck* of our rigid boots resounding in the quiet streets. Had we walked without speaking, no one would have noticed us making our way from the slopes to the hostel. But silence was not Sullivan's strong suit.

She talked. No, she didn't just talk. She Sullivan-ed. In this stoic mountain village, where qualities like order, modesty, and privacy were prized, Sullivan's voice cut like a drill sergeant's wake-up call. I walked alongside my striking friend, mostly invisible and perfectly content that my more common appearance, small frame, and sober countenance made me a less obvious foreigner. Even in the comfort zone of my college back home, I shirked the spotlight, leaving the bulk of performance assignments to more extroverted classmates and happy to help behind the scenes when others elbowed their way onto the lighted stage.

"You realize people are staring, right?"

Sullivan stopped and propped a hand on her hip, eyebrows arched. "Lauren. Sweetie. This is the churchmouse version of me. Back home, I'd be speaking twice as loudly and stopping to say hey to every last one of these folks. They should be happy I'm putting this much effort into being sensitive to their culture!"

As a recovering churchmouse myself, I knew how inaccurate her self-assessment was. Age and increased confidence had allowed me to reach a sort of functional introversion, but I still tended toward a more subdued disposition than Sullivan's. She stood in tall, loud, shiny contrast to all that was Austrian, while I tried to move, unseen, around the shadowed edges of the culture.

It was at the beginning of our second week in Sternensee that Craig Peters—the lanky, sixty-year-old former competitive skier from Minnesota who now directed the Bible school—interrupted our evening in the lounge to introduce us to a new arrival. His name was Sam. He'd come late because of passport problems. He'd be with us for the rest of the semester and would be rooming with Rudy.

There was a moment of awkward silence after Craig left the room. Sam stood there with a backpack over his shoulder and a suitcase at his feet. He didn't seem insecure, just curious as he glanced around the lounge, taking off his jacket and scarf.

"So this is Sternensee." He grinned and held out his arms in a what-do-we-do-now gesture. There was confidence in his stance and in the tilt of his chin. A couple of the guys rose to greet him and offered to show him to his room.

Sullivan's elbow connected with my ribs as they exited. "One— those eyes!" she said. "Lashes to die for!"

"Sullivan . . ."

"Two—that sweater. Those khakis. Loverboy's got style."

I angled a disapproving look at her. "Loverboy's been here thirty seconds—"

"Three," she interrupted, a hand on my arm and her eyes on the door. "There's a chance this man is God's will for your life."

"Wow," I said, laughing. "If God's using you to prophesy my future, he does indeed work in mysterious ways."

Sam and his new friends walked back into the room, and Sullivan made a production of offering him some Ovo.

"I'm sure I'd love some, but I have no idea what it is," he said, eyeing the can of brown powder in Sullivan's hand.

There was something about his voice that caught my attention. Something sharp and smooth. A vibrancy. A sincerity. He gave Sullivan a lopsided smile as she went on about the health benefits of nutrient-rich Ovomaltine and America's loss for not having discovered the chocolate malt drink. A few seconds into her speech, he held up a hand to stop her.

"I don't mean to be rude," Sam said, his smile seeming to soothe some of Sullivan's discomfiture, "but I don't think we've officially met. I'm Sam."

"Sullivan." She shook the hand he extended, then giggled and said, "Where are my manners? Fly a Southern girl to Austria and her entire upbringing goes out the window."

"Not bad manners at all," Sam said, releasing her hand. "And I'd love to have a cup of that . . . stuff you're offering."

While Sullivan prepared the drink for him, the rest of us introduced ourselves, welcoming him into our little group. Though he'd just arrived, he subtly took control of the dynamics that evening. When Sullivan attempted to insert herself into a more prominent role, he shifted the conversation to include all those present. It was an admirable trait—one that flowed from Sam naturally. The students seemed drawn to it. They engaged with him in a slightly more energetic way than they had with others, their guards lowered by the sincerity of his interest.

I watched from my chair in the corner of the room, tamping down the single-girl question that seemed ubiquitous to first meetings with charming single men. *Is it him?*

I instructed my mind to pipe down and shook my head at the silliness of the question. I hadn't flown to Austria to meet potential mates, and I was not one of those women who counted on marriage to seal their self-worth. But as I observed the stranger weaving himself into our tight-knit group within minutes of his arrival, I couldn't help the curiosity that swelled in spite of me.

Sam was just beginning his second cup of Ovomaltine, served again by a somewhat deflated Sullivan, when he looked at me and said, "Lauren, right?" I nodded. "Tell me about you."

∽

It didn't take long for Sullivan to decide that Sam was interested in me.

"He's not interested, Sullivan," I said one day, as we rode the ski lift to the top of Hochkőnig.

Sullivan would have none of that. "He's smitten."

"Sullivan . . ."

"There are a few things in this world at which I'm mediocre, Chickadee. Reading men is not one of them."

I laughed. "But humility makes the cut."

Sullivan turned in her seat, making it lurch and grind. "He talks to everyone—"

"That's what I'm saying—"

"But when he talks to you, there's something different." She paused dramatically. "I'm going to overlook the fact that your smile right now is mildly condescending," she said, "and will instead let you in on the fruit of my keen observation."

"Is there an eject button on this chairlift?"

"We've established that he has impeccable etiquette. He looks straight at a person when he talks, and he listens with his eyes and his ears. Very rare—very rare indeed. But when he talks to you?" She paused, ostensibly to let the suspense build before going on. "Notice this next time—when he talks to you, he leans forward a little. Not much. Just enough to tell anyone watching that this woman—this woman with the fair skin and sleek hair and the . . ."

19

"Crooked eyetooth."

"Oh, hush. It just gives you more character."

"Right."

She went on undeterred. "The way he leans in, all attentive and enraptured, tells anyone watching that this woman right here has his undivided attention."

"Enraptured?"

"The subtext is: 'Don't interrupt—this is important business.'"

"Sullivan," I laughed, "we've got to get you home to Savannah so you can go back to meddling in your own life." She raised an eyebrow, and I patted her knee. "I'll watch for the lean."

"You'll find I'm right."

⤜≋⤛

It bothered me to admit it, but I had to conclude that there was some genius in my friend's assessment of Sam's body language and intentions. By the fourth week of the Christschule semester, I knew when I headed for the slopes in the afternoon that Sam would arrive in the ski shed outside the hostel right after Sullivan and I got there. He'd join us on the long walk through town and, yes, lean in when he spoke to me. He'd drift in and out during our time on the slopes, sometimes going solo, other times joining the Norwegian contingent for some high-octane descents, but the moment we headed for home, he'd be there, skis on his shoulder, ready to go.

Sam brought to our friendship the same steadfast drive he brought to his studies and his goals—a focused, no-nonsense energy, a pursuit of well-iterated objectives. Living in such close quarters, I had plenty of time to observe him. He was an avid learner. Not the type who challenged professors for sport or asked questions merely to draw attention to himself. No, Sam Coventry was engrossed by the subjects he'd come to learn about. He was eager in his quest for knowledge,

20

often stumping our professors with his theological queries or baiting them into debate with the intensity of his disagreement. I admired his zeal and knowledge, but sometimes wondered at the rightness of his methods.

***

I'd been minding my own business in the downstairs lounge, curled up in one of the more comfortable chairs in a hostel furnished more for practicality than luxury. I looked up from the copy of *Pride and Prejudice* I'd taken from the lost-and-found shelf.

"Adam and Eve—fact or fable?"

Sam stood there, smiling. He lowered himself into the chair across from mine with a muffled groan. He caught my raised eyebrows. "Took the black slope with the Norwegians and they decided to go off course. Big mistake."

I winced. "The kind that ends wrapped around a tree?"

"The kind that ends with one ski pointing downhill and the other pointing toward the summit. So . . . fact or fable?"

"Adam and Eve?" I asked. He nodded, his expression expectant. "And you actually expect me to have an educated response?"

Another nod. I laughed and dropped my head onto the backrest of my chair to stare at the ceiling and think. I found myself doing that a lot when I was talking with Sam.

When I looked back at him, he was still watching me. "That depends. Serpent and apple—fact or fable?"

I'd grown accustomed to the flutters his smiles elicited, but I still wasn't sure I liked them. "You can't answer a question with a question," he said.

"Sure I can."

"I want to know what *you* think."

"Why?"

"I have to have a reason?"

"It seems to me you always do."

"Really."

"Why do you part your hair on the left?"

"Cowlicks."

"Why do you wear so much khaki?"

"To simplify mixing and matching."

"Why did you move your mattress onto the floor?"

He raised an eyebrow.

"I've got sources."

"Because I don't want to get too comfortable," he said, smirking.

"See? Reasons."

Sparring was a communication style to Sam. Sullivan suspected it was a flirting style too. But when we'd gone a couple rounds about biblical figures and theological sticking points, we tended to settle into less lofty conversations.

"So tell me something I don't know about you," he said. He leveled his best Sam-stare at me—casual, interested, and analytical. Part of me missed the high grounds of our theoretical sparring. They felt safer than the personal questions.

"You can't just throw out that broad of a net and expect me to know how to answer."

"Good point. So tell me what you think I should know about you."

Vulnerability fluttered again. "Why?"

"Because I want to know."

"Why?"

"You realize the 'why stage' happens during the Terrible Twos, right?"

I glanced out the window that faced the street and focused my attention on the mountaintops in the distance. Sam sat across from me, elbows on his knees, leaning forward. I wasn't sure why his interest felt so daunting or why my defenses went up when he delved too deep.

Sullivan had called me on it after witnessing a particularly reluctant exchange. "Your hard-to-get routine could land you in never-gotten purgatory, Chickadee." I'd responded with vigor, asserting that being "gotten" was not the only means to a meaningful life. She'd looked at me askance. "Listen, when the lady doth protest too much, it makes me wonder what's behind the resistance."

"I'm not resisting."

Raised eyebrow. "Really?"

Sam's eyes were still on me when I turned back to him, his curiosity and trademark energy evident in his gaze. He'd been nothing but genuine since his arrival at Sternensee, but there was something about his interest, as flattering as it felt, that flashed memories across my mind—like slides on a shadowed screen. Juvenile laughter. Whispered dreams. Unspoken emotions. Flames. Embers. Ashes. They warned and whimpered from the past.

But Sam lived in the present—in a clear, unshadowed Now—and I wouldn't let my ghosts deprive me of this challenging unknown. I squared my shoulders and looked Sam straight in the eyes. "I stole money from my mom's Mary Kay drawer."

He looked confused. "You stole from your mom's—"

"She sold Mary Kay products and kept the money she made in her desk drawer between trips to the bank, and when she and my dad cut off my allowance for three weeks because I said a bad word, I stole money from the drawer to see a movie with my friends."

A smile deepened the creases around Sam's eyes. "You stole from your mom to see a movie?"

My smile matched his. "It was *Beaches*—well worth the guilt."

"Shame on you."

"Now tell me a secret about you."

"Hey, I never asked for a secret."

But Sam was a storyteller, and the invitation to recount the tales of his youth led him down trails both entertaining and crystallizing in

23

the weeks we spent together. I realized as he unveiled them one after another that the integrity that defined him was a purposeful pursuit, and though his history was typical in so many ways, his dreams were the stuff of trailblazing legends.

∼

Part of life at Sternensee was sharing daily chores, and when Sam and I were assigned to do dinner dishes together, neither of us contested it. As Sam pushed racks of plates and cutlery in and out of an industrial dishwasher and I washed pots and pans in a deep, stainless steel sink, we let our conversations skip naturally from topic to topic.

"So what are you going to do when you graduate?" Sam asked during one of our last evenings doing dishes together.

"With a degree in communications? I'm thinking I'll be doing more of this for a while." I held up my sudsy hands. "Then I'll move up the corporate ladder to short-order cook. Or maybe I can drive a school bus if I play my cards right."

Sam stopped in the act of drying a dinner plate and leaned a hip against the counter. "What's the dream?" he asked.

I shrugged. "I honestly don't know." I pushed back a strand of hair with my wrist. "I love to write but . . . I don't know."

Sam stepped closer. "What's the dream*?" he repeated, drawing out the word like it gave it more significance.*

"What's yours?"

"This technique again?"

"If it ain't broke . . ."

"To make a difference," he answered. I could tell from his tone that he'd given it some thought.

"But what's the dream*?" I parroted.*

He acknowledged my imitation with a nod and got back to drying plates. "To be a pioneer," he said after a few moments of silence. "Do something unconventional. Stray a little from the traveled path."

"There's probably a reason why that path is traveled."

"Or it may be because no one dared to be unconventional before."

I'd never been much of a risk taker. I found a comfort in predictability that Sam probably wouldn't understand. "Honestly, when I think about the future, I don't have a driving ambition. You know—that one thing I need to do or I'll never be satisfied."

"So writing is . . . ?"

"Something I enjoy. I'm not sure I can make it into a career, though."

"And when you were growing up? What about then?"

I hesitated. "Seriously?" I asked, playing for time. He nodded, and I knew my answer to this query would open the door to a more intimate conversation. I paused long enough to make sure I'd be okay with that.

"If this is too personal—"

"No," I said, interrupting him. "It's fine." Mere weeks before, I might not have verbalized an honest answer to this question. I may not have acknowledged it even to myself. But there was something about Sam—the steadiness of his friendship and the openness of his interest—that made me able to recognize and speak it. "To be truthful," I said, still hoping he was safe, "all I've ever pictured myself being as an adult is a mom. Just . . . a mom."

"Just a mom? No husband."

"Of course a husband." I rolled my eyes and saw him flash a grin.

"You can do better," he said. There was no judgment in his expression. Just certainty.

"Than being a wife and mother?"

"You can be that and more. I tend to view my future as a 'both-and' scenario."

"Except that I don't know, right now, what that 'and' might be."

He nodded. "I think it comes to us when we need it to. Not a moment before." He shrugged. "But what do I know? I'm still waiting for my marching orders."

I nodded. Both-and. If Sam believed it to be true, I figured it was a concept I needed to consider.

＊

"You realize you'll soon be living in the shadow of my educational achievements," Sullivan said after her essay on New Testament anti-heroes earned a higher grade than mine.

"You realize theology isn't a competitive sport," I answered, a bit miffed that my relationship with Sam was having such a detrimental effect on my grades. The truth was that he'd become a distraction. At some point in the weeks we'd spent together, this undefined relationship had become a jeopardizing thing—to my studies, my concentration, and my equilibrium.

"My theory," Sullivan drawled, "is that all this pussyfootin' around the true nature of your feelings is depleting the mental energy your studies require."

We were sitting in the bedroom we shared under the hostel's eaves.

"We're not pussyfooting." I stuffed my essay into a folder and tossed it on the bed next to me, unwilling to acknowledge my friend's rightness. "We're exploring."

Sullivan pulled a cardigan out of a drawer and shrugged into it, muttering under her breath. "You two are seriously testing my atten-tion span."

"Are we moving too slow for your entertainment needs?"

"You're moving too slow—period. Time's a tickin' and I'm seeing no evidence that you're ready to commit." She sat at her desk and gave me her sorority sister stare.

"Because we're not."

"Well, what's the holdup?" My hesitation was inconceivable to her.

I shrugged. "I guess we're being wise."

"Or you're being scared. You'd sooner take on a black diamond slope blindfolded than speak honestly of your emotions."

"I'm not scared."

"Say that again with conviction."

I looked her straight in the eyes. "I'm not scared." The words sounded hollow even to my ears.

"I know I'm meddling, but I just need to ask . . ."

"Sullivan . . ."

"Are you attracted to the boy or not?"

"I . . ." The directness of her question took me aback. "I don't know."

She seemed unsatisfied with that. "You don't *want* to know." She leaned forward in her desk chair and pursed her lips. "What is it you're afraid of?"

Though I wanted to back away from the bluntness of her interrogation, I held my position. "Again—I'm not afraid."

"Tell me this, Chickadee," she said after a beat. "When was the last time you really loved someone? In a romantic way, I mean."

"I'm not sure I—"

"Gracious, you can be cagey. Have you ever loved someone or not?"

I didn't like the question. It grated over unmarked graves in fragile spaces of my past. I stared at my hands. "Maybe?" I cleared my throat. "Yes."

"And?"

I shook my head. "It didn't work out."

The cuckoo clock in the hallway outside our bedroom ticked in the silence, metronoming the parade of recollections and regrets marching through my mind.

"Sam's great," I said after a few moments, sitting up straighter. "He's . . ." I shook my head again, confused and frustrated. "He's

great. And . . . and yes, I think I like him." My own laugh startled me.
"Welcome to junior high," I said.

"Some things we don't outgrow."

"Listen, if I had a list of 'ideal husband' traits, he'd probably check every item on it. And I do love being with him. I do. I'm just not sure how to categorize this . . . thing. Besides, the semester is short and we're living in this bubble. Who knows if what we have could survive in the real world?"

"So you're playing it safe."

"So I'm playing it safe."

Sullivan moved to sit beside me on the edge of my bed. "Here's what I know. If you are meant to share your heart in a til-death-do-us-part kind of way with a man who is likely debating some obscure piece of the Scriptures with a poor sap downstairs at this very moment, I'd hate to see you squander it for the sake of"—she mimed air quotes—"'playing it safe.'"

"But how can I be sure?" I whispered.

She straightened. "Just so you know, I'm going to open the door and leave when I'm done saying what I'm going to say, because I've been holding on to this quote for a long time and I'm a big fan of dramatic exits."

I bit my lip to stifle a giggle. "Okay . . ."

Sullivan stood and moved toward the door. "'To love at all is to be vulnerable. Love anything and your heart will be wrung and possibly broken.'"

"Steel Magnolias?"

"C.S. Lewis. Your hero. Chickadee, you can keep your heart safe or you can lay it on the line and mend it when it breaks. A heart unrisked is a heart unshared—and yours is too good to waste."

She opened the door and stepped out of sight.

three

IT WAS A RARE THING FOR ME TO HAVE A MORNING AT HOME, but a *bandh* had erupted just after dawn, making my commute to the language school in Bhaktapur unsafe. These protests, some of them spontaneous and others well planned, were frequent occurrences in a country where there were few diplomatic means for people to be heard. From other expats in the city, I'd gleaned a bit of an understanding of this society that seemed to teeter on the brim of chaos. The side effects of decades of mismanagement and power grabs were intricately woven into every hardship and challenge that existed in Nepal—from its devalued currency to electricity shortages to the tenuous truce between Nepali castes and tribes.

Sometimes the *bandhs* were about political matters. Other times they were protests about unjust verdicts, Maoist demands, and incompetent leadership. Like gunpowder sifting through the government's hands just inches from an open flame, it seemed that the capital was perpetually on the brink of more protests that would send screaming, sign-carrying, and tire-burning crowds into the streets and squares of Kathmandu.

Though Ryan had previously enjoyed the delayed start of classes on *bandh* days, an unpleasant meeting in Miss Moore's

29

classroom had changed that. We'd sat him down afterward and tried to get to the bottom of the problems we'd only just discovered.

"Can you explain this?" Sam asked, holding up the report Ryan's teacher had given us. It detailed unfinished homework, tardiness, and a disrespectful attitude.

"Nope." Long, wavy bangs nearly covered his eyes. He looked from Sam to me, no sign of remorse in his gaze.

"What's with the grades?" There was a muscle twitching in Sam's jaw.

Ryan looked down and flopped back in his chair, feigning calm, arms loosely crossed. "I got behind, I guess."

"Sit up straight, son."

"Sam . . ."

"Lauren." His tone was sharp. So was the look on his face. It ordered silence. "Sit up straight," he said again, his words clipped.

Ryan hesitated. Then he shifted to a more upright position in his chair. He glanced at me before looking down at his hands.

"This has been going on for months and we're just hearing about it now?"

"You weren't home."

I leaned in. "But I *was*. Ryan, I could have helped you if you'd told me you were struggling."

He smirked. "With math?"

The conversation had deteriorated from there. Sam had pushed for answers and Ryan had clammed up. I'd tried to emphasize responsibility, challenging Ryan with the promise of rewards, but Sam had opted for outlining consequences instead. "We're not going to breathe down your neck every day, son. Either you shape up or we pull you out of soccer. Simple as that."

Ryan was on academic probation now—just one failing grade away from being held back a year—and *bandh* delays were no longer a break in schoolwork for him. They were an extra chance to finish his assignments before looming deadlines. I could feel his tension reaching me from the dining room as he polished the Renaissance paper due that day, procrastination once again fueling his frustration. I'd offered to proofread it for him. He'd refused. He always did, now.

When Ryan's school called to let us know that it was safe for the students to come in, he shoved his paper into his backpack and headed for the door.

"You think you did a good job on it?" I asked as Ryan was tying his shoelaces.

He shrugged, then slung his backpack over his shoulder and walked out without a word.

It would be awhile longer before the road to Bhaktapur was open, and I busied myself while I waited for the call. The language school was about an hour out of the city, and though my job teaching English to Nepali students was technically part-time, it seemed to consume much of my days. The commute was tedious and the teaching uninspiring, but the work granted us visas to live in Nepal. It gave Sam the ability to work where his passions lay. I envied him the luxury.

"Sam," I'd begged soon after our arrival, "is there any other way? What if I apply to teach at Ryan's school? Or another international school in the city?"

"I'm not sure that would fit our ministry platform."

"This isn't ministry—it's a visa requirement."

"Bhaktapur needs a teacher, and the students there are all Nepali. Think of the inroads . . ."

"But the commute—"

"Nepali students, Lauren. The people group we came to reach." I couldn't fathom the depth of his love for these people.

"I could bike to Ryan's school in fifteen minutes if I taught there. They have a curriculum in place. They have textbooks. Their educational system is—"

"God didn't call us to work with other expats." He paused. "Lauren, I know this isn't easy. I know it's a huge sacrifice."

"Do you?"

He took my hands in his. "He'll give you what it takes. Both of us. He'll give us both what it takes to do this work."

"Or maybe he gave us a house this close to Ryan's school as a sign . . ."

"Think about it." I knew from his smile that his vision would trump my desires. "You get to have influence over the Nepali students in your classes. You get to shape their thinking. Do you realize what a powerful position that is?"

He didn't understand my hesitance. Though he felt called to the Nepali people, I felt called to protecting our son. I wanted to be home for him. I wanted to stay sane for him. I wanted to connect *with him*. He'd already withdrawn in so many ways. The time, stress, and dissatisfaction of the position in Bhaktapur felt like another impediment to dragging him back to us. But there was no convincing Sam of that. His ministry compass was unwavering.

So I'd given in to the Bhaktapur obligation. Not willingly. Not graciously. Though my students were hardworking and committed to learning—motivated by the broader world that would open to them if they could hone their English skills— exhaustion, frustration, and a reluctance to be there impeded the "connection" Sam envisioned. We interacted between classes, our conversations polite and our topics unimportant. My failure dismayed me. I wanted to be more than this. More noble in my motivation. More selfless in my efforts.

"Hang in there," Sam would say when I showed my unhappiness. "God'll get you through this—he hasn't failed us yet!" He couldn't possibly sympathize with my onerous reality when his was rich with dreams fulfilled and bright with purposes achieved.

I dawdled on Facebook while I waited for the all clear to head to Bhaktapur. Suman worked in the kitchen, washing the dishes we'd left in the sink and swatting at the flies that made it into the house when she went out to bring the slop bucket to our chickens. Sam had insisted that hiring her was an important contribution to the economy and that it would mend some of the fences other expats had damaged by failing to invest in the lives of locals. Though I welcomed the help with cooking and cleaning and tried to schedule her hours around my teaching schedule, on days like this, when we were both home at the same time, it felt a bit like an intrusion. I felt useless and "unwifely," because those chores other women resented were not mine to choose four days a week.

It was a petty and ridiculous complaint. I knew that. But in a country where there was so little and life was so narrow, I missed the luxury of choice.

I picked up the laptop and escaped to the Sumanless sanctuary of our bedroom. Not exactly a sanctuary, by any Western definition. It was . . . sufficient. Barred windows allowed sunlight in. Colorful shawls hung on one wall, their patterns a welcome relief from the grey-green paint that covered rough plaster. A few pictures, some of them framed, and a painting of Mount Everest Sam had picked up on a trip to Dharan.

Sufficient. That's what life felt like in Nepal. And though the "lacks" of my new life had proven to be a challenge to my attitude and outlook, Sam had thrived in them, as if the deprivations were a badge of honor. He saw them as life-enhancing opportunities. Maybe faith-proving too.

I propped myself up against the braided straw mat that served as a headboard and opened Aidan's message. My fingers hovered over the keys as I pondered the approach to take in my response. Lighthearted? Excited? Nonchalant? Nostalgic?

I took a deep breath, aware of the tingle in the far recesses of my consciousness. I couldn't quite identify its source. Intrigue? Yes. Excitement? Perhaps. And also something that felt like a warning bell.

I hadn't thought of Aidan in so long. Hearing from him—and preparing to communicate with him—was like revisiting an old, familiar, me-shaped place I'd long forgotten about. It was compelling and daunting.

> Aidan, hi. I'm not sure what to write . . . I joined Facebook three days ago, just so a friend would get off my case about connecting with a group of people she and I used to know. Then I found the note from you. I don't know how you found me, but . . .

I hesitated. Just a few lines would be enough. Right? Acknowledge his message. Chalk it up to a surprising cyber encounter. Move on.

> . . . but it's good to know you're out there.

I pushed return to start a new paragraph and was dismayed

to see the message move out of the box I was typing in and into the thread below his initial line of text.

"What?" I tried to undo the action and erase the message by the usual means, but there it was, sent before I'd taken the time to really consider it. I reread my own words, relieved that I sounded less nervous "on paper" than I felt. *It's good to know you're out there.* Sullivan would call it a nonstatement. She despised those. Unsure of the proper etiquette for cyber messages, I hesitated again, then quickly typed,

All the best, Lauren.

I hit send, logged out of Facebook, and closed the browser window.

It was late afternoon when I got back to Kathmandu. As I made the hour-long journey home from Bhaktapur, there were still traces of the morning's *bandh* in the street outside the parliament building, a stack of burned-out tires near the gate and a couple bicycles shoved off to the side, probably abandoned when military trucks arrived on the scene to clear the protesters.

In my first few months in Nepal, I'd used my commutes as bonus time to observe my new world and its people. I found the Nepali striking. Their blend of exotic features and serene expressions had captivated me despite the hardships of learning life in a new country. But somewhere along the way, the hardships had snuffed out my desire to see and sense. I'd lost the tranquility appreciation required. Now I could share buses with these people—these beautiful, surprising people—and never really pause to look into their faces. I missed feeling curious, and I berated myself for letting the burden of foreignness steal my fascination.

Because of the disruption to public transit, I'd opted for a taxi instead of the usual bus home. The car was small—a scrappy, four-cylindered Maruti as dirty inside as outside. But it was neither the size of the cars nor the horsepower of their engines that made Nepali taxis fierce. It was the driving. It had taken me just a few days in the country to understand that drivers here navigated like bats, guided by the constant bleating of horns that replaced the rearview mirrors and blinkers of more Western civilizations. They ducked and weaved through potholed, crowded streets, sometimes coming within an inch of collision, with the dexterity of tightrope walkers, each move predicated on the sound of the cars around them.

By the time I got home, I could feel a layer of dust on my face and plastered to my eyelashes, the tightness in my lower back from shock absorbers that had absorbed nothing. I dropped my book bag on the bench just inside the door and followed the smell of food into the kitchen. Suman had left warm samosás and a salad on the table, ready to be eaten when Ryan's soccer game was over. I popped one of the boiled, vegetable-filled pastries into my mouth and covered the rest of the tray with tinfoil.

A few moments later, I wandered into the dining room with feigned casualness, lifted the laptop's lid, and opened Facebook to Aidan's page. It felt unseemly to scroll through someone else's communication with people I didn't know. There were bad cell phone pictures of some sort of event, a George Carlin quote, and two links to political articles. Not for the first time, I wondered about the value of a site designed for public exposure.

There was a red 1 next to the message icon at the top of my screen. Something vaguely unsettling scratched at my consciousness, much like Muffin, our Nepali mutt, had scratched at the front door when he was a puppy. It was a nearly imperceptible thing, barely audible above the growing hum of anticipation.

Letting out a long breath, I moved my fingers over the trackpad and clicked on the message icon. I leaned forward to read, my eyes skipping ahead in their hurry, then going back to savor each of Aidan's words.

> ren. it's you. this is . . . surreal. what is it? twenty years? twenty-one? you're here (and by 'here' i mean on a computer screen) and we're . . . talking? kinda.
>
> i'll be honest. i took a look at your facebook page and laughed out loud. you've got to work on the 'internet presence' thing. no pictures? no 'about you' answers? no memes or rants or 'which dwarf are you' surveys?
>
> you know i'm kidding. i should be proud you're on here at all. you're the girl who resented having to use electric typewriters, and here you are using modern technology. whodda thunk? you're officially the new spokesperson for virginia slims commercials.
>
> would love to know more. how. who. where. you know the drill.
>
> this is . . . surreal. guess i already said that. it's a little weird too. much to say. too much for the few minutes i've got right now. i'm glad to have found you. 'glad' doesn't cut it. thrilled. sobered. a little nervous too. talk soon, ren. it's been too long.

It had been twenty-two years. Twenty-two years and what felt like a couple of lifetimes. But the words on the screen still sounded like his voice. A little sarcastic. A lot irreverent. And in my mind, a little raspy—deep and lazy. I felt a surge of adrenaline and caught myself smiling dumbly.

I clicked reply, eager to respond, then realized I had no idea where to begin. He'd asked about the how, who, and where, but those categories felt restrictive. So did the clock ticking away the seconds in the kitchen. I had a parent-teacher meeting to get to and needed to drop Ryan's soccer cleats off on the way. If we'd had a car, the entire trip would have taken fifteen minutes. But we didn't.

What we did have were three bicycles. Sam's was about ten years old and mine was closer to twenty, with threadbare tires and unpredictable brakes. Its headlight only occasionally worked and its chain had a tendency to come out of its sprocket. It was to three-speeds what go-karts were to Ferraris, but I rode it because it got me where I needed to go. And in the warm season, I took an extra T-shirt along so I could shed the sweaty one when I reached my destination.

With only minutes to spare before I headed out, I read Aidan's words again and tried to formulate an answer, frustrated by the bottleneck between my mind and my fingers. I finally began, trying to keep the tone casual.

Surreal? Yes. Honestly, a bit intimidating too. There are so many questions I want to ask . . . Where do you live now? What do you do? I try to picture you at forty-one, but can't get past the huge mess of hair, the here-comes-trouble grin, and defiant strut in my memory. I suspect all three have changed in our two decades of silence.

You asked about me, and I've only got a few minutes before I need to run, so here are the basics: I'm living in Kathmandu (long story) with my husband and my son. I'm teaching some English classes (a visa requirement) so Sam can be a trailblazer—quite literally. He works with tribal villages in a remote district of the Karnali Zone (far up in the western Himalayas). It can take them six or seven days just to get there. Talk about the ends of the earth. He and his partner, a Nepali man named Prakash, trek out there to visit them, one village per trip, with all the practical help they can carry strapped to their backs.

And then they just do life together. A guy from Wyoming, a guy from Kalikot, and these beautiful tribal people who live in unbelievable poverty. I think Sam's done more emergency medicine than your average med student back home. And survived more near misses than your average thrill-seeker. He's transforming lives. Loving people to faith in very practical ways. (You knew I'd marry a good Christian boy, didn't you?)

And me? I'm doing well, though life here is a little different. It makes this reconnecting feel all the more jarring—planet "then" and planet "now" colliding in a place that is still foreign to me. I crave a familiar context.

Heading out the door. Am I supposed to sign off like a real letter or is this kind of communication different? Educate this novice.

❧

The fan woke me out of restless, muddled sleep again. The light in the hall came on and the answering machine downstairs beeped to life. It was just past three in the morning, and though I wanted nothing more than to turn off the lights and try to sleep again, Ryan needed his soccer uniform washed. Several days of rain had left the vacant lot his team used as a soccer field a muddy swamp. I'd tried to handwash his mud-caked warm-up pants and jersey in the sink since the washing machine was useless during a blackout, but they still looked more brown than black.

I wasn't going to earn any mother-of-the-year awards from Ryan, he'd made that much clear, but if I could send him to the informal game they were playing against the British school tomorrow morning looking less like a vagrant and more like an athlete, there was a chance I could score a few points.

There were various tasks I tended to in the wee hours after the whirring fan woke me—like pumping water to the roof, running the vacuum, and using the stand mixer. It all depended on what I'd gotten accomplished before the fan had last gone quiet. There were days when Sam would shake his head at the dark circles under my eyes and ask if there was something he could do to help me get more done before the next power outage. I knew he meant well, but the message his offer sent felt far from supportive.

"It's stupid," Ryan had blurted during one of Sam's weeks at home. The dullness of his voice had an impatient edge to it. It was nearly nine at night, and he'd been halfway through a homework assignment when the battery power on his laptop ran out.

"Son, it's been this way since we got to Nepal. You should be used to it by now."

"But Miss Moore's going to give me an incomplete if I don't get it done."

"I can talk to her," I offered.

"Or we could get an inverter . . ." my son muttered under his breath.

It wasn't an extraordinary demand. Most Western families in Kathmandu owned at least one of the devices that accumulated electricity when the power was on, allowing them to use lamps and small appliances when it went out again. But as common and practical as the systems were, Sam's commitment to living frugally ruled out such extravagance.

We would not be one of "those" families who brought to a developing country the luxuries of the Western world. "We're here to live among them, not above them," he'd said on more than one occasion.

He didn't look up from the book he was reading by a lantern's light. "We don't need an inverter."

Ryan's eyebrows came together in a frown. "It's due tomorrow, Dad. And now I can't finish it!"

Sam put down the book and gave Ryan a look. "If you'd worked ahead . . ."

"If we had an inverter!"

"If our Nepali friends can live without them, so can we."

"A bunch of our Nepali friends have them!" Ryan exclaimed, glaring at his father.

I jumped in before things escalated. "You can use my laptop, Ryan. It's still got a couple hours on it."

He rolled his eyes before casting a dismissive glare in my direction. "My report is on *this* laptop, Mom," he said, slamming down the lid.

Sam spoke in the teacher-voice he preferred for this kind of skirmish. "How long have you known about this assignment, Ryan?"

"It wouldn't matter if we—"

"Would it help if I sent a note in with you?" I asked. He gave me the usual disappointed look. The one that left me feeling incompetent and dismissed.

"Can I go to Steven's?"

"Son," Sam said, "it's too late."

"But they have power."

"You can't go biking across town and disturbing the Harringtons at this time of night."

"They won't mind."

They probably wouldn't. Eveline, the British woman Prakash had sent to greet us when we'd first arrived in Kathmandu, loved that our sons had struck up a friendship. And with Nyall keeping crazy hours as an ER doctor at the Patan Hospital, I was confident a late-evening arrival wouldn't bother them at all.

"It shouldn't be this complicated," Ryan said, shoving his laptop away. I could see his shoulders stiffening and his jaw clenching.

"The power will come back on by morning . . ." Sam began.

"The report is *due* in the morning!"

"Son—"

"Ryan, I'll wake you as soon as it's on again. Okay? You can get up early and finish it before school."

"But I don't want to get up early!" he growled at me.

I felt myself flinch even as Sam got out of his chair. "Ryan, you will not speak to your—"

Ryan pushed away from the table so abruptly that his chair fell over. He grabbed his laptop and stalked out of the room. "I hate this place!"

Sam stood there for a moment while I stifled the impulse to run after our son.

"Let him go to Steven's," I said.

"Lauren, he needs to learn discipline."

Anger surged. I tamped it down. "He needs to pass this class."

He frowned. I recognized the disapproval.

"You're right," I said, striving for persuasion. "He needs to factor the blackouts into his planning. But he's on academic probation, and if he fails again . . ."

"We'll take him out of soccer before we let him repeat the year."

That he would even consider depriving Ryan of his only joy in life was horrifying to me. "Sam, just this once. I'll call Eveline and make sure it's okay."

His nod was nearly imperceptible. I went to the kitchen and reached for the phone.

From the few conversations I'd had with Eveline, I suspected that Ryan's countenance was different when he was away from us. "He's a delight," she'd said as we stood on the sidelines watching our sons play just weeks after our arrival. Steven was the only schoolmate Ryan seemed to connect with, though I had no idea what they talked about other than soccer and video games. "He's well mannered and polite."

The words didn't describe the boy I saw at home. I'd have given a lot to catch a glimpse of the Ryan we used to know—the more civil and content son we'd lost in those last months before our world-upheaval. "I'm glad to hear that," I said to Eveline. "We don't get to see 'well mannered and polite' very much."

She gave me a searching look. "Taking it out on you, is he?"

"Taking . . . ?"

"The change," she said. "The newness of all this." She laughed a little as we looked out at the mud pit the school called a soccer field. There was a butcher stand just a few feet from it where two goats appeared to be following the game, while another, cut in quarters, lay exposed to the elements on a small wooden countertop. Electrical cables and phone wires hung in huge, tangled clumps from straining utility poles on the far side of the pitch where stray dogs fought over the contents of a discarded plastic bag.

"Newness is a bit of an understatement," I said.

Ryan headed the ball toward the goal and kicked the ground when it bounced off the crossbar. A couple teammates yelled encouragement, which he dismissed with a wave of his hand. "He's certainly competitive," Eveline said.

I looked at her and weighed the benefits of honesty. "He's angry."

"With good reason." She smiled.

"Did Steven struggle too? When you first came."

Eveline pursed her lips, then shook her head. "No. No, I don't recall anything out of the ordinary. Forgive me for making it sound so simplistic, but some people just find it easier to adjust to change."

I thought about Sam. And I thought about me.

"Steven took it all in stride. Monsoon season. The food. This mud puddle they play on. But I've seen others who haven't fared as well."

Ryan ran by in hot pursuit of the other team's top scorer. He didn't look at me or acknowledge our cheer when he stole the ball away.

"He'll come around," Eveline said, sensing my discouragement. "This kind of transition requires a sort of—elasticity. The ability to bend and stretch."

My smile felt cynical. "And if a parent doesn't have it either?"

"It can be an acquired trait."

I gave her words some thought. Acquired implied pursued. And pursued implied wanted. "If one's heart is in it," I said.

"Yes." She nodded. "The heart needs to come first."

My laptop was on the dining room table. I unplugged its power cord from the wall and headed back upstairs with it. Might as well be productive as I waited for the wash to finish so I could hang Ryan's jersey out to dry.

I installed myself on the roof. The air was thick with pollution even at this hour. Nyall Harrington had told me that breathing in Kathmandu was like smoking a pack of cigarettes a day. As a doctor, he made it a point to get Steven and Eveline out of the city once a month for a long weekend, if only to give their lungs a reprieve from the toxic cloud that hovered over the capital. Ryan and I hadn't left once—not for any kind of extended time—and I wondered what damage had already been done and if our lungs would recover if we ever left this place.

I went through the usual clicks on the laptop and found a message waiting for me. I hesitated, but only briefly.

well, ren, you've always been a bit of a mystery, but you threw me for a loop with this one. kathmandu? i get the husband and i get the kid (pictures please), but the third world thing is a mind twister.

it's strange, this reconnecting. i haven't seen you in— how many years? but it's like i hear you when you write. or i imagine i do. i'm having some trouble distinguishing between memory and reality. that's the thing with cyber reunions.

quick picture of my life. i'm single. spent a few years not single, then decided i function better solo. hurt less people that way too. my art is going strong. it actually took a bit of a breather for a while, but . . . well, it's happening again. feels like a dam has burst sometimes. remember the koi pond at old man riley's place? (most ridiculous thing i ever saw.) when the police showed up with a front loader and told him the retaining wall he'd built to redirect the stream was on the neighbor's property? by the time he'd finished screaming bloody murder, half the neighborhood had turned up to watch the festivities. and when that front loader dug into that wall . . . that's what the art thing has felt like. a furious flow. note the alliteration. it feels . . . invigorating. if you look on my facebook wall, you'll see some of my stuff. i'll send you more pics if you'd like to see them.

your turn—enough about me. how in the H-E-double-hockey-sticks did you and your husband end up in nepal? geez, ren. every time i ask a question, a hundred more slam me. sequence seems boring, but we have to start somewhere, right? what i really want to know is how you've changed. who you are now. but that can come later. we've got nothing but time. sorta. that's another thing i don't know. do you have the time? or even the inclination? i guess that's a better place to start. no hurry . . . i'm not going anywhere.

I read the message again. Then another time. The cadence of his words. The quirks of his train of thought. With every sentence he wrote, I remembered more of him.

The washer began to drain. Ryan would be up in a handful of hours and his uniform would be clean. At that moment, it didn't seem to matter.

Aidan—I love that you still call me "Ren" . . .

Your question makes it sound so simple. "Tell me how you ended up in Nepal." Really? Then you tell me how you became a painter. There are no quick answers. No easy ones either. The "how" that brought our family to Kathmandu would take volumes to explain. The term "journey" is cliché, but it's the only one that really applies here.

Nepal was a surprise. Ryan had just turned six when my husband became convinced—just convinced—that the next logical step for our family would be to raise enough funds to leave the US and move to Kathmandu. It took us awhile to sort it all out. A few more volumes needed there . . . We've been here for a little over two years of an initial four-year term. Sam wants there to be more after this one, but . . . I'm taking it a day at a time. Sometimes an hour at a time.

This journey unfolded in unexpected ways. I've found that's the nature of life-travel: imagine the best, plan for the safest, and brace for the jarring "otherness" you couldn't have predicted. Otherness—disappointment or mystery? It's all in your mind-set, Sam would say. His perspective's the architect, and I tend to be its victim.

I glanced back over what I'd written and took a deep breath to still the quickening in my spirit. He'd always had this effect on me—an adrenaline rush, word-fueled and art-expressed. It had begun again as I'd read Aidan's first message, his return into my life inspiring literary risk and verbal rediscovery.

Aidan, it's . . . good . . . to reconnect with you. Weak word. I know you understand. You talked about Old Man Riley's bursting dam and what you've been doing with your art. It feels like an apt description of this communication with you too. I haven't written much since I've been here. Not fun stuff, anyway. Too much of my life is wrapped up in grading the words of others. But these e-mails? (Messages? Not clear on the Facebook terminology.) These feel like my own "bursting dam" . . . and I've only written to you—what—three times? I find myself wanting to start on those missing volumes, not one message at a time, but in the "fierce flow" you described.

You asked too many questions. I'm sorry I couldn't answer them all—or any of them thoroughly enough. But it's going on 4:30 a.m. here and Ryan will be up in less than three hours, so I'll leave this first draft untouched, though I'd love to go back and edit.

Are you well? Are you happy? Basic question: What do you do for a living, assuming art still isn't a money-maker? Start there . . . or anywhere. I want to know.

Not sure how to sign off. Deep breath. Trust. Click send.

I let my hand linger on my laptop's warm surface. Indistinct emotions swirled in my mind. I wanted to explore them—I feared what I would find. So I hung Ryan's clothes out to dry and took the laptop downstairs to charge while the electricity was still on. And then I headed back to bed.

four

Sam and I took the chairlift to the top of the mountain again on the day after graduation and hopped off in a place transformed by spring's arrival. The winter's snow had melted and a wooden platform now spanned the "landing pad" that became a muddy mess by midafternoon every day, when the sun had warmed it long enough to thaw it.

While hardcore hikers went off in the direction of paths that projected from this point into the ridges and pastures revealed by May's milder temperatures, Sam and I wandered straight up from the lift to an outcropping that gave us a broad and unimpeded view of the Sternensee valley.

I'd known this moment was coming. In part because of the subtle crescendo of touch and topics that had led us to this point, and in part because of the imminent end of our time at Christschule. Though I'd been hesitant at first, Sam's persistence had proven the consistency of his intentions. I was ready for us to finally have it out—braced, for sure, but ready.

We talked about the graduation "ceremony" that had happened just the day before, its pale imitation of pomp and circumstance laughable but sincere. We talked about what we'd learned and how we'd grown. We talked about the weather when other topics ran out, while

49

the hardest conversation we'd likely ever had loomed, inescapable, at the end of every silence.

Sam chewed on the stem of a weed and I said something about his Farmer Sam look. He informed me that he considered the comparison a compliment.

"I'll introduce you to my farmer friends when you come see me in Wyoming," he said.

"I'm seeing you in Wyoming?"

He turned toward me and removed the stem from his mouth, a gesture that meant business. "You ready for this?"

"That depends entirely on what 'this' is."

"Us."

My eyes tunnel-visioned onto his face. "Oh. That 'this.'"

"Sullivan has talked about it. The rest of the school has talked about it. Dr. Peters took me aside and asked me about it a couple days ago, but you and I still haven't broached the subject, so . . ."

"So now's a good time."

He nodded and a smile deepened the laugh lines around his eyes. Though I'd known this moment would have to come before two different planes took us to two different lives in two different regions of a vast continent, I was surprised by the tension I felt gathering in my chest.

Sam looked at me the way he usually did, with appreciation, curiosity, and enjoyment. That direct gaze that had drawn me in on the night of his arrival held no hesitation. Sam wasn't the type to ask for permission. Not to chart his own intellectual course, not to question traditional convictions, and certainly not to speak his mind. Though the greatest decisions in my life had most often been motivated by discontent or deadlines, in Sam's, they had been the fruit of passionate exploration and rational analysis. So while he undoubtedly approached this conversation with a well-pondered certainty, I approached it with a dubious curiosity . . . and enough nerves that I thought of sitting on my hands to hide their shaking.

"I didn't come to Austria with the intention of meeting someone like you," Sam said.

"But Sullivan came with the specific intention of meeting someone like you. You've been a tremendous disappointment."

"Lauren."

I rubbed my face and let out a sigh. "Bear with me. I'm not very good at this kind of thing."

He chuckled and let the silence stretch a little. Just enough to leave me wishing he'd speak. When he did, his voice had the academic tone he used for serious discourse, and I braced myself for the answer I'd have to give when his exposition was over.

"I like certainty," he said. It was a thesis statement. I braced for what would come next. "I can't remember a time, even as a kid, when I didn't have this sense that there was something extraordinary waiting for me. Around the next corner. I've predicated my life on this . . . I don't know . . . on this expectancy. Like I've been waiting for it—whatever it is—to present itself to me. So I came to Austria wondering if this is the place where I'll get my marching orders. If this is where God will say 'Do this!' and I'll finally understand what all this has been leading up to. And yes, I've learned a lot, but instead of a 'Do this!' to set me off in a direction I'm sure of, I got . . . well . . . you."

I felt myself frown. "I'm sorry to be a letdown."

"No!" he said hurriedly. "No—that's not what I'm saying."

I tried to still the voices whispering disquiet in my spirit.

"I'm sorry," he said, urgency and sincerity in his eyes. "This isn't supposed to be this hard." He took a deep breath and frowned in concentration. "I'm just going to go on, okay?" When I nodded, he did. "This—this friendship completely took me by surprise. I've got to admit that I've always prided myself in being able to skirt the usual pitfalls of places like Christschule, the attachments that distract from the real purpose of being here. Then I met you—that first night when Sullivan was so determined to serve me Ovomaltine—and I . . . I felt something."

I laughed at that. "The Great Intellect himself admitting to *feeling* something?"

He laughed too. It was one of the defining traits of this relationship and perhaps the first thing that had drawn us to each other. "If anything has ever made me doubt my intellect, it's this!"

"Ouch."

He put up his hands to mitigate the sting of what he'd said. "In the sense that I've always been able to think my way to a conclusion, but . . . not in this case." He paused and I realized I desperately wanted him to take my hand. "Not in our case."

I bit my lip. "Please go on."

He smiled at that. I smiled back. "I didn't want this to turn into anything else," he said, staring out. He shifted so he could face me. "I'm not saying I was right. It's just that I've seen too many people with huge potential to make a difference lose track of their goals when they met someone they cared for. I don't want to be that guy. I want my relationships to support who God made me to be—what he made me to *want*—not distract from it."

"And what have you concluded about this—about you and me?"

"That's the problem," he said, shaking his head. "I haven't concluded anything yet. And . . ."

"And time's a tickin'," I said, imitating Sullivan. I realized that this was more than a relationship-defining conversation for Sam. It was a vision-comparing necessity.

He hesitated. The man whose behaviors and words were the embodiment of conviction stumbled a little—just enough for me to grasp the enormity of this moment for him. "I know you love God. I've seen it in the way you love others, and I've heard it in the way you pray. The commonsense insight you bring to topics I tend to overthink is . . . refreshing."

"Refreshing, huh?"

He smiled. "It's good for me to see things from a different angle."

"That's me. The different-angle girl. Your commonsense alternative to Sullivan's different-planet girl."

"Indeed."

I smiled. "So . . . about this 'us' business . . ."

I loved the way he chuckled. As intransigent as he was about theology and responsibility, there was something about his laughter that attested to a lighter side—a less unyielding side.

He leaned back and focused on the clouds for a moment. "This is—hard."

I tried to tamp down a stirring insecurity. "What do you need to know?"

He sighed. "Okay. Here it is. Before I can talk about anything else, before I can talk about us, I need to be sure of you. Of the reality of your faith."

Something that felt like indignation overtook my insecurity. As sincere as his expression was, his words sounded like doubt to me. Doubt about the authenticity of my faith or the strength of my commitment. I was a little miffed too. I'd wanted this conversation to be about how irresistible I was, and now it felt like an exam I needed to pass before we could proceed any further.

"What are you asking exactly?"

He must have seen a darkening in my expression. "Wait—I said that wrong."

"I've only known you a few months, but I'm pretty sure saying things wrong isn't something you do."

"It is when I'm in completely uncharted territory." He reached for my hand—finally—and held it firmly in both of his. "Forgive me. When things get confusing, I tend to run for the analytical high ground. It helps me keep things straight."

"It also makes a conversation about really personal things feel like a job interview."

"It's not." He squeezed my hand and I squeezed it back. Our gazes locked and spoke and restored trust. "Lauren—believe me. This is so much more than . . ." He frowned and shook his head. "Than an interview." He brushed a stray tendril of hair from my face and I found solace in the gesture. "I'm doing this all wrong," he said. "Can I back up for a minute?"

I nodded. He closed his eyes and gathered his thoughts, then he began to speak again—softly and intensely, some of his concentration yielding to a more joyous recollection. He talked about the precise moments when pivotal realizations had dawned. Not just an acknowledgment of traits he liked in me, but a full appreciation of their value.

Hope unfurled slowly in my mind.

"I know we started out like sparring partners, but you've got to know how quickly that changed. Those debates were just an excuse for more time with you."

"You still wanted to win."

"But if it meant time alone with you, I didn't mind losing as much."

"Keep talking."

He recalled the first time he'd noticed my sense of humor, the first time he'd heard me articulate an unusual spiritual truth, the first time he'd noticed my loyalty to relationships, the first time he'd wanted to hold my hand, and the first time he'd found the courage to reach for it.

"It took my appetite away," he said, remembering our first meal at the Alpenblick Gasthaus. "There was such a strong urge to . . . to connect with you, that I couldn't eat until I'd touched your hand." He shook his head. "It felt juvenile, but . . ."

I recalled the silence that had preceded the gesture. A trace of uncertainty in his eyes. The question asked with fervor and sincerity. "Is it okay if I hold your hand?"

"I remember," I whispered. He brought my hands to his lips and I heard children giggle as they hiked past our vantage point.

Sam launched into a somewhat condensed version of the dreams I'd heard about for nearly five months. He had no desire to walk the well-traveled paths worn bare by the small-thinking believers who had come before him. But he knew he couldn't do it alone. He'd discovered in me, he said, an element that felt like completion. Like wholeness and possibility.

"I . . ." He hesitated again. It took me aback. Sam wasn't the tentative sort. "I'd love to see what this relationship could become," he said. "I've prayed—" He laughed. "I'm praying right now!"

"I can tell by the sweat on your forehead."

"I haven't given a lot of thought to the *type* of woman I'd want to pursue, but I've always—from as early as I can remember—I've always known that she'd have to love God as much as I do. That's why I got tangled up in the faith stuff back there. Because it's the only real standard I've ever had."

"That's a pretty tough thing to measure."

"I know. I know it is. But my faith—it motivates everything. You know that about me." Anticipation lit his eyes again. "I just need to hear you say you feel the same way." He held my gaze, waiting for my answer.

"You make it sound like faith is a career plan."

"No—that's not what I mean." He shook his head and seemed to search for the right words. "But what we do for him is *evidence* of the relationship, right?"

"I tend to think that who we *become* because of our faith is more important than what we *do* to—I don't know—to prove it."

"Two sides of the same coin," he said. "If we're truly committed, he's going to use us—right? In ways we can't imagine." There was excitement in his smile.

I reached past the semantics to our common faith identity, itemizing the spiritual pillars on which our beliefs rested. They were all there—our foundations complementary or shared. The smaller things mattered less when the same certainties sealed our spiritual unity.

"I love God," I said. "He's been there—since as far back as I can remember. But coming here?" I let the fullness of a deeper faith wash over me. "Coming here has made me experience him in a more . . . I don't know. In a more intense and intimate way. So do I love God?" I looked Sam straight in the eyes. "I love him as much as I know how to, right now. But Sam, whether it's as much as you do isn't something I can quantify."

His hand tightened on mine. "Would you be willing to give up everything—*everything*—if he asked you to?"

I felt something constrict in my spirit. "Everything?"

He leaned in close, excitement in his expression. "Everything."

"God is the center of my life," I said, squeezing the hand that still held mine. "And I'm not done learning. That's all I can tell you. And if it's not enough . . ."

His smile was wildly hopeful. "It's more than enough." The look we exchanged seemed to blot out the sounds and sights that surrounded us. He let out a quick breath, eyes still on mine. "You live like you ski— with caution, for sure, but with . . . I don't know. With eyes wide open. And I know I need that in my life."

"Huh."

"I've given this some thought."

"I'd be disappointed in you if you hadn't."

"Lauren." He cupped my face with his hand and I nestled my cheek into it. As his thumb skimmed back and forth over my skin, his warmth and conviction settled me. He brushed the hair from my face again with his other hand. "Will you let me pursue you? Court you. In a romantic, marriage-minded way?"

I searched his face for hesitation and found only resolve and something that looked an awful lot like love. I looked into his eyes and saw a person I trusted. He was more than my "checklist guy." This man with steadfast vision and ardent heart. This man with genuine compassion and avid mind. He wanted a relationship with me. He was committed to seeing where it led.

The knight and stallion stories of my childhood, the roses and poetry daydreams of my youth seemed irrelevant atop a mountain in the Austrian Alps, face-to-face with a man who had seen enough of me to know me and wanted me enough to pursue me. I focused on the vision of a lifetime with Sam as my fear morphed into temerity.

I smiled and expectation tingled through my spirit. "Are you sure?" I asked.

He nodded. Lopsided grin.

I hunched up my shoulders and giggled. "Okay!"

⚮

We sat across from each other on the couch, surrounded by a crush of peonies, hydrangeas, and garden roses. There were vases on the coffee table and sideboard, and buckets lined up against the far wall over-flowed with the peach, pink, and white blossoms. Every vine and sprig of greenery we'd been able to collect from our yard and the neighbors' sat in pails and bins filled with water.

We were two days away from what was shaping up to be a watermark event in the little town of West Lorne, Indiana, and Mom had finally shooed my aunts and uncles and cousins and grandparents out of the house for the short drive to church.

"Mom," I'd said to her a few minutes earlier, emotion quivering in my voice, "I've been surrounded by people and chaos for three days straight. Can you go to the church for a while—and take everybody with you? I just need a few minutes alone with Sam."

I wasn't much of a crier—never had been, really. So when my mom saw my emotions teetering, she knew this was serious. She immediately set a trip to church in motion and added enough items to the "prerehearsal to-do list" that I knew my boisterous extended family would be gone for a while.

The front door closed, the chaos receded, silence descended, and the tears that had threatened moments before evaporated in the sudden stillness. There we sat, Sam and I, surrounded by enough flowers to stock a botanical exhibit. We just stared at each other for a few seconds, relishing the hush. Amazement and exhaustion dueled in Sam's eyes. Amazement at the frenzy that had electrified my parents' small home since our arrival and exhaustion from the frantic pace of preparing for a wedding more elaborate than either of us had wanted.

"Are we having fun yet?" Sam asked.

I tried to giggle, but it came out sounding like a groan. "This," I said, "is what I tried to warn you about when you asked me to marry you."

"It's just a little chaos," he said, failing to sound blasé.

"Aw, honey. You won't see true chaos until Sullivan gets here."

He shook his head. "I can't even imagine." Sullivan's presence in our lives hadn't ended when we'd left Sternensee, and I knew Sam was still trying to make his peace with that fact. At least he'd gotten to the point where he could utter her name without visible twitches. Bless his heart.

He opened an arm and gave me a grin. "What are you doing way over there?"

I scooted over and he wrapped me into his chest. I sighed a long, relieved breath and nestled my face into his neck. This—this was the sanity I'd missed for the past few days. The time to be—to hold—to breathe.

Sam kissed my temple and we slid down a little on the couch, relaxing into the silence. "Two days," he said, his chin propped on the top of my head. I loved the sound of his voice and had since his first evening at Sternensee. Hearing it through his chest, punctuated by the beat of his heart and wrapped in the leathery-clean scent of his cologne was a heady sensation.

I whispered, "Still want to marry me?"

He leaned me back to answer the question with the kind of kiss *that left no illusion as to his intentions. His weight, as it settled over me, was a potent expression of his strength. I looked up into his eyes and felt contentment, like warm honey seeping through the static in my mind. It didn't matter, at that moment, whether Grandma would finish hemming the bridesmaids' dresses in time or the bouquets would get assembled or the church pianist would beat the flu. All I knew as Sam's lips settled over mine again, as his arm burrowed under my back and his breath whispered over my face, was that this was the man with whom I'd spend the rest of my life.*

I pushed at his chest and squinted up at him. "You got your vows finished?"

He squinted back. "What'll you do if I don't?"

The metronome counting down to our wedding redoubled its ticking in my mind. I pushed Sam off so I could sit upright and focus. "You've got them written, right? Seriously, Sam, with everything we still have to—"

"You'll hear them in two days," he said, leaning in again.

I pushed him away. "Sam."

He sat back and let out a deep sigh, crossing his arms and contemplating my expression. "They're written," he said.

Of course they were. Thinking he might have procrastinated was a testament to my precarious state of mind. "Can I hear them?"

He laughed and shook his head. "Not a chance."

"Come on . . ." I attempted a seductive smile. "What's a couple of days?"

"Exactly."

I sat cross-legged on the couch, facing the man who would become my husband, trying to capture the moment in such a way that I'd be able to revisit it, years from now, when memories of this vibrancy and longing would be a healing thing. I had no illusions about marriage being easy. I'd witnessed enough of them to recognize that truth. So I entered my own with eyes wide open, eager for the joys and challenges of twoness as I relinquished the freedoms and frustrations of oneness, confident in the vows that would seal us to each other.

"Did you mention anything about obedience in your vows?" I asked, mock threatening. "'Cause if you say anything about you commanding and me dumbly obeying, I assure you my Auntie Lou will get up and march her walker right down that aisle and out the door before you're done with your little speech."

"I didn't say anything about obeying," he said, taking my hands and looking too earnestly into my eyes. "But I had to say something about ironing my underwear. It's a wife's duty," he said, his voice rising in a bad imitation of a charismatic preacher, "to iron them boxers and darn them socks and scrub them floors and quiet them shriekin' babies so a poor man can think!"

"Are you done?"

He leaned in close enough that our noses were touching, adding in an intimate voice, "I haven't even started on the topics of submission, head coverings, and the evils of contraception."

I rolled my eyes and laughed while he swiveled and lay down on the couch, feet dangling over the far armrest, his head in my lap. We'd had that conversation, of course. The one about submission and obedience. I'd heard the arguments against the vows all my life from irate women who found them belittling. We'd even discussed it in a class at Christschule, and the resulting debate had sent Sullivan into apoplectic disbelief.

"Puh-lease!" she'd finally exclaimed. "Are you telling me that I'm the only clear-minded individual in this room who sees the chauvinistic bias of verses written for a primitive civilization? We—have—evolved." She held the last word long and low. "Y'all are crazier'n an outhouse rat . . . and I am mindin' my language!"

I'd learned that frustration tended to deepen Sullivan's accent, and it was reaching unparalleled depths. But when she said "y'all," a

Southernism she considered cliché and had banned from her vocabulary, I knew she was clinging to the last shreds of her civility.

I understood the discomfort the traditional vows inspired. I'd wrestled with them myself. But this was Sam. As difficult as it might have been for me to make those promises to anyone else—this was Sam. I trusted his heart. I trusted his commitment to care for me in the Christlike way he did everything else. I could promise submission and obedience without qualm. Joyfully, even. This was the marriage I desired.

"You're an obnoxious man, Mr. Coventry," I said, running a hand over his short, bristly hair. "But I'd be honored to darn your socks and iron your boxers."

"Much obliged, Mrs. Coventry." He took my hand from his head and held it to his lips. "Mrs. Coventry," he repeated against my skin, his voice softer this time. He strained his neck to look up at me. "We made it," he said.

"We made it."

What our time at Christschule had done for our spiritual development, the year since then had done for our relationship. When we'd returned to the States—Sam to Wyoming and me to Indiana—the only certainty we had was that we both saw something special in our friendship and were committed to seeing where it led. Beyond that, we had no idea of how things would play out.

We tried to see each other every six weeks at the very least. Either he came to me or I went to him. We met each other's families and friends, we deepened our understanding and love for the other's world. We argued and debated a host of issues—politics, art, philosophy, religion. Sam's knowledge base was so much broader than mine that I willingly surrendered, in the end, when topics were beyond the scope of my understanding. That scope itself was a source of disagreement. I considered it respectable, but Sam's occasional rolled eyes intimated that he didn't share my assessment.

Despite our differences, we were diligent in our journey toward marriage, enlisting my pastor to walk us through the process. It felt like no personal, spiritual, or emotional stone had been left unturned.

I let my fingers explore Sam's face, the ridges of his lips, the indentation of his temples. This good, honest, earnest, respectable, and godly man was more than I'd ever dreamed I'd find. He was fearless in his convictions. Unapologetic in his faith. Uncompromising in his persuasion. Passionate in his dreams. Indefatigable in his commitment to help others and love well.

I met his gaze with affection and amazement overflowing my eyes. He smiled. He'd seen these tears before. "Thank you for marrying me, Sam," I whispered. And as he shifted our positions so we lay tightly wrapped on my parents' plaid couch, his closeness cradled my dreams, his warmth confirmed my desire, his sureness blanketed old fears with love's invincibility.

It took nearly six years for us to conceive. The first was filled with expectation. "Wanna give it another shot?" Sam would say, leering, as I slipped into bed. I'd laugh and mumble something like, "Well, if we have to." Our eyes would meet as we brushed our teeth or poured coffee or ate our toast the next day, and I'd say, "Do you think it took?" with excitement in the words, and Sam would lean in for a kiss and say, eye to eye, "Indubitably."

By the second year, we'd started charting my cycles on the calendar I kept in the kitchen's junk drawer. Though we were dutiful in our attempts, part of me hoped that our pregnancy would come from the spontaneous, less methodical intimacy that still, when our guards were down, sent us focused and yearning to our bed, our couch, or the living room floor.

Year three saw doctors' visits and dire predictions and medical options that would insert science into our increasingly taxing pursuit of family.

Sam laid out three pages of spreadsheets on the table after dinner one night, and I knew before he started speaking that this moment would bend our charted course.

"Just over thirty-one thousand in combined college debt," he said. "Another five years at the rate we're going."

I nodded, aware that the income I was making as a freelance writer was doing little to lessen our debt. I sat across from him at the table and felt waning hope stooping my shoulders. "I could get another job."

He shook his head. "And quit again when you get pregnant?"

"*If* I get pregnant." We tended to live on different sides of the optimism divide. He'd anchored his bunker to a rocky outcropping of "It'll happen if it's supposed to," and I'd erected a tattered shelter on the "What if God doesn't want it to happen?" shifting slope of doubt. Neither of us had found our way to the "Trust and you will receive" mind-set of more emphatic dreamers.

Sam must have felt my faltering hope. "If he wants us to—"

"I know, Sam." I berated myself for the sharpness of my tone. This wasn't Sam's fault. It was mine. My "inhospitable womb." My recalcitrant body.

He ran a hand over his face and went back to staring at the figures on the pages in front of him, lined up like sentinels between reality and dreams. "We can try the treatments . . ." His voice held a tinge of defeat, though I knew he intended it to sound firm and hopeful.

"But we can't afford them." The resignation in my voice masked a yearning to hear him answer with a confident "We'll make it work," or a passionate "Money can't stand in the way of becoming a family."

But Sam had an accountant's mind. He approached finances from a pragmatic point of view and saw the eradication of our debt as a crucial precursor to whatever adventures the future held. His eyes sought the safety of the numbers on the spreadsheets he'd designed for reassurance. For support. For ammunition? "I just don't see the wisdom in—"

"Buying a baby?"

I saw his determination falter. The subtle droop of his shoulders. A slackening in his face. "I want a baby," he said so fervently that I had to believe him. "But with our current budget? Lauren, we can barely afford to begin our family the natural way. And if we add more debt . . ." He shook his head at the irrefutability of his analysis. "If we do that, there's no way we'll make it out of here in the next decade," he said, his voice subdued but resolute.

"Make it where?" Resentment crept its serrated edge into my voice. Since I'd first met him, Sam had had a glorious, albeit vague, vision of global impact, but try as I had to pry details out of him, he had never spoken of precise goals and destinations. Only in the ideals of a life of purpose and selfless investment. All he knew was that he had been called to something more, and he lived in that growing conviction, anticipating the marching orders he thought would become clear when we were finally debt-free. Both his dreams and mine were predicated on money—and at that moment I realized how starkly different they were.

Sam had been halfway through a degree in finance when we'd met in Austria, and though his driving goal even then had been to be a force for change in a broader scope, he'd gone back to a college he couldn't really afford to finish the degree he needed in order to move forward. After a couple years working in accounting for a nonprofit organization on the outskirts of Indianapolis, he'd come to the reluctant conclusion that our college debt wasn't going to pay itself off and that any save-the-world endeavors were contingent on that.

So Sam had gone over to what he called the dark side. He applied for several "real" accounting jobs and finally landed one in Muncie. The thankless work was made bearable only by the clients whose impact extended beyond North America to Africa, Asia, and South America. He drew a degree of comfort from knowing that his number crunching was contributing in some way to cultures outside his reach. Still, the zeal of his calling to needy parts of the globe seemed only deferred, not quenched, by those small connections with a vaster world.

And now it felt like we were sacrificing our family to Sam's "call," as hazy as it was.

"Where exactly do you think we're going, Sam?" I asked again, my dreams of motherhood groaning under the weight of his conviction.

"I don't know," he said, weariness in his voice. "Wherever God calls me."

"Us."

"Us." He leaned across the table and took my hands in both of his. "Of course, us . . ."

I squeezed the hands that held mine with what felt like contrition. "I want a baby. I want 'us' to be you, me, and at least one baby."

"I want that too . . ." His grip tightened on mine.

"But not enough to invest in it? It's just money, Sam."

"It's money we don't have."

We locked eyes, silent. There was certainty in his gaze. And determination. I pulled my hands free and moved to the living room's picture window, crossing my arms over the empty womb that had sucked the joy out of our lovemaking and the brightness out of a future I could no longer envision. We lived frugally in a modest house, our thermostat set low. We walked rather than drove as often as we could and used coupons like currency. We shopped at Goodwill and spent vacations at home. We had an ironclad ten-year plan for financial independence that was strangling my greatest desire. My acutest need.

"I guess we could take out a loan," Sam said from the table, his voice barely loud enough to reach me. Just loud enough for me to hear the reluctance that invalidated the promise.

I couldn't say anything, just then. Not yet.

Sam watched as I returned to the table and cleared the dinner dishes that were stacked to the side of his neat and sterile spreadsheets. I loaded the dishwasher, left the slow-cooker to soak, and wiped down the counters.

Sam was still at the table when I headed toward the stairs. He was staring off, his hands flat against the folded spreadsheets in front of him. I paused at the foot of the staircase and turned, forcing my eyes toward him, trying to inject serenity into the burning void I felt. "It's okay, Sam," I said, willing the sarcasm out of my voice. I wanted my statement to be sincere. "If it's supposed to happen, God will make sure it does." Something in my spirit flinched at my own words.

Sam straightened a little where he sat at the table. He nodded. I went upstairs.

Years four and five were marked not by change so much as by crescendos. Sam increased our revenue by working up the ladder in the firm. I volunteered as an English substitute for the Christian school associated with our church and eventually began teaching three high school classes in journalism, poetry, and short story writing. And as our careers expanded more by chance than by intent, our conversations drifted from pregnancy to projects and from procreating to projecting five, ten, fifteen years forward. We were ahead of the game in paying off our debts. We tried to laugh more. We purposed to breathe more. Our social circle settled and stabilized. Though none of the friendships were as galvanizing as I might have wanted them to be, they dragged us out of the predictability of our well-crafted life, and I was grateful for that.

I got up early on a Saturday in May for a run to the drugstore. When Sam woke up and turned over, he found me sitting on the bed next to him, trembling with excitement. He checked the alarm clock, as if it would hold an explanation for my cheerful, silent, and upright presence on a weekend morning.

He frowned. "Am I supposed to . . . get up? . . . or . . . be somewhere?" He ran a hand over his face and looked around the room. Then he squinted at me again. "Are you okay?"

I leaned over and whispered, "We're pregnant" against his lips.

"We're what?!" He shot out of bed and stared, slack-jawed and arms akimbo. Then he covered his head with both hands and said again, aghast and elated, "We're what?"

When I giggled, he threw himself at me, pinned me down and secured my face between his hands, our noses almost touching. "Say it again," he said, and tears flooded his eyes when I repeated the words. "Honey . . ."

"I know."

He wiped a tear from my cheek with a shaking thumb and smiled with the kind of abandon I hadn't seen in him since . . . since I could remember. He kissed me. Passionately and exuberantly. Then he slid down the bed, pulled up my T-shirt, and stared at my belly, a goofy grin aimed straight at my navel. He kissed my stomach and laid a warm hand over the spot, looking up at me with tears still brimming in his eyes. "Honey . . ." he said again.

Then the calm, rational, wise, and unflappable man I'd married nearly seven years before leapt off the bed and let loose with a demented sort of happy dance—a howling, arms flapping and legs pumping symphony to answered prayers.

I'd never loved him more ferociously.

five

I HEARD RYAN BANGING AROUND IN THE KITCHEN. THE slam of a cupboard—he'd gotten his bowl. The swish of the pantry curtain being pulled back—he had the cereal. The rattle of the fridge door opening and closing—he'd taken out the milk. The scrape of a wooden chair against the dining room's tile floor—he'd seated himself at the table. The silence—he'd turned on his iPod and was staring out the window at the chickens as he ate.

I slipped into my house shoes and pulled on a robe. Ryan didn't look away from the window when I padded into the dining room with my cup of coffee and sank into the armchair in the corner. It was an unusual place for the chair, but we'd discovered that it was the spot in the house where the neighbor's Wi-Fi signal came in strongest.

Ryan stared out the window and I stared at him. His iPod was turned up loud enough that I could hear the hisses of sibilants and the steady boom of the bass. He looked down long enough to shovel a spoonful of granola into his mouth, then went back to watching the chickens—Hannah-Grace and Geraldine—pecking at the corn in the bottom of their pen.

He had his father's features. Sharp and classical. He'd inherited my brown eyes and fine dark hair. He wore it longer, like the shag skateboarders had sported in my youth. He had his soccer uniform on this morning: black shorts and a black-and-white jersey, his prized Manchester United jersey pulled on over it. It was red and threadbare, a memento of our stopover at Heathrow on our long flight to Nepal.

It had taken all my powers of persuasion, after we arrived, to convince him that the shirt would last longer if he didn't wear it at night too. I'd darned the holes in his armpits and around the frayed hemline several times. My ministrations had left the sweatshirt looking lumpy in spots—besides being faded, stained, and stretched out of shape. But Ryan loved it. And there were so many things in his new life that he despised that I was committed to salvaging that shirt for as long as I could.

Soccer had been the catalyst that had eventually allowed Ryan to engage with others. It had taken a few months, a time span extended by the sullen reticence he brought to social contact. A long period of adaptation that seemed to chip away at his boyness. The culture, the food, the lifestyle, the unsafe water, the foreignness . . . Although many of his peers lived in a tidy Western bubble nestled in Kathmandu's chaos, we lived in an uncomfortable no-man's-land—foreigners faking assimilation. Dual alienation.

What this culture, his parents, and his home had failed to give to Ryan, sports had. Predictability, safety, purpose, and a semblance of belonging. He would probably have denied that his team afforded him those comforts. He was still guarded in his interactions with his peers. Yet there was a sureness in his step when he left for practice that spoke more of soccer's significance than any admission could have. I wanted to celebrate it, but as his life became increasingly wrapped up in the sport, I wasn't sure whether soccer was saving my son or stealing him from me.

I love you, Ryan. I'm so sorry you're hurting. I know I should have fought for you. Forgive me. Please, forgive me. I wanted to say the words. I wanted him to know how deeply his pain grieved me. But words felt disloyal.

I leaned forward in my chair and knocked on the table to get Ryan's attention, signaling for him to pull an earphone out.

"What?"

"Good morning."

An eyebrow went up. I knew he was tapping a foot under the table. I smiled. "Good morning," he said back. His greeting lacked a little—a lot—in warmth and sincerity. I'd long decided not to judge him on form.

"Tell me about the game."

He shoveled a spoonful of granola into his mouth and chewed slowly. "It's this thing where we kick a ball into a big white square."

"Ryan." He kept chewing. "Who are you playing?"

I already knew the answer. The distance of the game was the sole reason I wasn't going.

"Panauti," he said.

"Do you think you'll win?" I hated—*hated*—the stilted tone of our conversations. I could interact with strangers more casually than I did with my own son. I missed the days when . . . No. Missing and wishing were an exercise in futility. Still. These conversations wounded me.

"Yup."

"I wish I could come cheer for you," I said, certain my presence at his games meant nothing to him, but determined to keep up this part of the mom bargain. "You going to Steven's afterward?"

"Yup." He shoveled the last spoonful of granola into his mouth and pushed away from the table. "Nice talk."

"You need a ride to practice?" I called as he sauntered into the entryway to retrieve his sports bag and a jacket.

"On what—your bicycle?"

Sometimes I forgot, just briefly, that I wasn't a suburban mom anymore.

"I'll be back tonight." He threw his bag over his shoulder as he headed out the front door and slammed it shut behind him. The lock hadn't worked right since we'd moved in, and a hefty pull seemed to latch it better than a softer approach. Still, Ryan's exit felt more like a slap than a slam.

I was getting used to the feeling.

As Suman didn't come on weekends, I had the house to myself. I let Muffin in and he cocked his head when I said, "Don't tell Sam." I figured it didn't hurt to pretend to be an inside dog every once in a while. I lay on the couch and graded twenty-five papers on ethics in journalism written by my advanced English students. It wasn't light reading. Some of it was downright difficult, given the writers' often deficient grasp of the English language. But it was a distraction from the Facebook icon flashing on the back wall of my mind.

I turned a few lights on when darkness fell and lit a couple of candles when the lights went out. I read a chapter from a book on Christ-centered living, then, with "ethics" and "godliness" rattling around in my brain, grabbed the laptop, picked up a candle, and made my way to the bedroom upstairs.

I lay in bed and scrolled down Aidan's Facebook wall, past memes and get-well wishes and news headlines, clicking on every picture of his art that I could find. Stopping to take it in. Wondering how much more powerful his creations would be in person.

We were in grade school when he started showing me his drawings. I knew little about art, except that I liked what he drew. In middle school, his art teacher asked his parents to let him stay after class for private lessons. But Aidan wasn't interested. He had better things to do than hang out with an adult trying to teach him something he already knew. Aidan was a lot of things growing up—many of them extraordinary. But "humble" and "compliant" didn't make the list.

By high school, he had divided his life into three specific categories: art, girls, and nothing good. He painted in the garden shed behind his mom and dad's house. In part because of the convenience of the location and in part because it got him away from cloying parents who suffocated him with kindness. Aside from an unfortunate incident when Aidan, in a mildly inebriated state, had knocked the paint thinner he was using into the candle he'd lit for "mood lighting," the arrangement had worked out well. They'd rebuilt the shed for their Child Wonder, and Aidan had installed a dead bolt on the *inside* of the door.

Depending on the part of West Lorne one came from—and depending on the relationship one's daughter had with "that Dennison boy"—Aidan was either considered an unsung prodigy or an unrepentant heartbreaker. Few knew, as I did, how interdependent those two facets were.

And in the midst of all the drama—in the center of the insanity that was Aidan's life—stood I. We'd been friends since grade school, an unlikely pair joined by the sensibilities that moved us. The writer and the artist. The introvert and the show-off. The good little girl and the bad-news boy. Calm waters and stormy surf. He showed me every piece he ever created long before he unveiled it to others. He watched my face and gauged the quality of his work by the way I responded. Those were the most intimate moments of my youth.

Aidan came to me with his girl problems and I went to him with my insecurities and confusions. While I common-sensed him, he live-a-littled me. The leather-jacketed guy with the awful reputation and dangerous vibes was the safest place on earth for me. Right up until he wasn't anymore.

ah, ren. there's something mystical about receiving your messages. thank you for clicking send without editing or whitewashing. we're both artists enough to recognize the value of rawness—quirks, warts, bad metaphors and all. maybe not the warts. there are products for those. (joking) please . . . i have no room in my life for sterile communication, so don't start now.

husband's name: check. kid's story: sorta started. ren at age . . . 40? not nearly enough info on that. but the picture is getting clearer. it's like the framed prints i hung on the walls of the shed for inspiration. remember those? when it got really cold and i turned on the space heater, condensation would cloud the glass. but if i stood there long enough for the space heater to do its thing, i could watch the colors and lines and textures taking shape again. that's what's happening with you, i think. i'm watching the condensation clear. another tortured metaphor. tell me when to stop.

tell me about your students too. i'm sure you're a fantastic teacher. and more about ryan. and about life there. seriously. leave out no detail . . .

you asked about work. i've made the rounds since you last knew me. did construction during and after college. got a degree in graphic arts . . . did you know that? just barely, mind you. i might have—maybe just a little bit perhaps, in some innocuous way—used my powers

73

of persuasion on the professor whose design class i was failing my last semester at iu. 'powers of persuasion' . . . euphemisms abound. she was a 'she,' by the way. just to keep things clear.

after construction, i put in some time as a landscaper. when i was (gasp) married, i became an utterly respectable art editor for a magazine known only to graphic artists. seemed like a great idea at the time. got me nowhere. and then i made the mistake of prostituting my first love (art) for the sake of my second love (money). got into painting, but not flowers and trees and unicorns and stuff. blank walls. in houses and offices. and siding too. the occasional faux-finish gig just barely kept me from shooting myself, but i liked being my own boss so i kept at it and made decent money in the process. pretty much stopped Painting (note the cap) for the sake of painting.

and then . . . i quit. four months and two weeks ago. went back to that first love and moved to pennsylvania. just over an hour from downtown new york. sold my car. burned my overalls. got myself an agent who's been shopping my stuff around. my website is almost ready to unveil. we're trying to plan a 'real' exhibit for this summer and maybe find some other ways to get my stuff out there.

just had this moment. one of those 'ah' things that stopped my thinking in its tracks. didn't realize how incredibly much i'd missed you until just now. i know there's tons of catching up to do, but . . . you already know me better than anyone. so all we're doing, really, is adding shadows to the painting. the rest is already there.

you said you're new to facebook. so you might not know about this little thing called instant messaging. if we're ever on at the same time, we should try it. what's the time difference anyway? it would allow us to actually converse. what a concept. or would that be too weird?

I closed the lid of the laptop with a little more force than I intended. *Converse.* My heart lurched. I wasn't sure why. Writing messages to Aidan felt safe. The cloak of time and distance made the exchanges feel more mysterious than real. The thought of instant messaging felt frightening, somehow. Too immediate. Too translucent.

Though I'd decided, before reading Aidan's message, that I'd wait until morning to answer, my fingers itched to start writing a response. Still, I hesitated. Would he be able to tell when I was on? Could he initiate instant messaging and know if I ignored it?

I carried the laptop—along with a blanket—up to the roof and installed myself in one of our creaky lawn chairs. The clock said 10:00 p.m. Twelve fifteen p.m. in Pennsylvania. Aidan would be at work. I figured I might as well answer now, while communicating was safe. I'd write our overdue newsletter and tend to our month's budgeting as soon as I was done.

I love your imagery, Aidan. Didn't I always tell you a writer lurked inside there? And you wasted your time painting . . .

Thanks for the details. I can't imagine the courage it must have taken for you to quit your job and change your life. To move to PA and commit to doing something with your art. I know the impulse probably came out of a couple decades of desire, but still . . .

There it goes again. A memory broadsiding me. That's been happening a lot these last few days. We were driving around town in your grandpa's car. I can't remember exactly where we were going. The windows were down, so it was spring or summer. I think we were listening to that horrible grunge stuff you played just to annoy me. Or maybe you actually liked it. I was never sure. You were spewing this long, impassioned monologue. Something about your parents wanting you to go to college and get a teaching degree and you wanting to lose yourself in painting. You spouted off all the reasons they'd given you for getting a "real" education so you could land a "real" job. You were pretty riled up, as I remember it.

Next thing I knew, you pulled into a parking spot— careened into it and slammed on the brakes is more like it—and you turned in your seat to face me and screamed, "I—am—my—art!" at the top of your lungs. Do you remember that? A bit dramatic, at the time.

Somebody came running out of Eddie's Pizza Shop to see if everything was okay, and I told them you were practicing for the school play. I thought then, as I do now, that the only reason you screamed was to stop yourself from crying. That's how much you loved your art.

And now you've shoved off into a phase of life where you truly can experience what it is to be—your—art. I'm proud of you. Is that condescending? I don't intend it to be. I've been stalking your Facebook page and poring over the pictures of your work. It has evolved in profound ways and I'm glad you're seeking a broader audience for it.

You asked for more on Ryan. Coming to Nepal was . . . hard on him. I'm actually not sure if it's the adaptation that was hard or just the fact that we forced him to come. I guess we didn't force him, per se, except that Sam and I decided moving here was what God wanted us to do. And since Ryan belongs to us . . .

God—there's a messy topic we haven't raised yet. Do you think it would be as messy today as back then, when you gave me such a hard time for attending youth group and going to church and praying about things? I'm guessing it would.

Ryan. Before our change of life, he was a vivacious and affectionate child. The apple of many eyes. (Bushels of apples.) It took us a bit more than four years to get here. Not all happy ones, though we knew this was the right move at the right time. He started to get in trouble. Nothing Aidan-esque. But just not like him. We sought counsel for him and for ourselves, and then we discovered that the funds we'd raised were sufficient to head out. "Sufficient." I've come to hate that word. It smacks of: "If you were a better person, you'd think it was enough."

We got here. And, in many ways, Ryan left. He's thirteen now. I love him with every cell in my body. But I don't know how to reach him. I've tried. And, yes, I've prayed. Go ahead and say it—you always have. "Prayer's great until you find out God's a mass hallucination." Except that prayer has gotten me through every day of my life since you and I said good-bye in my parents' backyard. So, yes. I pray.

That got a bit dark.

Got to run. If I can figure out how to do it, I'll attach our last family picture. Ryan's the kid using hair as camouflage. That red sweatshirt is a story in itself . . .

I've got to tell you. I've had no desire to use my writing creatively for—a long time. Too much "prostituting my true love," as you put it, for the sake of, in my case, ministry and income. But hearing from you. No, reengaging with you. It's stoked that fire again. Maybe not a fire. Embers glowing brighter. I need to tell you "thank you."

✑

Sam would be home on Sunday. Three weeks gone and one week home. We'd made that pact. Either with God or the devil. But he'd be home on Sunday.

During my first months in Nepal, the days preceding his returns had been buoyed by a livening in my spirit. I gleefully announced his return to the other moms at soccer games. They knew the intervals of his absence, but it still felt good to say it out loud. I delighted in making plans. "When Sam's home, this week . . ." "Why doesn't Sam give you a hand with that . . . ?" Better yet were the sentences that could include both men in my life. "Sam and Ryan are at a game, but I can give him your message." And the ultimate joy was speaking words like, "We've got plans as a family tonight, but maybe some other time?" Family. Oh, the decadence of the word.

I'd spruce up the house to make it as welcoming as possible: spotless stove, clean rugs, ironed sheets, small vases of sweet peas on bookshelves and tables, and the aroma of incense in every room. Then I'd turn my efforts on myself. Our cement shower and its trickle of warm water were hardly a spa, but I waited for the time of day when I knew the hot water would be in greatest supply. I deep conditioned, I exfoliated, I pumiced. All with eyes and mouth conscientiously closed, lest I swallow a drop of water and be ill for any portion of Sam's seven days home.

But time had passed. I'd learned through recurrent surprises that one of the many Nepali traits Sam had embraced since our arrival was a loose relationship with punctuality. Being ready a little early for his return was one thing. But seeing his arrival time come and go, then waiting for hours for him to walk through the door? What good were smooth legs and ironed sheets if the spirit was resentful?

And now I waited again for Sam to come home. I knew the circuit of stores I'd need to visit to stock the pantry's shelves, but what had once been an exciting precursor to his return now felt more like a chore.

It was rush hour in Kathmandu, but in the area where we lived, just outside the pulsing heart of the city, it was a less frantic thing. Still, the surge in traffic made walking the narrow, sidewalk-less streets an exercise in strategy and panoramic vision. My goal was to stay a step ahead of the taxi veering to miss a truck, the cyclist dashing through the two-foot space between my body and the fruit I was inspecting, and the dispassionate stray dog that picked the moment I stepped over him to take a piece out of the man carrying bricks from a demolition site. I weaved my way to the bakery with my senses trained on the sounds and movement around me, pausing to press my hands together and bow with a quiet "*Namaste*" to those who knew me.

Every so often I got a glimpse of the progress I'd made since our arrival in Nepal. Things that used to bother me did so more rarely now—like people who cut in line without the slightest hesitation. I'd grown accustomed to the holy men, the sadhus, bathing mostly naked at communal taps, and to the smell of the sewage-polluted Baghmati River that had made me gag during my first weeks in Kathmandu.

I could mostly take it all in stride now, except on frustrated days when my inability to speak the language got to me. I'd taken classes for a while, but the basics I'd learned were in the official Nepali tongue, and in a country where 145 languages and dialects were spoken and in a city where thousands of foreigners lived, I might as well have stuck to English.

The bakery was a small shop at the end of a narrow passage-way lined with propane tanks. Bina started her day at three in the morning, preparing croissants and raisin buns and square yeast breads called *Krishna Pauroti* in a surprisingly modern oven at the back of her shop. Two small children covered in flour stared at me with a sullen sort of interest as I ordered with gestures, nods, and the few words of Nepali I could apply to the task.

Then it was off to the grocery store, a two-aisled space stacked floor to ceiling with a complete inventory of basic house-hold needs. In my first weeks in Nepal, the thought of shopping for groceries had been a terrifying thing. Few products looked familiar and fewer yet had labels I could read. But the store's shelves held less mystery now, and after more than two years, I could navigate through it without the meltdowns and near panic attacks of my first months in the country.

I carried my loot in several large bags and retraced my steps, my agility hampered by the weight of the groceries, and my *Namastes* somewhat handicapped by their pull on my arms.

Once home, I heaved the bags onto the table in the middle of the kitchen and flinched a little as Suman got to work put-ting the groceries away. With Sam coming home, my nesting instincts were in overdrive, and there was something about our housekeeper's familiarity with my space that felt more intrusive than usual.

"I'll take care of it," I said lightly, taking a two-kilo bag of lentils from her hands. She looked at me. "It's okay," I said, nod-ding and smiling to add meaning to my words. I pointed toward the pantry, then at myself, miming putting things away. "I'll take care of this."

Suman looked at the clock. There was a half hour left in

her day. A pot of *dal bhat* simmered on the stove. Lettuce and cucumber soaked in a bath of diluted iodine in the sink. All our pitchers were full and lined up on their shelf.

"You don't have to stay," I said, articulating each word carefully. There was no telling how much English Suman understood. She'd worked for foreigners for nearly thirty years and she must have picked up some language in that time, but she kept her proficiency close to the vest.

Suman nodded her head no, as the Nepali did. I nodded my head yes. She nodded her head no. Nonverbal communication could be a confusing exercise in a country where identical gestures held opposite meanings.

"*Namaste*," I said, wishing her good-bye, then I turned up the wattage on my sincerity and said thank you with all the deep appreciation I could muster. "*Dhanyabad, Suman. Dhanyabad.*"

I went back to the kitchen after she left and unpacked the groceries myself, taking an extra moment here and there to rearrange a row of cans or combine two half-finished bags of sugar. It was my silly attempt at regaining possession of the space before my husband got home.

⁂

running ragged here. trying to get a commissioned (sorta) piece finished by friday. kitschy coffee shop in soho wanted something for a save-the-planet campaign (how original) and since my agent is a customer . . . it'll be good exposure at the very least. i'm going with a sort of postapocalyptic concept. desolate landscape where greens grow out of structures made from landfill trash. i know. always the upbeat thinker.

i'm sorry about the ryan stuff, ren. i truly am. i realize

i have no context, but i don't get it. i always knew you'd be an awesome mother. wait—not awesome. that's a cheap word. like elvis on velvet. i knew you'd be an attentive, devoted, and affectionate mother. i guess it's because, in some strange, not kinky way, you mothered me. don't frown and roll your eyes and look at me like i'm an idiot. like when i used to tell you you'd be published someday. i'm being sincere here.

you were a friend to me. and because of who you are— you were something of a mother too. patient. affirming. chastising when necessary. and mostly able to take my immaturity and jackassery in stride. i have no doubt that you've been a good mother. and i'm sad things are rough with ryan. life gets in the way of our best intentions and efforts, sometimes, doesn't it? maybe that's just me. i want you and ryan to be good. i have a feeling you will be.

prayer. i saw how you just snuck that topic in. there you go shoving your faith down my throat again (kidding). i actually have a few things to say about it. trying to figure out how much and how. no time for that right now though. i have a postapocalyptic 'agenda piece' (blech) to finish.

but i'm attaching another one before i hit send. did it a couple months ago and i think it's right up your alley. i call it 'hope.'

pop quiz: describe your life there in one word. just one. you're a wordsmith, you can do it.

this is . . . wild.

a.

There was a small version of a painting at the bottom of Aidan's message. I clicked and found that I was holding my breath. The digital picture of Aidan's *Hope* opened in a new window on my screen. I let out a slow breath.

I should have known before I clicked the thumbnail what my reaction would be. How many times had I entered the garden shed to find him sitting on the stool he'd positioned facing the back wall so the sun filtering through the dirty window could illuminate the piece he was creating. And how many times had my eyes glanced off his work in progress, then swung right back to it, captured by something almost tangible that reached out of the canvas and demanded . . . not just attention . . . engagement. A sort of visceral, enveloping response to lines and colors and the texture of intimacy.

The first landscapes he'd painted had been anemic foreshadows of the work he'd produce in his late teens: psychotic collages that articulated emotion. Mixed-medium portraits that merged erratic shapes and slashes of color into faces that seethed with history. His abstracts were focused and concise. His still lifes imbued with intrinsic authority. Some teachers called his work artistic arrogance. Others called it unconventional brilliance. I suspected both sides knew that time and training would make *Aidan Dennison* a name to remember.

And there I sat, nearly twenty two years later, catching my breath as *Hope* unfolded on my screen, top to bottom, like a curtain. Given the title, I'd expected something bold shifting from dark to bright. Or something redemptive that spoke of coming things. I remembered how creatively stunted Aidan's work had always made me feel.

The colors of the painting were dulled and the textures flattened by the computer's screen. Still, the harrowing depths of jagged emotion reached out to me, their danger muted by just a hint of light, as if a waking sun had skimmed raised ridges in the dark and left them morning-tinged.

I ran a finger over the image, disappointed by the smooth, cool surface of the screen. I composed a dozen responses in my mind. Tried to type a few and clicked delete. The last ten days had birthed a flurry in my soul. An awakening. And I was still learning how to function in its grip. I felt torn between two planets. Each with its own mystery. One more captivating than the other. The other more real and breathing.

I typed four words and clicked send.

You are astounding. Still.

Then I logged out. Turned off. Put away. And determined to live, at least for a few hours, dead center in the "real and breathing."

⁓

Muffin let out a happy bark, letting me know Ryan was back. The poor dog was completely unaware that his love was unrequited. We'd found the mixed-breed dodging traffic at rush hour one evening, a couple months into our new life in Nepal. He was about four months old and malnourished.

We'd picked him up and carried him home, hoping he would give Ryan a boost—maybe coax some nurturing and affection out of him. But Ryan had studiously ignored the new member of our family, kicking him away when he begged for attention and shutting him out of the house. I'd been taken aback by Ryan's refusal to connect. But there wasn't much about my son that made sense to me these days.

He came clattering through the front door.

"Good day at school?" I asked when he came into the kitchen and headed to the fridge to get some yogurt.

"Yeah."

"Your dad's coming home in two days."

"I know." He was spooning some of the yogurt into a bowl.

"What would you like to do while he's here?"

"I don't know."

"We could go up to Swayambhunath. See the monkeys."

"That's okay."

"Is that a no?"

"Yeah." He moved into the dining room and sat at the table to eat. I continued my unpacking in the kitchen.

"Do you have any games while he's home?"

"Tuesday."

"That'll make him happy."

"Whatever."

"You might want to start on your homework right away. The power's been on for a while, so it could go off anytime . . ."

"I know."

I went into the dining room and sat down across from him, wondering if Aidan's question might begin to bridge the conversational gap that broadened into a chasm in the days preceding Sam's returns. "Ryan . . ."

He sighed but didn't look up from his yogurt. "What, Mom?"

"If you had to describe our life here in one word—"

"Mom . . ."

"Come on. One word. How would you describe it?"

He looked up from his empty bowl. I was startled by the direct eye contact. How I loved the gold flecks in his brown irises. The smattering of freckles over his nose. The hint of peach fuzz growing on his upper lip. I couldn't remember the last time we'd looked at each other this directly for even a moment. The realization seared me.

"Why do you want to know?" he asked in the expressionless

85

tone he used for all his interactions with me. His voice had deepened noticeably in the past few months. I wondered if it cracked sometimes. I hadn't heard him talk enough to know.

"A friend asked me," I answered. "And . . . I'm stumped. But I thought you might have an idea."

"I don't know," he said, pushing his chair back and picking up his bowl to return it to the kitchen.

I hung my head. Tensed my shoulders, then released them. Valiant attempt—nothing gained.

Ryan was heading out of the kitchen when he said, almost too quietly for me to hear, "It sucks."

He'd disappeared when I turned. I looked at the empty doorway through tear-filled eyes and loved him till it bled. I guessed Nepal required two words to describe it.

I let a couple minutes pass before following him upstairs. His bedroom door was open. He was standing by the desk, looking out.

"Does it still?" I asked, standing there like an intruder hoping not to be kicked out.

He looked annoyed when he turned. "Does what still what?"

I took a tentative step into his room. "Does it still suck as much? Living here."

I wasn't sure if what I saw was a smile or a sneer. Whatever it was, it wasn't pleasant. There was a painful clarity to that moment. Me standing by the door, groveling for connection while he leaned back on his desk, arms crossed, offering only silent spite.

"I just wondered if after two years . . ."

"I'm happy?"

"Happier." It seemed the best I could hope for, but the look on his face dispelled my cautious optimism.

He bent over to retrieve his book bag and heaved it onto the desk. "I'm so happy," he said in a high-pitched, artificial voice.

"Ryan."

"Isn't that what you want to hear?" He sat at his desk and swiveled away from me, pulling a notebook from his bag and opening it in front of him.

"No," I said. "What I want is to hear *you*. We haven't talked—really talked—in so long, and . . . I don't want to hear pat answers, I want to hear *you*."

He picked up a pencil and tapped it on the desk. *Tap, tap, tap. Tap, tap, tap.* Hearing my son would require words, and it seemed we'd run out of those. There was a pain in my chest. Intensity and futility.

"Does it still suck as bad?" I tried again, hoping irrationally for a glimmer of "better" in the debris of "worst."

Tap, tap, tap. Tap, tap, tap. He breathed slowly. Deeply.

"I hope it's getting better. Really, Ryan. I hope it is." There was a desperation in my voice that I couldn't quite mask. I stopped myself from wringing my hands. Just barely. "With your soccer friends and your grades coming up and just . . . getting used to everything here. And with your dad coming home soon. That's a good thing—right?"

He stopped the tapping and turned on me, incredulity on his face. "I'm supposed to be happy that Dad's coming home?"

"I . . . yes. I want you to be glad when Dad comes back."

"Why?" The question was unflinching. So was the stare he leveled at me.

"Because . . ." But there was no reason worth expressing. As much as I longed to see contentment in my son, as much as I dreamed of hearing him laugh out loud again—because it would signal growth and healing—I knew the yearning was just as much about myself. My conscience. The permeating guilt that I had stolen Ryan's life.

"Because it's what a mother wants for her son," I said into the brittle silence between us. It didn't soften.

"Maybe you should have thought of that when—" He stopped himself midsentence.

Our eyes met and held. His combative and mine pleading. The stare-off shamed and wounded me.

"I'm glad he's coming home," Ryan said in the same contrived tone he'd used before. He dropped the pretense. "Now can I start my homework?"

"I love you," I said, emotions rendering my voice inaudible. I cleared my throat and tried again. "I love you."

Tap, tap, tap. Tap, tap, tap.

I left his room.

six

Sam came through the front door covered in snow.

"Daddy!" Ryan shrieked, nearly knocking a plate of mac-and-cheese onto the floor in his hurry to get down from the table. He raced to the entryway and hurled himself at his dad.

"How are you doing, kiddo?" Sam asked, crouching down to give his son a hug. Ryan was already recounting the day's events, eyes wide and animated as he talked mere inches from his father's face.

"There's a new kid in my class and he brought a gerbil to school because we were studying dodents—"

"Rodents," I interjected, mopping up some spilled milk.

"—and he bit the teacher on her pinky."

"The new kid did?" Sam asked.

"No," Ryan said so dramatically that I again considered trotting him out to talent agencies. "The dodent did!"

"I think you mean rodent, kiddo."

"And then we weren't allowed to touch him anymore."

I went to the door and gave my husband a kiss. "Thus ends the story of the first grade dodent," I said, pulling Ryan back a step or two so Sam could shrug out of his snow-dusted jacket. I instructed Ryan to head back to the table.

"But—"

"Now."

"But I'm telling Dad about—"

"Ryan."

He ducked his head and skulked back to his seat.

"Tough day?" I asked Sam, brushing a few flakes from his hair.

"Just long." He took a sheaf of colored pamphlets from the messenger bag he kept his papers in and dropped them on the dining room table. "You should take a look at these," he said as he lowered himself into a chair.

"Sure," I said, serving him a large portion of dinner.

Sam's hours at Brinkman, Crooks & Krause, a small investment firm near Muncie, had grown longer with the beginning of the year. He never complained, though I knew he got no real pleasure from the job. Sam was a hands-on man who preferred human interaction to theory, and concrete results to protracted processes. Still, he gave to the job all the focus it required, displaying the commitment that had drawn me to him during our months at Christschule.

Sam listened as Ryan prattled on about the new boy in his class and the rodent that bit the teacher. His eyes were focused on his son, but the light dancing in them seemed a little too bright even in response to Ryan's animated expansion on the classroom incident.

I glanced at the brochures Sam had dropped on the table. Then I took a step closer and splayed them out, leaning in for a better look. Suspicion stirred in me. Sam broke eye contact with Ryan just long enough to flash me a smile loaded with excitement and adventure.

As something vaguely reluctant settled into my stomach, I lowered myself into the chair at the end of the table. The brochures were four-color odes to Nepal—majestic mountains set against stunning blue skies, the deep-rutted faces of elderly people, and the gap-toothed smiles of beautiful children. There were facts about cultural events and weather and local industry and Everest treks. The pamphlets were intended for tourists, and part of me was relieved at that. Still, as I read through the information and contemplated the beauty of the places and people, I wondered how they related to the light in Sam's eyes.

We didn't talk about the brochures until Ryan was tucked into bed. I got a cup of tea and Sam poured himself some coffee, then we stood a little awkwardly by the dining room table while the silence stretched into tension. I had no idea what Sam was thinking, but I knew the brochures still lying where he'd dropped them were part of the answer.

"I met a guy called Prakash today," Sam finally said. "He came in with the pastor from the United Church. Wanted some advice on starting a 501(c)(3)."

"Okay."

"He's an amazing guy. Not even thirty. Comes from this remote Himalayan village in Nepal." He pulled a pamphlet from the bottom of the stack and dropped it on top. I glanced down at the picture of exotic children posing in front of a brick building. Mountains soared in the background. "He started a school for kids like these," Sam said. The excitement in his voice and the animation on his face were startling. "Come here." He took my free hand and pulled me toward the living room, installing me in one of our wingback chairs and pulling the other one up so he could sit across from me.

"He went to the capital—Kathmandu—to get an education," Sam continued, "but every time he went home, he felt this . . . this anger that the kids in the villages around where he grew up would probably never even learn the basics of reading and writing. And he got frustrated enough to do something about it."

The story was too compelling to be told sitting down. Sam pushed his chair back and began to pace in front of the fireplace, gesticulating joyously as he continued Prakash's story. "So this guy who's maybe twenty-six or twenty-seven decides to fix the problem. Now bear in mind, getting back to his village from the capital every time—every time—would take two full days on a bus, then four or five days walking over rough terrain and mountain passes." Sam shook his head, amazement in his expression. "If he wanted to start a school, he'd either have to carve out new roads in places where they've never

91

existed before—and for good reason—or find some other way of bringing in building equipment and school supplies."

"Let me guess—he found a way to do it?"

He threw up his hands, laughing in disbelief. "This kid from Podunk, Nepal, wheeled and dealed until he'd raised the funds and worked out the logistics to get eight crates of building and school materials delivered *by helicopter* to the village." He laughed again. "Who does that?"

"A boy after your own heart."

He smiled and sat in the chair opposite mine. "A boy after my own heart."

I laughed. Then I sobered up. "So . . . what are you peddling here?"

The expression on his face scared me a little. I could tell he knew that whatever it was would be a tough sell—and I had a feeling Sam's "path less traveled" was about to intersect with my "path of least resistance."

"Here's my thinking," he said. If the living room had been equipped with a blackboard, he'd have pulled out a piece of chalk and started drawing charts and sketches of the future he was envisioning. "He's just this . . . this regular Third World kid, and there's a school in Kalikot District now because he was dogged enough to make it happen. That gives me hope, Lauren."

"Hope?"

"Hope. The kind that says, 'Don't let anyone tell you it isn't possible.' The kind that says, 'You commit to the task and I'll have your back.'"

I felt myself frown and tried to undo it. I wanted to honor Sam's enthusiasm with an open-minded response, but something that felt like fear was building in my mind. "What task are you talking about, Sam?"

"Nepal," he said, somehow assuming the single word would clarify his thoughts.

"What about it?"

"I think . . ." He paused long enough to hurry to the dining room to retrieve the brochures. "I think this is it. I think this is where God wants us to go."

"To do what? Start another school?"

He shook his head. "I thought so. When Prakash started telling me about his school, I thought that's what I was sensing. But then . . ." He looked down at the brochures again, and I watched a smile that looked like passion blended with purpose spread across his face. "Look at these people," he said, holding up their pictures. "Prakash told me there are hundreds of villages in remote parts of the country that have never heard the gospel." He pointed at the faces staring out from the glossy pamphlets. "That's thousands of people just like these who have never been reached. They have huge needs—medical, educational, practical. Lauren"—he dropped the brochures, sat down again, and reached for my hands—"we could do that. We could be the people who reach them!"

"Sam . . ." I wanted to share his enthusiasm. I really did.

"It's Prakash's dream too. His next big project. He was in the office today trying to set up a fund with the United Church to keep his school running so he can devote himself to getting to the people in these other places."

"And our role would be . . . ?"

"I'm not sure yet. It was just one conversation, but as he told me about his project, I . . . Lauren, think about it. If he and I could do this together. Locate the villages and build relationships . . ."

There were so many questions and doubts swirling in my mind that all I could do was stare. Sam took it as an invitation to go on.

"I don't speak the language, but Prakash does. He doesn't have the fund-raising networks and practical resources, but I could find sponsors and aid. He said he wants to weave his way into these villages by living alongside the people and offering help—whatever they need. Extra hands tending to their animals? We can do that. New techniques for increasing their crops? We can do that too. Medical supplies? We can bring those in ourselves. And we can do all that while demonstrating God and faith to them."

"It's just . . ." I hesitated. "Sam, you've got to admit that this is all very sudden."

He nearly whooped. The man whose most defining trait was emotional stability nearly whooped with excitement. "But it's perfect!" he exclaimed. "It's the path less traveled, and relationships and humanitarian aid. It's . . ." He smiled. "Lauren—it's everything."

I let the silence settle for a moment, my eyes on his face, his on mine. After a few seconds, his shoulders sagged a little as the adrenaline rush of laying out his vision filtered out of his system. He stared at my face, expectation in his gaze.

"So . . ." I began. Then I stopped. I wasn't sure where to go with this. If someone had told me earlier that day that Sam would be coming home with a harebrained idea about working with villagers in Nepal, I might have been prepared for the scenario playing out in front of me. I might have had the time to plan a thoughtful response. Some follow-up questions. Different perspectives to consider. But they had caught me completely off guard—Sam and Nepal and this man called Prakash.

I looked into his face. It seemed lit from the inside with the energy of potential. In Sam's eyes was an invitation to an extraordinary adventure, a divine appointment he could practically taste. I reached forward and gripped his knees with steady hands.

"Honey," I said, "we're not moving to Nepal."

❧

Five weeks had passed since Sam had come home from the office with brochures in his hand, and still we'd reached no conclusion.

Far from being discouraged, he'd taken my initial dismissal as an invitation to persuasion. Under other circumstances, he would have carefully crafted his approach, like the logical thinker he was. But there was something less measured about his attempts at convincing me this time—a messy fervency perhaps fueled by the certainty that had struck him so immediately, but still eluded me.

I struggled to give him the space and spontaneity his arguments required, wondering when our roles had been reversed. The idealism of my youth was mired in the dailiness of marriage and motherhood, while Sam's sober rationality seemed to have been unshackled by this dream.

Our conversation had gone on, in fits and starts, for over a month. We lived like fighters circling the ring—Sam waiting for the strategic moment to launch a cogent thrust, and me in my protective stance, trying to imbue my deflections with support and reason.

Though we'd always started our days with prayer, it felt now like Sam was using those times to further press his agenda. It wasn't an overt thing—just pleas infused with a certainty that I'd come around once I realized this was God's will for me. And I felt guilty articulating trivial concerns about here-and-now matters when the direction of our lives seemed to hang in suspension. I frequently walked away from our morning intercession feeling more frustration and confusion than I had before we prayed. It saddened me.

On one Wednesday evening in February, we started the usual conversation in the kitchen while I cleaned up from dinner. We continued the disagreement in the living room, then moved the argument upstairs when it became clear that our hushed exchanges weren't helping Ryan with his spelling homework.

That's where things escalated, as they too often did. "We've been talking about this since we were in Austria!" Sam tried to keep his tone measured, but the edge of his voice had a telltale jaggedness.

"I know."

"Am I remembering wrong? Didn't you want to get involved in ministry too?"

"I did—I do!"

"Then—" He held out his arms in incomprehension. *"Then why are we still arguing about this?"*

"Because this thing you presented to me like it was a done deal is huge! A huge decision. A huge upheaval. This is more than a couple idealistic kids plotting their future on a mountaintop in Sternensee. I don't know how to say this to make it any clearer than the last ten times I tried, but it's more than just you and me now. I am not going to leap into something this . . . this life-altering without being as sure of it as you are."

"Lauren . . ."

"We have a son."

"And this could be the best thing for him. Think of all the experiences he'll have!"

I'd done enough online research to be fairly sure the "experiences" wouldn't all be pleasant. *"I need to see a plan, Sam. A concrete, rational plan."* I knew as I said the words that I needed far more than that.

"I'm working on it."

He'd been in regular contact with his new friend from Nepal since their first encounter in his office, trying to hammer out the details of the precise role Sam could play in the work he was doing there. I could tell when he'd received an e-mail from Prakash by the vitality in Sam's eyes and the excitement he exuded like a force field. I recognized the passion growing in him and resented it. I just couldn't figure out why.

"I don't know how to make you see this from my perspective," I said. I was leaning against the dresser that bridged the gap between our two bedroom windows as Sam crammed agitated pacing into a space that seemed too small for it. *"This has been so . . . so sudden."*

Sam stopped his pacing and faced me, hands on hips, apparently at a loss. *"And that makes it wrong?"*

I took a deep breath and blew it out slowly. For someone who avoided confrontation at all costs, the past few weeks had been an energy-sapping thing. "We've always talked about doing mission work. I know that—I was there. And it's still something I can envision us doing. But there are thousands of ministries out there for us to consider, Sam. And after one brief encounter that came out of nowhere, you've become *fixated* on this one. Like it's the most obvious thing in the world. Forgive me if I need a little time to think it all through."

He stared at the ceiling.

"How can you be so convinced that this is the right time and the right project for us?" I asked.

He sighed and scratched the back of his head a little too vigorously. "We've been over this."

"And I'm still confused." And frustrated. And angry. "You're assuming that all the thoughts and details that are apparently completing the picture in your mind are in my mind too, but they're not! All I hear is you saying, 'We're packing up, we're moving to Nepal, and it's going to be great because God's told us to go.'" I threw up my hands in exasperation. "I need more than that—Ryan and I need more than that!"

"Why?" He leaned in, arms outstretched, every inch of his body expressing his incomprehension. "This has never been in question. We've always said—even in our wedding vows!—if God calls us, we'll follow. Wherever he calls us, we'll follow." He said the first word again, giving extra emphasis to the second part. "Where—*ever.*"

I motioned to him to calm down. "And I'm not recanting what I said on our wedding day," I said, trying to keep my voice calm and measured. "But I can't just manufacture the same level of certainty you seem to feel for this . . . this . . . thing."

"Calling."

"What?"

"Not a 'thing.' A calling."

I cringed. Inserting God into the negotiations felt like unfair advantage.

Sam resumed his pacing. There was perspiration on his forehead and a tightness in the carriage of his shoulders that made him look feral. He was not a choleric man. In all our years of marriage, I'd only seen him lose his cool three times, all three for valid—even noble—reasons. So his anger on this night and others took me aback. I wondered if my doubts were reason or revolt, if my questions were moving the conversation forward or strangling it before it could conclude.

"My wedding vows were sincere." My voice shook with repressed frustration. "I still want to follow where God leads. But Sam . . . don't you think that if God called you, he would have called me too?"

"Maybe he is and you're not hearing him."

I took a couple deep breaths and stifled a retort. "Let's slow down a little. Okay? Take our time. Talk to a few people. You've always made lists of pros and cons. Let's do that with this too." I stepped over to where he stood and grasped his shoulders, forcing eye contact. "I'm not trying to stand in your way. I'm just . . ." He resisted a little as I framed his face with my hands. "I've got to be sure of this. Can we give it more time?"

He took my hands and held them. "How much time do you need?"

I felt the slow burn of frustration again. "I don't . . . It's not . . ." I didn't know how long it would take. What pieces were missing. All I knew was the intensity of my hesitation. "Ryan is seven. He's just started school. He has friends. He lives in a familiar world with all kinds of safety nets—"

"And if we didn't have Ryan," Sam interrupted. "If we didn't have a son, would you be reacting any differently?"

I wanted to tell him that I'd pack a bag and be on my way to Kathmandu in a moment if we didn't have Ryan, but . . . "I don't know, Sam. This is sudden. And it feels like you're acting—I don't know—rashly."

"Passionately. About something that's important to me."

"Impulsively."

He sat on the edge of the bed, elbows on knees as he rubbed his hands over his face. "Think about it," he said, more calmly this time, looking up at me. "Think about all the world-changers whose work started with just that. An impulse they acted on. A rash decision their loved ones might not have understood." He shook his head in a sort of frustrated reverence. "David Livingston. Hudson Taylor . . ."

"Sam."

"I don't think I'm being impulsive. I think . . ." He stopped and breathed for a few moments, staring at the ceiling. "I think this is what I'm meant to do."

I moved to the bed and sat down next to him, my hand on his thigh in the only gesture of support I could muster. His arm came around me and I let him draw me in. "I love your passion, Sam," I said, turning into the warmth of his shoulder.

His voice rumbled through his chest. "But?"

I burrowed in deeper, closer to his voice, closer to the heart that beat so fervently for the less fortunate and always would. "But I need for us to take more time. Just so we're sure. You know?" I pulled back just far enough to see the pulse beating in his neck and concession on his face. "I just want to be sure. For Ryan's sake."

He nodded and tightened his arm around me. Some of the tension went out of his body as he propped his chin on the top of my head. I relaxed into his chest and felt his breathing slow.

I knew he was praying.

⁓

Squawking geese walked on the frozen lake, following Ryan's progress as he skipped, stick in hand, along the hardened ground. His blue jacket and bright yellow boots stood in stark contrast to the black-and-white scenery left by too many weeks of below-freezing temperatures. The long cold snap had been fun for the first few days, when school closings had allowed for fireside games and hot cocoa. But there are only so many rounds of Monopoly a family can play. Only so many finger-painting projects an eight-year-old can tolerate. "Can we please get a Wii?" our stir-crazy son had asked roughly fourteen times a day for the past two weeks.

So though the sky was overcast on this early-April Saturday and the fog far from inviting, an acute case of cabin fever and temperatures finally rising above freezing had made us venture out for goose-feeding and a bit of fresh air. I could feel my lungs celebrating the luxury.

Ryan walked ahead of me on our slow progress around the lake. Every so often, he stopped to show me a leaf coated with ice or to point at something the geese were doing. Sam had motioned us on after answering his phone back at the car. "I'll catch up with you," he'd mouthed. I wasn't sure who had called, but I had a fairly good idea of the topic they were discussing. I glanced over my shoulder—he was sitting in the driver's seat, still talking. He'd been doing a lot of that since bringing home those brochures of Nepal three months ago.

I loved watching Ryan when his mind and body were released from the restrictions of schoolwork and planned activities. The looseness in his gait, the frequent changes of direction and focus, the eyes-wide-open contemplation of the world . . . They spoke of a lightheartedness I couldn't imagine—a lack of preoccupation I envied.

I watched him insert his stick into a discarded Coke can and lift it into the air, then flick it at an oak tree. It hit the trunk with a bright clatter, and he did a little victory dance, mouth open in imitation of a cheering crowd. He ran over to retrieve the can and launched it again, this time in the direction of a sign that warned against walking on the ice. The can sailed past the sign onto the frozen pond and scattered the geese still hoping to be fed. He looked at me and covered his mouth with a blue-mittened hand.

I shook my head. "Ryan . . ."

"I was aiming for the sign!" he said, running over to me and pointing back in the direction of the painted warning his missile had missed.

"And now there's a Coke can in the middle of the lake."

"I can go out and get it!" He stopped in front of me, eyes wide with the adventure he imagined. "I can go out really slowly, and if I hear cracking, I'll come right back."

"You're not going out on the ice, Ryan."

He pointed at the can with his stick and put on his best responsible expression. "But I put the can out there! Now I have to go get it before the geese eat it or something."

I crouched down in front of him. "When was the last time you saw a goose eat a soda can?"

His forehead wrinkled as he frowned, deep in thought. "Sasha—at Brendon's party."

I gave him my stop-fooling-around look. "That was a dog and a cupcake."

"But it could have been a goose."

There was no contradicting that kind of logic, not when it was so earnestly expressed. He looked at me with the sort of conviction he brought to endorsing the health benefits of Wii games and the nutritional value of donuts. "Mom," he said with confidence, my agreement apparently a foregone conclusion, "we can't leave a tin can out on the lake."

I'd always wanted children—I'd imagined all my life what motherhood would feel like. But nothing had prepared me for the surges of love that overtook me at random times. There were moments, like this one, when feelings so fierce I forgot to breathe made me want to grab my son and hold on so tightly that he'd know the full force of my devotion. Oh, how I loved this little human being. His laughter fed my soul. His tantrums and demands sturdied it. His love heartened it.

On this day, a protective rush exacerbated the already powerful emotions. Sam and I were still at odds. His passion and my reticence formed an uncomfortable, combustible dichotomy. I despised the tension and its toll on our marriage. But as I took in the details of Ryan's upturned face, I felt the repercussions of a possible mistake like a physical ache. I had to be sure before we moved forward with Sam's plans. For Ryan's sake, I had to be convinced.

We were standing by the railing throwing stale bread to the geese that had stranded themselves in Indiana for the winter when Sam joined us. Ryan ran up to him, pointing at the ice.

"Dad, we have to go out there and get the can!"

Sam followed the direction Ryan was pointing. "It's pretty far out there, kiddo."

"But if a goose eats it, it could die!"

"The goose or the can?"

Ryan furrowed his forehead. "What?"

Sam found a spot where the embankment was gradual enough for him to reach the edges of the lake. Ryan yelled instructions at him. "Go really slow, Dad! If you hear cracking, you have to run right back, okay? Dad, take my stick in case a goose gets mad!"

Sam was a good sport. He took a couple steps out onto the ice and hopped once, just to make sure it would hold his weight. Then he shuffled out far enough to reach the can with Ryan's stick and send it clattering back to the shore. Ryan whooped and did his victory routine again, exchanging a vigorous high five with Sam when he joined us.

We ambled on to the park's designated barbecue area, where a small deck projected a few feet over the lake. "You want some bread?" Ryan asked, waiting for his dad to join him at the fence.

"You go ahead and feed them, buddy."

"But Dad!"

I pulled a piece of stale bread from the bag I carried and handed it to Sam. "If you can't beat 'em . . ."

He smiled as he took the bread from my hand, then tore off a piece and threw it to a smaller goose that hung back a bit from the rest.

"That one's not looking too good," he said as he tossed another piece. My husband the rescuer.

Ryan could have stayed out there for hours, despite the cold. He was fascinated—enraptured, really—with animals and always had been. Sad? Mad? Stubborn? Sickly? All I had to do was mention a trip to the petting zoo, the pet store at the mall, or to the lake to feed the geese, and my little guy perked up.

I handed Ryan his fourth slice of bread and instructed him to break it into smaller pieces so it would last longer.

"I know, Mom," he said, drawing out my name. It's not like I hadn't told him the same thing with the first three slices.

I tousled his hair with my purple-mittened hand. "When it's gone, it's gone."

"Okay." And he chucked half of the piece at the feet of the loudest goose.

Sam leaned on the fence next to his son and propped a foot on the lowest rung. I delighted in the similarities of their profiles. Same high cheekbones and deep eye sockets. Same classic nose. I was contemplating the similarities in their personalities too when Sam said, "Ryan, Mom and I have been talking and we want to tell you about something we've been thinking about."

I felt the bottom drop out of my stomach. "Sam . . ." I wasn't ready for this conversation.

Ryan's face brightened. "A puppy?"

"No," Sam said, mock-aggravated. "We're not getting a dog!"

Ryan went back to feeding the geese. "Shoot."

I tried to subdue the impulse to tell Sam to be quiet. We'd talked about this. We'd agreed that it would be good to very slowly introduce Ryan to the possibility of change. I'd initially resisted the notion, unwilling to put our son through the prospect of a difficult transition if we ended up not going after all. But Sam had convinced me of the value of this step, of the benefit of giving Ryan time to consider the possibility of a life-change we might choose for him. I just hadn't expected this talk to come so soon.

As we stood by the frozen pond, I felt a chill that had nothing to do with the quickly cooling air. Sam sought my gaze and held it for a moment. I nodded my agreement, though a bit reluctantly, and moved to stand closer to him. A unified front. That's what we'd agreed on. He turned to lean back against the top rail of the fence and took my hand, drawing me nearer. I leaned into his side, arms crossed against the chill. His arm around my waist wrapped me closer to his warmth. "Remember that story we used to read to you?" he said to Ryan. "The one about the family that moved to Africa to bring Jesus to the people there?"

"The lion story?"

"Sure. The one with the lions and elephants."

Our son held out his hand for another slice of bread. He tore off a huge piece.

"What would you think about us doing something like that?" My voice was deliberately calm and noncommittal.

Ryan's arm froze midthrow. He looked from Sam to me, then back to Sam. Then he frowned. "You mean, like, Africa?"

We'd agreed not to mention Nepal until we were convinced that was where we were heading. "We're not completely sure of the place just yet," Sam said. I loved the softer tone he used when he talked to Ryan about important things. "But we think God might want us to move to another country."

"A faraway one?"

"Maybe," Sam said.

Ryan tossed the piece of bread he was holding with a little less enthusiasm and turned toward us, traces of confusion on his face. I crouched down beside him and took one of his hands. "It's not a for-sure thing yet," I said quietly. "But we want you to know that we're thinking about it, because it involves you too."

Sam came down on his haunches next to us and smiled his beautiful father-smile. "You know how sometimes we get this feeling that something's going to happen?"

"Like I might get sick if I eat another cookie?"

I pinched my lips against a giggle.

"Or like you know it's going to be a really good game—even before the game starts," Sam continued, a smile in his voice. When Ryan nodded, albeit a bit dubiously, he went on. "Well, Mom and I have wondered for a while if we might end up in another part of the world, telling people about Jesus. And I have that same kind of feeling that it might be a really great thing."

"You mean, going somewhere?"

"Yup. Going somewhere."

"Will they have soccer?"

"We don't know yet," I said as casually as I could. "But we want you to be thinking about it too, because we're not going anywhere without you!" I kissed his face and he wiped it off.

"I don't want to go somewhere." He turned and threw more bread at the waiting geese.

Sam and I looked at each other, both still in a crouch while the subject of our concentration ripped another piece from the slice he held in his blue mitten. We groaned back to a standing position like seventy-year-olds. "Just think about it," I said.

Ryan shook his head. "I don't want to go somewhere," he said again.

"We're not going anywhere quite yet." That was the problem with explaining theoretical situations to children who saw the world in immediate, immutable terms.

Sam stepped closer to the rail to throw his last piece of bread onto the frozen surface of the lake. "We're just giving you time to get used to the idea," he said, gripping the top of Ryan's head in his large hand and giving it a shake. "We don't know what's going to happen yet."

Ryan's chin jutted out a little as he too released his last piece of bread. He watched the geese leap toward it, wings flapping, barking in their comical show of bravado.

I met Sam's eyes and shrugged. We'd opened the conversation. It would take time and persistence to see where it led.

As we headed to the car, there was a bit less lightness in Ryan's zigzags and distractions. He stopped every so often to look back at us with something that looked like suspicion in his eyes. I held Sam's arm and huddled close.

seven

ONE DAY UNTIL SAM CAME HOME. I HAD MY PRE-RETURN list taped to the fridge door—tasks to be accomplished before Sam got back. I plugged away at them during each three-week absence, but those I disliked or resented had the annoying habit of staying there, glaring at me from the rainbow-colored note-pad as I scratched off the items above and below them.

So on this eve of Sam's return, I glared right back at the "Write newsletter" and "Finish accounting" lines on my to-do list. I would not even *think* of Facebook until the items were both checked off. They were excruciating endeavors for me. The first because I despised begging disguised as reporting. The second because I'd married a financial guru. If only I'd have thought of including "And you will do all the entering of expenses and income into our monthly budgeting plan" in my wedding vows. Hindsight.

About six months into our life in Nepal, the giving that fueled our ministry had decreased. Forgetfulness. Lack of con-nection. Personal difficulties. We didn't know what was causing the funds to dry up, but we were keenly aware that we'd be power-less without them. I'd had to find the right time to suggest to Sam that we engage in the type of communication he despised—newsletters and mass e-mails. "Just so people know what we're accomplishing."

He didn't like the concept. I think he saw it as lack of faith. His God was above all a provider and a miracle worker. He wanted him to show up without our effort—to prove the validity of our work through unsolicited, generous donations from people and churches whose only motivation was the work God was doing.

So I'd taken the communication burden onto myself, with a bad attitude and a resentful spirit. Only Sullivan's enthusiastic approval seemed to make the tedium bearable.

"You may not realize this," she'd said on a Skype call after reading one of my newsletters, "but if it weren't for your reporting, we'd have no idea whether Sam was playing midwife to a poor sixteen-year-old villager or painting his toenails in the Kathmandu Hilton!"

Sam always came home with dramatic stories to tell, but his experience helping a Nepali girl give birth in the bed of an ox-drawn cart while her husband tried to get them to the nearest clinic had made for a particularly entertaining letter.

"He'd rather stay in a tent than at the Hilton," I said.

"One of the many ways in which Sam and I are different."

"I'm trying to think of ways in which you're *similar* and drawing a blank . . ."

"Skin," she said. "We both have skin. It may not seem like much, as similarities go, but imagine the mess if all those organs were hanging out unrestricted."

I laughed. There were many reasons I was grateful to have reconnected with Sullivan. Laughter was one of the greatest.

She'd left the mountain village after our semester abroad with an acceptance letter to a Southern bastion of education. Though she'd flown to Sternensee on a whim, eager for an adventure to spice up a "leisurely yawn of a life," she'd discovered a passion for learning in the intimate, single-purposed atmosphere of

Christschule. Where to invest that education hadn't come to her quite as clearly. As she'd hopped off the ski lift on a sunny day near the middle of our semester abroad, she'd pointed a pole at the sky and declared, "I'm going to be a counselor!"

She'd gone on to study psychology and had lasted nearly a year. ("It's not as conversational as I thought it would be.") She'd switched to teaching and only made it to her first class-room experience. ("Too much nose-wiping and not enough fun-having.") And when an up-and-coming second-year at her father's legal firm had asked her to the company's New Year's celebration, she'd found a calling and a Collin that required nei-ther studies nor second thought.

They wed within a year, a pink-saturated affair ("'It's my signature color'—get it?"), were living apart after four years, and now were married only in legal terms. Sullivan's abandonment of a dreary career path had collided midflight with Collin's escape from his sexual identity. He was now a well-respected lawyer for big-money, conservative clients in historical Savannah. His marriage, such as it was, cloaked a guilt-ridden private life that afforded Sullivan an existence as carefree and comfortable as she wanted it to be.

"Do you ever feel like he has all the fun?" Sullivan drawled. "Sam gets to play a real-life Robinson Crusoe, inventing this and fixing that and—for heaven's sake—birthing teensy Nepali babies while bouncing along a rocky mountain path. I'd be sur-prised if there wasn't a giant *S* tattooed on his chest."

"There's an *E* on mine," I said. "It stands for 'everything else.'"

"Don't fool yourself, Chickadee. You earned him that *S*. The stories are great and you honor your husband when you write about them, but your 'everything else' is the reason he gets to do what he does."

I let that sink in for a moment. "How did you know I needed to hear that?"

"'Cause I would too, in your shoes . . . sensible and rubber-soled as they are."

"Are you attacking my footwear again?"

"Your next care package may or may not contain a more glamorous alternative."

"Sullivan . . ."

"I want you to know that I'm not just partnering with Sam in all of this. You know that, right? I'm cheering for you too."

With the memory of that conversation in my mind and one day to go before Sam's return, I opened the laptop and pulled up a new document. One newsletter and one financial report. And then Facebook.

To prove to myself that Aidan wasn't the sole reason for my interest in Facebook, I opened the message waiting for me from Sullivan first.

> I'll keep this brief. My Dudley is getting a new hairdo this p.m. and if I'm late, the only beautician who can groom his little stub without gagging will move on to another mutt. But you need to know that the gang's been talking and we have an idea to run by you. I'm not going to tell you what it is just yet, but I think you're going to LOVE it. Love it, I say! I'm just giving you a few days of heads-up to anticipate it, since your life there is so boring. What with the monkeys and the monks and the civil unrest. "When it comes to pain, you're right up there with Elizabeth Taylor." That's my *Magnolias* quote for the day. Aren't you loving Facebook??

I laughed and shook my head. What had I done in those intervening years, when Sullivan's bright, ferocious energy had been out of my life?

I'd often wondered if any man could live in her wake for a protracted amount of time. It was moot musing, of course, as she seemed perfectly content in her pseudomarriage to Collin Geary. One of her favorite *Steel Magnolias* quotes was "The only reason people are nice to me is because I have more money than God." She said it flippantly, usually after she'd secured an outrageous favor from someone who barely knew her. But Sullivan lived according to another quote from her favorite movie: "An ounce of pretension is worth a pound of manure." As flamboyant as she was, she wielded her influence humbly. Still, I wondered if her primal brightness could exist tethered to another soul.

I responded to her message with a quick one of my own.

The monkeys are quiet, the monks are sleeping, and the protesters are taking a break. I've just finished writing newsletter number forty-nine. Let me repeat that. Newsletter number forty-nine! Elizabeth Taylor has nothing on me in the pain and suffering department. I can assure you I'd rather be taking three-legged Dudley to the beautician than trying to be pithy for the nearly fortieth time! (You realize they're called groomers, right?) I'll entertain the gang's idea. Send it along.

My cursor hovered over Aidan's latest message. I hesitated to open it. It seemed . . . inappropriate, somehow, to be so caught up in preparing for Sam's return home, yet yearning for contact with a friend from my past. Though I knew there wasn't anything illicit about our communication, something about it frightened me. We knew each other with a fierceness that felt exhilarating and dangerous, yet somehow entirely innocuous. Even as teen-agers, we played in the soft sand at the edge of the precipice, watching each other take flight with others while blissfully una-ware, most of the time, of how close we were to falling. Ours was a contorted, visceral mismatch that left bystanders bemused and us infused with a "take on the world" energy we wouldn't have found with anyone else.

In its adult, digital form, the friendship felt just as powerful. Perhaps more so because of the depth and breadth age lent to juve-nile connection. I remembered, again, Aidan's promise to "say something" about prayer. Curiosity got the best of me. I clicked on Aidan's message and his words popped up on my screen.

> really, ren. you shouldn't have put so many words into your comments about 'hope.'
>
> humbled by the 'astounding.' honored by the 'still.' it echoes.
>
> i realize you have a full and busy life and i know this message comes quickly on the heels of the last one. let me know if it's too much. but . . . i guess i've said it before: there isn't much room in my life right now for hesitancy of any kind.
>
> i need to unpack this tidbit of information for you. in the interest of, i don't know, context. and full disclosure. or some other legal term that means, 'you were one of the first people i wanted to tell.' it might take a few minutes of your time. if you don't have it right now, just close this window and come back when you do, okay? or never. no obligations here. none.
>
> i had a pretty terrible headache on labor day.
>
> there. don't you feel enriched by that fact?
>
> just kidding.

i had a headache that felt like someone inside my head was using a sledgehammer to get out. i'd been drinking the night before and figured it was a bad hangover. then it got worse. sledgehammer to battering ram worse. i called one of the guys from work—my drinking buddy—and asked if he was sick too. i must have made some gnarly sound when i was talking to him or maybe i passed out. he tells me he was there within five minutes. called 911.

so while most of the world on this side of the ocean was celebrating with cookouts, i was being poked and prodded and injected and iv-d and scanned. the pain was a few steps the other side of hell. i can't express it. ren, i know you know this. there comes a time when all you have left to do is pray. i discovered how true that is while i lay on a gurney on labor day.

the bottom line is a little thing called glioblastoma multiforme. by little, i mean the size of an orange. (never trust a fruit whose name has no rhyming words in the english language.) by thing, i mean tumor. they tell me it's stage four. they tell me it's the nastiest kind of critter.

so . . . that's where i'm at. and i wanted you to know. i went home after they stabilized me and gave me a list of specialists to see asap. and you know what i did once i'd showered and put on clothes that didn't smell like hospital? i sat down at my computer and typed your name into facebook. no matches. did some googling. no hits.

then i had my head cracked open. barbarian surgery. and tried to get back to seeing straight and not walking into doorways. my mom came out to see me through surgery. suggested you might be married. duh. called the old high school in west lorne. found out mr. foster still taught there. old geezer knew way too much about all our comrades in arms, including you. lauren coventry. back to facebook and still nothing.

so i continued the unbuilding of my life. quit my job. moved to pa because my parents are here now and . . . well . . . i'll be needing some help at some point in the (hopefully) distant future. they own a couple rentals. one down the street from them. guess who got evicted after his diagnosis?

i weighed my medical options. duke. johns hopkins. mayo. learned way too much about way too many alternative approaches. and every time i had a minute to reflect on the time i have left, i typed your name into facebook again. then a few days ago, bingo. as if you knew.

and here we are.

not sure why i needed you to know about what's happening. so badly. except that this—whatever 'this' is—feels death-defying.

i know that raises more questions than it answers. most of the words that whip around the globe from you to me and me to you probably do. but this is . . . me. this is my battle. it's why i don't want to wait to answer your messages. or tackle the next painting. or watch the next sunset. or capture the next snowflake. (sappy but true.)

this isn't a bribe, by the way. 'i'm sick so you have to . . . whatever.' no pressure. and please, no pity. i'm going to kick this beast's patooty. (language cleaned up just for you.)

now you know. sigh. now you know.

Night had fallen. Ryan had called to tell me he was sleeping over at Steven's because his mom was out of town and Nyall had been called into the hospital for some kind of emergency. I'd told him to be back by noon tomorrow, when Sam would be home.

I hadn't moved from the bed in what felt like hours. The laptop was still open, Aidan's message still displayed. I'd read and reread it, my breath catching, my throat constricting, my eyes filling and overflowing with tears. Aidan. Not Aidan. We hadn't spoken in two decades and I'd mostly forgotten him in the intervening time. But finding each other again had disintegrated the distance, and it felt like he'd never been gone.

My mind churned with questions and writhed with grief. I'd started a message twice, then erased it. Wordlessness consumed me.

When my initial reaction had subsided enough for me to think more clearly, I started again, soon overcome by emotion.

Aidan, I just read your message . . . I don't know how to start. There's a rock in my stomach. It speaks of grief and incomprehension and fragility and fear and fury. I've tried to find the words to express it, but this is a visceral thing words can't unravel. I wish you were close. I need to read your face when you say things like "cancer" and "malignant." I need to hear your voice when you utter words like "prayer" and "death-defying" and "peace." I need to watch you breathe.

You sound . . . braced. And aware. Who is there for you? How is your heart as you face this battle? What treatment will you undergo? So many questions. I Googled glioblastoma for thirty seconds, then stopped. What do you know, Aidan? And what do I need to know too?

Silence. I don't have the words to describe it so you'll understand its mass. There's this abyss that yawns between the friends we used to be and the adults we're still becoming. And the memories in these messages—the places, smells, tastes, and emotions—have formed elusive stepping-stones that allow us closer. Just close enough to feel more keenly the void of absence. I venture out, hoping something will materialize under my feet, and there it is. There you are. But still too far to see. And hear. And reach.

There's an insurrection swirling in my mind. Not you. Not Aidan! You go ahead and pray. I'm going to scream for a while. And believe. And hope. And love.

And love.

I probably shouldn't send this. It's as tangled and bent and broken as my thoughts. But it's real. Speak to me, Aidan.

I'm right here—still.

Ren

My sleep was restless, shot through with the darkness of death and loss. I battled the specters of futility and helplessness. With the laptop beside me on Sam's side of the bed, I propped myself up every time I started out of a tortured half slumber to see if Aidan had answered my message yet.

The sky was brightening when I reached out to lift the laptop's lid again. And there it was. There Aidan was.

i wasn't sure of how you'd respond. but as i read your message, i realized how sure i'd actually been. there are few people in this world whose words can be a healing thing . . .

there's no way of saying this without coming across like an egocentric jerk, so i'll just throw it out there and trust you'll understand. thank you for feeling so strongly. about me. that in itself is a validation of my postdiagnosis impulse to find you. i say impulse but we both know it was more of an obsession. you've seen me go through enough of those to get how excessive they can be. think kelly in ninth grade. think jack daniel's (preferably out of the flask in the inside pocket of my so-cool denim jacket) in tenth grade. think kelly and jack and drag racing down main street at midnight in eleventh grade. think aidan-never-should-have-survived-high-school. so yeah. i was going to find you or die trying.

quite literally.

which brings me to the question of why, which brings me to the subject of you. ren—hear me clearly. tracking you down was not a cowardly ploy to drag someone with me through the hell of what the docs say might be two more months of life. six if i'm lucky. it wasn't an attempt to guilt you into 'being there for me.' (though a certain episode in our history would make that a logical assump-tion.) but it wasn't a casual reaching-out to give an old high school classmate a news update either.

do you remember how this . . . how 'this' really started? the notebook you'd always leave under the desk in mrs. dailey's classroom. i wrote 'hi' in it one day and you wrote 'hi' back. not sure how long it took you to figure out who was sitting in that desk when you weren't in it. but the 'hi' expanded and curled into this swirl of words. ended up filling the inside cover of your notebook. then we started leaving loose notes. and this normal, two-kids-grow-up-in-the-same-small-town-and-go-to-the-same-schools thing . . . it turned into something else. and when i took the time, lying in that hospital bed on labor day, to look back over a life most accurately painted in the color beige (sigh), i saw bursts of bold, bright, primal colors. all yours.

i know i'm dying. (haven't gotten used to writing that yet . . .) i'm going to try to beat the odds, but at some point . . . the odds are going to get me. and i don't want my dying to be another shade of beige layered over a lifetime of beige. i need it to have color. just a few splotches here and there. just enough to keep me anchored to the vibrancy of life as i get absorbed, kicking and screaming, into death.

that's why i needed to connect with you.

you know what? what i said earlier is a lie. this is entirely self-serving. it's about me needing you and not caring enough about you to leave you out of whatever hellish death-throes lie ahead.

but i never regretted writing that single word in the notebook back in mrs. dailey's class. i dragged you through the kind of turbulence that had you begging to get off, half the time. but it was color and vitality to me. and now i've dragged you in again. i'd like to say it's a selfless effort to offer you the ride of your life, except that it's the ride of my death.

i'm sorry, ren. it's just now striking me what a narcissistic jerk i am. not the conclusion i was reaching for when i began this note . . . and i fear that the ren who chastised and calmed and accused and placated and rebuked and appeased and ultimately cared for me when i was an impulsive, obsessive kid will sacrifice herself for this cause too, despite the family and obligations and life you have now.

geez. i don't want you to do that for me. no self-immolation—please. just the occasional word to anchor

me again. the splash of color. that's all i was hoping for
when i tracked you down.

i'm well taken care of here. my parents live two
houses down. (so much for being a grown-up.) medical
care is great. chemo done just over a week ago—i hope.
i'd just . . . i'd be really grateful for a now-and-again
splash of you . . .

still.

a.

I rolled onto my back and closed my eyes, feeling waves
of contradictory emotions washing over my mind. Concern,
frustration, fear, helplessness . . . inspiration, joy, need. Similar
sentiments to what I'd experienced when Aidan had roused
me from a deep sleep, our junior year, by throwing pebbles of
increasing size at my window. It was the sound of fissuring glass
that had finally startled me awake.

I'd tiptoed downstairs and gone out through the garage—a
safe distance from Mom and Dad's room.

"What the heck, Aidan? You cracked my window!"

He was shivering, hands shoved into his pockets, his T-shirt
wet with sweat and steaming on the frigid November night. His
eyes were a bit wild.

"Are you drunk?" I demanded. I'd told him the last time
he'd turned up like this that I wanted nothing to do with him if
he was inebriated or stoned.

"Maybe," he slurred.

I took in his thin T-shirt and jeans, then noticed his bare
feet. "Aidan, really? No shoes?" I was about to launch into the
sermon I reserved for Aidan's top three misbehaviors—cheating,
speeding, and getting drunk—when I looked into his face, finger
already brandished, and was halted by his expression. I paused,

my arguments deflating, then took his arm and pulled him into the garage. I couldn't take him into the house without risking a parental firestorm, so I turned on the space heater my dad used for tinkering at his workbench and installed Aidan in the passenger seat of the family Chevy. I rolled down the window to let some heat in, then reached for the blanket my dad always kept in the backseat.

"I don't need that," Aidan said, swatting at my hands as I tucked the fabric around him.

"Yes, you do," I said calmly, trying to read the expression on his face.

He stopped resisting and I finished the job, then cranked up the heat a little more and went around the car to crawl into the driver's seat.

Aidan's eyes were closed and the shivers now came in bursts. I lay my head against the backrest and watched as they slowed, then ceased. After long minutes had passed, during which I suspected Aidan might have dozed off a time or two, he finally opened his eyes and stared straight ahead. I was still sitting sideways in the driver's seat, my legs pulled up.

"You know," I said into the dark silence, "it would be really great if you could start having your crises during daylight hours."

He smirked a little reluctantly. A few more minutes lumbered by. I'd figured out early in this contorted thing we called a friendship that I didn't need to pry information from Aidan. If he came to me, he was planning on speaking. Eventually. I just had to find the patience to wait for him to be ready. He'd done for my self-control what no number of groundings and lectures had before.

I was dozing off myself when he spoke. "My parents are splitting up."

I thought I must have heard him wrong. If someone had

asked me to list three things I was sure of, I'd have said God's existence, my dad's beloved Cubs losing, and Aidan's parents never divorcing. Russ and Janet Dennison were pillars of our rural community, active in our small-town government and in the Baptist church, avid volunteers for important causes, and despite the fact that their son might have spent more time in detention than he actually did in class, well respected and envied for the strength of their bond.

"What do you mean, 'splitting up'?"

"I mean," Aidan said, anger and consternation washing over his face, "they're . . . splitting up." He looked at me as if he expected me to explain it to him.

"What happened?"

"I don't know!" His voice rose and I motioned for him to keep it down.

The next few minutes were a halting account of what had transpired that evening. He'd come home past his curfew, fully expecting to be grounded again, and had found his parents locked in conflict—his mother in tears and his dad bristling with anger. They'd sent him upstairs and ordered him to stay in his room, but he'd crept back to the top of the stairs to listen.

He swiped at his eyes with the back of his hand and turned his head farther away from me. "Dad said something about getting a divorce," he said in a broken voice. "And Mom told him he'd have to tell me himself, because she'd have no part in breaking the family up."

I squeezed his arm and tried to think past the confusion in my mind. "Aidan, people have arguments all the time. Maybe this'll blow over. You know how it goes—parents get angry, they say stupid stuff, and then they figure things out."

He turned and looked at my hand where it gripped his arm. "My dad went up to the attic and came down with a suitcase," he said. Tears choked off his voice, his emotions heightened by the alcohol in his system.

"Aidan . . ."

"And I . . ." He swallowed hard again. "And I lost it."

I'd seen him lose control before, so I had a vague idea of what it looked like.

"What did you say?" He shook his head. "Aidan."

"I told him to go to hell." His eyes were haunted as they connected with mine. "I said I hated them both and that I was moving out anyway. Dad yelled, 'Go to your room right now, young man!'—something like that—and I flipped him off and ran down the stairs and out the door." Something that looked like absolute brokenness washed over his face. He fisted his hands and tried to control the emotions quaking through his body. "I didn't know where to go," he said, the words strangled and rushed. He gripped my hand where it lay on his arm. "I just—I didn't know where to go."

I'd never seen him so weakened by emotion. I didn't know what to do. How to comfort him.

The car's console separated us, but I tried to bridge the gap. I laid a hand on his face so he'd know I wasn't embarrassed by his tears. I stroked his arm and tried to speak soothing words about "maybe" and "tomorrow" and "we don't know." He dismissed my hopefulness with a shake of his head and tried to push away my hands when emotions welled up in his eyes again. But I couldn't back down. I couldn't leave him alone with so much pain and fear.

I leaned in close so he couldn't look away and poured all the confidence and calm I could muster into my gaze. "You're going to get through this, Aidan." He tried to avoid connection, but I cradled his cheek in my hand and brought his eyes back to me. "We'll figure this out," I said.

I wasn't sure who first kissed who. There was surprise, wide-eyed hesitation, then an unspoken mutual surrender to the solace of insentience.

What followed was a fumbling flight from a reality we were too young to grasp, warm breaths and reaching hands. Looking back the next day and for many days after that, I was grateful for the tight confines of my dad's prized sedan. Cup holders and gearshifts had kept a full expression of our shared grief from tarnishing a friendship that was—we realized at that moment—more primal and pure than we could possibly articulate. It was the wordlessness of that night that had ultimately defined and deepened what drew us.

And then, by common, unspoken consent, we'd drifted back from the brink to a more practical intimacy. The kind that soared in art and words, but left our teenage spirits free to make the mistakes hardwired into our needs. I tried to erase the memory of our lapse in judgment and berated myself when I failed. But as his parents' passions cooled and wiser minds prevailed, we saw their reconciliation as a fresh, new milestone in our own relationship, one in which bygones could be safely forgotten and a less murky foundation laid.

But the murkiness had not been entirely abolished. It had merely lain dormant for twenty-some years. I was discovering again that love, like grief, doesn't die. It bleeds until it can no more. Then, pale and listless, sleeps.

eight

It took us three more months to decide to pursue Nepal in earnest, after breaking the idea to Ryan by the lake. Three months of praying together, then inviting our friends and family into the prayer circle. Three months of conversations that crescendoed into arguments and decrescendoed into a tenuous truce only relieved by the promise of more talks.

They usually started with Sam asking the obvious. "Are you still struggling with it?" We'd be driving home from church. Or pulling our trash cans up the driveway. Or wrapped up in each other as our bodies cooled.

"Yes," I'd answer, hoping the single word would be enough.

"Can you tell me why?" Or something to that effect. I think he sincerely wanted in on my thought process, but my own mind demanded a response from me so often during the day that the added pressure of Sam's question felt like badgering.

We'd read books and interpreted them completely differently. We'd spent time in independent prayer and come together afterward to find our "signals" didn't match. We'd asked our friends and family for their input and gotten no consistent answers. Just exhortations to be careful, to take our time, to think it through.

And when three months had passed without a consensus, Sam had done exactly what I'd granted him permission to do when I spoke my wedding vows. "I love you, Lauren," he'd said, his voice resonating with a clarity I hadn't heard in a while. "There is no doubt—no doubt—in my mind that this urge to do ministry in Nepal is from God. I know you have reservations. I understand and respect them. And all I can ask is for you to trust me on this. To trust me and to trust God, because this call feels like a fire in my gut . . . Honey, if it's from him, how can we second-guess it?"

I sat in the wingback chair in the living room, hands folded in my lap, ankles crossed, and watched the energy of conviction endow his movements and voice with authority and certainty. And while I tried to school my features into a thoughtful expression, my mind reeled with the emotions I'd been battling since he'd dropped that sheaf of pamphlets on the dining room table months ago, fissuring the foundation of our lives. I thought about the financial hurdles, the administrative nightmare, the relational upheaval and logistical insanity of pioneering a ministry, securing our finances, leaving our home, and setting up life in a Third World country we only knew from books and documentaries.

And I thought about Ryan. I grieved over Ryan. I rebelled because of Ryan. My sweet boy. My fragile boy. My obedient boy who had come to us a few weeks after we'd presented the possibility to him and said, "I don't want to go to that country you talked about." His chin had quivered, but he'd dug deep to find the courage to say again, "I really don't want to go there."

So when Sam sat me down to tell me to "trust me and trust God," I took deep breaths and tried to still the panicked racing of my heart. I dug my fingernails into my palm to quiet my body's unease. I listened as Sam described again the vision that had sublimated a vague desire into overwhelming devotion to a people he didn't know. I fought my protective instincts and surrendered them to the commitment I'd made nearly fourteen years before.

And when he kneeled in front of me, wrung out by the intensity of his belief, and begged me to embark with him on this wild and illogical *journey of faith, I felt a threshold rise out of the ashes of my fear and chose, weeping, to step forward with my husband.*

~~~

Eleven months passed. Months in which Sam's single-minded pursuit led him headlong into roadblock after roadblock. With each rejection and obligation to redirect, his confusion had grown deeper. His passion hadn't waned. But it was muddied now with incomprehension and a crippling sense of powerlessness.

Sam had a long list of objections to the way things were customarily done in missionary circles. Chief among them was a narrow-minded, linear approach to ministry endeavors rather than the enthusiastic, flexible, and unboundaried vision that drove him. When friends pointed out the advantages of working under an established organization that would provide structure, oversight, and practical support, he countered with grandiose statements about the vastness of God's structure, oversight, and support.

Our church elders had their qualms and expressed them in a meeting that turned contentious by the end.

"How do you know this is of God?"

"Is anyone else involved in this kind of work?"

"What mission organization will you go with?"

"How do you propose to raise the support you need?"

"What is your timeline?"

"What is your strategy?"

Sam's adamance about going it alone, without the obligations of a sending agency, seemed visionary to him, but it wasn't shared by the elders he consulted. "We'll happily reconsider if you change your mind about joining a recognized organization," our head elder concluded.

Sam's jaw was set. "I don't understand how God would have given us this clear—I mean *clear* idea of what he wants us to do—then ask us to slam on the brakes while we jump through the hoops of a man-made agency."

The meeting ended there. So did our attendance at that church.

Ryan's coach had moved him to defense for the game, and I could tell he was frustrated. The variation of soccer his U10 team played was a comical version of what idols like Messi and Beckham did on World Cup stages, but most of the nine- and ten-year-olds' hearts were in it. None, it seemed to me, as intensely as Ryan's.

Nearly a head taller than most of his teammates, his footwork and bursts of speed set him apart from his friends. Ryan excelled as a striker and was wasted in the backfield, and everyone but his new coach seemed to know it.

There wasn't much predictability left in our lives these days, and I cherished these spotlit evenings on the soccer field when life took on the appearance of normal. We brought halftime snacks when it was our turn. We stood on the sidelines, blazing heat or pouring rain, and commiserated with other parents. We cheered. We yelled at the refs. We bellowed ridiculous encouragement: Run faster! Kick it in! Don't give up! Keep on 'im! As if the boys didn't know what they were there to do.

After almost three years of being locked in personal and strategic wrangling, there was something about the simplicity of spectating that nourished my soul.

I watched Ryan as he scrambled to the sidelines for a quick drink from his water bottle during a pause in the soccer game. He seemed focused and somber, a little more so than the rest of his teammates. Not for the first time, I wondered if I should be concerned.

We'd tried to include Ryan in the labyrinthine progress our path to Nepal was taking. He helped me stuff envelopes, and he went with us to meetings—something I didn't entirely support—but Sam believed our *whole family needed to be seen standing together as we anticipated our move. At first Ryan had whined about the obligation. "I don't want to meet new people all the time." Or about the sacrifices his participation required. "But I have a game on Saturday!" Or about being sent to Sunday school classes where he didn't know anyone. "I want to go to* my *Sunday school. At* our *church!"*

As the months wore on, his whining turned into a more pointed dissent. Sometimes the silent, glaring type. Other times, the "It's not fair!" yelling type. And when either was punctuated with the extra oomph of a slamming door—car or bedroom—it felt all the more distressing.

Every so often, we'd pull out a book of interesting facts about Nepal after dinner and go through some of them with Ryan—just to give him a feel for the culture's qualities and quirks, hoping something in them would whet his appetite for the life awaiting him. He suffered through our attempts at engaging him with visible discomfort. Still, we persisted, wanting our son to anticipate with us. More often than not, he ended our conversations with a soft, "I still don't want to go."

He would come around. Sam was sure of it. I was a little less convinced, but eager to believe his predictions were true.

A phone call from my mom, gently letting us know that she was seeing changes in Ryan, had sent up a flag. I'd been deliberate since then in observing the nine-year-old whose life seemed to revolve around his friends and soccer.

The changes in him were subtle but unmistakable. Until recently, he'd leapt out of the car in the mornings and gone running into school, backpack bouncing. Now he got out more slowly and walked with a sort of lethargy toward the tall, wide doors of his school. He'd usually exited those doors in the afternoons surrounded by a group of friends— talking, laughing, and planning adventures. But now he came out quite awhile after the initial rush, with just a friend or two . . . or no one. Before, he'd been quick to volunteer the highlights and frustrations of his day when he crawled into the backseat. Now he got in, answered a few questions, and fell silent when they stopped coming.

Inside our home, he was generally obedient and polite. When I'd ask him if he was giving some thought to moving overseas, he'd shrug.

"Can you tell me why you don't want to go, honey?"

"I like it here."

I'd look into his face and hope he saw my love. "I get that, Ryan. I like it here too."

"Then why do we have to move?"

"We don't have to. We want to. We think this could be a really great thing for our family."

"What if it isn't?"

It was a question that plagued me too. "God wouldn't call us to something that would harm us."

He was a child, and these hypotheticals were well beyond his ability to comprehend, but I could see him contemplating our circumstances as seriously as a nine-year-old could. I prayed he'd come around.

On a cool March evening, as I watched Ryan protecting the goalie in his bright blue soccer cleats, arms and legs at the ready, eyes on the ball, I saw something different in him. Something leaner. It was hard to put into words, much as I'd tried to express it to Sam—not really a physical thing, though his body was changing as he grew up. I felt like he'd lost a bit of the childhood that rounded his movements and softened his features. He played with the speed and agility he'd always displayed, but there was a sharpness now to his demeanor.

Sam came back from a chat he was having with one of the other dads and handed me a cup of coffee from the thermos we'd brought. He'd always been a vocal supporter, and this evening was no different. He called encouragement out to Ryan as the other team's striker charged the goal. The parents lined up along the field with us let out a simultaneous roar. "Get 'im, Ryan! Get 'im!" Sam bellowed. Ryan crouched down a little as the other player approached and prepared to pass the ball to a teammate, but instead of shooting out a leg to intercept the pass, Ryan lunged headfirst into his opponent. Like a human battering ram, he swept the boy off his legs and slammed his upper body to the ground. To my horror, he started pummeling him in the face and shoulders, his blows infantile and aimless.

While Sam and I stood frozen, one of the coaches ran out to the field and pulled Ryan off his opponent, forcefully holding him away as Ryan wiggled in his hold and finally broke free. He yelled, "Get off me!" at his coach, kicked some grass at the other player who was now sitting where he'd fallen, then swiveled and ran off the field toward the locker room.

Sam and I just stared—first at the mayhem as coaches from both teams converged on the boy Ryan had mowed down, then at each other. I had no idea what my expression was, but Sam's went from shock, to bewilderment, to fury in the few seconds it took him to process what he'd just seen.

He took off for the locker room in a half run, tension in his gait.

Neither spoke a word as they came out of the locker room, skirted the field, and headed for our car. Ryan didn't look up. He walked with his head down, his hood pulled up, and his hands burrowed into his pockets. Sam carried Ryan's sports bag, his face set. He stopped long enough to exchange a few words with the coach while Ryan continued his pained walk toward the car. I sat in the passenger seat and Ryan crawled in the back. Sam sat behind the wheel after he'd closed the driver's door and said nothing.

After a few moments, he turned the key in the ignition and we drove home.

There was no postgame analysis going on as we entered the house. No instructions to finish his homework or come to the kitchen for a snack.

"Living room," Sam said, and Ryan, still in his coat, made his way to the couch.

I didn't know what to do. We had never, in all his life, had to confront him about that kind of behavior. I wasn't sure if Sam wanted me involved or if this would be better handled as a father-son moment. I figured I should be there just to lend words, as neither of them seemed inclined to speak. I finally heard Sam inhale and braced for what he'd say.

Ryan burst into tears before Sam started to speak. The rigidness of his carriage melted into sobs as he curled up on the couch and leaned sideways against the backrest.

I glanced at Sam, wanting to go over and comfort the boy whose crying was convulsing his body, but Sam shook his head. He moved to the chair by the fireplace and sat, elbows braced on his knees, eyes on his son. We let Ryan cry until the sobs had receded into hiccups. Still, his face was turned into the couch, covered by the hood of the coat he hadn't yet removed.

Sam leaned forward and scratched the back of his head in a gesture of frustration. There was incomprehension and anger on his face.

"What was that, son?" he asked, his voice tight, his eyes seeking Ryan's.

Ryan started crying again.

"Sam . . ." I pleaded. He shook his head again, more firmly this time.

"Ryan, I need you to stop your crying. Now."

Ryan glanced at his dad around his raised hood, fear in his eyes, and I could tell he was trying his hardest to stem his tears. But I could also see, wedged into the sadness and shame on his face, the glint of something steely and unyielding. He looked away and I could hear him working on his breathing, trying to take steadier breaths.

It wounded me to watch him agonize. I wanted to go to him, to pull him against me and stroke his hair, to whisper calming words into his ear. But Sam had made his wishes clear, and the intensity of his expression brooked no argument.

"What was that, Ryan?" Sam said again, when Ryan's breathing had settled.

"I don't know." His voice was small but defiant.

"Did you know that kid?"

He shook his head.

This time, Sam's voice was commanding. "Ryan—look at me."

The eyes our son turned on his father were scared but challenging. I felt tears forming in my own. This wasn't my Ryan . . .

"What—was—that?"

Ryan threw up his hands and cried, "I don't know, okay?" His eyebrows were drawn fiercely together and I could see him calling on every ounce of his willpower to stop from bursting into tears again.

"It had to be something! Ryan, you don't just . . . attack another player like that! Do you know what that looked like? And how many people saw it? What were you thinking?"

"I didn't mean to," Ryan yelled, eyes wide and stunned. He seemed to catch himself and squared his shoulders as his eyes narrowed into angry slits. "The stupid coach!" he spat. "Why'd he make me play defense?"

"You'll be lucky if he lets you play at all after that stunt."

"Fine! I don't care anyway!" He got up and stormed toward the stairs, ripping at the zipper on his coat.

"Sit—down!" Sam's voice was as fierce as I'd ever heard it.

Ryan turned and yelled, "No! You can't make me!"

"Ryan . . ." I stood up and took a step forward, appalled by the turn this confrontation was taking.

He turned on me. "No, Mom!" And I saw fresh tears forming in his eyes. "He can't make me! You can't make me!" He turned and rushed up the stairs to his room.

I turned on Sam. "Really?"

Sam was still sitting. His face pale. His jaw set. "You saw what he did. He needed to be called on it."

"But not like that! Not in the state he's in!"

Sam's voice was still hard. "He needs to understand how inappropriate that behavior was."

"He's a kid. He has a lot going on . . ."

"He assaulted another player. And he did it in front of—"

I had a moment of clarity. "In front of other people?"

"Yes."

"Really? That's your greatest concern?"

Sam opened his mouth to answer, then closed it, staring at me. He shook his head. "What are you saying?"

I came at him then. "I'm pointing out that the greater concern here should be that a kid who has never behaved this way before just stood in this room and yelled at you." I was done hiding my tears. My voice rose another notch. "And before that, he sat there and sobbed for a while. And before that, he tackled some kid on the soccer field with the kind of . . ." I couldn't find the word. "Ferocity the kind of ferocity I have never, ever seen in that boy."

"Lauren . . ."

"So you go right ahead and sit there fuming because the other parents saw the missionaries' kid losing it in public. You go right ahead, Sam. I'm going upstairs to talk to our son because there's clearly something major going on that we—should—care about."

I marched out of the room and up the stairs before Sam had a chance to answer.

It took me a few moments to compose myself before entering Ryan's bedroom. "Ryan?" I pushed the door open a crack. He lay on his side, facing the wall. His coat was in a heap on the floor by his bed. I felt the bottom fall out of my resilience. My little boy.

He flinched when I touched his hair and moved his head away. I paused, my hand suspended. I prayed. *Please, God. Please.* I sat on the

133

edge of his bed and laid my hand against his hair again. This time he didn't flinch. He didn't move away.

We sat in silence as several long minutes ticked by, me stroking his hair and him utterly still. When I thought I could speak without losing my composure, I said as softly as I could, "What's going on, honey?" Silence. He shifted against his Transformers pillow. "Did something happen at school?" He shook his head. "Is it something Daddy and I did?" He didn't move. "Ryan, I'd like for you to look at me. Can you do that, please?" I let another minute pass, my hand now in my lap, and listened to him breathe. He finally turned to face me, knees drawn up. His eyes glanced off my face, then looked down and away.

I slipped off the bed onto my knees and brought my eyes even with his, propping my chin on my hands. "So," I started quietly, trying to keep any trace of anger or disappointment out of my voice. "I'm guessing there's something that's making you unhappy." He glanced up, then down again. "Am I right?"

He nodded against his pillow.

"Can you tell me what it is?"

I saw fresh tears flood his eyes as his chin began to quiver.

"Ryan?"

His eyebrows came together in a frown. "I don't know," he said. This time his eyes locked with mine, spilling their tears over the bridge of his nose, down his face, and into his hair. He hiccupped a little and curled into a tighter ball. There was confusion and fear on his face. "I don't know what it is, Mom." And he started to cry in earnest again.

I shushed him and told him I loved him, that all the changes were hard on me too, that I was grieving about leaving our home and that I understood how sadness can look like other things sometimes—like anger or disobedience. I assured him that Sam and I loved him and that we'd figure this out together.

I saw movement by the door and knew Sam stood there. He loved his son. He had loved him and protected him since that moment nearly ten years ago when he'd stood in our bedroom and done his happy dance. I looked up at my husband and hoped my gaze conveyed my trust. He came into the room and lowered himself to the floor beside me, his legs bent and an arm draped over Ryan's blanketed form.

We all stayed like that for a while. There would be time later for more questions. Time for apologies and for reweaving the thin fabric of our family's happiness.

That's what I thought.

"I know these past few months have been hard, son," Sam said.

Don't say "but," I thought. *Please don't say "but."*

"But God wants us to help kids like you in Nepal, and temper tantrums like the one you had tonight aren't going to change that."

Anger tingled across my face. *Please, God. Please,* I prayed again. And even as the words surged through my spirit, I felt my son withdraw from Sam . . . and me.

~~~

Sam's projected departure date came and went, and still we struggled on. Desperation, a fickle emotion, seemed to either pummel or propel us. For Sam, it was about getting to Nepal and launching full-throttle into the work he'd already been pursuing as much as he could from a distance. His exhaustion was physical, in part because of the hours and effort he was putting in to shore up enough support, and in part because the unrelenting optimism that fueled his work was such an energy-sapping, soul-depleting thing to maintain.

For Ryan, the desperation was much more subterranean. We hadn't seen much of his anger since the soccer incident. He'd mostly kept it under wraps from that day forward. But I could see it in the quick steely flash that would brighten his eyes for a moment, then be replaced by a dullness I found more alarming than the temper. It was in the clipped words, mutinous glares, careless shrugs that seemed to come at random. Some days he was the Ryan we'd always known. Responsive and talkative. Then something would trigger his darker disposition, and he'd sink into what seemed a deliberate withdrawal from enjoyment and connection. I was sure the weariness that sagged his shoulders and slowed his steps in those moments was the side effect of such a young soul living with so much dread.

It was Ryan who fueled my desperation to get to Kathmandu. Watching my son disappear into a harder, quieter, deader boy felt like my undoing. I would tell Sam he had to speak to him—father to son—since mother to son didn't seem to be effective anymore. Maybe he could coax some answers or at least a reaction—any reaction—out of him. And Sam would climb the stairs to Ryan's room. I'd listen from downstairs, trying to read significance into creaking floorboards and portions of words.

As time passed and we remained stateside, supporters who had started sending donations stopped—perhaps because the grand plan Sam had outlined for them didn't include years of living in our old house, in our old town, with little evidence of an imminent move across the world. Some called to explain their decision, promising to resume giving when we finally got to Kathmandu. Others never called or wrote. Their checks just stopped coming.

Still, Sam labored on with the tenacity of a man whose very existence revolved around the completion of a singular goal. I hurt for him. I hurt for the frustrations that tightened his shoulders and the disappointments that bowed them. I hurt for the joyous, dynamic, convicted presentations he gave to tiny groups and individuals whose watch-checking and blank faces eviscerated his efforts. I hurt for the forced optimism in his voice on days when we seemed to be losing more ground than we gained. I hurt for the troubled gaze he cast on Ryan when he didn't realize I was watching.

We delved deeper into our past and located every former friend and colleague we could think of, presenting our cause and praying for that miracle.

It came in the form of Sullivan.

After I sent a tentative introductory e-mail, she came sweeping back into our lives with a squeal of delight, a flurry of questions, and a little black book (blue, in her case) filled with the contact information of corporations and individuals looking for tax deductions. She saw the passion in Sam's eyes and the determination in mine and said, "Well, hey—let's get this show on the road!"

The plane had started its descent a few minutes earlier. I strained against my seat belt, trying to lean far enough over Ryan's sleeping form to see out the window. Only clouds. Sam stirred on the other side of me and grunted as he stretched his legs.

"See anything?" he asked.

I shook my head and adjusted the brightness of the small screen embedded in the seat in front of me. I was halfway through the second movie of this leg of the trip. It wasn't exactly riveting, but it kept my mind occupied. Though Sam and Ryan had fallen asleep shortly after takeoff, exhausted by the thirteen-hour flight that had taken us from Chicago to Abu Dhabi, I'd remained awake. I liked to think it was the excitement of landing in a little over an hour that had kept me from sleeping, but I suspected it was an emotion of a much different nature.

The relief that had come over me when we finally got on that first flight had sharp edges. We'd succeeded. We'd drummed up a small army of partners who believed enough in what we had envisioned to put their enthusiasm and pocketbooks behind it. We'd exited the long process of preparation on bruised knees, our prayers finally answered, but our hearts injured by the protracted battle for miracles that had always felt just beyond our reach. And now that our headlong leap was approaching its landing, though I tried to muster the exhilaration that should cap such an extraordinary moment, all I felt was a disheartening blend of weariness and wariness.

I knew they were the logical conclusion of our years-long toil—the missionary version of post-traumatic stress: erratic, hair-trigger responses and unshakable flashes of disturbing scenes. Like driving away from the house in which we'd welcomed and raised Ryan. Like dropping off the remainder of our furniture, some of it wedding gifts, at the Salvation Army a couple days before our flight. Like saying good-bye to my dad over the phone, knowing I wouldn't be there when he went in for bypass surgery in just a few weeks. Like watching Ryan say good-bye to his friends, then run back to the van with a desperate anger stiffening his legs.

And here we were. Thirty thousand feet and falling. Exhausted by over twenty hours in the air, but so close . . . so close. A hint of panic tightened my lungs. I breathed deeply, shut off the screen in front of me, and leaned over Ryan again to see out the window. The clouds had broken. Nepal was finally in sight.

As our plane continued its descent over lush green hills and brown valleys, clusters of homes began to dot the landscape, nearly camouflaged against the brown earth save for their geometric shapes. Then came larger buildings. Tall, rectangular, multistoried forms with gaping windows. Yellows, greens, grays, and terra-cottas. They seemed arranged randomly, in clumps that lined serpentine roads—a small river here, a patch of trees there.

"Ryan," I said, excitement and trepidation in my voice. "Ryan, wake up!"

He was frowning before his eyes even opened, but even his most laborious attempts at a poker face failed when he followed my gaze to the airplane window and saw Nepal materializing out of the mist.

"Would you look at that," Sam said behind me. I thought I heard something catch in his throat and turned to find tears gathering in his eyes and a huge smile on his face. He grabbed my hand and held it tight. I squeezed it back and let my eyes travel over his face. The maverick, the tenacious visionary, the indefatigable pursuer.

Ryan stared mutely out the window. From the heights where we flew, the landscape and structures looked Seussian. His eyes moved quickly, taking in the details that appeared and disappeared as the plane flew forward. I could feel something growing in him, something he might have expressed before our calling had extinguished his communicating.

"What do you think?" Sam asked.

"It's fine," Ryan said without conviction, his eyes never straying from the Nepali countryside unfolding under the plane's wings.

Sam and I exchanged glances. At least he hadn't said, "It sucks."

Tribhuvan International Airport was a small collection of buildings on the east side of the capital, with one runway, two terminals, and interminable lines. A sign along the long walk from the plane to the security checkpoint had tried to warn us. The vodka advertisement, clearly intended for foreigners, read, "Things to be done take time in Nepal, so relax & chill out."

We waited for over an hour to clear customs, a process lengthened by the need to purchase our visas on the spot. There was neither urgency nor efficiency in the procedures, and the passengers who appeared to have been through this before merely surrendered to the system and leaned on walls or on their carry-ons, biding their time.

The small terminal resonated with the sounds of barely contained chaos. It was in a mildly shell-shocked state that we found the luggage area and waited for our bags to appear. I tried to school my features into something blasé as I began to grasp how different this world was from the one I'd spent nearly five years now trying to escape. I'd expected the language to be an adjustment, but there was so much more to this foreignness than that. It was in every nuance of every space, person, and object I could see. In every sound. In every aroma.

It was like being shoved, slowly and irrevocably, into a tidal wave of newness that felt destabilizing and taxing.

Already, Sam was trying to communicate, buoyed by his online exploration of the language. I marveled at his temerity. He *Namaste*-d everyone he approached, smiling and bowing, asking questions and getting answers he couldn't understand.

I, on the other hand, was just trying to keep it together. Marrow-deep fatigue weighed me down—limbs, heart, and mind. The noise pummeled me. The chaos abraded me. I rested a hand on my eleven-year-old's shoulder and he didn't pull away. He stood close to me, closer than he normally would, his discomfort drawn to mine.

When a porter had loaded our nine suitcases onto his cart, we moved out of the dark terminal into a dusty, horn-saturated sunlight and crossed the narrow street. A wiry middle-aged man stood on the other side with a sign that read Couentry. Close enough. Sam waved and he came toward us, hands pressed together, offering a terse but cheerful *Namaste*. He led us to the beat-up Mitsubishi van wedged into a too-small parking space and loaded our fifty-pound bags into the trunk and rear seat as if they weighed nothing.

"We go," he said in a high-pitched, sharp voice. "We go! We go!"

Ryan and I climbed into the backseat and Sam rounded the van to the passenger door, realizing when he got there that it would be on the left side in this country.

He laughed as the uncle Prakash had sent to meet us careened down a wide, encumbered boulevard, slamming on the brakes, accelerating wildly, whiplashing us with abrupt turns and lurches, all the while sounding his horn and blurting words none of us understood.

We knew he'd drive us to the home Prakash had arranged for us. We knew we'd be met there by the wife of a doctor who had championed Prakash's school. We knew she'd be able to give us a crash course in living Nepali. We knew we'd see our friend when he arrived in the city three days later, fresh from the exploration of potential target villages.

That's all we knew.

"What is your name?" Sam yelled at our driver over the noise of the racing engine.

He merely smiled and nodded and forged ahead.

Sam tried again, articulating slowly. "Your name," he yelled. He pointed at himself. "Me—Sam. I am Sam."

The driver nodded and smiled again.

"You?" Sam asked, pointing at him.

"Binod."

"Binod?"

"Yes, yes!" Binod said, pointing at himself.

"It's very nice to meet you!" I watched the exhilaration pour from Sam's countenance.

"Binod!" our driver answered.

He veered off the main road onto what could only be a back alley. It was narrow, deeply potholed, and crowded with men on motorcycles, women carrying children on their backs, and mangy, wandering dogs.

Binod lay on the horn and bounced us through passages that seemed too small to accommodate the width of our creaking, quaking van. Pedestrians leapt calmly out of our way, then filled the gap we left in our wake. A man pushed a bicycle into our path and didn't stop to glance at the big white hunk of steel surging toward him. Binod slammed on the brakes and dodged, narrowly missing a cement step jutting out from a dilapidated building.

"Wow," Sam yelled over the noise. I thought I could hear a hint of fear in the excitement of his voice. "This is . . . crazy!"

Binod took his eyes off the road to smile in Sam's direction, hit a pothole the size of a crater, and snapped his attention front again, shifting down but barely slowing as he breached an intersection.

We turned onto a wider road, this one lined with stores and shoppers. We hurtled by a man with a mountain of fruit on the back of his bicycle, barely missed another carrying huge bundles of clothes on his head, and finally turned down a narrow, quieter alley with just inches to spare on either side of the van. We pulled up in front of a seven-foot metallic gate, and Binod jumped out, coming around the van to open our doors.

"Welcome home," I said to Ryan, hoping the smile that was sapping the last of my energy looked sincere and cheerful.

He stumbled out of the van and threw up.

When Prakash had told Eveline about our arrival and explained that he'd be gone for the first three days of our stay, she'd immediately offered to help out. It was one of the qualities that had drawn me to this no-nonsense English woman, whose sturdiness of spirit was a comforting thing. She'd been waiting when we drove up and had immediately tended to our taxi-sick son.

In the days before we landed, she'd purchased a few of the basics we'd need and had loaded our fridge with food her housekeeper had prepared for us. She'd also gathered dishes and cooking materials at an expat flea market and had arranged them in our rudimentary kitchen.

"Oh, no—don't drink the tap water!" Eveline exclaimed when Sam poured himself a glass of water from the kitchen tap.

He froze with the glass halfway to his lips.

"You'll be sick for days. Feces in the water."

Ryan looked at me with saucer eyes.

Eveline went into the pantry and came out with an armful of water bottles. "I got these for you to use until we can get you a filtration system. The last family took theirs with them."

Our house's previous owners had been friends of Eveline's, so she was able to give us the kind of tour that pointed out both the obvious and the less obvious. She told us that toilets in Nepal wouldn't evacuate soiled paper and showed us the small garbage cans where we should throw it instead. About the third step from the top that was taller than the others ("Tripped over that one myself!"), and the spot in the dining room where the neighbors' Wi-Fi was strongest.

"I'm not sure we're comfortable using someone else's signal," Sam said.

I glanced at him. Dead on his feet and still a bastion of morality.

Eveline invited us on a short walk into town. "It will keep you upright and moving. You'll never get over jet lag if you nap on your first day. And more importantly," she added, "the sooner you get the lay of the land, the faster this planet will feel more like home."

Planet. The word rang true. Beyond the foreignness of sights, sounds, and odors, there was an otherness to this place that felt like a physical dislocation. Every one of my senses perceived it, but I knew I'd be incapable of accurately articulating it. All I could do, as Eveline had suggested, was try to wrap my mind around the reality of it.

So we went upstairs to change into clothes more suited to the heat, in bedrooms we all knew would have to become home somehow. Ryan stumbled over a step and caught himself, the weariness of two days of travel a visible burden. He walked into the bedroom he'd chosen—a high-ceilinged space with a view on our courtyard—and turned to close the door. Our gazes locked and held, exhaustion in his and, I hoped, expectation in mine. I whispered a prayer when the latch clicked shut and locked him out of sight.

When we met Eveline in the foyer again a few minutes later, there was a sense of purpose livening my steps. I looked into Sam's eyes and knew his dark circles matched mine. So did the resolve in their depths. The questions we'd wrestled with since his first meeting with Prakash were moot now. This was our new world. The ramifications of our choice loomed large in the jet-lagged vacuum of my mind, so I clung to the certainty Sam had proclaimed from the start: this was the *right place for us. This was God's place for us.* I patted Ryan's drooping shoulders and squared mine.

Then we all left the house and stepped into the sunlight.

After our walk and after Eveline left, telling us that it was late enough for us to go to bed, the three of us sat in the living room on the couch she'd secured for us, just staring straight ahead. Then Ryan started to cry.

"Ryan," I said, squeezing the knee of the stoic eleven-year-old whose tears fell silently onto his cheeks. "Ryan, what's going on?"

He swiped at his eyes with his sleeve, digging deep for self-control. "There's poop in the water!" he blurted out. We'd been bombarded with so much "different" in our first stroll around town—the stray dogs, the lawless driving, the *Namaste*-ing, the mysterious foods, and unrecognizable language. But I had to agree with my overtired son. Of all the newness, "poop in the water" won the prize.

While Sam began a weary lecture on filtration systems and preventative measures, I shuffled upstairs and began to unpack.

⁓

As we all came to grips with the alienness of Nepal in the days that followed, Eveline continued to offer her assistance, her gentle spirit a balm in our change-saturated lives. She soothed our culture shock with a positive perspective and offered practical solutions to myriad small challenges. After a few days setting up our household and acclimating to the new time zone, she offered to go with us to Ryan's school and help with the formalities of getting him enrolled.

"That over there is going to be a gymnasium," she said as we walked down the paved laneway to the gates of the school. A crane stood in a vacant lot where the walls of a half-finished structure stood under an overcast sky. Just beyond the new construction was a muddy expanse of land bookended with goalposts that had seen better days.

"Is that a soccer field?" I asked, mostly to point it out to Ryan.

She nodded. "The students use it all the time for gym and intra-murals. Even in monsoon season, when it doubles as a mud pit! My son, Steven—I'll have to introduce you to him, Ryan—plays on the soccer team."

Ryan's eyes stayed on the field until we turned a corner and entered the gates of the International School of Greater Kathmandu.

Part Two

PRESENCE

nine

SAM WOULD BE HOME BY NOON IF ALL WENT ACCORDING TO plan, a phrase that was downright laughable in a country where plans were better made in retrospect, and Ryan would hopefully be home shortly before that. I felt Aidan's message like a veil over my thinking. A veil tinged grey with resurrected murkiness. With Sam's return, my focus needed to be clear—locked full and unhindered on the man I'd married.

So before putting the laptop away, I opened Aidan's message again and typed a few words. I hoped they would be sufficient.

Aidan—time and words fail me again. Sam returns today and will be home for a week.

I'm grappling with the ramifications of "this." Not in any way regretting reconnection (please believe that) nor wanting to shirk the gift, the honor, the pain of inviting me into this chapter of your journey. You compare me to a splash of color in the beigeness of your life, and I realize how luminescent your imprint on mine was. Is. Present tense.

So there is nothing selfish about this precarious, bright, fluid place you've brought me to. It has galvanized my life with a richness and vitality that is so unique to you. To you and me.

So I stand with you. I weep with you. I fear with you. I grieve with you. I hope with you. And though you've only hinted at your faith, I want to say I pray with you. I am not going anywhere.

But I'm also intimately conscious of the danger of this bonded pain. I want to be sober in my perspective and grounded in my reality. There are two universes vying for my attention and I'm not sure how to balance them. But I'll live with that tension because it is the overflow of this tortured rediscovery.

I'll need to communicate less frequently in the coming week. It's hard and good and right. But I will read your words as they come to me, maybe jot a very brief response if time and presence of mind permit. I want to be clear so you'll interpret any silence correctly.

And since you said to ask . . .

I want to know about your treatment.

I want to know about the God piece.

I want to know about your heart.

I guess I've always wanted to.

Ren

Muffin didn't bark when the gate swung open.

"Ryan, Dad's home!" I called up the stairs, stepping out of my slippers and into street shoes to go outside and greet him.

What a sight he was, when he returned from his three-week excursions into parts of Nepal few foreigners saw. He carried his battered, oversized backpack deflated from the generosity of his time away. His hiking boots were caked with dried dirt, there was a tear just below the knee of his pants, and his jacket was faded with dust. Thick stubble covered his face and neck.

He smiled a little wearily as he ambled toward the front porch, dropping the backpack off one shoulder and holding his free arm out to me. I entered his embrace and wrapped my arms around his waist. He smelled of nature and pollution and too-few showers.

"Is that chili I smell?" he asked, tossing his bag onto our porch to be dealt with later.

"Really?" I asked. "That's what you're leading with?"

He hooked an elbow around the back of my neck and pulled me in for a kiss. I leaned, surprised by how much I needed it. "Suman made us chili for lunch," I explained when he pulled back to look at my face.

"Again?"

I turned to enter the house. "She insists that you need 'Western food' for your first meal home, and I think chili is the easiest dish in her repertoire."

"And I insist every time that I'm happy with traditional food—there's a breakdown in this communication," he said, smirking at our housekeeper's stubborn streak.

Ryan was standing in the kitchen when we came inside. Not in the entryway—as if he wanted to see his dad but didn't want to appear too eager.

"Hey, kiddo!" Sam grabbed him into a hug and kissed the top of his head.

"Hi." Quiet word, sullenly spoken.

"You doing okay?"

"Yeah."

Sam poured himself a cup of coffee from the pot I'd made, then looked at Ryan. "You got your book bag?" he asked.

Ryan knew the routine and knew there was no changing it. He retrieved his bag from the bench inside the door and moved—shuffled, really—into the dining room. They sat down at the table and Ryan showed him all he'd done in the past three weeks.

"You stink," he said. He always did.

"I'll take a shower once you've shown me your stuff."

Sam had determined early on in our Nepali life that his first minutes home after treks out of town would be all about Ryan. I suspected he feared that our son didn't understand the necessity of his absences. In those first few months, I'd seen the ritual as a good thing—a sign of his devotion to being Ryan's dad. He'd coax him into the courtyard to play catch or challenge him to a free-throw competition. Ryan would submit to it with the same kind of dark deference he applied to most things now, but every so often, I'd glimpse a brightening.

After Miss Moore's revelations about Ryan's academic standing, though, Sam had moved their reconnecting indoors and traded fun for academic scrutiny. Ryan still came first. Second, really, after Sam's beloved cup of coffee. But there was nothing connective in this altered ritual. And though I still saw fatherliness in Sam's concern for his son's grades, his attention felt tutorial, not celebratory or warm.

Sam pored over Ryan's schoolwork, expressing his affection with the time and focus that would otherwise be spent on the shower he so desperately needed. I listened to him asking questions about the papers Ryan handed him while I finished making cornbread. Every so often, he pushed a paper over with more willingness than others. "I got an 82 on this one," he'd say in his lifeless voice.

"That's fantastic," I'd hear Sam answer. "Where did you lose those eighteen points?"

Sam thought he was doing the right thing. No amount of reasoning could dissuade him from that certainty. He thought he was a good father to a difficult son. From all appearances, Ryan thought Sam was an absentee father to a screwed-over son. I suspected there was no bridging that kind of perspective gap.

It had taken me a few months to realize that each of Sam's returns seemed to push Ryan further into himself. Initially, when Sam was gone, there were moments when our son seemed to forget about being sullen—brief windows of time when I'd catch him grinning at something he was streaming on his laptop or when he'd sit at the dinner table and offer words that were neither coaxed nor reticent.

Now, the days before Sam came walking through the gate seemed to mark a deepening of Ryan's resentment—a more intense rejection of our lives in Kathmandu. It was expressed by silence. By distance. And every time Sam left, I got less of Ryan back.

It was a reality I struggled to accept.

≋

After a short shower, Sam joined us in the kitchen.

"Nice," I said after a kiss that was blessedly devoid of facial hair.

"Thought you'd like it."

"So—tell me about your trip."

It took Sam nearly three hours and several bowls of chili to recount the adventures of his latest excursion. He described the challenges of getting through a mountain pass obliterated by a landslide and of using a gap-toothed bamboo bridge to cross a deep ravine.

I had no delusions that Sam's work was a safe thing. While friends parroted easy truths about the center of God's will putting us beyond harm's reach, I lived with the certainty that life as I knew it, such as it was, was contingent on mud not sliding, viruses not spreading, wild animals not attacking, and Sam not over-risking.

I loved the vivacity in his voice as he told Ryan and me about his latest adventures.

"You should have seen them," he said around a bite of bread. "We trekked two and a half days from the last bus stop in the mountains to this village so far back into the valley that I thought we'd followed the wrong coordinates. And there they were. Probably fifty, sixty adults and children." He nodded his thanks for the coffee I poured and went on. "Prakash was great—always is. Talked to the village leaders first and explained what we were doing. They'd already heard about us from the time we spent just up the valley in December."

He talked about the horrible living conditions and the hopelessness of a people group that had been virtually amputated from the rest of the world when China closed the roads that led through Tibet to Nepal. Trade routes and cultural exchanges ended. So did their supply of life-supporting food and income.

Hearing about the lack of hygiene and basic medical care made me wonder how Sam and Prakash came away, trip after trip, without health crises of their own.

"There are piles of human feces in front of their homes," Sam said, describing the village in which he'd spent his weeks away from us.

"Gross." Ryan wasn't impressed.

"It gives them status," Sam explained. "Proves they have enough to feed the family in a place where an awful lot don't." He talked about the village elder, who had asked for a drawing of

God, and the difficulty they'd had explaining to him that God wasn't a visible being.

Sam and Prakash had made enough trips now that they'd developed strategies and contingencies. In most villages they visited, they were able to connect quickly, offering the food and medicines they carried and explaining in simple words that they wanted to get to know the inhabitants better. Then they just "did life" with them, forging relationships that allowed them to weave God's love and goodness into casual conversations. And when they left, it was with the promise that they'd return. Which they did—bearing Bibles and practical gifts that would make the villagers' lives easier.

Sam's face shone with enthusiasm as he told me the names of the men and women he'd met—their stories, their struggles, their small steps toward faith. He'd left the people of Kalikot District only days before, but he already spoke of them with longing, eager for the return trip that would cement their relationships and their understanding of God.

I heard the excitement in his voice and tried to quell the dissatisfaction that hampered my response. I loved witnessing the fulfillment he received from the work we'd so doggedly pursued. I thanked God that Sam could spend time in places few missionaries ever explored, living in squalid conditions and thriving from his interactions with the people he'd come to reach. I reminded myself of the important role I played in keeping our home and our family running, in reporting on the ministry, and in earning the visas that allowed for Sam's work.

Still—I envied the elation I heard in his voice.

We played Monopoly that evening. We knew the days when we'd be able to coerce Ryan into this kind of activity were counted, but at thirteen, he still had no option but to sit in the candlelight and walk his tin car around the board.

Tomorrow, we'd release him to leave the house again. Tomorrow, Sam would lock himself in the office he rented for a pittance from an NGO a few blocks away and start to plan his next foray. Tomorrow, we'd begin the post-reunion process of growing apart again.

But tonight—tonight we'd be a family.

Sam went to bed early and Ryan and I stayed downstairs. He worked on my laptop—he claimed it was faster than his—and though I felt the compulsion to check Facebook for a message from Aidan, I tamped down the impulse and focused on the thank-you cards I was writing.

Ryan let out a frustrated breath.

I looked up. "What?"

He turned the laptop around and pushed it toward me. "Skype," he said, shoving away from the table and heading upstairs. He knew the name on the screen and assumed this would take awhile.

I turned up the volume and clicked the green phone icon.

The camera light flickered on and a welcome face appeared. "Chickadee!"

I felt a weight lift. "Sullivan."

"Listen. I was just sitting here contemplating life," she said in her slow, lilting diction. "Well, not life so much as this little plan I've been hatching, and I figured the best way to break it to you is face-to-face . . . since you've been suspiciously absent from Facebook and all."

I laughed. "Suspiciously?"

"There are two things I have radar for, honey. One is rich

men with a loose grip on their checkbooks. The other is a friend who wants me to believe she's loving social networking, because it was my idea she join, but has no desire to get mired in its den of iniquity!"

"Can you say 'mired' again?"

She leaned in until I could see the pores in her forehead. "Are you mocking me?" she drawled, extra slow this time.

"I'm enjoying you."

"Where is that Don Juan of yours? He got home today, right?"

"Bed," I said.

"Good heavens, bed? Did I get the time difference wrong again?"

It was Sullivan's inability to accurately calculate a nine-hour-and-forty-five-minute time difference that had forced us to completely log out of Skype after a certain time at night and until we were fully conscious in the morning.

"It's just past ten p.m. Congratulations on a call finally made during a sane hour of the day."

"Old dog, new trick. I'm a fast learner if you don't mind explaining a long time."

"It's been forever, Sullivan. What have you been up to?"

"Says the girl who went out of touch for approximately sixteen years."

"Yes, but then I had to come crawling back. You know I"—I mimed a pair of air quotes—"'worship the quicksand you walk on.'"

"Nice! And smoothly fit into an unrelated conversation."

"I learned from the best."

Sullivan propped her chin on her hands and gave me a considering look. "Tell me about you," she said.

I raised an eyebrow. "Anything specific you'd like to know?" I stopped myself. "Wait—I asked *you* first!"

She dismissed it with a wave of her well-manicured hand.

"There is absolutely nothing noteworthy happening here. I live in the land of rare power outages, drinkable water, personal vehicles, and Piggly Wigglys fully stocked with Oreos and Ben & Jerry's. Exotic here is a trip to Thai takeout." She leaned in again and the camera struggled to focus. "That's why I call you at ungodly hours—to escape the First World monotony."

"While I'm stuck in Third World monotony. Different list, same predictability."

"So you've ventured onto Facebook twice, from what I've seen," she said, completely ignoring my rejoinder. "Once to create your profile and once to write a note to the Sternensee gang. They loved it, by the way, and weren't in the least surprised to learn that Sam was palling around with a bunch of tribal people. It also got their wheels turning about what we could do that would be a blessing to you."

"I get nervous when you start talking Christianese."

"Hush, I'm telling a story. So—we discussed something we could do for you and Sam, since we're all so impressed with what you're doing over there."

"Sarcasm duly noted."

"That wasn't sarcasm, honey. That was flair."

"I see a giant care package in our future."

"No, you don't," she said with a conspiratorial grin. "You see something a whole lot better."

I racked my mind. What could be better than a care package from Sullivan? "I . . ." I was at a loss.

"Plane tickets."

My mind whirled. "Come again?"

"We want to fly all three of you back to the States for a couple weeks. Get yourself a long, hot shower, some fattening food, and if you can fit it in, an hour or two with family." She giggled.

I shook my head. "Sullivan."

"Hush, now. We've pooled our nickels and dimes and we'll make the reservations just as soon as you're ready. You hear? We're flying you home! You pick the dates and the destination, and leave the rest up to me."

Part of me wanted to jump up and cheer. Visions swirled in my head—reunions with family and all those normal activities and treats that had taken on extraordinary significance since our arrival here.

The other part of me was already formulating a strategy to present this to Sam. How could I break this to him in a way that would seem exciting to him too?

"Well, I had an idea it might surprise you, but this speechless thing is a bit unexpected."

My eyes snapped back to the computer screen. "I . . . you're right. I'm speechless."

"Listen, I know this is a bit unexpected, and there's no hurry at all getting the details figured out. You and Sam give it some thought, and when you're ready . . . say the word!"

"Are you sure?"

"I am. We all are. Consider it our mea culpa for living in the land of plenty while you toil in the land of dysentery."

I laughed. It felt . . . rejuvenating.

We hung up a few minutes later. I turned out the lights and went up to our bedroom, wondering if I should wake Sam to tell him about our friends' extraordinary generosity. But he was sleeping so deeply that I decided it could wait until morning.

I lay in bed and pictured myself back in the States. Made a list of the first places I'd go. The foods I'd eat. The movies I'd see. I tried to plot a road trip that would allow us to see special friends and family.

I wanted to go back downstairs, log in to Facebook, and tell Aidan. I wanted him to know that we'd be on the same continent soon. I wanted to describe Sullivan to him in all her astonishing originality. I wanted to share this happiness with him. I knew he'd get it. Because he got me. And I wanted to figure out with him if there was a way we could meet—one last time before . . .

But my husband lay in bed next to me. This was my God-given, challenging, and good reality. I turned over, curled into his side, and listened to him breathe.

⁕

ah, ren . . . your husband is home. i want to hear from you every minute of every day, but your husband is home. it's right and good for you to be out of touch.

i'd love to see you as a mom and wife. i have images in my head of what that might look like, but every time i have a 'yes, that's it' moment, i realize the person in the scene is 18-year-old you. in my memory, you're arrested at that age. i know from your family picture that you've changed. but the 'voice' in your messages . . . it sounds the same. same relationship to language. same purpose to love and to know. you make me reach for deeper words and strive for clearer vibes. all while drinking in the simple something of your prose.

my agent, dan, and i are heading downtown in a couple hours to meet with a group that's interested in my stuff. the original plan was to have one of my pieces included in a calendar they're publishing to raise funds for the brain tumor association, but somebody with the bta saw my stuff and asked if i had anything else. i'm a little dubious about what i'm hearing—after all, i majored in disappointment and got a degree in cynicism. but dan said something about an aidan dennison collection, all proceeds to the bta. coffee-table style. asked me if i'd be okay with that—no compensation, but serving a good cause. i thought about it for—oh—a fraction of a second. then i heard myself say, 'i'll be dead by the time it's published anyway.'

that set me back a little. to hear those words out of my mouth. i've thought them before, but saying them. that felt like reaching a whole new level on my dig to six feet . . . part of me wanted dan to say, 'come on, what are you talking about? you'll be standing in stockholm receiving a nobel prize long after this thing is published.' there'd be two problems with that statement. one, there's no nobel prize for visual arts. two, no i won't.

there's a finality about death that's too extreme for me to grasp, most of the time. there's so much in life that can be undone that i can't fathom something that's just so . . . finished. no command-z. no undo button. just . . . the end of everything. it doesn't hit me often, but when it does . . . like when i catch myself projecting what i'll do next summer. or next week for that matter. it bends the edges of my universe, i guess. and of my courage too.

so dan and i are heading downtown to see if the multi-artist calendar can become a single-artist collection to gather dust on coffee tables and drop some cash into brain cancer research. i'm not gonna lie. i want it to work out. there's something poetic about posthumous publication . . .

it's the middle of the night there (i looked it up). i hope you're sleeping as i type. ren . . . when you use words like 'danger' and 'tension' to tell me about going out of touch while sam is home with you . . . it makes me wonder if there's discomfort or regret or guilt in this communication.

you would tell me, right? if there were, i'd stop writing. right now.

i'll be honest. hearing from you has . . . sated me. i really don't know how else to put it. might try to paint it though. so the prospect of a week without your words after so many years without them is a challenging thing. i understand and cheer your choice. but i . . . you know.

and since i've got time to spare before dan gets here, and since writing to you makes the distance and silence seem a bit less vast, i'll give your questions a shot: treatment—after surgery and some vague, dire predictions from my surgeon (whose bedside manner reflected the bedside table's), i embarked on a search for clinical trials that might—might—give me a few more days. months. maybe years? (i was in the dumbly optimistic stage of brain surgery recovery at the time.) found an insanely talented and astoundingly kind neuro-oncologist at sloan kettering (another reason i moved nearer to ny). he got me in for an appointment within two days. gave me a lightning-speed education, ran scans, the whole 509 yards. found a bit of tumor still there. devised a plan. so i did six weeks of radiation (every day) and a newfangled kind of chemo—five days on, twenty-one days off. kicked my butt. just finishing my last round of that. more scans next week, and we'll adjust. i'm stuck in a midair limbo between pessimistic hope and optimistic gloom.

i miss you.

the god piece, you ask. that's a different kind of limbo. not sure if my occasional prayer (horrors) is a postsurgical tick or the awakening of something that's been there all along. all i know for sure is that its mystery comforts me. i want god to be real. i want my brain to be tumor-free. i want my art to go viral. you're in there somewhere too. why is it that reconnecting with you has made me fear death more? not fear it. resent it, i guess.

and even as i write this, into the void of distance and time passed, i remember—vivid in my mind—the day you marched out to the garden shed, swiveled me around on my stool, stuck your finger in my face, and screeched, 'you will not—NOT—drink yourself stupid and get behind the wheel of a car.' you'd found out about a drunken game of chicken between my dad's mercury and chris adams's firebird. i'm sure i could see your whole face, but in my memory, i have this tunnel vision of just your anger-crazed eyes boring into me and your finger poking at my chest. 'don't ever risk your life or anyone else's just to prove you've got . . . !' (rhymes with 'malls.') or something along those lines. remember that day? i nearly wet myself right on the stool. you stood there, hands on hips, glaring at me. and right before you turned around to slam out of the shed, you yelled something i should really have embroidered on every throw pillow in my house: 'i'll kill you if you die!'

i remember thinking i should track down and beat up whoever it was who told you about the previous night's stupidity. i knew you knew i was an idiot—no mystery there—but i wanted you to keep figuring it out for yourself, without tattletales interposed. as pissed as i was at whoever had talked, though, it's your parting words that echoed in my mind as i picked up my brush and got back to painting.

they pretty much kept me from driving drunk again. that's how potent they were, coupled with your ren's-on-fire glare. 'i'll kill you if you die.' i'd love to hear you yell those words again.

that's where my heart is tonight.

god, we were so young . . . and now i don't know you from adam, yet somehow you never really left and so i do. shut up, dennison. she understands. don't write back, ren. just love the ones you're with.

I found Sam in his "prayer chair" on the roof, a cup of steaming coffee in his hand. He was looking out over the city he called home, the contrasting randomness of new and old construction, of poverty and wealth. The water cisterns perched on roofs. The clothes strung out to dry.

He looked older in the less forgiving light of morning. His laugh lines seemed deeper than when we'd first arrived, lengthened, perhaps, by exposure to the elements on his days outside the capital. He was thinner and somehow more serene. I watched from the top of the stairs as he took another sip, his every movement familiar and calming.

He saw me standing there. "Come sit by me," he said. He put down his mug and shifted over in his chair, motioning for me to join him.

"I'm not sure this thing is built for two . . ."

He gave me his "trust me" look and held out a hand. I settled into the chair with him—on top of him, really—and felt his arms come around me and pull me in. There it was again. The smell and feel and sound of him were as familiar as my own. I ran a hand over his close-cropped hair and traced the edges of his still receding hairline, wondering about Aidan's scars. "You think you'll ever grow it longer again?"

He took my hand and held my palm to his lips. "You think I should?"

"I'd like to see how gray it is. Always liked a distinguished-looking older man."

"If by distinguished you mean 'over the hill and coasting,' you've found him."

We let the silence settle for a moment. His palm traced circles on my back.

"Are you happy with the progress you're making out there?" I asked.

He nodded, lips pursed. "All things considered, yeah. Feels like we're laying a solid foundation. I'm telling you, Lauren— all those visions of big meetings and conversions by the dozens? They're nothing compared to a farmer inviting me in to share his *tarkari* and asking me why I've come to his village."

"How about the water pipeline for the place you visited two trips ago—anything new on that?" I got up and went to the corner of the balcony where a barrel overflowed with rainwater.

"Working on it. Correction, Sullivan's working on it. We should be able to get the equipment trucked in and a team there to install it this summer."

There was irony in the central role Sullivan's help had come to occupy in our ministry. Who would have thought, when we lived in Austria together, that she would become a linchpin in the ministry of the maverick who routinely dismissed her? I dipped a jug into the barrel and started to water the plants that lined the rooftop patio.

"Speaking of Sullivan . . . ," I said, feigning deep interest in plants I generally starved to death. "She called after you'd gone to bed last night."

He took a sip of coffee, clearly expecting bad news. "What is it this time? Red tape? Donors backing out?"

I took a deep breath and stopped what I was doing. "The Sternensee gang is buying us tickets for a trip back to the States." I said the words as casually as I could, scanning Sam's face for any sign of displeasure.

"They . . . what?"

I put down the watering can and took a step or two forward, trying to pick words that would appeal to his priorities. I wondered when I'd started managing his responses.

"They want us to be able to see our friends and family. We can pick our dates and Sullivan will book the tickets. Anywhere we want to go. Isn't that amazing, Sam? We could start at your parents' . . . maybe borrow one of their cars to drive out to Indiana and see mine." Sam's eyebrows were drawn. "I made a list of the people we'd be able to see fairly easily if we gave it two weeks—three weeks max."

"Lauren, it's a really generous gesture, but . . ."

"We've been here for more than two years, Sam. Our parents are getting older, and Ryan—it might be really good for him."

He put his cup down and moved to stand by the railing. "I wish Sullivan had talked to me before getting your hopes up."

"You were in bed. And since when do you need to screen my calls?"

He turned and leaned back. "We said we'd be here for a four-year term before heading back to the States."

"Because we didn't have the funds to fly back in between, but this would be entirely paid for." I heard my voice rising and tried to temper it. "I mean—it's a gift, Sam. No money out of pocket."

"It's not just about the finances."

"Right. It's about seeing family and friends and taking a

166

break. Come on—we've been here over two years. Surely we've earned a couple weeks off."

He looked at me as if that argument were ridiculous. "People aren't supporting us so we can take a vacation."

I wished I'd been surprised by his hesitance. "But this wouldn't cost them a penny."

He shook his head and held up his arms, as if it were all out of his control. "Even without the risk of offending our supporters, I couldn't leave Prakash here alone to continue without me."

"Two weeks. Three max!"

"I'm not comfortable with . . ."

I felt the dream slipping out of my grasp. "So maybe just Ryan and I go. I want you to come with us, but if you can't . . . Maybe just the two of us can head out for a couple weeks."

"It wouldn't be right."

"Why?"

"Because we came for four years," he repeated, talking to me like I was a child. "You, me, *and* Ryan."

"We did," I said, a hard edge to my voice. "We came for four years. And it's been hard."

"It's been challenging."

"Really? You're going to play semantics with this?"

He shook his head, frowning in confusion. "Lauren . . . what's the big deal? We planned to stay four years and we're still staying four years. Nothing has changed except Sullivan's offer."

"Exactly," I exclaimed. "That's what's changed. Last week we couldn't afford it and didn't want to offend our donors. Today we *can* afford it and we're not using money from our donors." I went over to him and pled my case. "Think about Ryan. Don't you think it would do him good to get a breather from all this?"

"He doesn't need a breather."

That chilled me. "Excuse me?"

"He'll come around. He's *coming* around. And taking him back to the States could actually be a detriment to that."

"You think he's 'coming around'?"

"Well, he's not getting any worse."

"When did not getting worse become the standard by which we judged our son's wellness?" I stared him down, hands on hips. "What if getting away from here for a while is exactly what he needs? What if it's exactly what *I* need, Sam? What if this is a gift from God and we're turning it down because we once said— before any of this was remotely a reality—that we were going to stick it out for four years? Correction: because *you* once said that we would."

"Lauren . . . ," he said with the same tone he'd used on Ryan when he was being disobedient. "You're being a little dramatic."

I froze. His gaze was as calm and sure as I'd ever seen it. "I'm sorry—did you just say I'm being dramatic?"

"Maybe not dramatic, but unreasonable," he said, attempting to pacify me. "It's not about the free tickets and it's not about Sullivan offering them. It's the principle of the matter."

"The principle being not ruffling anyone's feathers."

"The principle being that *we* committed to four years, and *I* committed to getting back to my villages before monsoon season hits."

"Okay, forget me for a minute. Forget the fact that I would love—*love*—to see my family again." And take a long hot shower and interact with people who speak my language and go places without taxis and overstuffed buses. I tried to bring Ryan into it one last time, hoping Sam's father-heart would soften out of love for his son. "Can we just do this for Ryan?"

"Look, we can go off on rabbit trails and argue the merits of this trip from every imaginable angle, but the bottom line is that it would be unwise to take it."

"This isn't an angle, Sam." I said his name more forcefully than I'd intended. "It's our son."

"And again, I think he's doing fine."

I felt my blood boil. "Well, *I* say he hasn't been fine in well over two years, and maybe we owe it to him to give him a break."

"He's an adolescent boy. It's a tough age regardless of where you live."

"But he's *our* adolescent boy, Sam," I said, leaning in in an attempt to influence his thinking. "He's dying on the vine." I took a deep breath and squared my shoulders in defiance. "And so am I."

His eyes snapped to mine. "Lauren, if you just take a step back . . ."

"No," I said. "You cannot use your lecturing-professor tone with me on this. Finances? Sure. Spiritual things? Have at it. But when it comes to how I'm feeling and what I need to make it to four years? You can't lecture me on that."

He frowned and crossed his arms. "Why are you getting so upset?" he asked.

I stared at him, searching his face for any sign of sympathy or conflicted emotion. There was nothing there but certainty. Tears stung my eyes. "Are you really going to turn these tickets down? Are you really going to put the"—I mimed quotation marks—"*optics* of a trip and a couple weeks of delayed ministry over something good that is being offered to us for free?"

"Maybe we both need to take some time and think it through."

Anger surged in me and I fought to tamp it down. The elation I'd felt since Sullivan's call yesterday was deflating into a painful reality. I should have predicted it. Part of me had. My reluctance to broach the subject with Sam had been about my fear that this would happen, that he'd dismiss the offer—along with my desperate need—and count appearances and ministry as more important than his family's sanity.

I nodded. "You go ahead and think about it, Sam. Go ahead and make believe you're considering the offer. I've never seen that lead to anything other than your decision standing." I swiveled and headed for the stairs, fighting the tears that made me feel weak. "Great to have you home."

My parting shot sounded petty, even to my own ears. I hated that it had come to this.

ten

Monsoon season had come early. It was wretched and gloomy. I'd seen heavy Midwestern rainfalls before, but nothing like this. Nothing like the sheets of precipitation that swept into us like solid waves. Suffocating humidity would gather during the day, exacerbated by an inescapable heat. The air would turn thick and clingy. Turgid with pent-up rain. And after gathering for several unbearable hours, the storm would break. The deluge would begin.

Some streets could fill in minutes with a knee-high, slow-moving stew of garbage, sewage, and dirt. Shoes and flip-flops were useless, sucked away by the lukewarm undertow. The rain would fall from afternoon through the night and most often let up around dawn. And the cycle would repeat: intensifying humidity, suffocating heat, paralyzing atmospheric pressure, then a thunderous release, engulfing, inescapable, and toxic.

Nothing could have prepared me for the reality of monsoon season. Neither the colorful descriptions from other expats nor Suman's dire warnings. I endured it with the fevered flailing of a drowning woman, clinging to the truth that each day got me nearer to its end and focusing on the silver lining of Sam's longer-than-usual presence in our home. And for the sake of Ryan, whose first few months had been an emotional monsoon already, I tried to talk down the fearsome floods that roared across the roof and poured over the gutters.

Sam stayed home for the worst of the season—a brief respite for us from his constant absences. He used the extra time to hole up in the office just a few blocks away, but he was home with us in the evenings. It was good to have him home. It was also a bit bewildering.

My breaking point came on a Thursday afternoon. I hadn't wanted to attend the recital at the Kathmandu conservatory, but one of my students was performing and I felt obligated to go. I hadn't felt well that morning and suspected it was the effect of too little sleep due to the intolerable humidity. I'd promised Ryan that I'd be home before dark to work on a science project with him. It was the first time he'd asked me for any help with his schoolwork since our arrival in Kathmandu—I would not stand him up.

I'd watched the skies from inside the conservatory, hoping the deluge would hold off just long enough for me to get home. My stomach churned with apprehension as time crawled by. In typical Nepali style, the recital went on longer than planned and I finally left early, tiptoeing out the door in the middle of someone's overwrought rendition of Vine's Sonata no. 1. It was a capital offense by music school standards, but I feared I'd already waited too long.

The skies opened as I was exiting the building and I knew most taxis would head for shelter rather than risk the flash floods that sometimes rushed Kathmandu's streets in a matter of minutes. I stood there, drenched in seconds by the wall of rain that beat me like a fire hose, unable to see clearly, shivering and helpless.

When a taxi finally drove by, I practically stepped into its path, ankle-deep in the street and waving my arms. It took several desperate attempts to make him understand where I needed him to take me. At first he refused, pointing at the sky as if I hadn't noticed the rain. I begged in English and threw in every Nepali word I knew. "Please. My baby." I made the sign of a mother rocking an infant, not caring at that moment whether it was entirely truthful or not. I needed to get home to Ryan. The driver finally conceded, and added something I didn't understand, making a categorical gesture with his hands.

We moved briskly despite the deluge obscuring visibility. I strained to see where we were going and suspected the driver was progressing more from muscle memory than by sight. Fear knotted my stomach and shivers quaked through my body, but a nearly hysterical fixation on getting home to Ryan kept me focused on the road ahead.

Two things happened nearly simultaneously when we were five minutes from home. We passed a high-riding truck that shot a wave of water under the taxi, and the motor just quit. One second we were progressing at an alarmingly unsafe clip, and the next we were stopped in the middle of the road, motor steaming. Much as he tried, the driver couldn't get the taxi started again. He screamed at me, I assumed blaming me for the watery demise of his sole income. He gesticulated and yelled and threw up his hands in despair while the churning in my stomach finally found release.

The diarrhea came in such a furious wave that I had no time to leap out of the taxi. There I was, being yelled at in a language I couldn't understand, sitting in my own excrement, immobilized by a terrifying monsoon—and still a five-minute drive from home.

Humiliation incinerated me as my stomach clenched in a cramp so intense I couldn't breathe. The driver didn't hesitate when he realized what was happening. He waded around to my door, still yelling, and dragged me out of the car and into the flooded street. He was gone before I was able to stand up straight again, my arms clasped over my stomach, the cramp slightly receding.

I stood there in the flooded street with diarrhea running down my legs, being pummeled by the torrents falling from the sky, racked with cramps and uncontrollable shivers, and there was nothing I could do. I had no cell phone—Sam considered them unnecessary—and whatever resilience I possessed had succumbed to my illness.

The terror and helplessness of that moment were a disintegrating force. I wailed. I wailed at the monsoon. I wailed at the taxi driver who had abandoned me so far from home. I wailed at the bacteria I'd probably caught from the toxic water I'd waded through for the past two weeks. I wailed at Sam for not being there, and I wailed at God for bringing me to this abominable country in the first place.

By some miracle, I made it home. Some of the roads were better than others, but I barely noticed as I walked and staggered, ripped again and again by cramps that had me doubled over or crouching. I was in so much pain and distress that I didn't bother to duck out of sight to relieve myself discreetly. I knew exactly what this was. I'd been warned about the bacterial infection since day one. It was the reason we showered with our mouths closed, filtered our drinking water, and soaked our fruit and vegetables in iodine. I'd taken all the precautions I could because I'd heard it was so bad, but I'd had no idea.

I was dizzy and fevered as I trudged on, oblivious to the stares of the few who dared to be in the street under such extreme circumstances.

It was our baker, Bina, who finally rescued me. She saw me stumbling by her window and came out into the elements. "You okay?" she asked. "You okay?"

I started to cry. I think she probably smelled my condition before she saw it. There was no hesitation. She placed an arm around my waist and half carried me the rest of the way home, pointing occasionally to make sure we were going the right way. I fumbled with the padlock on our gate and she took the key from my hand to unlock it herself.

Ryan had called his father at the office when I hadn't returned when I'd said I would. Sam heard the gate and came running, thanking Bina as he lifted me into his arms and carried me into the house. I caught a brief glimpse of Ryan standing in the living room doorway as Sam kicked the door shut behind us. "Get some hot water bottles, Ryan," he said, his voice soft but urgent.

He had to get into the shower with me to clean me. I was shaking so badly I couldn't stand without assistance. He dried me and helped me onto the toilet, wrapping a blanket around me. Then he carried me up the stairs to our bedroom, repositioned our bed as close to our bathroom as it would go, and took the two hot water bottles Ryan handed him, tucking them around me as he covered my still-shaking form with more blankets.

He helped me to swallow a pill with warm water and brushed the hair away from my face. I couldn't stop the tears, and the kindness in his eyes wasn't helping.

"You're going to be okay," he said, shushing me when the tears turned to sobbing.

When I could get a breath and control my voice, I looked him in the eyes and said, "I'm going home, Sam. You can stay here if you want, but I want to go home."

"Shhh," he murmured, stroking my shoulder. "We'll talk about it when you're feeling better."

It took three days. On the third, I found Sam cleaning out the chickens' pen. He took note of my clean hair and fresh clothes. "You look like you're on the mend," he said.

I tried to smile. "Almost got through the whole night last night."

Sam closed the gate on the chickens' pen and stepped closer for a better look. "You gave me quite the scare." There was no judgment in his voice. Only relief.

I took a deep breath. "I wasn't kidding, Sam. I want to go back to the States."

He started to smile, then realized I wasn't. "Lauren . . ."

I moved to sit on the front steps. The humidity was already building to this afternoon's downpour. I tried to speak with conviction and certainty, knowing that any sign of hysteria would invalidate my declaration. "I know this is the fulfillment of your dream. I know that, Sam. But it's . . . it's killing me. I don't want to be here. There's nothing for me here."

175

"It's only been six months—"

"I—want—out." My voice was hardening.

He lowered himself to the step next to me and said nothing for a while. "You've been sick . . ."

"Yes."

"And it's been a rough few months, I understand that."

"Yes."

"Maybe I should have been home more when we first got here . . ."

I almost laughed. "Sure—that would have been nice. But it wouldn't really have changed anything."

He turned toward me. "It's getting better, though. We're making progress. Can't you see that?"

I cringed. "Maybe."

"So . . . in another six months, think of how far we'll have come."

He was trying to be sensitive. I could hear it in his voice and see it on his face. The sudden thoughtfulness grated. "Not 'we,' Sam. This isn't about us. It's about me."

"What do you mean?"

I attempted a patient, rational tone and missed the mark. "I get it. I get that this is everything you hoped it would be. That you've made friends with people you can't exchange two sentences with. I get that you love your work and that you love the challenges of living in this country." I turned to look at him so he'd see exactly how serious I was. "But I'm going home."

I got up, went back into the house, climbed the stairs to our bedroom, pulled a suitcase from under the bed, and started to pack.

⁓

I lay on my bed between Suman's departure and Ryan's arrival, wearing nothing but my underwear and begging for the gods of electricity to turn it back on. The fan stood motionless next to the bed while humidity thick enough to trigger my claustrophobia covered me like a wet cloud. I yelled at Muffin to be quiet when he started barking, and the effort pushed more sweat to the surface of my skin. We were just three weeks out from the illness that had caused my epic meltdown, and I lived in fear that it would happen again.

"Oh, hush now! You know me, you loon."

The sound of Eveline's voice put a temporary end to the torpor that immobilized me every afternoon. I threw on a pair of shorts and tank top, clothes I would never wear outside our courtyard, and hurried downstairs to greet Eveline. It was a rare occurrence for her to come by the house—rarer still unannounced.

"Eveline."

She looked up and smiled, giving Muffin a good shove with her leg so he'd know who was the boss. "Well, aren't you the picture of monsoon morosity!" she said in her aristocratic English accent.

"Morosity?"

"That state in which we find ourselves after too many sweat-drenched nights and humidity-plagued days," she explained. "Even after all these years, there are still times when I feel exactly how you look."

I tried to hide my dismay. "So I won't get used to it?"

She patted my back as we climbed the steps into the house. "There are a lot of things we can learn to live with, Lauren, but monsoon season will always be unbearable."

"Would you like something cold to drink?"

"Water is fine—and you can pour it right down my back, if you wouldn't mind."

I led the way into the kitchen. "I'm surprised to see you."

"Well, a rather handsome little birdie suggested to me that you might enjoy some company." She took the glass I handed her.

"A birdie?"

She leaned in conspiratorially. "Rhymes with sham, luv."

177

I wasn't sure how I felt about Sam enlisting Eveline's help. I'd recovered slowly from my monsoon meltdown, hampered by the humidity, but there was a lingering fragility in my spirit that felt like a flaw.

"You could have called me," Eveline said. "When you weren't at the last couple of games, I figured you were traveling. If I'd known . . ."

She let the words trail off, and I knew they were meant to express her concern. An invitation to seek help when life spun out, as it just had. But I hadn't considered seeking help from Eveline in the depths of my illness or the slog of my recovery. I hadn't called anyone, not even Sullivan, when a halt in the deluge saw Sam leaving town again with excitement in his step. And I wasn't sure, as this displaced foreigner with the kind face and willing words offered her companionship, what my reticence was. It just felt like this life—this desert land—was mine to navigate alone.

"What exactly did Sam say when he told you I could use some company?"

If she heard the hardness in my voice, she didn't let it show. "Just that you'd hit a bit of a hiccup in processing life here."

"And he told you I got sick."

"He did. I suppose that makes you more officially one of us. You can't really claim to have lived here if you haven't spent a minimum of three days chained to the loo."

"It's a dubious honor . . ."

"Granted."

I wasn't sure what to say. If Eveline was here to cheer me up or counsel me, was I supposed to come right out and ask for her advice? We headed out to the front steps to sit. The faint breeze felt insufficient.

"Tell me what's been bothering you," Eveline said.

I contemplated putting on a resilient face and dismissing her concern. But I knew it wouldn't be convincing. "How did you do it?" I finally asked. "When you first moved here. How did you make your peace with this place?"

She thought for a moment. "Well, I just embraced it, I suppose. Not because I'm any kind of saint or cultural chameleon. I've been here long enough to know that some of us . . ." She paused and frowned. "I hesitate to speak in generalizations. It just seems some of us are wired to do better with change."

"I've done change before," I interjected, stung by what sounded like censure. This wasn't my first taste of newness.

"Of course you have. Change is inevitable in any life, I suppose. But this version of it—the kind that explodes any sense of familiarity—it's an identity-shifting thing. And I'm not sure what it is that makes some people more predisposed to weathering it than others. Some can take it in stride—thrive on it, really. And others . . . Others struggle more."

I let out a breath and wiped the sweat from my face. "And if we're not in the thriving group? We're doomed?"

"Heavens, no. It just may take a bit more time. More courage." She laughed.

"More courage," I repeated. I tried to imagine why Sam had sent Eveline to my rescue. She was a foreigner in Nepal, but she was also a high-profile doctor's wife, living in a gated community with amenities I only dreamed of.

"I'm sorry, Lauren! Here I am on a pick-me-up mission and running my mouth in a most discouraging way."

"No," I said, reaching out to pat her arm. "You're being honest. I'm just not sure what to do with what you've said."

"We're all different," Eveline said, "and we must each adapt at our own pace." She looked at me over the rim of her glass. "Sam certainly seems to be taking it all in stride."

"He is."

"Wonderful to see him so passionate about his work."

"Yes." I lacked her enthusiasm.

"Well, it's splendid. A man needs a mission."

"A woman does too."

She heard the edge in my voice and gave me a look. "Yes, of course."

"I don't want to be here," I heard myself say. If Eveline was surprised, she hid it well. She waited for me to continue. "I've been putting on a brave face and trying to be the good little missionary wife, but . . ." I looked at her and saw no reprimand. "This is hard, Eveline." I blinked against the tears I felt rising in my eyes. No more tears. I'd vowed to banish them after the monsoon episode.

Eveline nodded, looking out over our unkempt yard. "You're right," she said. "This is indeed hard. And there is absolutely no shame in realizing it."

"But . . ."

"No buts, dear. Not today. This is your chance to make a long list of everything you despise and tomorrow—tomorrow you can start thinking about the buts." There was nothing on her face but a sort of firm, compassionate expectancy. "All right, then. Make your list. Tell me what has brought you to your transitional knees." She said the last two words with enough drama to elicit a small smile from me.

"Really?" I asked. After weeks of trying not to speak of the challenges that were sucking the life out of me, I found Eveline's invitation strangely exhilarating. I sat up a little straighter and took a deep breath, still unsure.

She leaned in to say under her breath, as if there were someone else present, "I'd say to take your time, but the day isn't young and I have a feeling your list is rather long. So . . . off you go now."

I gathered my thoughts and began rather timidly. "It's not that I really want to leave."

"Yes, you do. Come on, luv. Tell me what's been hard."

I sighed. And then I started to enumerate my grievances. And though my list began with the obvious discomforts and lacks of a life in a Third World culture, it became clear that my greatest frustration was that it didn't need to be that way. Other expats had the luxuries that would make my new life in a frighteningly different place less taxing. And I had a husband who constantly reminded me that we were called to live *in* Nepal, not around it. Among the people, not above them. And though others, whether missionaries or diplomats and business families, might put their survival-comforts above the optics, we would not.

I understood Sam's desire to live as the Nepali did and his repeated assertions that we were already failing in that aspect—what with our three bicycles and kitchen filter and one portable heater and housekeeper and meat three times a week. This was the life we'd chosen—though we'd done so with incomplete information and theoretical temerity.

When I'd finished enumerating all that had depleted my tenacity, Eveline took my hands in hers and said, in her usual firm way, "You're stronger than you think, my dear. And those frustrations you've just listed? You can do something about quite a number of them."

I shook my head, fighting back tears. "Sam won't let us," I said, feeling guilt at the disloyalty of the statement.

"But they're such small investments in the larger scope of things—more water filters and better Internet coverage and another heater or two—maybe even a secondhand vehicle—and, for heaven's sake, an inverter for the electrical necessities. Surely, he wouldn't . . ."

I pulled my hands back. "He would. He has."

Eveline, who'd never before seemed to run out of words, said nothing for a few moments. "You've explained to him how much easier life would be?"

I nodded.

"Maybe if I ask around—someone might be leaving or upgrading . . ."

"He wouldn't allow it even if we could get those things for free."

I said, rubbing my hands over my face. I didn't try to explain Sam's reasoning. Eveline couldn't possibly understand the difference between a medical post and a nonprofit ministry.

"How many months has it been since you arrived?" she finally asked.

"Going on seven."

"And have you found any sort of niche that makes you feel useful?"

I heard the sincerity in her question, but it sounded like a mild rebuke. "No, I haven't really had the time to find a niche," I said, trying to keep the bitterness out of my voice.

"Well, there's no time like the present," Eveline said in her positive, no-nonsense manner. "What do you like to do?" She waited for me to make a list.

I drew a blank. I tried to think of activities I enjoyed, but every one that came to mind required more time than I could spare, more money than I could afford, or more energy than I could muster. She started listing off some options, but they sounded to me like just another drain on my already depleted life.

"How would you feel about assisting me with our expat ladies' group?" she finally asked. "I'm constantly in need of a right-hand person to help with our meetings and outings." I'd heard about the Expatriate Women of Kathmandu group. Eveline had invited me to join since our arrival in Nepal, but I'd balked at the notion. As most of the participants belonged to the business world or the diplomatic corps, I feared our modest lifestyle and complicated calling would make me feel too different—too unworthy of the group.

"What would you think of that?" Eveline persisted. "There would be, heavens, perhaps one activity per month. Some planning . . . some implementing. What do you think?"

I was so torn between her kindness and my reticence that I couldn't muster an answer. Eveline took the silence for consent. "Right then. Let's get back in touch in a few days and take a look at our calendars."

"Eveline, with my teaching job, I can't just—"

"A little variety will do you good!" She smiled expectantly. "You'll set your mind on different things and perhaps even discover something you like about this country."

"It's not the country . . ."

"It seldom is, luv."

After Eveline left, I sat on the step and considered her offer, feeling a nagging sense of dissent. Sam's assumption that a visit from a recent acquaintance would "fix" me galled a little. Did he think it was boredom fueling my desperation? Was it lack of hobbies that had sent me to him begging to leave?

When Eveline called a few days later with an invitation to help her plan an outing to Shivapuri Nagarjun National Park, I politely declined. I hadn't planned to. But the moment she'd started telling me about her upcoming field trip, I knew I would have to say no.

"I see," Eveline said, disappointment in her voice. "Maybe in a few more weeks, when you've settled in some more."

"I just don't think it's the right fit," I said. "But I'm so grateful for your willingness to include me."

I sat by the phone after she hung up and tried to discern what had prompted such a definitive refusal. Lack of social energy, perhaps. Or just not the "right fit." I wanted the answer to be something that simple, but I knew the truth was more obscure. More twisted. There was masochistic solace in enduring my pain in isolation—as if my solitary survival exposed how much I lived without. And in a strange, convoluted way, the notion felt affirming.

eleven

SAM WAS IN THE CITY. HE AND PRAKASH WERE MEETING with officials who might be able to supply the materials and equipment they planned to bring to Rambada. It was part of the ritual I'd come to expect when Sam came home. I'd made my peace with this reality—most of the time. I'd wait for his return, I'd celebrate his arrival, we'd try to function as a family for a day or two, something we disagreed on would come up, he'd apply his dispassionate logic to it, I'd argue my point, he'd stick to his guns, I'd concede defeat, and we'd spend the remaining days pretending there was no tension while ministry obligations stole him from our home.

Or maybe it was only me who sensed the distance in our postreunion cohabitation. Sam's mind seemed happily occupied by thoughts of saving Nepal one villager at a time. I suspected he never really strayed from that focus. Not when we argued, and not on those rarified occasions when he reached for me at night in what felt like a coercion of forgiveness.

When Ryan asked to sleep over at Steven's again, I snapped at him.

"Your father is only home for four more days, Ryan."

"So?"

I tried not to let his tone get to me. "So I'm sure he'd like to spend as much time as possible with you before he heads back out again."

He stared at me. "Can I spend the night at Steven's?" he repeated.

We locked eyes for a few moments, me trying to detect a trace of vulnerability in his armor and him probably wondering if I'd just hurry up and give in—like I usually did when Sam wasn't around.

"Come home by ten," I said.

"Why?"

"So we can have breakfast together."

A little more loudly. "Why?"

"Because your dad is only home for four more days," I said again.

"And that's my problem?"

"He's your father," I said, surprised by the passion in my voice.

Ryan shook his head and grabbed his jacket off the hook next to the door. "Tell him that." And he was gone.

I vented my frustration by scrubbing our floors and cleaning the chickens' pen and organizing the pantry . . . again. Then I sat in Sam's chair up on the roof and wondered how we'd gotten here.

It was a useless train of thought. We were here. Period. In this place. In this family. In this marriage. In this ministry too, though I had trouble celebrating that dubious blessing on days when it felt like it had stripped everything else from me.

With my resilience exhausted by keeping it together, I let myself be drawn back to a place of soul comfort. I opened the laptop I'd brought to the roof with me and read Aidan's last message again. I skimmed over the medical details of his treatment, the description of his faith, his recollection of the day I'd bullied him into giving up buzzed driving, and stopped, sobered, on his parting phrase. "Love the ones you're with."

Aidan. Sometimes I feel like the mark you left on my life is more crater than footprint. And I wonder how many of these messages it will take to fill it. And how much time we'll have to try.

Thank you for letting me in on your treatment and your heart. You say "maybe weeks" and I say MONTHS. YEARS! But that's my fervor speaking. I don't live inside the disease, as you do. Inside the discomfort of radiation and the nausea of chemo. Maybe that's the difference. Still, I'm believing in longer—much longer. Enough to fill that crater to the brim.

I do "love the ones I'm with." I do. But these days have been . . . hard. I catch myself wandering nearer to a pathetic sort of whine about my circumstances—a son who rarely speaks, a husband who seldom understands, a life that seems to diminish me.

It's not this country. I wish it were that easy. Nepal is beautiful in its brokenness. Its people are exquisite—kind, strong, and genuine. The lifestyle is organic and stripped down. I think you'd love it, as many Westerners do. I don't know why I haven't connected with this place and culture. That's not true. I have theories and suspicions. Mostly I have disappointment. In myself and in my woeful weakness. (Yes—I've noted the alliteration.)

Can I tell you about a friend of mine? Her name is Sullivan. She's a feisty, effervescent Southern woman who wields her irresistibility like Sam wields his Bible. She called two nights ago. Skyped. And . . . Aidan, she offered to buy us tickets to come home. She and a bunch of our old friends. For two or three weeks or however long we needed. Can you imagine? A trip home. A trip back to everything that's familiar. Maybe even to see you.

Sam refused to accept the gift. He has reasons— none of them worth trying to explain. And this anger, this small, petty, immature anger has plagued me since our conversation ended with his "no." It wasn't apologetic or sympathetic. It wasn't even falsely understanding. It was a dispassionate decree. We will not accept the offer of free tickets for a trip home to see our family.

So while you're wrestling with your demons—while you're battling a disease that has sublimated your art as it has undermined your strength—I've been moping around on my side of the globe. Pouting about plane rides and craving silly things.

And as I write the inane details of my life to you, I realize again how slight and wan they are. You've chosen weight and vibrancy and I've fallen into this. That's just one urge you've lit in me. To live more as you do. That and a desire, broad and mobile, for a face-to-face that fuels and frightens me. Twenty-two years without contact. Twenty-two years with only the faintest, occasional curiosity about where you might be. And then a rush of "this" and it's as if you never left. Thank you for that. I miss you too . . .

I sat motionless, my elbows propped on the table, my chin on my clasped hands . . . as if in prayer. I listened to the crows fighting over something on the roof. Heard the strident honking of horns on the street just up the alley. My seething had slithered into a darker, safer recess of my mind. I felt it there, stirring ever so slightly when memories of Sam's words revived it, coiled for a resurgence. Writing to Aidan had subdued it for a time, but I knew it would rush forth again if nothing in me changed.

I knew my resentment skewed my thinking, distorted my interpretation, and set my attitude on edge. I knew I needed to eliminate it. Not just ignore or control it. I knew the steps to take—prayer, repentance, apology, grace, reconciliation. But something treacherous prevented me from taking them, a strange hybrid of pride and guilt and juvenile insurrection.

Sullivan's offer and Aidan's illness had fused into a forward-straining energy that had felt indomitable until Sam's quiet dismissal. In its absence, I felt hollowed out and miserable.

I sat at the table while the sun swept shadows from one side of the room to the other, impervious to the falling temperature and the dimming of the lights. I sat there long after they'd gone out completely. Waiting. Berating myself. Urging my mind to calmness and my heart to stillness. Tamping down the rebellion that surged, righteous and impassioned, if I lowered my guards for even a moment.

Sam entered around suppertime. And still I sat at the dining room table, hands clasped, mind unsettled.

"Honey?" I heard him call from just inside the door. He found me moments later. "Why are you sitting in the dark?" He located the matches and the candle in their designated spot on the window ledge and soft light filled the dining room. "Are you okay?" he asked when he could see my face.

He installed himself at the other end of the table and leaned back in his chair, head cocked, considering me.

"I need to accept those tickets," I said.

Sam dropped his head.

I went on. "I realize that you might not feel the need to leave here yet. I also understand your concerns about the way an expensive trip like this might be perceived." I congratulated myself on keeping my tone low and measured. "I realize that you've made promises to the villages and need to keep your rotation going until monsoon season. I know all that."

He looked at me and frowned his confusion.

"But . . . I need to accept those tickets."

Disapproval flickered in his gaze. He sat forward and leaned on the table. "Lauren . . ."

I put my hand up to stop him, surprised to see my fingers shaking. My voice was strained and low as I said, "I have fought you on *nothing*, Sam." I locked onto his eyes and plowed on, determined to get this out now, while I still had the courage. "I didn't fight you when this 'calling' turned our worlds upside down. I didn't fight you when even our trusted friends tried to convince you that your approach to it was foolhardy. I didn't fight you when our savings were dwindling and you stopped working anyway. I didn't fight you when you bulldozed over our son's emotions in your zeal to get us here."

"Lauren," he tried again. But I wasn't finished.

"I didn't fight you when you decided that I'd be a part-time teacher so you could be a full-time missionary. Or when you decreed that we didn't need any of the luxuries other expats here call necessities. Or when you decided that your ministry required longer, more frequent absences. Or when that meant that I'd be left here for three weeks at a time, being mother and father to a disintegrating son. Or when you came back every time for seven days but started to drift out again after just two. I didn't fight you on any of that. But I want to fight you for this. I want us to accept those tickets and get away from here for a while. Please, Sam."

"We committed to four years—"

"Did you hear anything I just said?" I was appalled. "All I ask now, after years of getting here and two years of surviving here . . . All I ask now is that we accept a free gift and give ourselves a couple weeks away from a place that might have enthralled you, but has nearly destroyed this family."

"Destroyed our family?"

"You don't see it?"

"I know it's been hard, but we're doing okay." He saw my disbelief. "We are."

"I need to accept those tickets," I said again. More loudly this time. It didn't matter, in that moment, how he perceived the wellness of our family. All that mattered was getting away for a while.

He looked at me with a mix of concern and adamance. "Lauren, I hear what you're saying. I do. It's just . . . It's not sitting right with me," he said, as if he'd articulated an unassailable argument.

A shiver of anger ran down my spine. "I'm not asking it to sit right with you. I'm telling you this is something *I need*."

He scratched the back of his head, let out a slow breath, and tried again. "Maybe if we pray about it, we'll gain some more clarity."

"Tell me the truth, Sam. Do you have any expectation that a few days of prayer are going to change your mind?"

A muscle twitched in his jaw.

I don't know how much time passed as we stared across the table at each other. Sam's gaze was assured and unflinching, while I knew mine was stubborn but wavering—conviction and desperation locked in a standoff.

And then . . .

I felt myself concede even before my mind admitted its defeat. Everything I knew to be true about my husband pointed

190

to one conclusion: he wouldn't give in. His verdict would stand. Despite my desperation—despite the validity of my arguments and the urgency of Ryan's need—I again succumbed to the tyranny of submission. Frustration hardened into hostile resignation. I released the reprieve.

I tried to curb my anger as I looked across the table to where Sam sat. My wedding vows taunted me.

"All right," I finally said, depleted by surrender. I saw relief flash in his eyes. "We'll stay here because you want us to. Because you *command* us to."

My fingers were stiff with anger as I opened the laptop in front of me, pulled up Skype, and typed in Sullivan's name.

"You do realize it's six in the morning, right?" Sullivan's sleep-roughened drawl. She clicked the camera off before I could see her.

"I'm sorry, Sullivan," I said stonily.

"Lauren," Sam began, but I put up a peremptory hand.

I could hear bed linens shifting. "Lauren?" There was concern in Sullivan's voice. Sam ran a hand over his face and leaned back, staring at the ceiling.

"Sam and I are sitting here, Sullivan," I said, hearing how the hardness in my voice contrasted with the lightness of my words, "and we thought I should call you right away to tell you how much we appreciate your offer, but we're going to have to reject it." Reject. The word jarred with the rest of the sentence. Sam winced a little.

"I . . . okay?" Sullivan sounded confused.

"Please tell everyone how grateful we are. It's just that we can't have anyone thinking we're being frivolous. Same reason we don't have a car and a bunch of other things that aren't really necessities. We're missionaries after all. Saving the world one sacrifice at a time. That's our motto and we're sticking to it." I looked at Sam as I went on, allowing Sullivan no time for comments or questions. "So that's it from here, Sullivan. We're so sorry for waking you up and we hope you can get back to sleep."

I clicked to end the call, shut the laptop, and headed for the roof.

The tears came, rough and ragged, while I paced on the roof. But guilt now outweighed anger and frustration—not about my attitude or the way I'd spoken to Sam. I knew my resistance was warranted and protective, and I felt no qualms about it. But I had realized, halfway through my call to Sullivan, that I'd never really stood up to Sam. I hadn't ever fought for myself or my son, not with the intent of seeing it through and not in any of the crises and turning points that had fractured our family. I might have balked and doubted, but I had never stood my ground.

Looking back, I saw milestone after milestone when I could have challenged Sam, pointed out the holes in his reasoning, or contradicted his conclusions. When courage might have lent clout to my convictions. And now it was too late. I'd surrendered the right to stand up for myself and Ryan by failing to exercise it. I'd let my vows enslave me and my cowardice define me.

Now I was lost to this straitjacket reality in which even righteous rebellion had no place.

When Sam joined me on the roof, his shoulders were hunched and his eyes hollow. Surprise and sadness mingled in his gaze. I'd never believed more clearly that he loved me—nor had I ever resented it more.

"Can we talk?" he asked.

"I hate myself," I said.

"Lauren . . ."

I went over to the edge of the roof and stared into the

darkness. "I should have fought," I said. "I should have fought you the moment I noticed Ryan slipping away. I should have stepped between you and your . . . your divine appointment with Nepal at the first hint that it was sucking the happiness out of our son." I swiped at the traitorous tears undermining my courage.

"What are you—?"

I turned and leaned back against the railing. "It's been over two years. *Two years*." My own laughter startled me. It was humorless and pathetic. "Two years of hell in this place you call home." I shook my head at my own inadequacy and raised my hands in a gesture of defeat. "I didn't sign up for this, Sam. I signed up for you—and *you* were supposed to be the man who protected me and looked out for me and stood like a—a fortress between our son and anything that could possibly harm him."

Sam turned tortured eyes toward me. "I—Lauren, I thought . . . I didn't know."

"How could you not?"

"You never told me."

"Sam . . . I did. I *did*."

He cleared his throat. "When have you ever told me you were this unhappy?"

"What?" I was dumbfounded. "After the monsoon, for one! Have you forgotten the monsoon?"

"You were sick," he said. "I thought it was your illness speaking."

"And every other time?"

He grasped my shoulders and looked into my face with concern, but no trace of concession. "I thought it was just part of your processing."

I turned out of his grasp and wiped my tears with shaking hands. Took a couple breaths. And wondered how it had come to this. Aidan's voice rose out of the tangle in my mind: *"Love the ones you're with.*" I hated the words. I hated the conviction they shoved to the forefront of my thoughts. Love, at the moment, felt like the enemy.

I stood by the bird feeder and waited until I was sure I could speak. This was the life I had chosen—and rechosen—at every turn. This was the life to which I had committed. This was the man to whom I had submitted.

My loyalty to this marriage convicted and dismantled me.

"It's okay, Sam." My voice was thin but calm when I finally spoke. "I want to take those tickets Sullivan is offering with every cell in my body." My guilt receded as my grief increased. I seized the shreds of the commitments I'd made before discomfort, before displacement, before dissatisfaction. For better or for worse. Vows like a vise. I squeezed Sam's hand as I brushed passed him on my way to the stairs. "If you say we shouldn't take them," I said, "we won't."

"Lauren . . ."

"It's okay, Sam. Really. It's okay."

bit of a downer today. equilibrium is off. headache. taking it easy until we figure out what's going on. scan coming up, if i can get myself downtown. not until 10:30 a.m. that helps. no art for this boy right now, though, since being upright makes me nauseous. trying to get to the bottom of that and hoping new meds kick in. so . . . that means more time on the laptop. i'm okay with that.

sullivan. she sounds like my kind of people. i read about your free tickets and my mind flew all over the board. you coming to new york. showing you my favorite dives and haunts. slow-drinking a bottle of cabernet in a smoky bar i found off a back alley in brooklyn. talking. that's what i'd want. just—talk. no screens. no time zones and busyness. face-to-face and voice to voice. i'm telling you, i was cheering for those tickets.

then i read on. i've got to preface this by saying that i have no right to say it. all i know of sam is what you've told me. so i may be way off base here, but . . . what has he been smoking? (kidding.) i'm sure he's got enough compelling arguments to convince a grand jury, but to this guy lying on a couch in a city on the other side of the world, the thought of free tickets to see friends and family and, well, 'moi' sounds like a pretty appealing thing. tell me what time sam's school lets out and i'll go beat him up.

sigh . . . take yourself into consideration too. that's my cancer-brained advice. you're just as worthy as the dimwits you care for. me included.

i'm sorry you're hurting, ren. i wish i could make it right. would you consider skyping sometime? your call. i know it might be weird. if ever you feel the urge—you know where to find me. i'm artist.aidan, fyi.

remember the question we always had to answer at the beginning of creative writing class? what is the current color and texture of your mind . . .

mine's wedgewood blue vellum right now. with a faint ochre light shining through.

what's yours?

still . . .

a

I let Aidan's affirmation smooth a spirit wearied by emotion. If he was ochre-glowed blue vellum, I was the scabrous surface left behind by a lumbering glacier. I felt crushed, plowed, raked over. Pulverized sandstone.

I went downstairs, slipped on my shoes, and headed for the gate. Then I realized there was really nowhere to go. I craved quiet and order. A place to hide away. Until now, I'd found a pale facsimile inside my home—mostly quiet, mostly orderly. But now even it felt hostile and unsafe, inhabited with a good so stark it left no room for need.

A hammock swung between two trees in the far corner of our yard, hung there in the early days when we'd dreamed of an inner-city oasis bursting with marigolds and jasmine. But Sam was the gardener in our family, and with his frequent absences, our oasis aspirations had turned dull and modest. A few sweet peas here. Some pink *makhmali* there. And a hammock that swayed, deserted in a corner, the vestige of ambitions past.

I installed myself in the hammock, my eyes on the tangle of branches intersecting above me. I wanted to pray. I wanted to seek counsel and solace as I had since childhood in the swells and silences of communication with God. But somewhere in the last few weeks, I'd lost the words. To some degree, I'd lost the inclination too. I feared the loss and cheered it. Feared it because I felt bereft without it. Cheered it because it forced me somewhere new—somewhere uncharted. The danger felt liberating.

≈≈

Sullivan's eyes were wide and anxious. "What was *that*?" She stared at me through the screen.

I didn't even try to laugh it off. I lacked the energy for subterfuge. The last couple of days had been a testament to that, and I'd resorted to saying nothing, the poor man's version of self-control.

"Everything's okay," I said to Sullivan. "I just wanted you to know. We're fine. Hit a rough patch there but . . . we're fine."

"Chickadee . . ." Botox fought the frown trying to draw her eyebrows together with concern. "You need to put in some time practicing your facial expressions in front of a mirror. What I'm seeing is a lot of things, but 'fine' isn't one of them."

I hung my head. "We're *going to be* fine," I amended.

"Anything I can do from eight thousand miles away?"

I shook my head. "I think we're just hitting the two-year mark and responding differently. That's all."

"You realize those tickets weren't a package deal, right? You need to get away for a while, just say the word. Or you and Ryan."

"I'm just tired," I said to Sullivan. I tried for a courageous smile. "It'll pass." The optimism in my voice sounded genuine even to my ears. Practice makes perfect.

"Lauren . . ."

I thought a change of topic might steer us in a less precarious direction. "Everything okay with you? And Dudley?"

She laughed that deep-throated, rich laugh that spoke of Sullivan's less public side. "That's an obvious deflection, my friend, but yes, we're doing well."

We talked about sunny things for a few minutes, then the conversation drifted to her efforts to secure the thousands of dollars still missing from our water fund. That was something else I'd come to resent—that blurred line between ministry partner and friend. I needed the latter, on this day more than others, and as Sullivan caught me up on her fund-raising efforts on our behalf, I felt again the sting of something stolen from me.

"My friend is dying," I blurted when she took a breath during a soliloquy about the hypocrisy of the rich. The words came out in spite of me and with no warning. Panic coursed ice down my spine.

197

"Come again?" She squinted at the screen in front of her and I knew she saw my fear. "Lauren?"

I couldn't stop the shuddering breath, both visible and audible to my friend on the other side of the world. Sullivan's expression turned serious and sincere. "Is this about the tickets?" she asked.

"No. Yes."

She leaned back a little in her chair and seemed to assess what she saw on my face. "Use your words, Chickadee. What's going on with your friend?"

It wasn't that I couldn't find the words. It's that there were too many. I inhaled—deep and reluctant and desperate. Then I exhaled my confusion. "It's an old friend. From childhood," I said. "And he's dying." I tasted the finality. "And I . . . Those tickets you offered. I was going to get to see him again before he . . . but Sam decided not to take them."

Sullivan's expression hadn't changed. Curiosity and compassion. "Tell me more," she finally said.

"Aidan. We practically grew up together. He found me on Facebook when I signed up and—"

"Wait—*the* Aidan? The one you talked about at Christschule when you and Sam were . . . ?"

Long-forgotten conversations in our room in Sternensee surfaced from the confusion of my mind. I'd only mentioned him once, when Sullivan's frustration with my reticence to accept Sam's advances had pried his name out of me. "Yes," I conceded twenty-some years later. "That Aidan."

She shook her head. "And he's dying?"

"Brain cancer."

She looked away from the screen for a moment, thinking. When she turned back toward her laptop's camera, she said, "How long have you been back in touch?"

"Not long. A few weeks."

"And Sam knows."

I shook my head and hoped Sullivan couldn't sense the guilt that cornered me.

"Sam doesn't know," she amended, frowning.

I rushed to my own defense. "I just haven't figured out how to tell him."

"Chickadee, if Aidan is merely a friend, what's the hard part of telling Sam?"

I didn't know how to respond. Sullivan seemed to sense my disquiet. "Unless it's something more . . ."

I shook my head. "No—no, Sullivan. Really. We've just known each other since we were kids and . . . it's a lot to explain." I sighed and ran a hand over my face, exhausted by too much intensity. "I just need to make my peace with . . . with all of this."

"How often do you think of him?"

"What?"

She was as serious as I'd ever seen her. "During the day—how often is he on your mind?"

"Why are you asking—?"

"He knows you. He needs you. He reminds you of easier, happier times, and he's far enough away that he feels safe." She shook her head and sent me a compassionate smile. "I'm only asking the questions you'd ask me if the roles were reversed."

Guilt tingled at the edges of my consciousness. "It's not like that."

"With the stress you and Sam have been under—"

"It's not like that."

Sullivan let a few moments pass. I could tell she wanted to say more and was grateful when she didn't.

"Listen," she finally said, kindness in her expression and a bit more firmness in her voice, "friendship and death—these are universal themes. Sam may have made his mind up about the tickets, but if you told him about Aidan, do you think he'd at least reconsider then? Surely he'd understand the importance of such a friendship."

I thought about the life we'd lived since Sam's first encounter with Prakash. "He might have forgotten," I whispered. "About the value of relationships."

Our eyes met across the thousands of miles that separated us, and she sensed what I couldn't admit.

"This Aidan. You're sure it's a healthy thing?"

I looked at Sullivan and felt tears come to my eyes.

"Chickadee . . ."

twelve

Sam had been holed up in our bedroom for most of the afternoon, hammering out the tasks that needed to be accomplished before he headed out again tomorrow. We'd gone to church that morning, as we always did. It was a small gathering of the English community under the leadership of a loosely Anglican pastor from Ireland who requested that we simply call him Justin. The services were casual and flexible, easily driven off script by lengthy periods of sharing or prayer times extended by an urgent need among us. It felt good to disconnect, for that one morning per week, from the tedium of grading and worry and make-do strategy.

Ryan tagged along because he had no other option. We made him take out his earbuds when we reached the gate of the school that housed our eclectic bunch. He sat hunched throughout the service, occasionally needing a prod to get him to stand at appropriate places. Sometimes he dozed. Most of the time he sat blank-faced, eyes on nothing, or staring out the window at the construction crane that towered over the half-built gym. I think I'd have preferred a scowl or a forced smile. Anything other than his absence.

When the pastor asked for prayer requests, Sam rose to speak. I pasted on my "peaceful wife" expression, knowing the spotlight that shone on Sam would catch me in its peripheral glow. He gave a brief update about his upcoming travels, mentioned a couple of specific prayer requests—the traditional missionaries-on-Sunday fare.

I listened to his smoothly modulated voice and wondered when his words had ceased to be inspirational to me. A prayer time followed. I fought the resentment that surged as good people uttered heartfelt pleas for Sam's important work, praising his determination and praying for his stamina. Eveline included me in her typically sturdy petition. "And be with Sam's family as they persevere through his absences," she said. I hated the swell of self-pity weighing in my stomach and reminded myself of greater needs than mine. Of cancerous lesions and counted days. I despised my shallowness.

It was day six of Sam's time at home, which meant our meals were shorter and our words sparser. It was hard to engage in casual banter when we lived most of our lives in different worlds.

And now we were off to Swayambhunath, a collection of shrines and sacred places known as Monkey Temple, founded on a steep hill in the fifth century and topped by a stunning white stupa on which Buddha's eyes and eyebrows were painted. On our first trip there, shortly after our arrival in Kathmandu, the monkeys that ran wild around the temple had coaxed the first delighted smile from our son on Nepali soil. We hadn't seen many of them since then. Still, we returned to this place periodically, not only for its beauty. I think we saw it as a glimpse into our past.

Sam had allowed us to take a taxi this time, a gesture I attributed to his imminent departure and the slightly less than pleasant nature of his weeklong stay. Other times, we'd forgone the taxi and made the eight-mile trip on foot, deliberate in our commitment to live as the Nepali did—some of them, anyway.

We took Swayambhunath's 365 steps slowly on this day,

stopping to browse through vendor displays whose prices varied depending on the number of foreigners navigating the long stairway. Smaller stupas formed a playground for the monkeys who darted in and out of reach, scanning the crowds for low-hanging shiny fare or snatchable food.

Though Ryan had once been enthralled by the dashing, chattering few, I now caught him watching mostly the older monkeys who sat out of reach, a distance from the path, observing monks and travelers with a dispassionate stare.

We circled the white dome festooned with prayer flags hung on wires that radiated from the center, peering into the small temples that lined it, taking in the gifts left by the devout to appease a stern god. Monks from the nearby monastery rang bells as they circled the stupa, while tourists stepped in for close-up pictures of their serene faces.

All I could think of was Aidan. How he'd want to sit and absorb the sights and sounds. How he'd already be plotting the medium he'd use to extrapolate immobile art from bustling reality. How he'd lose himself in contemplation for minutes at a time, as he had so often in our youth, then leap from that focus into a completely irrational burst of hyperactivity.

We took the shaded back steps down to the World Peace Pond and found a bench to sit on while we ate our sandwiches. Ryan wandered a few steps off and crouched against a wall. His expression was blank and distant. He didn't move when the first monkey, an older female, slid off the wall a little ways down and sidled up to him. He pulled off a piece of his sandwich and tossed it lightly in her direction, eyes forward, emotionless.

When she had captured the forbidden food, other monkeys ventured nearer, chattering to each other, eyeing the crouching human who continued to tear off chunks of bread and lob them in their direction.

I watched as a faint gleam of light appeared in Ryan's eyes. He lowered himself completely to the ground, legs crossed, and continued to feed the simians from his bag. As they grew braver, he finally turned his head to look directly at them. There was a brief face-off while they seemed to consider each other, then the monkeys moved closer in a gesture of trust.

Sam took a breath and I knew—I knew—what he was going to say. He'd point at one of the multilingual signs lining the space where we sat and say, "That's illegal, son. No feeding the monkeys." I lay a hand on his arm and motioned toward Ryan. I hoped Sam saw what I did. A softening in his countenance. A slightly lighter bearing. A hint of *presence* in that time and place. Sam nodded and looked away.

"Do you think we did the wrong thing—coming to Kathmandu?" he asked.

The question had been hanging between us since our conversation on the roof. I sensed the weight of the moment and paused to consider a measured reply. "To tell you the truth, I don't know."

"But . . . we got here. Right?"

"I know," I said, sighing. That simple fact had always been at the center of Sam's arguments.

"How many people told us it couldn't be done? I know I keep coming back to that, but . . . if God hadn't wanted us to make it here . . ."

My concession was reluctant. "We'd still be home fund-raising."

Sam nodded and swung his gaze toward Ryan again. "I know my traveling has put a lot of pressure on you and Ryan."

A pregnant silence stretched between us. It was I who finally broke it. "But your work can't be done from Kathmandu."

Sam's relief was a nearly palpable thing. He reached for my hand. "Thank you for understanding, Lauren."

I wanted to tell him that I didn't, but I knew any demands would be futile. I wanted to tell him that this on-again, off-again version of marriage couldn't possibly be healthy. I wanted him to understand the full extent of the sacrifices soul-saving work was imposing on Ryan and me. But I'd loved him long enough to know how useless the words would be.

"I've been looking into getting away—just the two of us," Sam said after a few minutes.

I glanced at him, trying to curb my hope. "You have?"

"There's a hotel in Nagarkot. It's the off-season, so the prices are good. We could go for a couple days next time I'm home." He looked at me. "Would you like that?"

Like. Beige word. "Are you sure we can afford it?" I hated the question the minute it was out of my mouth.

"We can. I think this is important."

"And Ryan?"

"This time"—Sam smiled—"we can actually say yes without hesitation when he asks to stay at Steven's."

A part of me that had been disappointed too often doubted the sureness of his offer. "What about work?"

He shrugged. When he turned on the bench to look at me, I saw vulnerability. It startled me. "The work will keep," he said. "This is about you and me."

I scanned his face for signs of reluctance. I saw nothing but sincerity. We watched as orange sunlight crept up the wall against which Ryan sat, then leapt off into night. My husband wanted to get away with me. He was willing to spend our money—his own investment on his own terms—for me. While I'd been trying to repress the yearning to flee this place for a couple of weeks, Sam had been planning for us to leave it together for a weekend, without compromising the principles that made him who he was.

"I'd love to go to Nagarkot," I said.

Aidan . . . how are you feeling now? The nausea and fatigue. Are those normal? I worry about you. The frustration of not being able to do anything for you—that's what keeps me awake at night. Being too far.

I'm concerned that I might have sounded petty in my last message. Or critical of Sam. Actually, petty is exactly what I was . . . He turned down Sullivan's tickets and I dug out my rebel flag and started waving it like a lunatic. I climbed my barricade and blustered. "I'm going to take those tickets whether you want me to or not!" Very mature, wife-of-the-year stuff. But sometimes I feel like Sam has a simple equation he uses to determine the right and the wrong of things. And it often feels like I don't appear anywhere in it.

Regardless—I shouldn't have made Sam sound so callous when I wrote to you. He's not. He just marches to the beat of a drummer who doesn't exist on Planet Lauren. He could climb Mount Everest unassisted and still have the energy to preach a sermon from the top. Not me. I'm not cut from that cloth. The unspoken missionary rules state that I shouldn't admit it, but there's no way around it. I'm just not strong—not in that way.

So, update: He told me yesterday that he's made plans to take me away the next time he's home. A place called Nagarkot, up in the mountains. Famous for its views of the Himalayas. Sam, who won't spend twenty dollars a month so we can get fast enough Internet to stream stuff for Ryan, is booking us a room in Nagarkot. Different planet—different drummer. When will I learn?

I guess that's the danger of having reconnected with you. This figment from the past reenters my life and communicates more in a handful of messages and art than others have in years of face-to-face. And gets me. The figment understands who I am after twenty-some years of separation, while those closest to me in proximity and relationship remain baffled. I'm wrestling with that one.

Sam leaves tomorrow for the next three-week installment of Sam's Great Disappearing Act. And after that, Nagarkot. Something to look forward to feels good.

But it also officially closes the "free ticket" chapter of my life. And that hurts. Aidan, you have no idea how . . . fervently . . . I wanted for that to happen. I guess I let my hopes rise too fast. It's a habit I've been trying to undo for most of my life.

I hate to think of you going through all of this virtually alone. You've said that's how you want it, but still. You need someone there . . . don't you? How do you process the emotions that must be a huge part of this fight you're engaged in? I imagine your art plays into it, but even that—even that must not entirely quell the uncertainty and . . . fear?

Thinking of you, Aidan. Praying, pleading, and believing.

My hand drifted over the stubble of close-cropped hair on Sam's head. His backpack stood propped against the bedroom door. He'd spent the evening as he always did the night before his departure: packing and planning as his excitement visibly increased. There was new energy in his steps as he climbed the stairs two at a time to get his clean clothes from the line, fresh vitality in his voice as he described the next expedition over dinner, and a general brightening of his expression as he connected by Skype with a couple of important donors. There was no denying the way these journeys galvanized him. He came alive with purpose and expectation, and the transformation in him was astounding.

There was a scar on the back of Sam's head. Small and mostly faded, it was at once a source of gratitude and a call to prayer. The large stone that had fallen from a cliff and glanced off his skull could have done serious damage. Just a couple inches closer and . . . But Prakash had quickly disinfected the wound and taped it shut, then they'd gone on their way ministering to others under unimaginable conditions.

Sam adjusted his position, glancing at me through barely conscious eyes as he shifted higher on the mattress. He was asleep again before he'd completely settled. I watched the movement behind his eyelids and wondered what he was dreaming. Did Ryan and I figure in the stories playing out on the broad screen of slumber, or were his dreams populated with the people and places I'd never known? I wondered what a hindrance I'd been to Sam's work. Guilt stirred. Then I remembered his uncanny ability to be utterly present in the immediacy of need, regardless of the challenges in other spheres of his life. I was certain my failures as a wife and missionary had had little impact on his ministry.

I walked Sam to the gate the next morning, trying to install a bottle of clean water in the loop on the side of his backpack. He was fresh-shaven, his clothes were clean. He radiated a sense of purpose and excitement.

"See you in three weeks?" he asked as a taxi pulled up just outside our gates.

I nodded. "I'll be waiting."

He dropped his pack into the rear seat and was preparing to climb in when I grabbed his arm.

"Are we okay, Sam?"

He frowned. "What do you mean?"

"You know what I mean. With the . . . the arguing. Are we— are we okay?"

I wanted him to tell me how concerned he was. I wanted him to say that our arguing had scared him too, that he was starting to see that my needs were different from his, that he was seriously considering changes that would make my life easier, that we'd talk about those tickets again when he got home.

Instead, he smiled and said, "We're fine, Lauren."

"Okay."

He looked more closely into my face. "Aren't we?"

I nodded and forced a smile. "Sure. Sure—we're fine." That old refrain.

Sam gave me a kiss good-bye, then framed my face in both his hands, staring into me. "I love you, Lauren."

"Love you too."

And he was gone.

I scratched the top of Muffin's head and headed back to the house. Ryan was upstairs sleeping. He'd said his good-byes last night. I needed to get ready for my day of teaching, though the prospect was utterly unappealing.

I found my laptop in the dining room and carried it up to the roof.

LCC: It's eight a.m. here. Just past nine p.m. where you are. How are you, Aidan? Do you feel any better?

AD: ren . . .

I gasped when Aidan's word showed up on my screen. Got up from the chair and laid the laptop on the small table next to me. Backed away. Adrenaline made my heart race, and confusion numbed my brain. I was so new to Facebook that I didn't know how to process the single word that had appeared under the lines I'd written. A message sent awhile ago that had just landed out of cyberspace? Or . . . was he actually there, speaking to me in real time?

I took stock of where I stood and rolled my eyes at my stupidity. A grown woman on a roof in Nepal cowering from a word she had read on her laptop. If Aidan was truly sitting at his computer on the other side of the globe, as I suspected he was . . . to my novice mind, it somehow felt more substantial. More real. Aidan was there. Right there—beyond my screen.

The realization sent me forward again. As I picked up the laptop and settled back into my chair, I saw more words from Aidan appear. My breath caught. He was speaking to me in that moment from a world away. I was speaking directly with Aidan—no delay. The notion intimidated and exhilarated me.

I watched more words unfurl across the screen, then took a deep breath and typed, the pseudoproximity stunning me. Tears stung my eyes. This felt—finally—like a reunion.

AD: ren . . . heart's beating fast here. are you on right now?

LCC: Yes. I'm a little unnerved.

AD: because?

LCC: I don't know. This feels . . . different.

AD: different bad?

LCC: Different great. In a reach-through-the-screen-and-hug-Aidan kind of way.

AD: easy there. these things aren't built for that.

LCC: Giggle. First real-time giggle. Why haven't we done this before?

AD: those pesky time zones.

LCC: Maybe a little trepidation too. This is . . .

AD: real.

LCC: Yeah. Real.

AD: geez, ren.

LCC: Aidan, how are you feeling? I spent half the night up worrying about you.

AD: better than when i wrote earlier. still fuzzy, but less than before. i'm just worn out, ren. managed to finish multimedia self-portrait this afternoon, though. in ten-minute increments, then back to the couch for a bit. felt disjointed and i didn't like it, but i got the thing done. let me see if i can take a pic and send it.

LCC: I'm pretty sure cancer patients are supposed to focus on beating the odds, not launch art collections and plan publishing projects.

AD: i'm pretty sure their friends are supposed to support whatever floats their boat. (kidding—there needs to be a sarcasm emoticon on this site.)

LCC: No need for labels. I've spoken Aidanese long enough to interpret it accurately, I think. Still—I wish you'd give yourself more time to feel better before pushing yourself to paint.

AD: that's the point, ren. i've learned a thing or two about time since labor day. biggest one is that you don't know how much there's left. i don't want to squander a second of it. just in case.

LCC: Sigh. How do you wrap your mind around this?

AD: what—knowing i'm dying?

LCC: I want to say, "Stop saying that," but . . .

AD: but this is my reality. right after i was diagnosed, i had this romantic notion that i'd just go on living like nothing was wrong. i'd do the art thing and travel the globe and love and learn and laugh, and when my time came, i'd just drop dead and be done.

LCC: Aidan.

AD: and then i decided that i could do most of that and still try to show this beast who's boss.

LCC: You've never been very good at sitting back and taking it.

AD: don't take to threats very well either.

LCC: Who cares for you when you're not doing well?

AD: i think i told you i live two doors down from my parents. if i need anything, i call them.

LCC: What if something happens and you can't call?

AD: i have a sneakin' suspicion my dad installed nanny cams in all the rooms so they can keep tabs on me.

LCC: Seriously?

AD: geez, ren. always the gullible one. no, not seriously. i'll find a way of getting their attention if i need to. (you get an f in aidanese, by the way.)

LCC: Think you'll be able to get to the hospital for your scan tomorrow?

AD: counting on it.

LCC: Heart?

AD: heart's okay. my mind tells me it will be good to know where things stand. don't want that pea-sized spot getting any grape ambitions.

LCC: Smiling. It won't. I've been praying it into submission.

AD: god, ren. this feels good.

LCC: Yup.

AD: i wish you were here.

LCC: Not sure how to answer that sufficiently, with just words on a screen. This is where art might say it better than words can. Try that one, will you? Paint something that says how intensely

I'd love to be there for you. In person. None of this technology needed.

AD: don't cut it.

LCC: I'm not.

AD: it found you, didn't it?

LCC: Color and texture.

AD: just like that?

LCC: Spit it out.

AD: i'm leaning toward . . . okay, this is weird. driftwood. greenish-brown.

LCC: Battered?

AD: polished. big nuance there. battered into something better.

LCC: Again with the imagery. You're going to have to become an artist or something.

AD: see what i mean about time being too short? couldn't possibly capture it all.

LCC: But you can't be sure. Right? You could have years and just not know it.

AD: i keep trying to convince the docs of that fact, but they give me their whatever-makes-you-feel-better look and move on to other topics.

LCC: What do they know?

AD: smirking. yeah, what do they know?

LCC: You ready to get some sleep?

AD: got to admit it. i'm tired right now. last spurt of creating might have overdone it a bit.

LCC: Plus the exhilaration of "talking" in real time with me, of course.

AD: of course. especially that.

LCC: Get some sleep. You have an important day tomorrow.

AD: but i'd rather keep talking to you.

LCC: There'll be time for more of this. Lots of it.

AD: optimist.

LCC: Good night, Aidan. Let me know how tomorrow goes? I'm rooting for you.

AD: always have. deserved or not.

LCC: Still do.

AD: still, good night, ren.

I packed my messenger bag with what I'd need for today's classes and headed out the door. And I thought of Aidan.

I got my bike out of the crowded shed by the gate, knowing I'd have to ride it through town to my bus stop, as another fuel shortage had limited taxi service. And I thought of Aidan.

I pedaled down the busy street to the main artery that curved through downtown Kathmandu to the place where I'd catch my bus to Bhaktapur, pushed hard across intersections where no vehicles slowed for cross-traffic, narrowly avoided pedestrians who stepped off the sidewalk with no concern for oncoming bikes and cars, held my breath as I rode through black billows of pollution belched out by trucks and cars alike. And still I thought of Aidan.

I boarded the bus with a layer of city dirt on my skin and stood in unbearably close quarters with other passengers crammed into the aisle. And still I thought of Aidan.

I walked ten minutes from the bus stop to the language school, hurried down the hall to my classroom, and launched into a bland lesson on reflective verbs, complete with excerpts from classic literature and a rudimentary PowerPoint I'd thrown together the night before. And still I thought about Aidan.

At the end of my fourth class, I lingered for a moment

making small talk with young people whose grasp of English far surpassed my grasp of Nepali, asking them about their families and their plans for the coming semester, and still . . . I thought about Aidan.

I was sure I made it up the hills faster and wove my way through the horn-saturated traffic more agilely on the return trip, urged forward by my desire to get home and write to Aidan so the message would be there for him when he woke up—before he headed into New York for his scan.

The electricity was out when I entered the house, but the laptop had been plugged in and was partially charged. I accessed the neighbors' Wi-Fi and logged in to Facebook. Four in the afternoon in Nepal, just after five in the morning in New York.

I was about to start typing when . . .

AD: ren.

LCC: Aidan? I just triple-checked my time-zone converter. What are you doing up so early?

AD: i went to bed early, remember?

LCC: You should be sleeping.

AD: time enough for that when i'm dead.

LCC: Consider yourself glared at.

AD: a little gallows humor from the guy whose life expectancy depends on heading into a tube later this morning. i want to hit the paints for a while before i go.

LCC: How are you feeling now that you've slept a little?

AD: honestly?

LCC: Of course.

AD: i'm a little freaked out about this one.

LCC: More than others?

AD: i'm five months out. last chemo treatment over. if there's no improvement . . . worse, if there's growth . . . not much more in the arsenal to throw at it.

215

LCC: Sigh. And you're sitting there alone in the wee hours contemplating the unknown.

AD: lying here. and yes.

LCC: I'm sorry, Aidan.

AD: actually, you're helping.

LCC: Because words appearing like magic on a screen are ever so comforting.

AD: because they're you. they make you here. when are you going to stop being you and tell your husband to give you the bleepin' tickets?

LCC: Bleepin', huh? My, how you've changed.

AD: again—just trying to be sensitive to my missionary friend.

LCC: Did you ever in your wildest dreams imagine I'd become a missionary?

AD: sure. right after i pictured you becoming a nun.

LCC: Laughing. Not sure that's a compliment.

AD: sam should be happy my first prediction was a dud.

LCC: I don't know. Those tickets caused the kind of blowout that might have made him wish for celibacy . . . but that's over now. We're staying put. I hate it. But it is what it is.

AD: probably the right thing.

LCC: I'm sorry you're scared, Aidan. I know I would be too.

AD: ren, i've got a bad feeling . . . like it's about time for my luck to run out.

LCC: You'll have answers in a few hours, and then you'll know how you should feel. If my prayers all the way over here in Nepal have anything to do with it, you're going to be celebrating with a snifter of something expensive.

AD: i'll drink to that.

LCC: Remember when you made me taste vodka?

AD: i remember you spitting it out all over me.

LCC: Good thing it's odorless.

AD: good thing i liked you. like. present tense.

LCC: And I like that we get to talk in present tense again.

AD: me too. geez, ren. me too.

LCC: What kind of piece are you working on? Wish I could sit and watch you paint like I used to.

AD: yeah, i should probably drag myself out of bed and get sketching. i think it's called 'still' . . . and you're invited into my art any time.

LCC: I miss you, Aidan. I think I miss being young with you too.

AD: same here. you have no idea.

LCC: I'll let you get to your painting.

AD: thanks, ren.

LCC: Please, please, please let me know when you're home again. Sam's gone and Ryan's in and out. I'll check often. Praying you through, Aidan. Still.

AD: bye . . .

I sat by the laptop awhile longer, rereading the two previous exchanges with Aidan and wondering why we hadn't chatted in real time sooner. I loved his long, descriptive messages and the way he wove our history into what he wrote, but there was something about the concurrence of chat that seemed to have decreased the distance just as it had increased the emotions.

I was surprised at how deeply I felt his fear as today's scan approached. And how intimately I felt the painting he was creating even as I sat there contemplating the technology that had brought us back together.

I started to pray for him—more an instinct than a conscious thing. But something stopped me. A feeling I couldn't quite identify. Something that simultaneously shied away and stomped its foot. I tried to pray again, but the words in my mind felt stilted.

Ryan came slamming through the front door a few minutes

after five and went straight to the fridge, as always. I put on my mom-after-school hat and performed our daily ritual.

"Hi, Ryan."

"Hi."

"There's leftover fruit salad in the green Tupperware at the back."

"Got it."

"Steven's mom called. She said they're postponing your next game because the other team has lice."

"That's fine."

"Dad got off okay this morning. He said to say good-bye to you."

"Cool."

I hesitated only briefly. "Ryan, do you miss your dad when he's gone?"

That got his attention. He looked up from shoving fruit salad into his mouth with a soupspoon. Suspicion drew his eyebrows together. "Why?"

"Just curious."

I was getting used to his my-mother-the-idiot eyerolls, but this one seemed particularly heartfelt.

"I guess I wonder because . . ." I hesitated. "You never really seem to enjoy it when he's home, and you don't particularly seem to care when he leaves, so . . ."

"Maybe it's easier that way."

I hadn't really expected a response from him, so when it came, it brought me up short.

"Easier. What do you mean by that?"

He shrugged and shoved another spoonful into his mouth. "Just easier," he said around it.

I watched him chew, buoyed that we were talking, but frozen

by the surprise of this exchange. "I know it takes awhile to adapt every time."

He swallowed and shook his head. "That's not what I mean."

"Then what *do* you mean?" I could tell he was angling to leave.

Ryan dropped the empty Tupperware in the sink. "If you don't really care, you don't really miss it. Right?" He looked at me and I saw flashes in my mind of all he'd lost with our move to Nepal. His classmates, his teammates, his neighborhood friends, his grandparents, our house . . . his universe. "It's just easier," he said again, his voice tinged with cynicism. Then he was gone.

thirteen

EVEN THE PILEUP OF UNANSWERED MAIL COULDN'T KEEP MY
mind focused during the first evening of Sam's absence. As I
wrote thank-you notes to our donors and graded the tests of an
intermediate language class, my mind was torn between Ryan's
final words to me and Aidan's impending verdict.

If there was one thing we had taught our son—quite unwit-
tingly—it was that loved ones leave. Or that we leave them. We'd
robbed him of stability when we'd made the decision to move
to Kathmandu, then we'd ended up staying in our hometown
for nearly five years, in an uncomfortable state of suspension
between impetus and completion, with no specific end goal in
sight. We'd lived in a temporariness that discouraged investment in any form of newness and generally kept us from a sense
of presence in the here and now.

Eventually, we'd taken off for a country none of us had seen
before, leaving limbo behind and clinging to the oft-repeated
expectation that things would settle down once we got there.
We'd get installed in our new home, we'd make friends, and
nothing much would change for the next four years. But that
wasn't the way things had happened, and an eleven-year-old
who had lost stability, then lost his friends, had found in his new
world even less predictability. Sam's three-week trips away from

home for nine months of the year had probably felt like the last straw to a boy who had already lost so much.

"It's just easier," he'd said. Easier, indeed. Part of me envied Ryan the ability to switch off his needs. It struck me that I'd actually done something similar with Sam. I couldn't be dependent anymore, not with the ministry and absences that stretched our lives thin. I felt my need like a self-perpetuating, diminishing force. Embittering too. And at some point in the past few months, I'd squelched it.

Then Aidan had found me, and in the reuniting I'd discovered again the nourishing power of connection—and had more fully understood the damage of its absence.

I stayed downstairs until past eleven, waiting for Ryan to come home from wherever he was. The part of Kathmandu where we lived was mostly safe, but I still didn't like my thirteen-year-old biking through town after dark. I lit some candles when the electricity flickered out and moved two large cans of frozen water from the freezer to the fridge, hanging the usual "Don't open the fridge while the power is out" sign on its handle. I put on a sweatshirt and wrapped up in a blanket. Then I waited, laptop open, for Ryan or Aidan—whoever would appear first.

AD: ren?

LCC: Aidan.

AD: you're there . . .

LCC: Been waiting all day. How did the scan go?

AD: long. and repeated.

LCC: They repeated the scan?

AD: twice.

LCC: That doesn't sound good.

AD: it's not.

Halted breath. Dread like a physical force descended over

me. I didn't know what to write. I couldn't see his face or read his expression. Helplessness wrung me. Not for the first time, I cursed the distance and the cold, sterile, impersonal glare of my laptop's screen. And even as I asked another question, I felt a tentacled fear grip me. It took him too long to continue.

LCC: Tell me what's going on, Aidan.

AD: . . . i'm sorry. not quite sure i want to write this.

LCC: Aidan.

AD: not because i don't want to tell you. it's just that . . . writing it makes it real.

LCC: Please, Aidan. What did your doctor see on the scan?

AD: i do have a brain—that's the good news.

LCC: Can you please not make jokes? Not now. Tell me.

AD: it's growing.

LCC: The tumor?

AD: that's a silly question, ren.

LCC: How much?

AD: nearly double since last month.

LCC: Oh, God.

God, no. God. No. I stared through tears at Aidan's words on the screen. *Nearly double since last month.* I berated myself for not knowing more. What did this mean? Why was it progressing so fast? Who was there with Aidan? That was my gravest concern in that moment. He couldn't be alone.

LCC: Are you alone?

AD: yup.

LCC: Are you okay being alone?

AD: aside from a fast-growing tumor, you mean?

LCC: . . .

AD: i'll be okay. just need awhile to absorb this.

LCC: Tell me what your doctor said. How worried was he?

AD: she. she was more pissed than worried. this wasn't

supposed to happen on this protocol. ren, i told you i had a bad feeling about this one.

LCC: But there's still stuff they can do, right? I hate not being able to see you. I hate it so much right now.

Aidan, are you there?

Aidan?

AD: skype? please.

He gave me his username again and I clicked on my Skype icon with shaking fingers, moving to the chair by the dining room window for optimum signal. The wait for connection was interminable. My fear of seeing Aidan face-to-face was as keen as the terror of losing him. A battle erupted between my heart and mind—the visceral, desperate need to get as close to him as I could and the cautionary voice that urged restraint and promised greater pain.

Aidan accepted the call. I heard him click on. Saw flashes of a room—ceiling, painting, lamp. And then his camera settled on a face I hadn't seen in twenty-two years. My mind desperately inventoried what it saw. Signs of age. Hollow eyes. Thinner lips. A bandana covering his bald head. But Aidan's face. Aidan's—face.

"Easy there," he said with a sad smirk that took my breath away. "I'm not a ghost yet."

I'd forgotten that he could see me too. I pulled back a little and tried to school my expression into something that wouldn't add my terror to his. "Sorry." I saw myself smile in the small screen embedded in the Skype window. I wondered if he could tell how strained it was. Then the enormity of being able to see him struck me again. I stared.

"Older, huh?" he said.

"But still you."

He seemed to be engaged in the same activity I was. He leaned in, scanning the picture of me on his computer's screen. And despite the death knell of his verdict, I couldn't help but wonder if I looked a mess. I put a hand to my hair.

"Don't," he said.

My own gesture shamed me. "I'm sorry."

He smiled again. "Still you."

"Yeah?"

"The shorter style suits you."

"A case of temporary insanity a couple years back," I said, blushing despite the untenable circumstances. I savored the sight of his face on my screen. Though he'd aged, his eyes held the same depth. His smile the same mischief. His skin was more wrinkled and somehow lived-in, but he was Aidan. My friend.

"Tell me what your doctor said," I prompted.

He nodded and looked away, biting the inside of his lip. When he'd gathered his thoughts, he looked back at me, his gaze just shy of meeting mine, as the camera was above my picture on his screen. Just when it looked like he was about to speak, he leaned back and ran his hands over his face. He seemed older when he leaned in again.

"It's good to see your face, Ren."

Tears blurred my vision. He saw them and smiled that sad smile again. "That's what I've missed," he said.

"Watching me cry?"

His laugh lines deepened. I found them beautiful. "Watching you love me."

Any semblance of composure I'd maintained until then drained out of me. "Tell me what she said," I repeated as tears fell down my face and my throat constricted.

"Aw, Ren. Geez. I'm so glad you're back in my life." He squared his shoulders and sat up a bit straighter. "Doc said we need to go in and clean it out again. She's trying to schedule the surgery as quickly as possible."

"And then more chemo?" I tried to stem my tears, not wanting my distress to add to his.

"She doesn't know. This thing is . . . Nobody knows what works on this kind of tumor."

"But there's more they can try, right?"

He sighed. "I don't know. We've thrown the best stuff at it already, and—"

"And it grew."

"Pea with grape ambitions. I called it."

The enormity of being able to see him struck me again. He sat with his eyes on the screen in front of him and I saw only fatigue in his face, not the paralyzing sadness I'd expected. He'd lived with the reality of his mortality since the diagnosis five months before, and while it was all coming at me so fast that I was reeling, he'd already had time to absorb some of the direness.

I wiped under my eyes, rubbing off the mascara that had run with my tears. "What's in your mind right now?" He seemed lost in thought. It was an expression I remembered well.

"You used to be better at letting a person sit in silence."

"I'm sorry." Age seemed to have increased my impatience.

"No, it's good. It's good. Just feels like we're running out of time too fast to give silence too much space . . ."

I tried to convey hope and optimism with my eyes. It made me feel like a fraud. But he was off in his thoughts again, his gaze unfocused and slightly averted from the screen. I didn't interrupt him this time. I watched him blink and breathe. I tried to still the emotions still rioting in my mind. I watched his face as I had for countless hours as he painted in his parents' shed.

He seemed to snap out of it after a couple of minutes. His expression shifted to matter-of-fact. He cracked his neck from side to side and took a deep breath. "Still there?" he asked a bit sheepishly.

"Still here."

He sat back and crossed his arms, concentration drawing his eyebrows together. "I don't know how to answer your question. If you'd asked me what I was thinking when I first heard the diagnosis, I'd have had no problem. Terror, anxiety, despair, anger—lots of anger. But . . . I don't know anymore."

"Have you told your parents about today?"

"Not yet." He paused again. "I'm really not looking forward to surgery again." There was weariness in his voice.

"Painful?"

He chuckled. "I'm not sure there are strong enough words to describe it. Plus the short-term effects."

"Did you have any last time?"

"Just peripheral vision and balancing stuff. Nothing major. But you never know."

I had to ask. "Do you have it in you to fight some more?"

He considered that for a moment, frowning. "Yeah," he said. "Yeah, I do."

My voice was raspy. "I wish there was something I could do for you . . ."

"I know you do," he said, smiling. "If there's one thing that defines our friendship, it's you wanting to help me."

"Interesting."

"What?"

"I'm not sure I agree with you."

"What—you're going to argue with a guy who's fighting a pea-to-grape tumor?"

"No, I'm going to set him straight."

"All right, lay it on me."

"What defined our friendship—"

"Defines. Present tense."

"Right. What defines our friendship is . . . familiarity."

He looked at me sideways through the screen. "Explain."

"Just—knowing."

"Knowing." He seemed to mull it over for a moment. "Yeah, that's about right."

His gaze grew distant again and I wondered if he was remembering what I was. It was the night before graduation. We'd been out with friends to celebrate, and Aidan had predictably had a little too much to drink. I drove him home in my dad's car and told him I'd see him at the ceremony the next day. I couldn't help myself. Just as he was closing the door, I said, "You know, the one advantage of going to different colleges is that I won't have to come to your rescue every time you get drunk anymore." He gave me a look. "Maybe you'll find yourself a cute little blonde to do the honors and call it an upgrade. Tell her good luck from me, okay?" I motioned for him to close the door and drove away.

I should have known that I'd be woken by the sound of stones hitting my bedroom window a few hours later. I didn't take the time to look outside and confirm that it was him. That familiarity. I just knew.

My mom poked her head out of their bedroom as I headed downstairs. "Aidan again?" she asked. I guess she knew too.

He was waiting by the garage door when I stepped out in my pajamas with a blanket wrapped around my shoulders. "I brought you something," he said. He seemed calm. Determined.

"What are you doing here, Aidan?"

He turned and headed back down the lane, toward the car his grandfather had loaned him for most of his senior year. I followed him in the dull light of a full moon. He opened the back door and pulled out a fourteen-by-eighteen canvas, holding it with its back to me. I looked at him suspiciously, wondering what kind of manipulation would follow. He knew my soft spot was his art.

"Can we go sit on your mom's bench?" he asked.

"I . . ." Suspicion dueled with curiosity. "Sure."

He seemed calm as we walked around the house and down my mom's rose-lined path to the bench under a maple tree. He sat us down and propped the painting, still averted, against his knee.

"What's going on here, Aidan?"

"I'm sorry about prom night," he said. There was a seriousness and sincerity about him that I'd seldom seen before.

I laughed. "Is that what this is about? That was weeks ago. I don't care about prom night."

"I do." He said it forcefully. "I shouldn't have taken you to prom and spent the night making passes at Darcy."

"It's not like I expected you to have eyes only for me."

Those eyes were riveted to mine with a frightening intensity. "We're graduating tomorrow."

"I'm aware."

"And my parents are moving to Pennsylvania."

"Again—aware."

"And you're—"

"Aidan."

He squeezed my hand. "Listen to me."

There was something so purposeful in his gaze that I complied, curiosity and alarm battling in my mind.

"I've been working on this," he said. "And I want you to have it as a grad present. Or something."

He turned the painting around and handed it to me. I held it up to catch the light from the full moon. Something clicked in my mind. I knew.

He said, "It's called *Kindred*."

Though it was far from dawn, the light of the moon illuminated a painting of such soul and clarity that it took my breath away. A woman's hand rested palm-down on the surface of a multihued liquid. His use of reflection and depth was stunning, as if a universe of northern lights hovered above the painting, its aura captured in the shadow play across the surface. The hand barely skimmed the surface, but fragments of the liquid's color seemed to have seeped over the skin, coloring it gradually from fingertips upward. The symbolism was arresting. He had painted with such conviction that the piece was nearly three-dimensional, natural lines and nuances exchanged for brash strokes and hues charged with meaning.

He'd never painted anything more powerful.

We'd decided long ago that I'd never ask him to explain his work. As an artist, he valued the mystery of audience interpretation. But on this night, he dispensed with our agreement.

"You're more than the girl who drives me home when I'm half-sloshed," he said as I contemplated his painting. The intensity of his voice startled me. I looked from the suspended, painted hand to him and saw something in his face that made my breath catch. He went on before I could say anything, his eyes averted. "I know you think you're only good for rescuing me or talking me down when I get stupid or telling me I'm good at art."

"Well, I do have some experience with—"

"Is that really all you think this is?"

I wasn't sure what to say. I wasn't sure what to think either. I knew our friendship was more than a series of rescues and exhortations. It was rich with words and shared passions, saturated with a minutia of life that somehow took on substance and value when we experienced it together. He was the first person I wanted to talk to when something went right or wrong. His dizzying trajectory seemed to keep mine straighter. He knew me with a fidelity and lucidity that were rare and intimate.

"No," I said. "It's more than that." I felt the next day's milestone and its implications settling over me.

"This," he said, laying his painting on the ground and jutting his chin toward it, "is what this feels like to me."

I searched the dimly lit surface for the meaning he'd infused into each ridge and hue.

"You calm me," he said. "And you . . . I don't know . . . you make me think twice. And I don't know if I've ever done anything for you, but . . . I hope it would be this." He motioned at the color filtering over the skin in the painting. "I'd like to think I brought you something—you know—colorful?" What had started as a statement had ended in a question.

He grabbed my hand where it lay in my lap and held it firmly. I looked into his face, unsure and disconcerted. The night was warm. The silence was complicit.

"I think I love you," the earnest boy in front of me said. And I believed him. I knew I loved him too.

"Aidan," I said, prepared to temper his fervor with a dose of reality.

He reached an arm along the back of the bench and leaned in, his ardor beautiful under the soft light of the moon. "I don't want to lose this," he said. He brushed a hand against my face and wove his fingers into my hair. And everything in me seemed to sway. I wanted to lean and wrap and rest. I shook my head, denying his plea and my compulsion to accept it. "Aidan. This is . . ."

"I've known since the night in your dad's garage," he said. I stared wide-eyed, realizing in that instant that I had too.

I felt completion when he kissed me. A void filled and sealed. A yearning sated. My arms wove around his neck as we strained toward each other, our breaths ragged with desire and despair. We slipped off the bench and into the damp grass, rendered mindless by an ache ten years growing. Sacrilege and sacrament wrapped in urgent need.

I'd lost my grip on time and reality when Aidan pulled back and said, "Let's ditch college." He didn't realize as the words came out of his mouth how irrevocably they would change our lives.

They reached me through a fevered haze, and I think I felt their warning before my mind could register it. "What?" He'd applied and been accepted. He was leaving in two days to work a summer job on campus and save up for his tuition.

"Let's ditch college." His face was luminous with adventure. "Go to New York. Get a studio. I'll paint, you'll write." He framed my face in his hands. "Ren—let's do this!"

I pushed into a sitting position and turned on him. "What?"

"You and me." He reached for the painting and turned it toward me. "You and me, Ren. I told you—I love you."

I shook my head, finally understanding where this was going. "Aidan—I can't ditch college."

"You're a writer, Ren. Just write."

"I—"

I saw his smile dim a little. As I searched his face, I realized this was about more than his feelings for me. This was about his fear of starting fresh, about losing the universe he'd grown up in, and about wanting to hold on to the one person who'd consistently been a source of reason and support. I loved him. I couldn't remember a time when I hadn't. But I couldn't dispel the certainty that Aidan's wild idea, as intoxicating as it was, was neither viable nor sustainable. I wanted the dream as desperately as I feared it. It was my love for Aidan that made me reject it.

"I can't go to New York with you and just . . . write."

"Why not?"

"Because I'm eighteen. Because *we're* eighteen."

"College sucks."

"You haven't tried it." I heard the firm, persuasive tone I'd so often used to talk him down from far-fetched plans. Whatever the nature of the love he felt for me, this plan was little more than license to quit—permission not to attempt something he wasn't sure he could pull off. I would not be his escape from a future he couldn't yet imagine.

With the taste of his lips still on mine and the warmth of physical hunger still heavy in my limbs, I saw with devastating clarity the only choice I had to make. "You have to go to college," I said, the hardness in my voice masking my staggering loss.

"Ren . . ."

I tried to sound unequivocal as I sealed our fate. "We're not ditching college. We're not going to New York. You're starting your job in two days, and I'm doing exactly what I've been planning on for the past few months."

His expression shifted from passionate to distraught in an instant. "But . . ." I saw disbelief hollow out his gaze. He pointed at the bench where we'd sat minutes before. "But—we just . . . we said we—"

"You did," I said. I felt an intimate, impossible hope shatter. "*You* said it, Aidan. I didn't."

As my love for him screamed across my nerves and synapses in a physical ache, I watched him stand, pick up the painting, and walk away.

I grieved as graduation unfolded without him there. I grieved on the day I knew he left for college. I grieved as my new life began far from the place that had sheltered the simple richness of our love. I grieved, and then I could no more.

"Graduation?" Aidan asked from his townhouse in Pennsylvania.

I sat in Nepal and met his knowing gaze. "Graduation," I confirmed.

"You were a cruel, cruel woman, Lauren Clark."

"Lauren Coventry."

He looked up, startled. "Lauren Coventry," he repeated. He leaned forward and propped his elbows on the table where his laptop lay, rubbing his forehead with one hand.

"Headache?"

"Brutal. But it'll pass."

"Do you have medication you can take?"

He ignored my question. "You did the right thing all those years ago."

"I don't know . . ."

"You broke my heart—there's no denying that—but you did the right thing."

"I spent months going back over that night. I could have done things differently. I could have—should have—said things better."

He raised an eyebrow. "Remember me? I wouldn't have heard anything short of a sledgehammer."

I felt tears brimming in my eyes again. "I hurt you, Aidan. I shouldn't have hurt you."

He leaned in closer, until only his eyes and the top of his head were framed in the Skype window. "You did the right thing. And I think I loved you all the more for it."

I looked into the tired, haunted eyes of a man who faced death with solemn lucidity, and I felt his courage bathing me. "I love you too," I said with every ounce of conviction I should have used on our graduation night.

A flash of red in the doorway caught my eye. Ryan stood there, his jaw set.

"Ryan." Guilt flooded me. I blotted my tears and tried for a disapproving voice. "What are you doing home so late?" It sounded phony and scared even to my ears.

The look he gave me chilled me. "Who's that?" he asked.

I scrambled for an answer that would satisfy him. "My friend Aidan in the States. Come around here and say hi to him."

He stared a moment more, then swiveled and went up to his room.

"Ryan?" Aidan asked from Pennsylvania.

"I don't know how he got in here without me hearing him."

"Probably trying to sneak in so he wouldn't get in trouble."

My mind reeled. What had he heard? What had he assumed?

"Ren?"

I looked at Aidan, torn between the friend battling cancer and the son who may have heard too much and concluded something awful. "You have to go," he said.

"I do. Ryan is—"

"Go take care of things."

"I'm sorry . . ."

"Don't be. It's been good seeing you."

I leaned in, reluctant to hang up and eager to get upstairs. "You're going to get through this, Aidan. You'll have your surgery, they'll take it out, you'll try some new protocol. You're going to make it through this. I believe it."

He smiled in a way that made me really doubt for the first time.

"Talk soon," he said. Then he hung up.

fourteen

IT TOOK ME SEVERAL MINUTES TO GATHER MY THOUGHTS. I sat with my laptop closed and tried to sort through the fears and guilt, seeking an obvious path forward and finding none.

I heard no response when I knocked on Ryan's door. When I stepped inside, I found him under his fleece blanket, earbuds in, facing the wall. I stood there for a while, watching the light from the candle next to his bed flicker across the ceiling. Listening to the hiss of trebles escaping from his iPod. Wondering what misinterpretations and accusation filled his thirteen-year-old mind. I didn't know what to say and feared what might happen if I spoke.

Ryan must have sensed my presence. He twisted around and looked over his shoulder. When he saw me standing near the door, he turned back to the wall and pulled his blanket up higher. I was his mother—but the inroads the status should have granted me had dried up long ago. I had no idea how to communicate with him. So I went and sat on the edge of his bed, hoping, praying another stilted prayer that the right words would come to me. Ryan scooted away and shrugged off the hand I laid on his shoulder.

"Ryan."

No response.

"Ryan." More firmly.

He tried to stop me as I pulled one of the earphones out of his ear. "Mom!"

Unable to formulate the thoughts I needed to express, I fell back on an old standard and kicked myself for it the moment the words were out of my mouth. "Where were you tonight?"

He turned just enough that I could see the defiance on his face. I wanted to grovel for his understanding. The weakness of it stunned me. I buffered my emotions with an internal pep talk about the conversation Ryan had interrupted. Regardless of what he thought he'd heard, there was nothing wrong about Skyping with an old friend who was facing a grave illness. That's what I clung to as I stared into the abyss that separated me from my son.

"I don't know what you think you heard when you came in," I said quietly. He huddled deeper into his blanket. "I was talking to someone I've known since I was your age." I hated that I was making excuses to my son. "He's sick, Ryan. He has cancer. And he got some bad news today. We were talking about that when you came in."

"You weren't just talking." His voice was muffled by his blanket.

"Yes, we were."

He turned angrily toward me. "You told him you loved him," he snapped. "I heard you!"

I resisted the impulse to chastise him about his attitude and his tone. I didn't have the upper hand in this conversation—not while Ryan was imagining the worst based on a few snippets of a longer conversation. "What you heard is . . ." I didn't know where to begin. "Ryan, what you heard was the tail end of a call between two old friends."

"I saw your face, Mom!"

"I . . . What do you mean?"

His expression turned venomous as he remembered. "What about Dad? Are you going to tell Dad?"

I was appalled. "Ryan, there's nothing to tell him. You're completely misinterpreting—" I realized I needed to say the words. "If you think I'm having some kind of illicit relationship—"

"Shut up, Mom!" He pushed away from me, up against the wall on the other side of his mattress. "You're lying. I know you're lying!"

"Ryan!" The hardness in my voice was more about my guilt than about his lashing out.

"All you've done is lie! Ever since . . ." His chin began to quiver.

"Ryan . . ." My breath caught on the sob I was trying to repress. "What are you—ever since what?"

Something came across his face then—something so foreign it stunned me into silence. His eyes were suddenly clear and meeting mine with a directness that frightened me. He sat up, his back to the wall and his knees drawn up in front of him. "Get out of my room, Mom."

"Ryan—"

"No!" His face was flushed but his eyes—my son's eyes—were brutally cold. "You're a liar. A cheating liar! Calling this guy and telling him that you . . . That's gross, Mom! It's disgusting!" The words hit me like a physical blow. I thought I saw a shimmer of tears in his eyes right before he lay down, drew the blanket up again, and turned back toward the wall. "Leave me alone."

"Ryan . . ."

"Get out of my room!"

He lay immobile. I sat on the edge of his hard mattress wondering what I could say that would debunk whatever sordid conclusions he'd reached. I sat until I realized my arguments would only exacerbate the scenarios in his mind. I stayed until my legs could carry my weight again, until his breathing slowed and eased. His body relaxed. He turned and burrowed his face into his pillow.

≈

I didn't want to log in the next morning. I'd slept fitfully and didn't want new messages to further muddy the conflicts in my mind, but I needed to know that Aidan was okay. If the quiet, undistracted hours of *my* nights led to morbid thinking, I couldn't imagine how rife with fear they'd be for him.

I fought the urge to take the laptop somewhere private—unwilling to capitulate to the tinges of guilt that hovered on the edge of my consciousness. I'd spent the night begging God for peace and found myself still caged by nagging discomfort. The water came on upstairs. Ryan was in the shower. I opened the laptop on the kitchen island and logged on.

> i've got to tell you, ren, the last time i saw that kind of look on your face was when we got caught barefoot in your mom's big blue storage container. probably didn't help that we were wading around ankle-deep in grapes we'd spent your entire allowance buying. kids, right? and too many episodes of 'i love lucy' . . .
>
> sigh. that look worried me a bit. not sure how to say this, so i'll just blurt it: if this is harming you in any way . . . ren, i don't want you to be dragged into something that's uncomfortable just because the internet exists and i've got a thing in my brain.
>
> i'm being as serious as i know how to be right now. i'm still the stupid kid you knew in a lot of ways, but i hope—i *hope*—i've shed some of my trademark

self-absorption in all these years. you know, that breed
of stupidity that made it impossible for me to consider
that what was fun for me might not be good for you. like
turning seven pounds of grapes into homemade 'wine' so
we could sell it to our fourth grade friends. or ditching
college to run off with our art.

so. say the word. even if this is where our reconnecting ends—it's been good enough to make me feel . . . i
don't know . . . hemmed. does that make sense? the ragged parts and random pieces wrapped and sealed. there's
comfort in that.

i finally got off my butt after i hung up with you and
wandered over to the parents' place. i think they had a
feeling about this scan too. it hit them pretty hard, but
i don't think they were surprised. do enough internet
rescarch about glioblastoma and you'll come away with
pretty low expectations.

my mom ranted a bit about me going into the city
alone for this kind of thing. you know how she is. ranting
is her love language. my dad smacked me on the shoulder
and offered me a beer. we talked about my options. mom
teared up a couple times and dad gave her the usual look.
they're doing the best they can.

i assume i'll hear from scheduling tomorrow. they
went ahead and did what lab work they could when i was
there, so it should be pretty straightforward. we like to
say the second time is easier, but that's not true with getting your skull cracked open. and saying good-bye. not
sure that gets any easier either.

gotta get to work. insurance, as usual, is not wanting
to cover the next surgery. it's been an upward battle since
labor day's big surprise. i guess they've googled it too. a

forty-year-old in the fifth month of a three-to-six-month prognosis doesn't seem like a very good investment—even to me. and i've never been very good with numbers. so . . . calls to make. forms to fill out. advocates to contact again. i'd say it's a major headache but that's a bit redundant, considering.

don't harm yourself or your family for me, ren. stay close if you can. (please.) but i've got weeks and you've got years. this recovering narcissist wants you to know that it's okay. love the ones you're with, right? and if this hinders that . . .

i hope you're sleeping as i write. seeing your face and hearing your voice was—no words. i know you know.

still.

I knew he'd logged off long before, but I answered quickly anyway.

I'm waiting for Ryan to come down for breakfast now. Thank you for the message I found minutes ago. I know your concern is real. So is mine. I feel torn between conflicting needs and loyalties. All good—all essential—but perhaps not intended to inhabit a person all at once. I'm grappling with it, but not willing to let you go. Be assured of that, Aidan. There is an urgency to this reconnecting that stuns me. It's a good and a horrible thing. And vital somehow. So I'm not going anywhere. Just processing and measuring and not yet concluding. Part of me thinks there will be plenty of time for that later.

Tell me when you have any news, okay? And everything else. Tell me that too.

I'll check for you later.

I braced myself as the sound of Ryan's slippered feet reached me from the stairs. I got the baked oatmeal out of the fridge for him and was reaching for the yogurt when I heard him go out the front door.

"Ryan?" He was already down the steps and headed for the gate. I went after him. "Ryan!"

He pulled his bicycle out of the shed without looking around, and I moved past him to block his exit through the gate. "Ryan."

He stood there holding his bike, looking away, chin jutted out, waiting for me to allow him to pass. I reached for one end of his handlebar and shook it. "Look at me, Ryan."

He raised dull eyes.

"Tell me what you think you heard last night."

"I don't want to." He looked away again.

Sounding for all the world like someone who had something to hide, I said very slowly, "It's not what you think you heard."

"Okay." There was no conviction in his voice.

"Do you understand me? He's a friend from home."

"Can I go now?"

"We need to talk about this, Ryan!"

"I'm going to be late for tutoring with Miss Moore." He shoved past me and I watched him go. He opened the gate, pushed his bike out ahead of him, then disappeared from sight.

I sat on the ground right where I'd been standing. Muffin pranced around me, thinking it was time to play. I let my eyes skim over this place that had been our home for over two years. The house with its small, barred windows and gray paint. The garden with its wide array of barely living plants. The birds whose communications skills put ours to shame. All of us. It wasn't just Ryan who had gone virtually mute in recent months. Sam and I still talked, but our words rang hollow with lowered expectations and prejudged conclusions.

And into the dearth of meaning had come a vestige from the past, a man whose face-off with death had lent his waning strength more vitality than the three of us together could muster. I wondered about the timing of his reentry into my universe. I'd been so programmed all my life to see God's hand in coincidences that I wanted to assign this to him too. Could the random conjunction of Aidan's cancer and Sullivan introducing me to Facebook be anything less than miraculous? And what if I hadn't sought her out three years ago in an effort to get the family to Nepal? What if we'd never decided to make the move? Could Aidan have found me if I hadn't found Sullivan?

My mind reeled with the mysteries that orbited around a central question mark. My conscience demanded answers, exhausted by my studious avoidance of considerations like rightness and repercussions. In a sense, I'd lived the days since that first Facebook message just as Aidan had lived the first three decades of his life: in determined oblivion. And probably, as he had, with a high risk of regret.

I scratched Muffin's head and stood, walking back toward a house that felt like solitary confinement. I'd get dressed, give Suman instructions, head off to school, be a dutiful teacher, then head home and hope for signs of life from Ryan. I'd perform my rituals with the passivity of someone who has already given up. And into that blandness would come thoughts of Aidan—proof that I had been alive before this pitiful stranding.

Reminders that I wasn't dead from a man who would be soon.

The return from language school took longer than usual, an accident on the outskirts of the city having forced my bus to take an alternate route. I pushed through the gate and greeted the dog, eager to get to my laptop.

Then I looked up and found Sam sitting on the porch.

"Sam?" He'd only been gone two days. I felt a trickle of dread run down my spine. "Has something happened?" He came down the steps toward me. "Ryan. Is it Ryan?"

He held up both hands. "Honey—no. Nothing's wrong."

His arms came around me and held me close. "What are you doing back so soon?"

"I just decided to come home."

I leaned back. "But . . . your trip."

"Prakash is going on without me." He kissed me, I thought, with inordinate fervor.

"You just . . . came back?"

He cocked his head and gave me a look, his arms still around me and his face close. "I'm not sure whether you're surprised or disappointed."

"Surprised," I said, forcing a smile. "Just surprised."

He kept his arm around me as we walked into the house. "I've rescheduled our Nagarkot trip for this weekend—just you and me. We leave on Friday and get back on Sunday night. Is that okay?"

My thoughts should have been on the luxury of getting away. Instead, they were on Aidan. Two days before we left. Three days gone.

"This all seems a little rash," I said. I tried to lighten the comment by adding, "I haven't ever known you to be an overly spontaneous person."

He cringed a little. "Thank you?"

I stared at him as he poured some coffee from the pot he'd made and handed it to me. "What's going on, Sam?"

"I told you."

He was pouring himself a cup. I laid a hand on his arm to get his attention. "This isn't like you."

"Again," he said, putting the pot down, "I'm not sure if you sound surprised or disappointed."

"It's just—"

"Not like me. So you've said."

He moved into the living room and I followed. His backpack was just inside the door, his jacket draped over the back of the couch. He had reentered my life eighteen days before he was supposed to and my world felt off-kilter. He sat and put his mug on the coffee table, and I saw something that looked like confusion and determination flash across his face. "Here's what happened."

I sat in the middle of the couch and tried not to let my eyes linger too long on the laptop charging in the dining room.

Sam steepled his fingers and pressed his lips together, sure signs that he was measuring his words. "So . . . I got as far as Ghorahi. Met up with Prakash there and hopped on the bus to Nepalgunj. And I had this—I don't know what to call it." He looked genuinely bewildered. "It felt like a decision had already been made and I was just then hearing about it. I . . . I had to come home." He shook his head.

"You just . . . had to?"

He frowned. "I didn't want to. You know me—all I could think of was getting to the village, but then this . . . thought— urge—whatever it is struck me so strongly . . ."

"An urge?"

Sam shook his head in bewilderment again. "That's what it felt like," he said. "So—I got off the bus, told Prakash to go on without me, explained that I needed to head home, and rode another bus back to Kathmandu. Then you walked through the gate and made me wonder if I'd gotten the message wrong." He smiled.

"This is . . . this is pretty revolutionary, Sam."

"I know!" he agreed, a perplexed look on his face.

"Next thing we know, you'll be taking a vacation."

"This weekend," he said. "Nagarkot."

"Right!" I smiled despite the tension building in my mind. He smiled too. We sat across from each other and smiled. He was home. He'd moved up our trip. It all felt foreign.

This was the point at which I'd normally ask him about his three weeks away. But he'd only been gone two days and had spent those on a bus. It was also the point where he'd usually ask me how Ryan was doing. I cringed at the thought. Instead, we talked about our upcoming trip to the mountains and the e-mails I'd received. We talked about the weather and construction delays with the gym at Ryan's school.

I got up to heat supper, and Sam went upstairs to unpack. I stood in the kitchen, disoriented.

Sam came downstairs when he heard Ryan pushing his bike through the gate. He seemed as surprised as I'd been to see his dad standing on the porch as he walked up. He didn't sound like it, though, when he said, "What are you doing here?" That bored tone grated.

"That's what your mom said."

From inside the house, I saw Ryan stop short. "I bet."

Sam gave him a hug, which Ryan visibly resisted. "I decided not to do the trip this time. We'll watch your game tomorrow night, then Mom and I are going away for the weekend."

"Whatever," Ryan said.

"Any new grades today?" Sam called to Ryan's retreating back.

"Nope." He walked right past me on his way to the bathroom, neither looking at me nor speaking to me when I said hi to him.

"Ryan, say hi to your mother," Sam instructed in his firm daddy-voice.

Ryan went into the bathroom and locked the door.

"Ryan."

"Let him be," I said. "We'll figure it out later." I had a feeling we wouldn't.

I removed my laptop from the table and laid it on a shelf in the kitchen. My hand lingered on it—longing. When the bathroom door opened, I said, "Ryan, can you set the table?" He turned and walked upstairs. Sam wasn't paying attention. He was reading the news on his laptop in the living room, looking more relaxed and at ease than he'd been in a long while.

I squared my shoulders and breathed a prayer. *Please, God. Please.*

I was fairly sure he didn't hear it.

i'm scared, ren. that's the bottom line. been trying to focus on making the calls and filling out the online forms, but the only clear thing in my mind is this voice saying, 'this is it, dennison. over and out.' it's never been this strong before—the gut feeling that i'm staring at my ending.

i try to control the images that rush my defenses . . . but i never know they're coming until they're there. i see myself in a hospital bed as my brain shuts down. seizures. loss of speech and sight. crapping myself. thrashing. i see my parents next to me while nurses whisper that it's almost over. in the good scenarios, i'm unconscious and unaware. but in others, i can see and hear everything. i'm trying to scream or speak or let them know somehow that i'm still in there, but they don't know and there's nothing i can do.

it's hard to put your mind to medical forms when you're envisioning death. not some far-off, when-i'm-old last breath. one that could happen next month, next week, or in a minute. i've got to tell you there are moments when i just want to yell. scream. wasting energy i should be sparing on telling death that i'm not ready. i haven't said a whole lot of 'why me?' since this all started, but ren . . . why me? i'm forty. and, god, i don't want to die . . . then i think why not? and i try to comfort myself with ridiculous attempts at quantifying things. at least no wife will be losing a husband when i die, right? at least no children will have to go on living without a father. it would be so much worse if i had people who depended on me, but since i'm single and childless . . . it's less of a tragedy, right?

but it's my life. it's my life, damn it. and call me selfish, but i just don't want it to be over. i've never been able to imagine who i'd be past forty. felt like a downhill kind of ride from there on. but i'd give a lot right now to make it to forty-one. fifty's out—i'm not an idiot. but forty-one? c'mon, god, i say. i'll be a good little boy if you give me just a little bit longer.

and that part of me that always distrusted him thinks, 'that's what you're getting, buddy. a little bit longer.' truth is, i do want to see fifty. i want to learn to snowboard. i want to take a hot air balloon ride over the smoky mountains at sunset. i want to make it to france and sit in a quaint little bakery with a beret on my head and a croissant in my hand. and you. i want you to be there too. maid costume optional.

i know. seize the day, right? be happy for each sunrise. call me greedy, but i'm not satisfied with ten. or fifty. or five hundred . . . and then i ask myself how many would be enough.

sorry to dump on you. i just need somebody to know that i'm not this heroic optimist facing my demise with courage and serenity. i'm freaked out, ren. and, geez, i'm sad. sad is a weak word for it, but i know you'll understand.

and amid the bleak, dark hues of the morbid painting in my mind, you waft in like a dancing shimmer of gold. just as you did when i thought i was immortal all those years ago. i don't know if i'll be alive tomorrow. or the day after. but i know that finding you again has been . . . resurrecting. thank you for staying close.

I read Aidan's message twice. I begged for a miracle. I begged for more time. And I ranted against the distance and the lost years and the inevitability of all he dreaded. I had never yearned more powerfully to be in another place. To wrap his terror in my faith. To lay my hope over his fear.

Thank you. For your honesty and your emotions. I'm heartbroken and wanting so badly—so desperately—to be close. Is there anyone there you can go to when things get so dark? Any flesh-and-blood person who can receive your pain? How I wish it could be me . . .

It's nearly midnight here. The day has been . . . surprising. It's completely irrelevant in light of what you're experiencing, but it might affect my ability to communicate with you, so I guess you need to know. Sam came home. For the first time in our years here, he cut short a trip and returned to Kathmandu. I found him waiting for me when I got back from Bhaktapur. No reason. He just . . . I don't know . . . felt the urge. Just writing the words feels odd. So unlike him. But he's home—that's the bottom line. He went up to bed a little while ago to read and catch up on some sleep.

I've got to tell you that walking by this laptop when I don't have time to get on is a delicate form of torture. I find myself calculating the time of day in Pennsylvania, imagining what you're doing and wondering how you're processing this ache.

I don't know when you'll see this . . .

AD: well, if this is any indication . . .

LCC: Aidan.

AD: fancy meeting you here.

LCC: How are you feeling?

AD: you mean after the mildly macabre message i sent earlier?

LCC: Yes.

AD: i've got to tell you, ren. if there were any exit off this ride other than death, i'd take it.

I strained for something positive to write. Something healing or redemptive. I thought of sayings that were too trite and of song lyrics that were too sappy. I scanned the comfort-verses in my memory and found none that would appease Aidan's sober grasp of reality. My inability to help felt like a flaw.

AD: i know what you're doing.

LCC: I'm not doing anything.

AD: you're beating yourself up for not having anything to say.

LCC: Maybe.

AD: go ahead and admit it, ren. i'm the boy genius who can read your mind from seven thousand miles away.

LCC: Seven thousand?

AD: i may or may not have looked it up . . .

LCC: Boy genius indeed.

AD: i don't expect you to make this go away, you know.

LCC: The distance?

AD: the cancer. or whatever's going on with me. i don't write those things to you because you're supposed to fix it. i know what this is.

LCC: I know you do.

AD: so if i tell you i'm struggling, don't twist yourself into a pretzel trying to make it better. knowing that you know is good enough.

LCC: Okay. But you know I'll still try, right?

AD: knock yourself out. can you skype?

LCC: Maybe not tonight?

AD: no lipstick necessary.

LCC: It's not that. I think I should tell Sam that we're communicating before he stumbles on us having a Skype conversation.

AD: like ryan?

LCC: Still need to deal with that too.

AD: see how quickly i revert to being a selfish jackass? i meant what i wrote, ren. if this is harmful to you or to your family . . .

LCC: Hush. I'm dealing with it.

AD: such an attitude.

LCC: Is your head still hurting?

AD: not as much as it will be in a few days. got the call. surgery's on monday.

LCC: That's fast. Were you able to make some headway with insurance?

AD: still working at it. but . . . they can't collect from a dead man, right?

LCC: No, but they will if you live all those years I'm predicting! There's a guy in Oregon who's made it fifteen years!

AD: look who's googling now. my doc is on the insurance snafu. she's got a few strings she can pull with my hmo.

LCC: I'm praying, Aidan. For all of this.

AD: prayer. i'm still wrestling with that one.

LCC: Just took me several seconds to figure out how to answer that. Bottom line: so am I.

AD: listen, i'm willing to throw all i've got at this. don't get the prayer vs. medical thing, but that's not stopping me.

LCC: It made more sense to me a few years ago. Before . . . before a lot.

AD: speaking of a lot, sam's home, huh?

LCC: Yes.

AD: and you're . . . ?

LCC: I'm not really sure, actually. I guess I'd gotten more used to our three-week separations than I realized. It all feels a little off-kilter right now.

AD: you'll figure it out.

LCC: Your confidence in me is daunting.

AD: just poured myself a bit of jack daniel's. you should be here.

LCC: Tell me you're not going to light up a cigarette too.

AD: you know me so well.

LCC: Aidan.

AD: lauren. do the math.

LCC: Got it.

We chatted for a few minutes more before the awkward business of signing off. He assured me he was doing okay and I assured him I was praying. Then the messiness of my life overwhelmed me. I sat at the dining room table and let the lights and shadows whisper through my mind. Ryan, Aidan, and Sam. Anger, fear, and strength. Aidan would know how to weave them into art. All I could do was contemplate how completely they'd swirled into impossibility.

fifteen

IT SEEMED FITTING THAT A STORM BREWED ABOVE Kathmandu on the day we left for Nagarkot. The sky turned to roiling slate, and a cloak of atmospheric pressure hung heavy over the city.

Inside our home, a precarious life-as-usual teetered. I knew the faintest of emotional shoves would topple it altogether. I spent every waking moment trying to manage dynamics and predict outcomes, all while my mind and heart reeled from the life-and-death face-off playing out on another continent.

I snuck upstairs with the laptop when I could, confronting guilt with compassion. Aidan needed me. Aidan was dying. I would not walk away from him. I knew I had to explain the situation to Sam, but in every dry run I'd conducted in my mind, the words had come out wrong, more indictments than rationales.

Ryan continued to live around me. The darkening of his countenance was a nearly tangible force. His usual frustrated frowns had turned to glares. His disinterest had become distaste. His sullen words had been replaced by acidic, mono-syllabic retorts. His entire demeanor spoke of emotions stretched too thin.

I knew I should address the untenable tension—try again to release Ryan from the assumptions stooping his shoulders and hardening his expression—but I didn't know how to contradict his conclusions. I didn't know if I honestly could. I realized it was a fear of my own reality that kept me from confronting Ryan's.

As we walked away from the soccer field after his game, heading home, Sam laid his hand on Ryan's shoulder to give it a congratulatory squeeze. He flung it off immediately, twisting out from under it.

"Ryan—" Sam began, bewildered.

"Leave me alone!" Ryan yelled, sprinting off in the direction of our house.

"What's gotten into him?" Sam stopped and stared at the spot where Ryan had veered off the street to take his usual short-cut through a parking lot.

"He's been on edge," I said.

"Any idea why?"

It was an open door to a conversation I didn't want to have. "I don't know," I said, panicking. "Maybe something going on at school? Give it a couple days. It will probably blow over. Usually does."

"Well, it had better blow over quickly, whatever it is, or there will be consequences." Sam shook his head and resumed walking. "How long until he's out of his teen years?" He smirked.

"And you only get to live with this for a few days out of the month." I wondered if he could hear the sarcasm souring my words.

"I'll talk to him. This isn't acceptable behavior."

I stifled a retort about despair's tendency to stymie civility. "Give him a little longer," I suggested, though I knew Ryan needed much more than that.

For the first time since the light had gone out of Ryan's spirit, I found myself reassured by his silence. As long as he wasn't talking . . . But in those moments when Aidan drifted just beyond the center of my concerns, in those brief instants when I could see with a little more perspective, I felt the broadening distance between Ryan and me like the evisceration of my motherhood. I wondered how many causes one child could be sacrificed to. And I berated myself for becoming one of his tormentors.

Sam had grown increasingly bothered by the tension between Ryan and me. I saw the frowns that crossed his face when he didn't realize I was watching. He'd begin to scold Ryan for ignoring or disobeying, but I'd stop his diatribe with a glance or a hand on his arm, assuring him that it would pass. I wasn't sure what casualties it would take with it when it did.

"Come in here, Ryan," Sam said on the evening before we left for Nagarkot. We were cleaning up from dinner, and Ryan was on his way to his bedroom with a stack of textbooks under his arm.

He paused at the base of the stairs. "Why?"

"Because I asked you to."

"I have homework." His head was lowered. He didn't even bother to turn toward the kitchen.

Sam put his towel down and took a step toward Ryan. "Look at me when I'm speaking to you, son."

He looked around at his dad without moving an inch more than he had to. "Happy?"

I stepped in. "Ryan . . ."

Sam put up a hand. "You need to smarten up, young man. I've had enough of your attitude."

"Yeah?" He flashed his dad a challenging half smile.

Sam's hands went to his hips. "What has gotten into you?"

"Oh, I don't know," Ryan said in a voice so devoid of respect or remorse that I barely recognized it. I felt fear seeping into my blood as I waited for the words he'd utter next. He looked right at me, then he looked at Sam. I braced myself. "Maybe I just don't give a crap anymore." He turned to climb the stairs as relief weakened my knees.

"Ryan!" Sam barked.

He kept climbing.

"Ryan, get back down here this minute!"

He stopped at the landing. "What, so you can lecture me? Saint Sam and his stupid sermons? I'm done with those, *Dad*."

"Ryan Coventry, if you don't—" He took a step toward the stairs.

I grabbed his arm. "Let him go, Sam."

He looked at me dumbfounded. "I will not let him go." He squared his shoulders. "I have never—"

"We're going away tomorrow." I moved to stand between him and the stairs, feeling the urgency of that moment like an electrical current. "Let him cool off a bit. Maybe a few days away from us will do him good. Please, Sam." I squeezed his arm and tried to insert myself into his frame of vision. "Don't get into this before our trip. It can wait. Can't it?"

He pursed his lips and thought for a moment. "No. This needs to be dealt with now."

He tried to move past me, but I wouldn't let him. "Please, Sam." Unexpected tears flooded my eyes. Tears of fear. Tears of guilt. Tears of anger. Tears of helplessness. "Can we please not do this tonight? Please. I don't want to leave for Nagarkot in the middle of a crisis." I swiped at a tear on my cheek. "Please? Sam. Let's not make this worse than it already is tonight."

He frowned at me. "Lauren . . ."

"Please."

Sam stared long and hard. I could tell he was torn. He'd never been one to put off confrontations. He liked to lance the abscess and move on. But this particular abscess threatened my world in too many ways to address it just yet. After a moment, he let out a long sigh and covered my hand where it still lay on his arm. "Okay," he said reluctantly, as if the concession were costing him dearly. "Fine, we'll wait until we're back." He looked at me questioningly. "Are you okay? You're . . . are you okay?"

"I'm fine, Sam. Just . . . just a little tired."

Sam went upstairs as I sank onto the bottom step. I heard him stop outside Ryan's room and knock, then try the doorknob. "Can you open the door?"

"I'm doing homework."

I could almost feel Sam's frustration pouring down the stairs to where I sat. I heard the hiss of his breath being released. "We're going to talk about this, son. This behavior is not okay. Not in this home. So when your mother and I get back from Nagarkot, you'd better be prepared to tell me what's going on. You hear me?" There was no sound from Ryan's bedroom. "You hear me, Ryan?"

"Okay!" It was an exasperated agreement. But it ended a conversation whose continuation I dreaded.

When Sam tried to raise the topic of our son as we were getting ready for bed that night, I asked him if we could wait until Sunday evening to discuss it. I told him I needed the time to pray for guidance and shrank away from the guilt that followed my excuse. What I wanted was to go back and undo the myriad decisions and misguided actions that had brought our family to its knees. What I wanted was a life in which covenants were buoyed with freedom, not anchored to servitude. What I wanted was a way out.

I knew there was none.

The first boom of thunder shook the foundations of the city around three, just as I was zipping our suitcase shut. I didn't want to go. I worried that something would happen to Aidan while I was out of touch or that he'd have another hard day and not be able to reach me. As far as I was from him, the Internet brought us closer, and the thought of being disconnected was a nearly physical ache.

But Sam wanted us to get away. He thought we needed the time alone, and in those moments when I was able to think straight, I acknowledged how right he was. He'd come home because of a "sense" that it was where he needed to be, probably hoping the surprise itself would spark some life into the listlessness of our relationship. But his homecoming had been a taxing thing—our conversations hampered by foreignness.

If Sam felt it too, he didn't let on. As flagrant as the deterioration of our communication seemed to me, he appeared as calm and focused as he'd always been. Only his unexpected return spoke of a disquiet he hadn't yet stated in so many words. I suspected he was hoping our time in the mountains would allow us to connect in an undistracted way. Part of me welcomed the effort and expense. The other resented it.

The greatest silver lining of our time away was entirely selfish. I'd researched Nagarkot online—a popular mountaintop town where classy hotels housed tourists in search of Himalayan sunrises. Sam had told me nothing about the arrangements he'd made, and though I knew he wanted our time together to be the highlight of the trip, the anticipation of taking a long, hot shower in a real hotel far surpassed togetherness in my mind. I packed my shaving gel, razor, and all those items I'd seldom used because our bathroom at home was so utilitarian and our warm water so limited.

I logged on a few minutes before Sam was due home. Aidan knew about my plans for the weekend, but I wanted to say goodbye before we left. There was a short note waiting for me.

insurance came through. funding granted. huge relief. and in the midst of all the wrangling, an impulse i couldn't resist. it hijacked my best intentions of getting solid rest before monday's scalpel. just a charcoal sketch with some watercolors slapped on . . . in case i run out of life before i get the chance to do it in oil. i think it's called 'if.' and i think it articulates 'this': you and me and everything that entails.

my mom asked me yesterday how i'm keeping it together. i told her i'm not, a lot of the time. but when i am . . . i think it's you.

'night, ren.

I opened the attachment and sat transfixed.

There were three sketches on the screen, each one a portion of the bench outside my parents' house where Aidan and I had spoken on the eve of our graduation. Put together, they displayed the full width of the bench, shining white against a cushioning darkness. The outer pieces of the triptych had been colorized with watercolors. The center one was a smudged black-and-white. In the far left portion, the bench was barely visible where two bodies, only a narrow portion visible from thigh to chin, pressed close together, were locked in a kiss. In the central piece, the bench seemed abandoned, littered with fallen leaves and small branches. Its paint cracked and peeling. And in the third, the leaves and branches remained and two figures stood behind the bench. He faced front and she was turned toward him. His hand and hers were so close on the backrest that their fingers overlapped. The contrast of black-and-white in the three paintings was stunning. Aidan's use of watercolor to lend depth to the pieces on each end was rich and meaningful.

I absorbed the visual representation of our journey and felt its warmth spreading from my chest into my limbs.

> I'm so glad I logged on. Aidan . . . it's stunning. I'm sorry it cost you sleep, but the result is breathtaking. Such a succinct and profound expression of who we've been. I think you should rename it "Still." Thank you, thank you, thank you for painting it.
>
> My bags are packed and we'll be heading out in a few minutes, but I couldn't leave without saying a quick good-bye. We're leaving my laptop here, so unless the hotel has a public computer with Internet access . . . But you'll never be far from my mind. You know that, right? You haven't been since reconnection.
>
> I'll write again in a couple days, if not before. Don't do anything stupid while I'm gone . . .

I'd assumed that we'd take a taxi the forty kilometers from Kathmandu to Nagarkot, perhaps forgetting for a moment who I'd married. Instead we took a rickshaw to a downtown street corner, where we boarded an Ashok Leyland bus and got on our way, winding through fields and villages as we left the pollution of Kathmandu behind.

The bus was made to seat twenty-four, but by the time we began our ascent into the mountain, standing passengers had filled the aisle and hung out the door by handrails. Several more had climbed to the top of the bus, one of them carrying a goat, and I could hear them talking casually as we lurched our way around blind hairpins. I looked out the window as rice paddies yielded to pine forests, averting my eyes when we seemed to hang over the precipice and squeezed past vehicles coming the other way.

The bus belched black smoke when our driver shifted gears. The road got steeper. The space between houses became wider and the air seemed to clear. After a couple incidents that felt to me like close calls, I focused my imagination on the hotel waiting at the top—its clean, well-furnished bedroom and Western-style bath.

The bus stopped with a screech of brakes and I stepped off eagerly, taking in the landscape of terraced mountainsides and the weaving roads that connected them. The town was small and modest, its Western hotels a bit farther up the road. Rustic restaurants lined its main artery, while unpaved roads ran farther into the hills.

Sam asked for directions at a roadside bar, where a large cutout of "Bryan Adams, Live in Nepal" seemed incongruous. While most of the other foreigners seemed to be following the main street through town, Sam and I jogged left onto a smaller, unpaved road. He carried the one bag we'd packed for the trip and walked quickly and effortlessly despite the seven-thousand-foot altitude. As I followed, I took in the sights of the mountaintop burg where local poverty coexisted with foreign wealth: a boarded-up schoolhouse, a dairy store where farmers dumped fresh milk into large cisterns, a small temple whose mud and bamboo walls seemed to have succumbed to the elements. And everywhere, Nepali people, their skin leathered by exposure, their clothing colorful and bold. Their expressions were arresting—introspective and calm.

The smooth dirt path turned rutted and rocky.

"You sure we're going the right way?"

"Just up ahead," Sam said, his breathing barely labored. Mine was coming in short gasps, the altitude wreaking havoc on my stamina. But I trudged on, motivated by the comforts waiting when we got there.

"Here it is," Sam said. I looked up at the orange and brown building he was facing. It stood just off the road, where construction crews worked to replace large drainage pipes.

"This?"

Sam double-checked the paper he'd printed off before leaving home.

"Yep!" And he stepped inside.

The hotel of my dreams was actually a modest hostel that catered to hikers. The German owner led us up three flights of stairs to a long hallway and motioned to a room on the right. "Dinner served anytime after six," he said in a robust accent.

I tried to lower my expectations as Sam led us through the door, but I was still disappointed. Our room was small—bare walls, hard mattress twin beds, and a set of windows that overlooked the valley. Sam saw my expression. "This isn't too bad."

I pushed the door to the bathroom open and felt my expectations deflate. It had a sink and a toilet—but the shower was just a small hose protruding from the tiled wall right above shoulder level. I could sit on the toilet and wash my hair under the trickle of water it produced. There was a yellowed, handwritten sign that warned guests not to drink the water. Not for the first time, I cursed myself for letting my hopes get in the way of reality. I'd invented a weekend that would feed me in the small and meaningless ways I craved, and real life had dealt me something infinitely less idyllic.

The disappointment sapped what little enthusiasm I'd been able to muster, leaving me feeling bereft. When Sam said, "Great place for a getaway" in his usual, content way, all I could muster was a small smile and a nod. I pulled the thin, faded curtains back from the window and looked out over the valley to where the Himalayas should have been. A thick bank of clouds obscured the horizon.

Sam's arms came around me from behind as his chin settled on my shoulder. We stood looking out the window together. I knew what would come next and wished I could cover his arms where they crossed on my stomach with eager hands, then turn into his strength for the kiss he'd been saving for this moment. I wanted to want him. But his touch felt impersonal and formal.

Afflicted and reluctant, I turned into his embrace.

≈

"Do you remember Aidan?" I asked as we sat on a parapet overlooking the Himalayas, a statue of Sri Chinmoy in the alcove at our feet.

I'd realized at some point during the night that the "right time" to broach the subject of Aidan was just another figment of my imagination. I'd already waited too long. There would be no moment in the near or distant future when telling Sam about our communication would be a comfortable thing, so the sunrise in Nagarkot had seemed as bad a time as any.

Sam seemed to search his memory after I asked the question. "The guy from home?"

I nodded. "The artist. Remember?"

"I do. He wanted you to run off with him before your graduation, right?"

"He's dying of cancer." Every time I said the words, they felt more damning.

Sam's eyes were on me. "Okay."

I tried to school my expression into something sincere and guilt-free. "He found me on Facebook a few weeks ago."

"You're on Facebook?"

"Sullivan talked me into it."

"Okay." He was trying to hear me out.

"I just wanted you to know that we're communicating. It didn't seem right that you weren't aware of it."

"On Facebook."

I looked directly into his eyes, wanting to defuse any notion he might have that I wasn't being honest. "Messaging, yes. And Skype," I said. "We talked on Skype one time while you were gone."

He nodded and gazed out as the last hues of sunrise escaped what was visible of the mountain peaks. "What kind of cancer?"

"Brain." Something caught in my throat and I raised a hand to quell it. I swallowed hard and took a deep breath, willing myself to be emotionless and calm. "Advanced stages. It could be a matter of weeks." Sam said nothing, so I went on. "I hadn't heard from him since we graduated high school, and all of a sudden he wrote to tell me he was sick and . . . I had to write him back, Sam. He doesn't really have anyone."

"Where is he?"

"Pennsylvania. Near his parents."

"Married?"

"Not anymore."

"And you've been back in touch for . . . ?"

"A few weeks."

Silence stretched and tightened. A group of Japanese tourists chattered by. I watched a hawk soar high above the terraced mountainsides and hang immobile on an updraft.

"Are you in love with him?"

The question jolted me. "Sam, why would you ask that?"

He looked at me again. "Because it took you this long to tell me about him."

"You haven't been home very much."

"I've been home enough for a conversation."

"I didn't want to bother you . . . and I wasn't sure it was important."

"But now you are?"

"I . . . Yes."

"Why?"

"Because you're my husband and Aidan and I are still talking, and if he gets any worse . . . I just want you to know."

"Or maybe you're afraid I'd find out on my own."

"Sam—stop acting like you've caught me doing something illicit."

"What if I came to you saying that I'd found an old girlfriend and had been talking to her online? You might have some qualms too."

I wanted to tell him that Aidan was more than an old boyfriend. That he had been a part of me long before Sam and I had met in Austria. That he held places in my life that no one else could possibly fill. All true. All susceptible of validating Sam's suspicions.

"You're right," I said calmly, my self-control straining. "I probably would." I straightened and reached for courage. "So what do you want to know? Ask any question you have."

He let out a long, loud breath and trained his eyes on the mountain peaks barely visible through the patches of thick clouds covering the Himalayas. "What do you talk about with him?"

"His art—he's still painting. His disease. Death."

Sam bent a leg and turned on the parapet so he could face me. I did the same, wanting my explanations to be sufficient. "How often do you communicate?"

"Probably every day."

Surprise. "That seems like a lot."

"Not when you consider that every day could be his last."

I watched Sam absorb the comment and mull it over. "You've been different," he finally said.

That took me aback. "I have?"

He nodded.

"I'm surprised you noticed."

"So," he asked again, his expression more analytical than concerned, "are you in love with him?"

"Sam." Annoyance lent an edge to my voice. "Stop asking that."

He looked down and sat in silence for a moment. "I don't want to be suspicious," he finally said. "If you tell me you're not . . ."

"It's not like we're having—"

"Just tell me. Are you . . ." He shook his head a little, as if to clear his thoughts. I'd seldom seen him so cautious before. "Are you emotionally involved with him?" He looked right at me and I saw sincerity in his gaze. So very Sam. He expected the same from me.

Shame stunned me. I knew. Though I longed to assert—loud and clear—that our relationship was harmless, the truth was in the twinges of unease, the stirrings of guilt I'd quelled in recent days. It breathed in the pulsing space Aidan inhabited in my mind. In my consciousness. In my perspective and desires. He'd entered so subtly, so naturally and quickly, that I had barely noticed. And he was anchored there now.

But there was no place in this moment for remorse. I lacked the energy and courage it required. Aidan would be dead soon. And none of this would matter anymore.

I attempted a half truth. "He's someone I cared for. And I'm concerned about him. I think I'm grieving for him too. And I just—if communicating with me helps him to—to approach death with less . . . I don't know. He was—he *is* a big part of my childhood. Surely, you can understand that."

In Sam's place, I knew I would have distrusted my words. They were too jagged to be entirely sincere.

"Sullivan's tickets," he said. "Is Aidan why you were so determined to accept them?"

I hadn't expected him to make that connection. I chided myself for the lapse. "It might have been part of it. There was a lot more to it than Aidan—I explained that to you—but . . ." I expelled a long breath. "Yes, it definitely made me want it more."

"Okay."

There was one more issue I had to address. "Ryan overheard the end of a conversation a few days ago. I think he . . . I think he jumped to conclusions."

"About you and Aidan."

"And the nature of our friendship, yes. I tried to explain it to him, but . . ."

He nodded. "That's why he's been so angry."

"Angrier. I can't remember a time in the past couple of years when he hasn't been some degree of angry."

Silence stretched thin.

"Why didn't you tell me that's why he's been acting out?"

"Because I needed to tell you about Aidan first."

Something unsure fell over his features. I could see him fighting it, committing his extraordinary intelligence to making sense of my revelations. I gave him time, the one commodity I most wanted to preserve.

After a few moments, he drew in a breath and examined my face, perhaps looking for something contradictory or conclusive. He stared so long that I wanted to look away, but I summoned enough self-control to keep my eyes locked on his. "Okay," he finally said.

I was startled. "Okay?"

He got up and extended a hand to me. I took it and let him pull me to my feet.

"Sam—if you have any questions . . ."

"I trust you," he said, twining his fingers with mine as we started back toward our hotel. "Let's get some breakfast."

"So . . ." His long strides kept him just a bit ahead of me. I pulled on his arm to slow him down and he stopped to look at me. "We're okay?" I asked.

"I trust you," he said again. Then he turned and resumed our walk back to the hotel.

His statement had dismayed me, and I searched my heart to understand why. I wanted him to be worried. I wanted him to fear losing me. I wanted him to question me, then assure me of his love.

I wanted him to need me enough to fight for me.

sixteen

WE ARRIVED BACK AT THE HOSTEL AND I HEADED TO OUR room to freshen up while Sam went upstairs to get coffee and read the paper.

As I stood in front of the bathroom mirror wrapping a rough, line-dried towel around my head, the sight of my body halted my movements. With my arms raised to secure the towel, I took stock of what I saw and wondered when I'd stopped defining myself as feminine—a woman whose body and spirit had needs that went beyond perfunctory offerings.

I lowered my arms and stared into my own face as if it belonged to a stranger, noting the patches of dry skin, the new wrinkles around my mouth. I let my eyes drift down past the sun damage on my neck and chest. It wasn't Nepal that had robbed me of my womanhood. I knew it had started to wane long before our arrival. Still, as I contemplated this new incarnation of me and compared her to the woman I'd been before the strain of ministry, I wondered how dearly I'd paid for Sam's cause. For *our* cause, I reminded myself. A reminder and a charge. It rang hollow in my mind.

"We've got to head home," Sam said brusquely, entering the bedroom with a note in his hand and heading straight for the suitcase.

"What?" I reached for another towel and wrapped it around me.

He held up the paper in his hand. "Eveline called."

"Why? What happened?"

"Ryan didn't come home last night."

A shiver of dread ran through me. "What do you mean, he didn't come home?"

"They were at that movie night he told us about," Sam said, throwing our clothes into the suitcase.

"With the soccer team?"

Sam nodded. "Steven called home this morning. Told his parents Ryan stole some liquor and ran off at some point. No one knows where he is."

I didn't say a word as I dressed and collected the rest of our items, shoving them into our bag while Sam went to pay our bill. I'd already started down the road to town when he caught up with me. I flagged down a taxi. "We can take the bus," Sam said.

"We're taking a taxi."

He dropped our suitcase into the trunk and we headed back to Kathmandu.

The drive was interminable. I tried to squelch the images in my mind. Ryan getting mugged and beaten. Intoxicated Ryan wandering the streets, getting lost and panicking. Ryan stepping out in front of a car and still lying on the roadside in a remote part of town.

My lungs ached from the strain of breathing calmly. I wanted to curse at Sam for refusing to get a cell phone so we could be in touch with Eveline as we traveled. I begged the driver to go faster and Sam leaned forward to explain that it was an emergency involving our son.

Nothing registered on the hour-long drive back to

Kathmandu. Neither the towns we drove through nor the sights we saw. Neither the swerving to avoid bicycles nor the sudden rainstorm that drenched the road and made it slick. Sam reached across and gripped my hand. I knew he was praying.

We were driving past Ryan's school when I saw two police cars at the foot of the crane next to the new gym. A crowd pressed around them. I looked up and heard myself groaning, "Oh, *God*."

Sam followed my gaze and I saw his face go ashen. He stopped the taxi and we both got out and ran, ignoring our driver's yells to come back for our suitcase. I could think of nothing but the splash of red at the end of the crane's jib, high above the ground, and the closer I got to it, the clearer the details became—Ryan's legs straddling the outermost beam, his jeans torn at the knee, his clothes drenched by the downpour that had slickened the metal on which he sat. He seemed oddly relaxed, his arms swinging. My stomach plunged when I saw him casually adjust his position.

As we got closer, I began to hear his voice. I doubted my ears. He was singing. Bellowing at the top of his lungs. His arms beat an erratic rhythm as a voice I'd never heard come out of him before quavered in a drunken version of his favorite childhood song. "*Jesus loves the little children*," he wailed, "*all the children of the world*."

We were close enough now for people to see us. The crowd gathered at the base of the crane parted, and Eveline, who had been speaking with the police officers, hurried over to us. "We don't know how long he's been up there," she said, and I could hear the effort it took for her to speak calmly. "Someone called it in to the police about an hour ago and we came as soon as we heard. They're afraid to go up there and scare him into falling."

Sam brushed past her and went straight to the officers who

stood at the bottom of the crane. They showed few signs of urgency. He gesticulated and tried to make himself understood while Eveline hung on to me as if she was afraid I'd faint. I figured she'd seen my legs buckling as I'd run to the place where my son sat unsteadily above a ninety-foot drop.

There was a commotion by the school's main gate as several men came out carrying high-jump mats the students used in gym class. They placed the two thickest ones side by side right under the place were Ryan still straddled the jib's outer beam, then ran back inside as one of Ryan's teachers barked orders I couldn't make out.

I clung to Eveline, my eyes riveted on Sam as he climbed the crane, moving slowly and surely on the slippery rungs.

"*Red and yellow, black and white, they are precious in his sight,*" Ryan continued to scream from his dangerous perch. "*Jesus* hates *the little children of the world.*"

There was a nearly palpable halt in the nervous chatter around the base of the crane. Ryan had accentuated the verb so clearly that no one could doubt what they'd heard. That's when the tears came. My eyes had stayed dry when I'd shot out of the taxi and run toward my son. It might have been panic that had kept me from crying as I'd stood there with friends and strangers staring at me, as I'd watched my husband climb a treacherous structure, as I'd sent up the same desperate prayer I'd breathed on so many occasions before—*Please, God. Please.*

But when my son screamed, "Jesus *hates* the little children of the world" for all assembled to hear—that's when my defenses finally collapsed under the terror and guilt and shame and horror of the moment.

I pressed closer. "Be careful," I sobbed to Sam from the bottom of the crane. "Oh, please—*God, please.*"

My voice must have cut through the fog in Ryan's mind. He

stopped singing and twisted on the beam to look down, scanning the crowd before finding me at the bottom of the crane. "God?" he yelled, a hysterical edge to his voice. "You're praying to God to help me?" And then he laughed in a way that chilled me. "What a joke," he spat at me.

"Ryan," I pled. "Please don't move . . ."

He edged farther out on the crane's jib. His voice was shrill and cynical as he intoned a sort of chant. "*Please, Jesus*, help my son. *Please, Jesus*, make people send money. *Please, Jesus*, can we leave this eff'in' country? Oh, and *please, Jesus*, don't let anybody find out that I'm in love with some guy back in the States . . ."

Sam froze and I felt a wave of nausea cramp my stomach. He looked down at me with an expression I couldn't read. The silence all around me was deafening.

"Ooh—*burn*!" Ryan continued, his voice maniacal and shrill. "What, did you think it would be our little secret?"

"Ryan, I told you—" I heard the protest as it escaped my lips and hated myself. I hated that I was preparing to utter guilty excuses to a son who sat in mortal danger. How low—how horribly low—had I sunk? "Just come down from there, Ryan. Please. We can talk about this. We can figure it out. Please, Ryan. Come back down before you . . ." I ran out of breath and seemed incapable of drawing more into my terrified lungs. My legs buckled and Eveline held me upright.

Sam was almost level with the beam on which Ryan sat. "Ryan?" his voice was calm and firm. How I envied him the ability to master his emotions.

"Oh, hey, Dad!" He sounded cheerful and sincere, but his eyes were crazed.

"Ryan, I want you to scoot along the beam toward me. Can you do that?"

"Why, Dad? Why do you want me to *scoot along the beam*?" he mocked.

"Because it's dangerous up here."

A derisive smile contorted his face. "And you care?"

Sam flinched. I saw his grip tighten on the metal rung he was holding.

"I care, son," he said.

Ryan's voice rose another notch, hysterical and shrill. "You *care*?" And then he laughed. He laughed so hard he lost his balance and had to fall forward onto his stomach and clutch the beam to keep from slipping off. And still he laughed.

Sam blanched. I saw weakness and fear erode him in an instant. He kept a grip on the ladder, but there was indecision and lostness in his countenance, two emotions I'd seldom seen in him before.

When Ryan's laughter had run dry, he pushed himself back up to a seated position and seemed to take in the situation with fresh eyes. He scanned the crowd below, saw the police officers standing by, looked at me where I stood weak-kneed, and let his eyes slide up the crane to where his father clung hollow-eyed and desperate.

"Slide over this way, son," Sam said in a voice so soft I could barely hear it.

"'Son'?" Sarcasm dripped from the word.

Sam flinched again. "Yes, Ryan. Come over this way . . ."

"*Son?*" Ryan shrieked again, oblivious to his dad's prompting. "I'm not your son! Those little village kids? *They're* your sons, *Dad*!" He stretched out the last word in a sarcastic sneer. "Go save their souls. I'll be fine up here without you!" He paused, eyes wide and mouth agape. "What? Nothing to say? Come on, *Dad*, preach one of your sermons. The one on sacrifice—that's my favorite. 'If we don't make these sacrifices, who will?'" He quoted nearly verbatim from one of the sermons Sam had given while we were presenting our work in churches before Nepal. "It's all 'for the kingdom'!" he yelled, then dissolved into laughter again. At some point, the laughter turned to sobs. He lay forward on the beam and wailed while a crowd of our friends and strangers looked on.

"I love you, Ryan," Sam said, his voice shaky with emotion. "Ryan . . . God loves you."

Ryan pushed up to a sitting position and stared, incredulous, at his dad. "What?"

Sam took the question as a sign of softening. "He loves you," he said again, eagerly, reaching out a little farther toward his son.

I saw Ryan jolt a little—his eyebrows came together in anger and incredulity. His voice was sharp and cracked as he screamed, "He loves me?!"

"Sam, stop!" I shrieked up at my husband from where I stood, frozen, afraid the mere mention of God's name would cause Ryan to ratchet up again.

He looked down and held out a hand in a silencing gesture, then looked back to his son. "God doesn't care that you've been drinking. He doesn't care what you've said here. He doesn't care, son. He loves you."

There was a sneer on Ryan's face when he propped himself up just enough to say, "And you think that's enough?"

Sam must have drawn on every ounce of conviction he had to answer, "Yes! Yes, son, it's enough." He paused and I could see him desperately searching for something to say—something that would pierce through Ryan's insanity so he could coax him off that crane. "God's love for you is so much greater than anything you can imagine . . ."

"Shut up!" I heard a voice shrilling, then realized it was my own. "Sam—*shut up!*" I felt a chasm opening beneath me, as if the last shreds of my motherly instincts understood before my mind did the horrible mistake of using God's name to get to Ryan.

My son froze. He eyed Sam with something that looked like disbelief and anguish. Then he sat up straighter, swung a leg over the beam, and dropped.

～

Four broken ribs, an open femur fracture, a lacerated spleen, two crushed vertebrae, and a severe hemorrhage herniating his brain. Ryan lay in a medical coma, wrapped in a mess of breathing tubes, heart monitors, casts, and bandages.

My mind had been so focused on my son atop that crane that I hadn't seen the army of teachers and students that had stacked sports mats and empty boxes under him, moving them as he progressed across the jib. It was the improvised cushion that had saved him from what would have been a certain death.

He fell soundlessly, though I knew he was conscious when he swung his leg over the beam and let himself drop. He neither screamed nor clawed the air, as instincts would dictate. I watched his body plunge ninety feet toward the ground and felt myself die as he crashed into the pile beneath him. I didn't move as bystanders raced in. I didn't think as Sam slid down the crane's wet ladder and launched himself into the crush of people tending to our son. I didn't breathe as someone yelled, "Don't move him!" and Sam's voice, like a mantra, repeated, "Stay with me, Ryan. Ryan, stay with me!" into the silent shock.

My legs gave out, and Eveline, who still held me, helped me to the ground. "He's alive," she said. "He's alive." I heard a keening sound that swelled and agonized. There was a blur in front of me—Eveline mouthing words I couldn't hear, someone shaking my shoulders, arms lifting me and dragging me to a nearby car. Propping me in the backseat—door open. Then hurrying back to the place where my son lay inside a rescuing circle of friends and strangers.

Later, I'd remember Nyall Harrington arriving at the scene. He took charge immediately, barking orders when the ambulance drove up, then telling Sam to get in the car with me and meet them at the hospital. With Eveline at the wheel, we followed the Nepali ambulance, a plain white van equipped with neither lights nor sirens. Nyall was the first to jump out when we reached the emergency entrance.

He stayed by Ryan's gurney as they pushed him into the hospital. A nurse showed me where to sit. I was surprised to see Eveline still beside me. Sam on my other side. There was a loud fuzziness in my brain, like heavy rain on a metallic roof. I couldn't really hear past it. Couldn't think around its fury. The keening had stopped and I knew enough to be grateful for that.

The following hours were an indistinct series of updates and oblivion. I tried to listen to Nyall, but it felt as if my neurons weren't connecting. "What did he say?" I asked Eveline after one of his visits.

"He said Ryan's . . ."

I held up a hand to stop Sam's explanation. "Not you," I said, my voice clipped and acidic. Not the man who'd preached our son into a suicidal leap. "Eveline, what did he say?"

She looked from me to Sam, then back again. "They're working on him. Trying to determine the full extent of his injuries and stabilize his blood pressure. He's bleeding from his spleen and they'll likely have to remove it, but . . . he's alive." She smiled a bit tightly—determined in her optimism. "He's in the best of hands, Lauren. Really. The best of hands."

Hours passed. Sam sat immobile between Nyall's visits, lean-ing forward in his plastic chair, elbows on his knees, head in his hands. Eveline got us coffee from the doctors' lounge and went with me to the restroom when I wasn't sure my legs could bear my weight. Otherwise, she sat in silence, honoring the survival I hoped was happening just down the hall.

Ryan went into surgery and Nyall explained to us what would happen. There was something about splinting his femur, fusing his spine, removing his spleen, and relieving the pressure on his still-swelling brain by opening his skull. A specialist vis-iting from Germany would be performing the operation, one of the foremost experts in his field. "He's in good hands," Nyall told us. "I couldn't have picked anyone more qualified to do this sur-gery . . ." He paused. "You can thank God for that," he said.

I nodded and looked away. How nice of God to bring a good surgeon into our lives after failing to keep my son from jumping off a crane.

Nyall assured us that he'd be right next to Ryan in the oper-ating room. There was minute comfort in that, but comfort nonetheless.

Ryan got through surgery. "That's a strong boy you've got," Nyall said. Sam asked a few questions. He'd be kept in a medi-cally induced coma until the swelling went down. There would be more surgeries later. But for now—for now he was alive. I had to be content with that.

We saw Ryan in intensive care. Sam stood at the head of the bed, a hand on Ryan's shoulder. He whispered a prayer about healing and praise for his spared life, and it was all I could do not to yell at him again.

"Shut up, Sam," I mumbled instead, anger like a vise around

my emotions. He went silent, but I knew he was still praying. I sat on the other side of the bed and held my son's hand. Traced the ridges of his knuckles. Kissed his palm. Lay my cheek against its warmth and fought the urge to pray, unwilling to commit my son to an unpredictable and fickle God.

Nyall came by again after a few hours. He assured us that Ryan was doing well, considering, and warned us that we'd see little change until they stopped administering the drugs that were keeping him unconscious. "Are you giving him pain-killers?" I asked, afraid he might be suffering without our knowing it.

"He's well medicated. Won't remember any of this when he wakes up again."

Eveline flagged down a taxi to drive us home and told us she would stay until we'd gathered a few clothes and made the necessary calls.

Muffin met us at the gate, his cheerful welcome an affront. The bag we'd forgotten in the taxi was there too, probably dropped over the gate by a helpful soul. "Do you want to call your parents?" Sam asked.

"You call yours first."

"Okay."

It was the longest exchange we'd had since the accident.

I heard the Skype call being placed as I closed the door to the bathroom and turned on the tap in the sink. I glanced at my face in the mirror and saw my haunted eyes. Only a handful of hours had passed since I'd stood in the bathroom in Nagarkot feeling sorry for myself.

I felt bile rising in my throat and bent over the toilet to retch. My empty stomach convulsed in dry heaves. Tears. Burning tears. And sobs that strangled me.

Sam knocked softly on the door. "Lauren?"

I slid down the wall to the floor and covered my mouth with my hands, trying to stifle the overflow of my terror.

"Lauren."

"Give me a minute," I said on a forcefully settled breath. I heard him walk away.

He was sitting on the bench just inside the front door when I left the bathroom. The bench where Ryan would drop his backpack after school. The bench under which his cleats still lay, their bright green laces trailing on the tile floor. I walked past Sam without a glance in his direction. "Lauren," he said again.

I didn't know who or what to hate. Sam. Or his job. Or this godforsaken country. Or God himself. I went to the laptop on the dining room table. Sullivan answered after just one ring. Her voice rough with sleep.

"This had better be good," she said. Then she saw my face. "Chickadee . . ."

"Ryan . . ." I said. Then new sobs choked my words.

"Lauren. Lauren, honey. What's going on?" I could hear the fear in her voice. "What's happened to Ryan?"

I forced myself to breathe. Ordered my lungs to stop their quaking. After several moments, I said, "He . . ." The words I needed to say bruised me in an unimaginable way. "He's in the hospital. In a coma. He—"

"What? What happened?" I saw her reach for the light switch next to her bed and turn it on. She was disheveled and as awake as I'd ever seen her. "Was he in an accident? Was he hit by one of those taxis?"

"He jumped off a crane." Saying it made it more real.

"He . . . what?"

"He threw himself off the top of a crane, Sullivan. He's . . ."

"Oh, my Lord. Tell me what I can do."

I wasn't sure why I'd called her first, instead of my parents.

But her quick, practical response soothed me in ways I didn't understand. "Nothing. Not yet."

"Does he need to be medevaced? I can arrange it, Lauren. Say the word."

"I don't think we can do that yet. He's got crushed vertebrae. And his leg is broken. They took out his spleen and cut out a piece of his skull because his brain's so swollen."

"Oh, Lord. What are the doctors saying?" Her question was firm and unflinching.

"Just to wait, I guess. He's stable right now, but . . . we're just home long enough to make a couple calls, then we're heading back."

"Well, don't waste time talking to me! I'm going to put out a few feelers so I'll be ready the minute you need anything. You hear me? Whatever it is—medical help or evacuation. You call me the minute you need anything."

Her words lent me courage. "Okay. I will. I just . . . I just wanted you to know."

After we'd hung up, I stared at my contact list and tried to find the energy to call my parents. They'd be devastated. They'd want to fly over. They'd smother me with questions and concern. I didn't know if I could do it. I didn't know how long my sanity would last.

"Do you want me to call your parents?" Sam asked from the dining room doorway.

I shook my head.

"Water's heating for coffee. I'll be in the bedroom packing a bag."

I heard him climb the stairs. His step was slow and heavy.

I called my parents and listened as their tiredness yielded to clear-minded horror. All I told them was that Ryan had fallen from a crane in the construction zone next to his school. They assumed it was an accident and I didn't contradict them. They said they'd be on the next flight out, and I made them promise to stay put. I'd tell them if and when we needed them to come.

"Then we'll pray," I heard my mother's shell-shocked voice say. "We'll get the church praying too. You let me know the moment anything changes, okay?" Her voice caught.

"We're there in spirit, sweetie," my dad said in a broken voice, bringing fresh tears to my eyes. "Tell our grandson we love him."

I assured him that I would, though I didn't know when he'd be conscious to hear it. I sat in silence after we hung up. The mere thought of moving exhausted me. Though my mind seemed to be functioning again, my body still rebelled against the reality of Ryan's condition. My fingers directed the laptop's mouse almost in spite of me. It hovered over the browser's icon. Then my bookmarked pages. Then Facebook's blue *F*. I clicked and saw a new message from Aidan.

Aidan.

If we hadn't found each other again. If Ryan hadn't overheard the end of our call.

I caught myself. If Sam had been more present. If we'd stayed in Indiana. If I'd protected my son from his father's fanaticism . . .

There were too many ifs. I clicked the browser closed and shut the laptop's lid.

~~~

Ryan was still in intensive care two days later. It was a far cry from American ICUs, but enough to keep our son alive. Eveline arranged for meals to be delivered to us while Sam and I stood vigil. Steven took in Muffin so we wouldn't be tied to his feeding schedule. Pastor Justin came by to offer his support. He went to Ryan's bed and laid a hand on his leg. "Father," he said, eyes closed and eyebrows drawn. "Father, please heal this young man." Sam glanced at me as if he knew I wanted to leave the room.

We hadn't said much to each other in the two days since Ryan's fall. We'd spoken to our son as if he could hear us, assuring him that we were near and that he was in good hands, trying to lend him a hope we often didn't feel. The reflexes in Ryan's legs and feet weren't good. We'd been told a hundred times that we wouldn't know the full extent of his injuries until the swelling in his brain went down and he returned to consciousness, but I knew both of us were bracing for the worst. Paralysis. A protracted coma. Brain death.

Eveline came by early that afternoon, took one look at me, and declared that I needed to go home to rest.

"I'm okay," I said, but I heard the exhaustion in my voice.

"You're dead on your feet, luv," she said. "And this boy of yours is going to need you even more when he comes out of the coma. So why don't you give yourself a little break? Go home. Get a few hours of sleep in your own bed. You'll feel much better in the morning."

I looked from Eveline to Sam and back again, craving the reprieve but afraid of what might happen when I was away.

"You go home," Sam said. "I'll stay with Ryan and give you a call if anything changes."

I conceded. "I'll go after Nyall's visit." Eveline seemed satisfied with that.

We settled into quietness again after she left. I wondered when we'd lost our words. It was Sam who finally lanced our silence. "I know you blame me," he said.

I looked up, startled. "What?"

"For Ryan. I know you blame me."

I knew what I should say. Comforting words. Wifely words. *It's not your fault, Sam. He was upset and not thinking straight. I don't blame you.* But the fact was that I did. And I didn't know when I'd begun. Looking back, I saw the slow build of my resentment like an inexorable force, fueled by disappointment and duress. But none of that mattered much with Ryan still unconscious, the outcome still unsure.

"I don't want to talk about it," I said to Sam. I hated the petulance in my voice. But not as much as I hated the beeping and whirring of the machines attached to our son.

"If he hadn't been drinking . . ." Sam said.

"If he hadn't been *drinking*? That's what you're focusing on?"

"His alcohol levels were . . . No one can make wise decisions with that amount of liquor in their system."

I shook my head, torn between amazement and disgust. "You go ahead and blame the liquor, Sam."

"While you're content to just blame me."

"Boys need fathers," I said, not caring if my words hurt him.

"Lauren . . ."

"And kids need stability."

I could hear him breathing. I could feel his eyes on me.

"I . . ." He stopped himself and expelled a long breath. "If I had known how unhappy he was . . ."

I felt resentment turn into cold fury. "If you had *known*? How could you have missed it?"

"Lauren."

"What kind of sign did you need, Sam? What kind of unhappiness would have convinced you that our son wasn't doing well?"

He held up his hands. "Some of that is just normal teenage stuff."

"Look where you're standing!" I barked, pointing at the boy who lay in a coma. "It was more than *normal teenage stuff*! But how were you supposed to know when you were gone more than half the time?" I took a breath and landed a satisfying blow. "I'll bet you'd have done something about it if one of your villagers has been as despondent as Ryan!"

"Lauren . . . what are you saying?" Shock sharpened his words.

I shook my head in revulsion at his ignorance. "How many times have I tried to tell you that your ideal life was killing us? How many times have you sat in our home having forced conversations with a boy who hasn't really spoken since a year before we left the States? I used to marvel at your ability to see the best in things. The optimism! The faith! The single-minded pursuit of God's purpose for your life! Oh, please." I heard the sneer in my voice and didn't try to silence it. "If this," I said, pointing at our son, "is God's doing, you're just the type of father he is."

I saw his face go pale. He grasped the edge of Ryan's bed and lowered himself into the chair next to it, eyes averted, jaw set. He had that look again—the one that told me he was seeking solace from a higher place.

"I've tried to play along—you can't fault me for that. I've struggled and I've wanted to get out of this place. I've made all the right excuses to our son. 'Your dad's doing good work.' 'Your dad loves you and he shows it when he's home.' I've told myself to buck up and take one for the kingdom. I've tried to be quiet when you needed me to be and supportive when you wanted me to be. I did my best to help Ryan as long as he'd accept it, then I told myself that this work couldn't really harm him because, after all, the call came from God.

"I've got to tell you, Sam, I'm done. I'm done ignoring and excusing the damage your . . . your *vision* has done! And if this," I cried, pointing again at Ryan, "if this was part of God's big plan to reach the remote villages of Nepal, you can have him! I will not trust a God who would want this to happen, nor the man who sacrificed his child to a highfalutin, egocentric calling. You're on crack, Sam! God's mission is your crack, and you can't see your own addiction." My entire body was shaking with my fury. "I wanted to love you and him enough to stomach the collateral damage, but . . . I'm done. I am so completely and utterly done."

While Sam sat by Ryan's bed, his gaze on nothing and his shoulders slumped, I gathered my things and picked up my bag. Then I leaned over Ryan and told him I loved him in a voice roughened by my diatribe, hoping he hadn't heard the hate I'd just spoken. "I'll be back soon," I said.

I left Sam sitting in the hospital room and instructed my legs to carry me down the hall. They felt leaden and unsteady. My mind did too. And my heart—my heart felt atrophied. The truth was, my own guilt was eating me alive.

seventeen

THERE WERE TOO MANY E-MAILS WAITING FOR ME TO READ them all. Some names looked familiar, but others I'd never seen before. Our families must have put the word out about Ryan, and friends as well as strangers were reaching out to offer their support. I read a note from Sullivan—short and sweet—telling me about a private medical group that was willing to evacuate Ryan as soon as he was stable. I hit reply and froze. The date at the top of my message stunned me.

Though the past few days had given me more reasons to grieve than I dared contemplate, I felt a fresh wave of anguish wash over me. It was Monday. In my focus on Ryan, I'd lost track of passing time.

I closed my e-mail to Sullivan before I'd begun writing it and quickly opened Facebook. The number of notifications waiting for me surprised me. Nearly a hundred posts on my wall and forty-three messages. I clicked on the message icon, then on his name. His words unfolded in a series of notes sent hours apart across the span of my lost days. I skimmed what he'd written, unease gnawing at my mind. I paused on the last message, written just that morning.

finally asked one of your facebook friends about what i've been seeing on your wall . . . she filled me in.

geez, ren, i'm so sorry. i wish i could do something—anything—to help you. i hoped i'd get to hear your voice one more time before they stuck that scalpel into my head again, but you're caring for your son. there should be no other thought in your mind.

might be out of touch for a few days starting tomorrow. but you'll be here, ren. you've been . . . you've been everything these last few weeks.

attaching something i've been working on for months. probably years, off and on, and just finished this morning. consider it a parting gift. just in case. you know me well enough to understand.

praying for ryan. really. and for you.

I felt my spirit's backbone bow under the weight of Aidan's need, and I wondered how much more my heart could take. My mind flashed lightning fast through snapshots of our lives. The shed, the garage, and Mom's old bench under the tree.

The light in Aidan's living room was on when his face came up on my screen.

"Hi," I whispered, hoarse from self-restraint.

He stared hard into his screen. I tried to school my expression into something resembling serenity, but knew he'd see right past it. He didn't mention the circles under my eyes or my dirty, unkempt hair. I saw him take a breath and smile his Aidan smile. "Ren . . ."

I didn't trust myself to speak.

"Tell me about Ryan."

I hung my head. "He jumped off a ninety-foot crane," I said after a few moments had passed.

"Wait . . . jumped?"

"He was drunk. He was . . ." I rubbed a hand over my face. "Sam tried to stop him but . . . he just . . . jumped."

"Ren . . ."

The horror lashed me again. "I was there when he jumped . . . next to the crane."

"Good God."

"He was so . . . so *angry*." I bit my lip to contain an overflow of terror. Then I took a deep breath and gave him an abbreviated version of all that had led to Ryan's leap. I told him what Nyall had said to us, and Aidan's eyes grew somber. "We won't know any more for a while. Sullivan's working on getting him back to the States, but Sam wants to keep him here. He insists the medical care is just as good, but . . ."

"How are you coping, Ren?"

"I'm not." I laughed.

"Of course you're not."

I shook my head to clear it. "And here I am telling you about Ryan when you're heading into surgery in . . . how many hours?"

"Eight and a half. But who's counting?" He paused. "I'm going to be fine. Don't waste any energy worrying about me. I'll get through this unpleasant bit and then we'll know."

"Then we'll know," I repeated, trying to unfasten my brain from Ryan long enough to focus it on Aidan's plight. Within a couple of days, he'd know if he would live to see another season.

I wondered how much more my disintegrating soul could take. Then I chastised myself for making this about me.

"I didn't open the attachment," I said, trying to inject some hope into my voice. "I'll wait until you're well enough to Skype. You can explain the new painting when I see it for the first time."

"No, open it now."

I shook my head, suddenly certain that I needed to wait. As if the unrevealed art could seal Aidan's survival. "When you're well enough to Skype," I said again.

He didn't say anything. I wanted to offer hopeful words.

Certain words. To pray as I might have weeks before. But my optimism and my faith had both been crushed in Ryan's fall.

"Ryan's going to make it," Aidan said. The conviction in his voice was a welcome, solid certainty. "He's a tough kid, and if he's got your stubborn streak . . ."

"He does." The battle waged in doubts and accusations and empty promises raged on inside my head. "You need your sleep," I said into another lengthening silence. "I'll check in again when it's all over." I smiled and hoped it spoke of hope.

"I love you, Ren." His voice caught. "You know I always have."

I stared at his face, shamed by the emotions that clawed at my resolve and stole from the well of strength I had to save for Ryan. "Good-bye for now, Aidan." The words felt anemic. I wanted to say more, but wouldn't let myself. "We'll talk soon, okay? I promise."

Tears clouded his eyes. His smile was deep and soft. "Good-bye for now." I felt the emptiness of the words when he said them back to me. He stared at me a moment longer. Then he reached forward and disconnected the call.

～∾

I woke just past dawn, checked the clock, and threw back the covers. I had to get back to the hospital. What if Ryan had woken during the night? What if something in his condition had changed?

The laptop lay beside me. I'd called Sullivan before surrendering to sleep and had left it there in case of an emergency. "You keep me up-to-date, okay?" she'd said before I hung up. "And leave the rest of the details to me. It'll all be lined up the minute you give the signal."

I knew she was the right person to oversee Ryan's evacuation.

But we weren't there yet. I reached for the laptop to write a quick update to our parents, eager to get back to the hospital where my son maintained his tenuous grip on life. When the browser opened to my Facebook page, I felt myself coming undone— raw from the heart-wrenching trauma of Ryan and rent by the numbing uncertainty of Aidan.

His face swam into focus and I tried to blot it out. Ryan. Only Ryan. I pushed the laptop away as if it were an evil force, the physical evidence of my deceit. Guilt in successive waves washed over me. It stole my breath and redoubled my agony. I blustered to myself about love's purity and motherhood and fear and shame and need. I begged for the opiates of serenity and certainty. I could not endure whatever lay ahead while torn in my attention and my loyalty.

Aidan's voice whispered in the chaos in my mind. I pushed the laptop harder—off the bed and onto the floor—then clasped my throbbing head with trembling hands.

I would not. I could not. Not while my son . . . Inescapable realities battled like spasms in my conscience. My flaws. My failures. My selfish, savaged dreams.

A groan tore from my throat as I scrambled off the bed, tears streaming, and retrieved the laptop from the floor. My fingers shook as I wrote a note to Sullivan. "I'm going off-line. My boy is injured. He may be dying. And . . . I just can't. You have our phone and I'm attaching the hospital's. Can you keep our contact list updated? And my parents too. I know I'm putting a lot on you, but I just—I can't anymore." I knew she'd understand.

I gave her the number I'd promised, found clothes and pulled them on, then stormed down the stairs with the laptop in my hands and out the kitchen to the shed. I shoved it in the bottom drawer of Sam's tool cabinet and kicked the drawer closed with my foot. Then I clicked the padlock on the shed's door back into place and pressed it closed.

I returned to the kitchen empty-handed, determined and broken, freed and imprisoned. I was a mother. I—was—a—mother. Above all, with every fiber of my being, I was a mother.

There was no time to shower. I'd wasted too much already. With snacks, a bottle of water, and a change of clothes stuffed into an overnight bag, I headed out the door.

I walked past several beds in the ICU toward the space where Ryan lay. After six hours of sleep, my steps felt surer. My outlook clearer. I pulled back the curtain that surrounded Ryan's bed and found him just as I'd left him, breathing with a respirator, his shattered leg raised, his head and arm bandaged. His color still off—a grayish shade of pale. But he was alive.

I glanced at the chair where Sam sat. "No change?"

He shook his head. I looked at him, then. Really looked at him for the first time since we'd watched our son jump from that crane. He was unshaven, his face pale. He sat in the plastic chair next to Ryan's bed, his chin propped on clasped hands, his eyes on the machine monitoring our son's vital signs. I reached into my bag and handed him a granola bar.

"You haven't eaten," I said.

He pushed the bar back to me and shook his head.

"Sam, you've got to eat something." I found his reticence more annoying than concerning. "Starving yourself won't do Ryan any good."

"I'm fasting."

That got my attention. "A bit late for that." I hated the acid in my voice.

"It's never too late for God."

"That's great."

"Lauren . . ."

"Save it." I dropped my bag on the floor in a corner of the room and went to stand next to Ryan. I brushed the hair off his forehead and let my hand linger there. His warmth felt comforting. "I'm here," I whispered close to his ear. "I went home to get some sleep, but I'm back now, okay? I'm right here." I squeezed his hand and hoped he'd squeeze it back. Nothing happened.

"They'll try to wean him off the respirator in a day or two," Sam said.

"I know."

He rubbed the back of his neck. "But Nyall said not to get our hopes up. Sometimes it takes a couple tries."

"I was there, Sam. I heard."

He rose from the chair and came to stand by me. He lay his hand on Ryan's arm, just above mine, and it took all the self-control I possessed not to snatch mine away. I would not give him the power to scare me farther from my son.

"I'd like for us to talk," he said. I didn't like the sureness in his voice.

"I'd like for you to go home. Take a shower. Get some sleep. Eat. Or don't. That's up to you."

"Okay."

He stood immobile for several minutes. So did I. "Sam," I tried again. "Go home."

He nodded and lifted his jacket from the back of the chair. "Can we talk when I get back?"

I stroked the skin of Ryan's wrist with my finger and leaned close. "I'm right here, Ryan," I said again, hoping he could hear me.

Sam stood there awhile longer. Then he left.

We settled into a kind of routine in the days that followed. I took the day shift and Sam stayed at night. Our visits overlapped by a few hours in the morning until Nyall came by with the latest update. Sam would collect his things when Nyall left. We'd exchange shallow words, and I could tell he wanted to say more.

I relished the hours I got to spend with Ryan alone. He was unconscious and I was spent, but for the first time in a long while, I felt like his mom.

Eveline came and went, her presence unobtrusive and calm. A doctor's wife, she was unfazed by the contraptions encasing our son, unafraid to touch him and speak as if he heard.

"Come on," she said one afternoon, as we sat on either side of Ryan's bed in comfortable silence. She stood and took a couple steps, motioning me to follow her. "Come on."

I looked at Ryan. "I'm not sure . . ."

"Nonsense. We're not going far, and I'll give the nurse my mobile number."

I hesitated.

"When was the last time you went anywhere other than this room and your home?"

"I . . ." I couldn't remember.

"Right, then," she said, waving me to follow her again. "Let's go."

"Eveline."

"Let's go, luv."

I followed her out to the hallway, where she left her phone number with a nurse. Then we walked into the stairwell. "Where are you taking me?" I asked as we started climbing, uncomfortable with leaving Ryan unattended.

"To breathe."

She pushed through a door at the top of the stairs and led me out into the light of day. I squinted at the brightness and took in what I saw. "What is this?"

"This, my dear," she said, leading me by the arm to the edge of the hospital's flat roof, "is a doctor's best kept secret."

I looked past the buildings next door to the mountains outlined in the distance. A faint breeze carried the sound of horns to the rooftop and cooled my skin. Eveline was right. I needed to breathe.

I felt a broadening in my spirit as I scanned the view. Cisterns on roofs, clothes hung out to dry, earth tones that glowed against the morning sky. The aromas of food being prepared rose, faint but unmistakable, from the homes and streets below.

We sat on the edge of a protrusion in the roof. I inhaled deeply, then again, conscious for the first time of the tight muscles in my shoulders and the ache in my back.

"May I speak honestly?" Eveline asked.

I felt my shoulders slump and nodded.

She paused before going on. "Nyall and I were just talking last night about the toll of illness on the family."

I didn't want to hear the lecture, but I let her continue.

"People who have gone through what you have—they're under unimaginable stress. It's quite common for them to experience . . ."

"Tension."

"Yes. And conflict sometimes too. What I've seen of you and Sam . . ." She smiled, sincere and kind. "Trauma can be brutal on relationships."

"Even relationships that were already dead?" The words were out before I had the chance to censor them.

She looked surprised, then her expression gentled into genuine concern.

"Crippled at least," I amended.

"I'm sorry. I didn't know. I knew there were disagreements, but . . . you've hid it well."

I laughed and heard the cynicism in the sound. "We've gotten good at pretending to be everything we're not."

Eveline seemed to consider what I'd said. "So you came into these circumstances already fragile."

Fragile seemed an understatement. *Fractured* seemed more apt. "Yes," I said, too tired to divulge more.

"Lauren, dear, I know I'm speaking out of turn, but I just need to say this once, if you'll allow me."

I stared at the rooftops of Kathmandu until tears began to blur the image. I nodded my permission.

"Getting through something like this—it's almost impossible alone. It's too overwhelming, too ghastly, really. So if . . . forgive me for saying it this way, but if you still have any hope of saving your marriage, crippled as it may be, you've got to fight for it now. Despite everything else that is sapping your strength. I know something broken can be fixed. I've seen it happen. But you've got to start now, luv, before it's too far gone . . ."

Her words trailed off. I sat without moving or speaking for a while, weighing resentment and duty. Abnegation and commitment. A forcible reconciliation seemed to me a grievous thing—an artificial truce, mind-ordained and heart-rejected. If what Eveline said was true—and I knew that it was—I wanted my effort to be about more than just Ryan. I wanted to *want* a relationship with Sam. I just wasn't sure I was there yet.

"Nyall thinks Ryan might hear your voice, even in his coma," Eveline said, startling me. She took my hand and held it firmly in both of hers. "You might consider that he can hear your silence too."

I realized how long it had been since anyone had touched me to comfort—to heal—and pressed my gratitude into the hands that still held mine. "I know you're right."

"Ryan will need to know you and Sam are strong."

I nodded again, convicted by her kindness, but paralyzed by my anger. I remembered our conversation by the soccer field at the beginning of our life in Nepal. "I think you called it elasticity—when we'd just gotten here," I said to the woman who'd been more of a friend than I had realized until just then. "The ability to make do. To adapt."

"I talk too much."

I shook my head. "No. No, you were right. But I think some of us may have been born without it. The elasticity. The courage it takes."

"And some of us . . ." She stopped herself.

"And some of us choose not to use it?"

Her expression softened. "I was going to say that some of us seem to lose it along the way. For a host of reasons. Many of them valid."

I thought of Sam and his ability to take it all in stride—the different, the unpredictable, the uncomfortable, the untenable. He'd brought to Nepal the power of submission and to our family the inflexibility of mission.

And I'd brought to it all a reluctance to engage. To risk. To take a stand. I took another breath and headed back downstairs.

I woke up from a restless sleep to find Sam standing in the bedroom doorway. Only one reason for Sam's arrival home shredded across my mind. Panic surged through me. I threw off the blanket and crawled up the bed until my back was pressed against the wall, hands over my mouth to muffle the slow moan of the moment's horror.

"Oh, no!" I heard my own voice wail. "Sam, no!"

He came to the bed in three long strides, his face close, his hands pulling mine from my mouth. "Lauren, no. No, it's not Ryan!"

I felt the breath freeze in my lungs, hiccup, and hiss out. My face and limbs burned with the aftermath of shock. "He's . . . he's not . . . ?"

"He's okay," Sam said. He pushed the hair back from my face and leaned closer. "He's still unconscious," he half whispered. "Nothing has changed."

"Then why . . . ?" I racked my mind for a reason for his presence. "Why are you home?"

As the adrenaline of fear receded, the acid of my anger resurged. The grip that had been calming a moment before became a restraint again. I pushed him away and put some distance between us on the bed.

He opened his mouth to speak and closed it before he'd said anything. He rubbed a hand down his face and expelled a loud breath.

I glanced at the alarm clock. "Sam," I said, "why are you home? If you're staying here, I'll head back to the hospital. Ryan needs one of us to be there."

"We need to fix this."

"What?"

"This—us. Can we just—take a few minutes to talk it out?"

I shook my head, confused by his urgency.

"Nyall and Eveline," he said. "I'm sure they've noticed. And the rest of the staff."

"Our son is injured. Gravely injured. I'm sure they understand." I swung my legs out of bed. "You stay here and I'll go back to the hospital. I've gotten enough sleep. I just need to get some things together for—"

Sam interrupted me. "What can I do to make things right between us?"

I stopped in the process of pulling clothes out of my drawers, then straightened to face him. "To make things right?"

"I . . ." He hesitated. "What you said at the hospital. I heard you. From an . . . objective point of view, I can see it. I can look back over the past few months and trace Ryan's descent into . . ."

"Hopelessness. Anger."

"Yes," Sam conceded. "What I did, the failures you listed. I look back and I can see those."

I knew there should be a stirring of relief in me. A flutter of satisfaction. Maybe even of hope. "But?"

The man who had always seemed to find the right words was coming up short. There was a sheen of sweat on his forehead, and a muscle twitched in his jaw.

"But I also see the miracles that led us here, that led me and Prakash into those villages. I see those too—the miracles." He scratched the back of his head in his trademark gesture of frustration. Then he looked at me with sober eyes. "I know you wish we could undo it all. Go back and do things differently."

My voice was low and listless. "It's too late for that."

"But if we could. You'd want that, right? No Nepal. No ministry."

I thought of Ryan's journey. I thought of mine. "Yes."

There was a long pause. "But how do we undo God's direction? How do we doubt the miracles? God got us here—do we doubt him too?"

Before I could answer, there was a flash of clarity in my mind. Despite the circumstances, it stunned and anchored me. This wasn't God's doing. He hadn't pushed Ryan to the despair that drove him up a crane. Our failures had. Sam's and mine. The responsibility was ours. Every bit of it—with all its irrevocable, unimaginable damage.

"I don't doubt God." Just saying the words, I realized how long I'd been doing exactly that, how long I'd subjugated my prayers and my serenity to a misplaced blame on God. "I blame us, Sam—the mistakes we've both made in his name."

"But he called me," Sam said, a trace of his old passion under the roughness of fatigue. "We're here because he called us."

"Wait—Ryan may never walk again, but it's okay because God called us? Is that what you're getting at? You're saying that you and I can sit by Ryan's bed in the hospital room in which he's fighting for his life, and we can be happy and content because God called us to Nepal? So it doesn't matter that the son he gave us just jumped off a crane? It doesn't matter that you did more to cause it than to hinder it? That *we*"—I amended as guilt speared me—"that *we* did more to cause it than to hinder it?"

"How can you second-guess—"

"How can *you* dismiss our son's"—I flinched before I uttered the crippling word—"our son's *suicide* with platitudes about calling?"

"Because there's too much we'll never understand," he said loudly, throwing up his hands. "Maybe his jumping is exactly what God wanted! We don't know! But if we can just hang on to what we *do* understand, Lauren. Then we can face this together. Without the . . . the tension between us—the coldness. I want us to be united. To each other and to God. That's all I want."

I took a breath and held it, reaching into reserves I didn't have for the frayed remnants of my self-control. "What *I* want is a son who hasn't been martyred by ministry. I want a son who knows that he came first—before the strangers in a foreign mountain. I want a son who can still see God as I used to—as a loving, protective father who grieves for his children and tries to rescue them from the ignorance of those who harm them for all the 'right' reasons.

"You find peace by tracing Ryan's descent into hell and calling it okay because it's somehow balanced by your ministry? That's not faith, Sam. That's insanity. That's negligence and abandonment! So we can sit in the same hospital room and you can pray to your God all you want. I'm going to pray too. I'll pray to the God I used to know—the one who gave us Ryan to protect. Who gave us a family to nurture. I'll pray to that God, and you go ahead and assuage your guilt with prayers to yours."

I grabbed a jacket off the back of the chair in the corner and walked downstairs. Sam followed, mute. His face was contorted by confusion and righteous certainty when I stopped to face him. "Tell me the truth, Sam. Did you come home tonight to work things out or to convince me to see things your way?"

"You're being unreasonable."

I smiled and shook my head. "I am. You've got me there. I'm unreasonable. You can stand there trying to convince me that it's God who wanted us to neglect our son. That what we witnessed three days ago—that *our son's suicide* and the desperation that drove him to it—were all part of God's plan, and I'm the unreasonable one."

Perhaps to prove that point, I decided to leave nothing unsaid. "You need to know this too, Sam. When Nyall clears him? We're going to take Sullivan up on her offer and get Ryan back to the States. I don't care what your Nepali friends or Nyall or Eveline will think. I'm Ryan's mother and I'm going to do what's right for him."

I saw disagreement, resistance, and resolve shifting like light patterns across Sam's face. I remembered Eveline's warning. Mustering the last vestiges of an exhausted resolve, I added,

"One more thing: I'm not walking out on this marriage. I committed to it—to you—for life. I don't like what it is . . . what it's become. But I want to try to fix it because I promised that I'd never let it die—that I'd never settle for the travesty we're living in. To be honest, I don't want to, but I'm going to try . . . for the promises we made before we knew how brutal life could be."

Sam's countenance brightened. I jumped in again before he had the chance to commend me for the choice I was making so reluctantly.

"But piecing us back together can't happen here. I'm taking Ryan to the States," I said again. "You can come with us. Ryan would want you to come with us, whether he admits it or not. But we're going either way."

I closed the door before Sam had the chance to respond. I walked to the gate and out into the street to flag down a taxi and get back to my son.

eighteen

RYAN COULD MOVE HIS FINGERS. IT FELT LIKE A MONU-mental victory. The swelling on his brain was receding, and his vitals had been stable for several days. His neurologist had decreased the drugs inducing his coma. "We need to get him breathing on his own," he'd said.

Sam called on Ryan's eighth night in the hospital. "His eyes are open." I was at his side in less than thirty minutes. He was confused—only semiconscious—and unable to respond to any of the nurse's commands. When the machines warned us that he needed more sedation, he faded away again. It would take time, they assured us, until he was able to tolerate the pain.

His doctors determined that it was time to wean him from the ventilator. The first attempt was a terrifying failure. His oxygen dropped and the medical personnel jumped into crisis mode to get him stabilized again. "We'll try tomorrow," his doctor said.

Nyall was visiting less often now, but when he did, he cautioned us to keep our expectations low. I fought the urge to celebrate too soon. Sam didn't. He saw each hint of healing as a precursor to the miracles he'd prayed for from the start. "God will restore him," he told Nyall. I envied his certainty.

The second time Ryan opened his eyes, I was sitting at his side. "Ryan?" His eyes moved toward me. I yelled to the nurse that he was waking up and leaned close, inserting my face into his line of vision. "Ryan, can you see me?"

I reached for his hand and squeezed it. His fingers moved. Not much. "Try it again, Ryan. Try squeezing my hand." They moved again, almost imperceptibly.

Tears blinded me and I swiped at them, unwilling to waste a moment seeing my now-conscious son. He frowned.

"You're in the hospital," I said as calmly as I could. His eyes met mine and held. "You—you took a fall. You're . . . you've got some injuries, but you're going to be fine." I rubbed his arm and smiled as hopefully as I could. "Steven's dad has been checking on you. Every day. And he says you're going to be fine."

Ryan blinked. "You're going to be fine," I said again, as much for my own benefit as his.

$$\approx$$

I could see his awareness returning as he drifted in and out of sleep in the days that followed. The respirator still kept him from speaking, but he could answer questions with blinks and expressions. Every so often, I'd catch a look of terror on his face. He'd blink twice to confirm it was pain, but something in his eyes told me it was much more.

The third attempt to wean Ryan from the ventilator worked. His doctor gradually reduced the oxygen forced into his body, allowing muscles that hadn't been taxed in a while to find their role again. His discomfort was visible as his lungs began to function on their own.

"What is your name?" his doctor asked.

"Ryan," he mouthed after an interminable wait.

Sam patted his shoulder while nurses tended to his needs. "You're doing great, kiddo," he said.

He was doing *better*. I'd grant him that. But while there was evidence of movement returning to his arms, neck, and shoulders, repeated tests of his lower extremities had yielded no encouraging results.

Ryan seemed to remember nothing of the events that had caused his injuries. He asked no questions and we offered no more information than we thought he could absorb. His thinking was still slow. His words still few. But he was alive and conscious. Alive and conscious. It was more than enough for now.

⁓

With Ryan moved to a regular room, Sam resumed a more normal schedule. We'd go to the hospital together in the mornings and try to be civil as we talked of trivial things. But I knew there were undertones we couldn't quite disguise. Sam would go home midday to work and return in the evening. He'd lay hands on Ryan and pray for him before he left the room, and Ryan would lie there enduring it, looking anywhere but at Sam.

Sam was just finishing up his prayer one morning when Ryan spoke. "I'm never going to be able to walk." It was a hoarse, despairing cry.

We'd tried to keep references to his prognosis vague, knowing he heard everything we said, but he'd likely gathered from our expressions when the nurses checked his reflexes that his inability to move his legs was more than a recovery delay.

Sam and I moved to stand on either side of his bed. I touched his cheek, wet with frightened tears, with the back of my fingers. "You don't know that, Ryan," I said. "You don't know that you won't walk again."

"I can't move my legs." A sob escaped, and I could see him

trying to contain it. With so many injuries, any movement seemed to cause him pain.

"Not yet," Sam said, his voice intense. "You can't move them yet. But you're just starting your recovery. Give it time, son."

"You heard what Nyall said yesterday," I added, forcing optimism into my expression. "The progress you're making—it's a good sign. And you're getting more sensation back, right? In your hands and shoulders?"

"Those are all positive things," Sam said. Our eyes met across our son's bed. We had to be hopeful for him. We—together—had to be hopeful for him.

"But I can't move my legs," Ryan sobbed again, unconvinced by the urgency of our reassurance.

"I know," I said, leaning close to shush him. I kissed his temple. "I know."

≈

We spoke of his suicide as an "accident" and of his paralysis as a "slow recovery." We talked about his soccer team. About the weather. The hospital food.

I'd officially quit my job at the language school three days after Ryan jumped from the crane. "You can't," Sam had said. "We need the visas."

"Not if we're going home."

He'd looked at me with disappointed eyes. "This is home."

I didn't try to deny it. This country was the center of Sam's universe. His passion for helping the needy in this place had long eclipsed his lesser homes.

Days later, the same argument continued at home, unabated by the time we'd already wasted to it.

"He needs specialized care," I said to him. "He needs

305

psychiatric help too. In a language he can understand. In a place that feels safe to him."

"He doesn't need psychiatry."

"Nyall agrees. Pastor Justin agrees. Everyone I've spoken to agrees. He needs that kind of help."

He crossed his arms and stared me down.

"We've got to take him back to the States," I said again.

"There are other options."

"Like what?"

"Like staying *here*. Trusting God to heal him *here*. Not insulting these people by taking Ryan to another country for his care."

I dropped my head back and looked at the ceiling, letting out a long, frustrated breath. No matter how many times we had this conversation, it always ended the same way. "It's the right thing for Ryan," I tried again.

He moved from the living room into the kitchen. "Let's not talk about this now," he said as he lit a fire under the water kettle.

I leaned against the door frame and watched him get the coffee from its shelf. He measured a few spoonfuls into the French press, then took a little out. Precision. Always precision. Then he stood by the stove and waited for the water to boil.

"You've said you want to talk."

He looked up. "I do."

"This is me trying to talk."

"About flying Ryan home. Not about us."

"Caring for our son is as central as it gets to *us*."

He paused. "You already know how I feel about it."

"Yes."

"And you disagree."

"I do."

"Then it seems to me there's little to discuss."

The kitchen clock ticked the seconds away. I wondered if our marriage was long past its potential for repair. For Ryan's sake, not mine, I hoped that I was wrong.

"Can you please reconsider?" I tried again. Stupidly perhaps.

"You're not seeing the bigger picture."

"I'm sorry," I said. "I'm sorry that my perspective is hampered by a boy lying partially paralyzed in a hospital bed."

"We don't know that for sure."

"We won't know anything until he's been through more tests, more procedures, more therapy. The best place for all that to happen is not here."

"How do you know?"

I shook my head. "Logic. Unbiased assessment."

The water boiled and Sam poured it into the coffee press.

"It's not just about Ryan," I said, gathering the shreds of my commitment to this man. "If we're going to put our family back together again . . . Sam, if we're really going to fix us, it just can't happen here."

"How do you know that?" His voice was getting sharp.

"I just know, Sam."

He shook his head and blew out a loud breath. "You're asking me to accept your opinion, no questions asked, without giving any thought to mine."

I remembered every time I'd surrendered to his reasoning, valid or not. "I've been giving in to your *opinion* for twenty years, Sam." My tone hardened to match his. "How dare you say this is unfair? It's the only time in our lives that I've demanded anything from you."

He looked at me as if the power of his gaze—its inherent authority—could make me fall in line again.

"This is the right decision," I said, unwilling to yield again and subjugate our son to my submission. "Doing this for Ryan . . .

doing this for us—removing us from the stress and pressures and memories in this place—it's right. I've considered your perspective and I've determined that mine is right."

Sam depressed the plunger, then poured some coffee into a cup. "You go," he said.

"What? Sam . . ."

He looked at me without emotion. "You and Ryan, go."

"You need to be there too."

"Why? He'll have the best possible care. You said so yourself. And you'll have Sullivan . . ."

"Sam." I was too stunned to speak for a few moments. I tried to appeal to his sense of logic. "You can't stay here without a visa, and I'm not going back to work."

"I'll find a way. There's always a way."

I raised my hands in utter incomprehension. "Ryan needs you with us. We need to get through his recovery together. If we're going to piece this family, this"—I stumbled on the word, but had to play this hand—"this *marriage* back together somehow, you need to be there too."

"I can't just pick up and abandon—"

"You can!"

The hardness of my voice startled him. "*You* can," he said. "I cannot."

Anger brought tears to my eyes and I fought them back. Sam would see them as weakness, and I wanted to be strong. "Can we compromise?" I said to my uncompromising husband. "Can you just commit to a while? Maybe just a year, for starters—twelve months, Sam. Because our son almost died and because . . . because it's the right thing." We'd figure out the rest later. I had to be okay with that.

Sam moved to the sink and looked out the window, but I doubted he saw anything. I was asking him to sacrifice his mission for his family, and I knew his battle raged deep and fierce. "I committed to you," he said without turning around. "When I married you. When we had Ryan. I committed to you both."

I leaned on the kitchen island, fearful of what I knew would come next. The *but* that had always seemed to defeat my rationales. The conviction. The divine directives that mocked my human needs.

"One year," he said. He continued to stare out.

"Try it again."

Ryan blew into the spirometer I held to his lips. I was gratified to see a slight improvement in his lung function since a couple of days before.

"Want something more to drink?" I asked as I put the device away.

"I'm fine."

"A blanket?"

"I'm fine."

I sat in the chair next to his bed and considered his expression. "And here I thought the promise of flying home might have changed your attitude." I smiled and hoped he would too.

He turned his head toward me on his pillow and I felt my smile fade. His jaw was set, his lips pinched. I stood. "Are you okay? Are you in pain?" I touched his arm and he pulled it away—just a bit, just enough for me to know.

"It wasn't an accident," he said.

I let the words settle. Mostly because I didn't know how to answer them. He turned his head and focused on the ceiling.

"Can you remember?"

Nothing.

"The hours before the accident . . . Ryan, are you starting to remember?"

"It wasn't an accident."

I sat on the edge of his bed and wondered when my words to my son had become so stilted. "You're right," I said. "It wasn't an accident. Can you look at me, Ryan?"

He shook his head against the pillow. "Did I jump from the crane?" His voice was tentative. Fearful.

I swallowed past my qualms. There'd been enough denial in our lives. "Yes. You climbed up the crane and . . . and you jumped off." I stopped long enough to control my breathing. He was talking. He was talking and I couldn't waste the moment on emotion. "You were upset," I said as calmly as I could. "The day of the—the day you got injured. You were upset and . . . and you'd been drinking."

He bit his lip, fiercely fighting for control.

"Do you remember anything else?" I asked, willing him to get it all out now—while he still had the courage to speak it.

He shook his head again. Then he said, "Dad . . ."

"Yes. He was there."

"You were in Nagarkot."

"We came back as soon as we heard."

A nurse came in and sensed the tension in the room. She backed out and we sat in silence for a while.

"You are not to blame," I finally said.

He pinched his lips together again as his chin began to shake.

"Ryan." I wanted to force his face toward me, but knew I shouldn't. This moment wasn't mine.

"Were you there too?" His voice was still hoarse from the breathing tube.

"I was there. Standing at the bottom of the crane."

He frowned. "I don't remember . . ."

"It's okay." He let me touch his arm. "Do you want to know?"

He shook his head again.

"All right," I said. There would be time for filling in the blanks. There would be time for restitching our lives. "You'll remember more someday. As your body continues to heal. You've been through so much . . . it's normal for you not to recall all the details." I lay a hand on his leg and knew he couldn't feel it.

His chin quivered again and he turned his head away. "I'm never going to walk. I—I jumped from the . . . and I'm never going to play soccer again."

I ached for him. I longed to wrap my faith around his uncertainty, but I'd learned in the chaos of our last few years how little I knew. How little I could predict.

"I wish I could be sure." I whispered the words and hoped he could hear them. "I want more than anything to promise you that you're going to walk again." I pictured his tattered red Manchester T-shirt. "To play again." I swallowed hard against the emotions, wanting my words to be heard and to matter. "But I promise you, Ryan—I promise you that we're going to do everything we can to get you well again. Whatever it takes. I promise."

I wanted so badly for him to believe me. To trust me. But how could he when I'd withheld so much of what I'd promised him before? By my inaction. By my spineless, will-less faith.

"I know you have no reason to believe me," I told him. He was still turned away. "I know I've said things and allowed things that . . . I know I've hurt you. Probably in ways I don't even realize. And I've been one of those who hasn't heard you." A tear ran down his cheek. I felt the guilt surge up again and freeze my lungs. I couldn't breathe.

Ryan must have sensed it. He turned his head and looked into my face. I saw anger in his eyes—that anger I'd so long tried to excuse away. And I saw trauma, too, the kind that made his shoulders shake.

I realized this wasn't just *his* moment—it was ours. In all its gruesome sacredness, this moment was our Truth.

Please, God. Please. The prayer rippled over my spirit and stunned me in its honesty. I neither feared, nor doubted. Somehow, I knew who heard it now. "I need you to know this," I said to him. "Ryan, please—don't look away."

He hesitated. It seemed interminable. Then he turned his head back to me. "It's my job to be your parent. It's my highest calling to be your mom. And your job—your only job, Ryan—is to be a thirteen-year-old boy. Happy or sad or angry or . . . or on top of a crane. I have failed you, and you have done nothing wrong."

He hiccupped on a sob and bit his lip, but didn't look away. I touched his face. The hair that escaped his bandage. "You have done nothing wrong," I said again.

For the hundredth, the thousandth time since his attempted suicide, I caught my breath and stared—just stared—at this battered, priceless extension of myself that I'd lost, in small concessions and false truths, along the way. I took in the minute details, the shadow beneath his lashes, the veins on the back of his hand, the sound of breath entering and leaving his still-tortured lungs.

"When I think that I could have lost you . . ." I closed my eyes and steadied my breathing. His gaze was still on me when I opened them again. "I'm sorry. For every time I should have protected you and didn't. Ryan, for every time I should have listened to you and didn't. For letting us stop talking."

He blinked at the tears in his eyes, but I didn't hide mine. They were the evidence of my heart for this boy. I'd hidden it too long. "We're all broken," I finally said. I took inventory of the bandages, wires, and tubes around his body and smiled. "Some of us in more obvious ways than others."

He rolled his eyes. It warmed my heart.

I took a deep breath and let it out. "We'll get help," I said. "We'll do the next thing—and then the next." I leaned in to kiss his cheek, expecting him to turn away.

He didn't.

nineteen

"LORD HAVE MERCY, I NEED SOME COFFEE!" SULLIVAN SAILED into Ryan's room in rumpled slacks, a wrinkled blouse, and matted hair. But her makeup was impeccable.

"Sullivan, what are you . . . ?"

She wrapped me in a Chanel-scented hug. "I told you I'd be here the moment you said 'Go,' and if I'm not mistaken, you said 'Go'!"

I'd called her two days ago with the news that Ryan had been given the all clear. "Well, I am tickled pink!" she'd exclaimed. "Let me round up the cavalry and get your family home!"

"So you're the cavalry?" I asked, standing in a Nepali hospital room with a woman so out of place that patients and doctors alike were staring.

She moved to Ryan's bedside and gave him a wink before saying, conspiratorially, "Do you really think I'd miss out on all the fun?"

He just stared at her, wide-eyed, and she looked back at me. "The spittin' image of his father," she declared. "Now—who do I talk to about our walking papers? We are leaving in two days, and not a moment later!"

Sullivan took Kathmandu and its hospital by storm. Unbeknownst to Sam and me, she'd spent the past few weeks securing every mode of transportation, piece of medical equipment, and document we'd need for a smooth departure from Nepal. She'd set it all in motion with the flair and aplomb only she could carry off, making new friends—though some reluctant—as she choreographed our exit strategy.

"Samuel Coventry!" She nearly scared him off his chair when she entered our home. He looked up from his typing to Sullivan, then me, then back again. "What's this I hear about you putting a time limit on your return to the States?" She propped a fist on her hip and raised an eyebrow in his direction. "Tell me! Why are you being so obtuse?"

Sam looked stunned. Sullivan's brightness was a bewildering force. Her presence. Her loudness. Her demands. They did not belong in Sam's life here, in a home encased in duty and sobriety.

Though the debate that ensued was civil, I could tell that being called out by a woman whose life and priorities were so different from his irked Sam. He spoke calmly, and Sullivan listened to his explanations. She countered them with common sense, but it was clear she never really expected him to cave in.

A few minutes later, she folded herself into the taxi I'd flagged outside our gates. "You knew going in that you wouldn't convince him to change his mind," I said.

"Some spar to win, Chickadee, but with people like that husband of yours, I just spar for sport," she answered. "The man's been living in a confrontation vacuum for too long."

She was right, of course. No confrontation. No call to reason. He'd led our family down this maiming path unchallenged.

Sam was still sitting at the table when I reentered the house. "I guess we should get packing," I said.

"I'm going to need more time. Two days is . . ."

"Sam." I shook my head. "We talked about this. We agreed on this."

"I can't leave now."

I was stunned. "But . . . you knew this was coming. You were there when I called Sullivan to tell her we were ready."

"I didn't expect it to go this fast," he said.

"You know her. Of course it went this fast."

"I can't leave now," he said again, more firmly this time.

I was starting to believe him. "Sam . . . Sam, please don't do this."

He went back to typing and I looked on, incredulous. "What is this really about?"

He paused but didn't look up. "I told you. It's the timing."

I shook my head. "There's more."

He finally made eye contact with me. What I saw in his gaze scared me. "I'm still not sure this is the right thing to do," he said, resolute.

I bit the inside of my lip and fought for control. "So this isn't just about delaying our departure."

His expression told me all I needed to know.

"But you agreed—"

He threw up his hands. "I was trying to appease you!"

"You were . . . *what*?"

"I knew you'd eventually come around if you . . ."

My blood froze. "Sam."

"If you tried to see this from a different angle. Once you got past the shock of what Ryan did and could think straight again . . ." He looked me square in the eye, and there was no mistaking his determination. "I have to stay. You go with Ryan so he can get the care he needs, and I'll follow through with the commitments we've made here." He looked at me with all the confidence, resolve, and influence that had drawn me to him when we met at Sternensee.

"Sam," I begged, "we agreed." I stared into his inflexible gaze and raised my hands in incredulity. "How could you let me think that you were coming with us?" The burn of humiliation traveled up my spine. "How could you let me think that you felt the same way I did?"

He leaned against the sink and crossed his arms. "I trusted God to change your—"

"No!" I raised a finger to interrupt him before he launched into another of his speeches on the importance of his work. "You don't get to use God to excuse your failures again." I fought the fury that tingled under my skin and made me want to scream. "We're parents," I said when I thought I could speak quietly. "We are parents! And if I hear you dismiss that one more time for the sake of—"

"God wants me here."

I stared at him. That fire was in his eyes again. I knew it well. "That—is—not—God." My voice and body shook.

I stifled a sob as I backed out of the kitchen, then turned and escaped into our unkempt front yard. I stood there—holding my head to keep from screaming—wounded and dazed. Desperate. *God. Please, God . . .*

My breath caught as lucidity struck me with such intensity that I reached for a tree to steady myself. As my hope dissolved again, I sensed God's presence—more powerful than my disillusion and more tangible than my grief—and realized he'd been there, waiting and unchanged.

It was *Sam's* God I had rejected, not mine.

I felt his comfort like a haunting peace. He was neither cruel nor demeaning. Neither neglectful nor tyrannical. The grandiose idol my husband served had eclipsed the God I'd known before surrender had lost him to me. He was still everything I'd believed him to be—my relentless, demanding, trustworthy, benevolent, and healing God.

A peace I hadn't felt in months settled over my spirit as I entered our house again. Sam was still in the kitchen, exactly where I'd left him. A mother's love and tenacity—the kind *God* had called me to before we'd even conceived Ryan—fueled my parting words.

"My God loves our son more than your work," I said to Sam. "My God longs to see him healed and smiling again. My God hates that we've blamed our failures—our negligence—on him. My God tells me it's time for us to leave, not because of this place but because of what we've sacrificed to it."

Sam didn't speak.

"I'll pack my bags tonight. There are two beds in Sullivan's suite, and . . . and I could use the space."

I gathered my things from the dining room table. "God has called me to be Ryan's mom," I said as I walked past Sam on my way to our bedroom. "And we're leaving in two days."

Epilogue

THE SCENE WAS APOCALYPTIC. SLATE CLOUDS ROILED IN A stormy sky as furious gales heaved waves against a jagged cliff. A woman stood above the chaos, flowing garments shredded by the force of nature's rage, hair plastered by the wind across her neck and brow.

She was luminous—as if a single, narrow shaft of brightness had pierced the chaos and alighted on her calm, uptilted face. Her eyes, hooded and serene, were turned toward the source. She stood with arms loose by her sides, her fragile frame arched forward by the wind rushing off the sea.

The colors and textures Aidan had used were stark—sharp and threatening and unyielding. He'd called his final painting *Faith*. I lay it in the grass on top of Aidan's grave, then knelt and traced the contour of his name.

A hemorrhage had snuffed the future from his life two weeks after his surgery. But it hadn't shortened it by much. Though the surgeon had removed the bulk of the tumor, some of it was inoperable, and Aidan knew his time was short.

It had taken a month, after our flight from Kathmandu, for me to log in to Facebook again. There were no messages from Aidan waiting there—as if he'd read into my silence all the words I couldn't say.

With my hand flat against the stone that marked his

curtailed life, I whispered, "Your mom made sure I got the painting." I hadn't intended to speak out loud, yet it seemed somehow fitting. "Thank you for leaving it to me." I'd found a note attached with masking tape to the back of the canvas. Two words: *i understand*. They bound my guilt and soothed my pain.

I skimmed the details of his work. The ridges of raised paint. The power and depth of color. The nearly audible roar of wind and rain and waves. They hadn't quieted yet—not in my life or Ryan's. Perhaps they had in Sam's, who'd assured me he'd return to the States so we could deal with our "disagreement"—his word still appalled me—when God told him it was time to leave his adopted land.

"I miss Nepal," I admitted as I knelt by Aidan's grave. I shook my head and laughed, and in my mind, he laughed too. Despite the turmoil that had stalked me in that place, its broken beauty had seeped its warmth into reluctant veins. I felt it pulsing still.

Ryan and I had flown out of Kathmandu together. Sam had come down to the ambulance bay with us for our departure, already dressed and packed for his next trek. He'd said his parting words to Ryan, told him he'd check in as often as he could. Then he'd looked at me and said nothing. There was no anger in his face. No accusation in his gaze. We'd talked so much already that there was nothing left to say. The chasm that yawned between his God and mine was an unbridgeable space.

He'd moved out of our house since then and gone to live among the people he had stayed to save. Independent, visa-free, and unconcerned. "God recruited me. He'll keep me here," he'd said in his last e-mail, his atypical compromise more proof of an irrational calling.

Sam's storm still surged around me. My storm. The one I'd fed by hoping and not doing, by allowing without questioning, by caving in, by sinning. I was learning to own my mistakes.

I was learning how to function in the remorse that ebbed and flowed like the battering waves of Aidan's painting. And shame. I was learning to live with my shame too.

"We're back in the States," I said into Aidan's absence. "Ryan's doing okay, I guess. He's in rehab, figuring out how to function without the use of his legs. But he was able to flex a muscle in his thigh a week ago, so . . . I guess we stay hopeful, right?"

I now lived in the unhurried South, in one of the bedrooms of Sullivan's vast home, where Ryan would join us when he was released. She'd already made sure he'd have all the help he needed.

I pictured my son on his hospital bed, long bangs covering averted eyes. "He's talking a bit more," I said. "Not much . . . and it's brutal when he does. I'm learning what I can undo and what I can't. And he's learning—I think he's just learning how to be hopeful again."

I propped the painting against Aidan's gravestone, stood back, and felt a tearing at my soul. A profound, piercing, solemn pain. "I want you to keep this," I whispered, tears again blurring my vision. "I know you left it for me, but . . . Aidan, it's you. And you were never mine."

Spent spirits hovered out of sight and reach. Releasing a slow breath, I squared my shoulders and closed my eyes. Then I turned, resolute, and walked toward a future I still could not predict and into a healing well beyond my tattered strength. *Please, God*, I breathed. *Please.*

I knew he heard.

A Note from the Author

THE PLIGHT OF MKs (MISSIONARIES' KIDS) IS FAMILIAR TO
me. As the daughter of missionaries to France, I benefited from
the best a life in ministry has to offer. But I also suffered from
some of the worst.

I am a fervent proponent of thoughtful missionary endeavors. I've seen them bring practical help and eternal hope to
jaded First World metropoles and imperiled Third World
tribes. It's the unintentional toll of a more reckless zeal, measured in broken families and wounded children, that gives me
pause.

In my twenty-five years of work with MKs, I've seen a
majority of them flourish, their relationships, careers, and faith
enriched by broad horizons and incomparable experiences. But
I've seen others—broken, cynical, yearning Ryans—blame their
abandonment and suffering on The Call.

My primary message, when I speak to churches, missions,
and ministers around the world, is simple: Evangelistic endeavors have too often resulted in collateral injury to defenseless
children, souls too young to distinguish between human failure
and divine directives. We've got to do better.

My hope is that this novel will be a cautionary tale, shedding
light on the plight of the MKs who struggle. And if it inspires
parents to make wiser choices to defend the well-being of their

families and their children, I'll consider the effort—and the potential backlash—worth the cost.

For more on the topic of MKs, please visit www. michelephoenix.com.

Discussion Questions

1. What were early warning signs that Sam might be prone to an irrational pursuit of ministry?
2. Is there anything Lauren could have done to foster a healthier ministry/family balance early on?
3. Lauren talks about losing Ryan by "small concessions and false truths" over the course of his childhood. List the concessions and false truths you see in the story.
4. Did Lauren have any other option than to follow Sam's calling to Nepal?
5. What are the factors in Lauren's life that made it so easy for her to enter an online relationship with Aidan?
6. How do you think the story would have ended if Aidan hadn't died?
7. Is there hope for Ryan and Lauren? Why do you think there is/isn't?
8. How does the church's naïveté about missionaries and their children potentially protect the kind of dysfunction the Coventry family experiences?

About the Author

BORN IN FRANCE TO A CANADIAN FATHER and an American mother, Michèle Phoenix is a consultant, writer, and speaker with a heart for Third Culture Kids. She taught for twenty years at Black Forest Academy (Germany) before launching her own advocacy venture under Global Outreach Mission. Michèle travels globally to consult and teach on topics related to this unique people group. She loves good conversations, mischievous students, Marvel movies, and paths to healing.

⁓

Learn more at michelephoenix.com.
Twitter: @frenchphoenix